# FINDING JODELLE

SEAL Team Hawaii, Book 7

## SUSAN STOKER

# CHAPTER ONE

Jodelle "Jody" Spencer hurried toward the older model Kia parked in a spot at the back of the lot at Waimea Bay. There were cars parked in every available space, and many vehicles were blocked in by others. Surf competitions at the North Shore were always that way. There simply wasn't enough space for all the competitors, tourists, and locals who came out to participate and watch. The two-lane Kamehameha Highway wasn't adequate to handle all the traffic either, which was a huge pain in the ass for the locals.

But the competitions brought in large amounts of money to vendors and shop owners in the area. Not to mention, it was exciting to watch the athletes take on the huge waves the northern shore of Oahu was known for.

At the moment, however, Jody wasn't thinking about the inconvenience of the traffic, or the competitors in the water, or the amount of money being made—all she could think about was Ben Miller. He was one of the high schoolers who came out to surf in the mornings, the kids Jody had a soft spot for. She'd started coming out to the popular surf spot in the mornings a few years ago, bringing breakfast sandwiches for the kids and encouraging them to get out of the surf on time to make it to class.

She was kind of like a surf mom to the group now. She delighted in their successes and did her best to soothe them when they struggled with school, surfing, or their fledging relationships.

Ben Miller was one of her favorites. He towered over her five-one frame at five-eleven. He had light brown hair, which he kept cut fairly short, a swimmer's frame, big feet that he joked about often, saying surfing was the only sport he could even halfway excel in because there was no way he could trip over his feet when they were planted on a board. And he had a smile that lit up his face and always made Jody feel good inside when she saw it.

But hearing that someone had seen Ben sleeping in his car, in the middle of the afternoon during a surf competition, had alarmed her. It was definitely out of the ordinary for the young man. He should've been on the beach with his friends, interacting with the professional surfers, flirting with girls, and volunteering his time.

Instead, he apparently had heat exhaustion from being inside his hot car.

Determination rose within Jody as she hurried through the parking lot toward where she'd been told Ben was being looked at by the medics.

"Easy, Jodelle," Baker said soothingly from beside her.

Jody had almost forgotten he was there, which would've made her laugh in any other situation than the one she was in now. Forgetting about Baker Rawlins was literally impossible —and not just because of his eye-catching size.

He was everything she'd ever dreamed about in a man... and more. He was honorable, and protective, and loyal. Not to mention gorgeous. His black hair liberally sprinkled with gray was longish on the top and shorter on the sides. He had a well-trimmed beard, and Jody had wondered more than once if it was soft or prickly. Dark tattoos lined his arms, his upper back, and chest. And he was muscular all over, from his arms to his thighs and even his ass.

In short...he was one of the best-looking men Jody had ever seen.

He was also broody, mysterious, and even a little scary. Somehow, those things didn't turn her off. Not at all.

But Baker was so far out of her league, it wasn't even funny. He used to be a Navy SEAL, for God's sake. Jody figured if the Navy didn't have age limitations for SEALs, he probably still would be. He was definitely in shape, even at fifty-two. And if the way he'd been helping his SEAL friends lately was any indication, he still had plenty of connections.

She should've been wary of that, of the secrecy surrounding everything Baker did, of how it reminded her a bit too much of her ex-husband, who couldn't tell the truth about anything if he tried. But she got a very different vibe from Baker than she had when she was with her ex.

She wasn't an idiot. She was fairly certain some things Baker did weren't exactly legal, but since he was using his connections to help others—instead of extorting money and messing with drugs, as her ex had done—she wasn't as concerned.

It was obvious Baker's friends respected him. And it was that respect that *really* made him different from her ex. Bobby had gotten off on making people fear him...even her. The first time he'd hit her, she was done. She'd packed her stuff, along with Kaimana's, and left.

She'd been afraid Bobby would come after them, but it turned out he was relieved to not have a wife and kid holding him back anymore. She hadn't asked for anything in the divorce, and he'd signed the papers without hassle. He'd been killed down in Honolulu when Kaimana was eight. A shoot-out with police when they'd come to serve a warrant for his arrest for drug trafficking.

His death had been a relief.

Looking at Baker from the corner of her eye, Jody knew without a doubt he wouldn't defile his body with any kind of drug. She'd never even seen him drink soda or alcohol, only water, and he always watched what he ate, telling her once he was too old to eat crap, that it would go straight to his gut. He sometimes surfed with her kids, and it was all she could do not to drool over his six-pack abs and incredibly toned physique.

No, Baker Rawlins wouldn't do drugs. Jody would bet everything she owned on that.

Her thoughts were jerked back to the present when they approached Ben's car. The teenager was sitting on the back seat, his feet on the sand outside the door, a medic crouched in front of him.

Jody tried to rush over, but Baker clutched her elbow.

"I need to check on him," she said, pulling on her arm distractedly.

"You get a medical degree since the last time I saw you?" he asked.

Jody frowned. "What? No."

"Then you need to stay back and let the paramedics do their thing."

"Let me go, Baker," she told him irritably.

In response, his grip on her only tightened.

He was beginning to piss her off. "Seriously—let go of my arm," she repeated. To her surprise, Baker did as she asked, releasing her elbow.

Only to step behind her, wrap an arm around her chest diagonally, and pull her close, so her back was pressed against his front.

Baker was literally a foot taller than Jody. She was used to

4

being the short one in whatever group she was in, but she internally struggled with her current feelings. She loved being in Baker's arms like this. Pressed up against him. But she was upset because he was preventing her from getting to Ben. From making sure he was all right.

"He's upset," Baker said softly into her ear.

Jody couldn't stop the shiver that went through her when his warm breath wafted over her sensitive skin. She reached up and held onto his forearm draped across her chest.

"If you go charging in there, he's gonna close down. Give the paramedic a chance to talk to him, try to find out what's up, before you go all mama bear on him."

"Something's wrong, Baker," Jody said, keeping her gaze glued to Ben. He was looking down at the sand under his feet. He had a bottle of water in one hand and the medic was taking his blood pressure. "He's a good kid. Happy. Outgoing. But lately, he's been withdrawn. Sullen."

"He's a teenager," Baker said in response.

Jody shook her head. "No. I mean, yes, he is, but that's not it. Something's going on with him. Look at his car—it's a mess. I know a lot of teenagers have messy cars, but not Ben. He keeps it pristine. And he's got clothes all over the back seat. That's not just a change of shorts or whatever for after surfing. And...is that a *pillow*? If I didn't know better, I'd say he's been living in his car. Which means something is *very* wrong."

She expected him to disagree, to try to convince her once more that whatever was going on with Ben was simply because he was seventeen. But to her surprise, Baker said, "Then we'll figure out what it is and fix it."

Jody turned her head to try to look at him. He didn't loosen his hold on her so the angle was awkward. She wanted to ask him what he meant by *we*.

In all the time she'd known him, Baker had never made

the slightest indication that he wanted to be anything other than casual acquaintances. He never lingered too long when he was surfing and she happened to run into him. Hadn't encouraged her interest in any way whatsoever.

And now here he was, holding her in his embrace and using the *we* pronoun.

Jody's head spun. He was confusing her, but she didn't know how to ask him what the hell was going on without embarrassing herself. He'd probably said it offhandedly, without thinking.

The medic straightened and began to pack up his kit. Ben chugged the rest of the water in the bottle and stood up. He opened the driver's door and slid back into the car.

Jody gasped in dismay, and this time when she tried to go to him, Baker released her. She ran the ten feet or so to the car and leaned into the open window. "Ben! Where are you going? You shouldn't be driving."

"I need to go, Miss Jody," Ben mumbled.

"What's going on?" she asked.

"Nothing," he said.

"Don't *nothing* me, Ben Miller," Jody chastised. "Talk to me."

"Nothing to talk about," he insisted.

Jody reached out and put her hand on the teenager's arm. He still felt too hot to her, but if the medic thought he was all right to leave, there wasn't much she could do about it. "I don't know what's going on, but I'm here if you ever want to talk. I know I'm old and not cool, but I'm a great listener. You need *anything*...I'm here for you. No questions asked. I mean it, Ben. Someone to listen, a hot meal, a place to stay... whatever it is, you come to me. Hear me?"

Ben's hazel eyes shot up then and he met her gaze. "I hear you, Miss Jody."

There was pain and confusion swirling in the young man's eyes, and Jody wanted nothing more than to haul him out of the car and give him a tight hug and never let go. But his walls were up, and there was no way he was going to get into a heart to heart right now. Not with everyone standing around watching. Not with tourists and his high school friends hanging out nearby.

As the medics went back to the beach and the looky-loos standing around also lost interest and began to disperse, Jody backed away from the car as Ben started it up. She would've tripped over one of the logs keeping cars in the designated parking area if Baker hadn't been there to catch her. When she had her balance once more, however, Baker didn't drop his hand from her waist.

Ben made eye contact with Baker and quickly lowered his gaze. He backed out of the spot, which was immediately occupied by a car filled with six tourists, obviously thrilled to have found a place to park.

Jody watched Ben's car leave in frustration.

"How long have you been here?" Baker asked.

Jody looked up at him and shrugged. "A while."

He snorted. "Which means you probably got here at the ass crack of dawn. It's three. You eaten?"

"I had a sandwich," Jody lied.

As if he had a built-in bullshit detector, Baker merely lifted an eyebrow skeptically.

"Fine. I haven't eaten, but I'm not hungry," Jody told him.

Without a word, he turned her toward the beach, where she'd left her cooler. "You're driving."

"No! I can't leave, I'll never get my spot back," Jody told him.

"I know."

Jody glared up at him.

He chuckled when he saw the look she was giving him. "You've been here all day, Jodelle. You need to eat, otherwise you'll be the next one the medics are having to look at. The kids you've taken under your wing are fine. And if we leave now, we've actually got a chance of getting to Waialua ahead of all these fuckin' tourists."

Jody stared at Baker as they walked. She wasn't afraid of tripping over anything; Baker's hand on her waist and the way his eyes constantly swept over the area assured she wouldn't. "What's in Waialua?" she asked.

"My place," Baker said nonchalantly.

Jody stopped walking altogether.

"What? What's wrong?" he asked, his voice hardening as he looked around, trying to figure out why she'd stopped.

"Your place?"

His lips twitched as he looked down at her. "Yeah."

"Um...why?"

"Because you need to eat. And you need to relax. And if you go home, you'll think too much about Ben, and you'll probably get a bug up your butt to go out and try to find him. If you're at my place, I can make sure that you get something nutritious in your belly and you won't head back out into the god-awful traffic that'll happen once today's competition is over."

Jody couldn't really argue with anything he'd said. She probably *would* throw a frozen meal into the microwave to eat and then break into the half-eaten pack of Oreos that was in her pantry. She wasn't sure if Baker was trying to tell her she was overweight or what. She'd also *definitely* worry about Ben, and seeing if she could find him wasn't a bad idea. She didn't have his address but could probably get it from one of the other surfers he hung out with.

"Jodelle, focus," Baker said, the humor easy to hear in his tone.

She looked up at him. "I don't understand."

"What don't you understand, Tink?"

Jody frowned. "Did you just call me Tink?"

"Yup. You're like a little fairy. Tinker Bell."

"Oh, Jesus. You know how annoying that is, right?" Jody asked huffily.

Baker only smiled.

"How would you like it if I called you Hulk? Or Gigantor?"

Baker leaned into her personal space, and Jody almost swallowed her tongue.

"You can call me whatever you want, Tink."

For a second, Jody thought Baker was going to kiss her, then he straightened and placed his fingers on the small of her back. "Come on, let's go get your cooler, see if we can find one of your kids, tell them you're headed out, remind them to be good, then we'll get the hell out of here."

In a daze, Jody let Baker lead her back toward the picnic table she'd made her home base and where she'd left her cooler. She had no idea what had brought about this change in the man. It was confusing...and exciting. But she didn't know what it meant, which scared the crap out of her.

When they arrived at the table, Baker picked up her cooler and nonchalantly put the strap around his free arm. Then he looked around for a moment, and upon seeing Rome, whistled loudly. The boy looked over at them, and Baker used his head to direct the kid over.

Jody could only shake her head in amusement when Rome immediately jogged toward them.

"What's up?" he asked Baker.

"Jodelle and I are headed out. You good?"

"Yeah."

"You'll let the others know?"

"Sure."

"Great."

"We're planning on riding the waves at Laniakea Beach at dawn patrol on Wednesday. Wanna join us?" he asked, using the slang for surfing first thing in the morning.

"Wouldn't miss it," Baker said. He held out his fist and

Rome gave him a fist bump. "Stay outta trouble," he warned. "Don't make Jodelle worry."

"We will, and we won't," Rome said with a grin.

"Don't stay too late," Jody warned, not able to help herself.

"I won't," Rome said. "You coming to the last day of the competition tomorrow?" he asked.

Jody opened her mouth to say that yes, of course she'd be there, but Baker beat her to it.

"Nope. You guys'll be on your own."

"Baker!" Jody exclaimed, but he kept his eyes on the teenager.

"No problem. The finals are tomorrow and we're stoked to watch," Rome answered with another smile.

Baker nodded at him. "We'll catch up to you later then."

"Later!" Rome called, then turned and jogged back to the girl he'd been talking to before Baker had summoned him.

Jody shook her head at the seemingly endless energy the boy had. Then she turned to the man beside her. "Seriously, Baker, that wasn't cool."

"Come on, yell at me on the way out of this craziness," Baker said, steering her toward the parking lot and her VW van. It was her pride and joy...as it had been Kaimana's. It was in pristine shape and she'd splurged to give it a funky, wild paint job, complete with flowers and peace signs.

All too soon, she found herself behind the wheel and backing out of the parking space she'd been lucky enough to score early that morning, before the sun came up and the tourists started descending on Waimea Bay.

She shook her head and chuckled.

"What?" Baker asked from the seat next to her.

Jody was grateful he hadn't insisted on driving. No one drove her baby but her. "I have no idea how this happened. Or even *what's* happening," she told him.

"What's happening is that I'm done fuckin' around."

Jody looked over at him in surprise. "What does that mean?"

"You'll see."

Jody frowned and divided her attention between the man lounging in the seat next to her and trying not to hit idiot drivers in front of her. She wanted to press Baker for more info. Wanted him to explain what he was talking about. He was acting so different today, and it was unsettling. Jody couldn't help but feel a zing of excitement in her veins too. Still, she refused to get too worked up. Baker couldn't be interested in her. She was too...normal. He needed a woman who was fit, prettier, more outgoing, ready for adventure. Simply *more* than Jody was.

She'd drop Baker off at his place, then go home to her small house. Things between them would go back to normal, and she'd continue with her somewhat boring and predictable life. Whatever had caused Baker to feel as if he needed to watch over her today would fade in his mind, and that would be that.

A pang of disappointment swept through Jody, but she refused to let it take hold. She'd gotten very good at keeping her real feelings from showing on her face.

She was a shadow of the woman she used to be...and that was fine with her. More than fine. The best thing that had ever happened to her had been snatched away cruelly, and she wasn't going to risk her heart or soul by caring so much for someone else ever again. It was safer, and more comfortable, to live on the sidelines. To merely be a spectator. Once Baker got whatever this wild hair was out of his system, he'd move on.

Satisfied with her train of thought, Jody glanced over at the man. She swallowed hard when she saw his gaze was glued on her, instead of the road in front of them. Uncomfortable with being the subject of his intense scrutiny, she said, "You're gonna tell me where to go when we get close, right?"

"Of course."

Jody nodded, turned her attention back to the road, and refused to read anything into what she'd seen in Baker's eyes.

Determination.

Stubbornness.

And a tenderness she hadn't seen turned her way since she was a newlywed.

# CHAPTER TWO

Baker held open his front door for Jodelle and couldn't stop the feeling of satisfaction when she walked past him and the door was firmly shut. The petite woman was the first guest he'd ever invited into his home...and having her there felt right.

From the moment he'd met her, shortly after she'd started coming to the beach to watch over the kids, Baker had felt a connection. He couldn't explain it, and honestly, it had made him so uncomfortable, he'd gone out of his way to treat her as nothing more than an acquaintance. But over the last year or so, she'd gotten even further under his skin without even trying. Watching his friends find and marry the loves of their lives...and seeing them actually make those relationships work...made him yearn for something more in his life.

He'd only ever had one long-term girlfriend. And that had been enough for him to be turned off of relationships for good. He'd treated Tabitha like gold, and in return, she'd emptied his bank account, taken out twenty-three credit cards in his name, and had actually plotted to kill him. It was like a fucking crime show. She'd played him, and he'd been so desperate for love at the time, to find what everyone else had, that he'd bought into her bullshit.

She hadn't even done any jail time either, which pissed him off to no end. Her daddy had hired the most expensive and successful lawyer he could find, and she'd gotten off with probation and some fines.

Baker had sworn off women from that point on. Refusing to spend more than a few nights with the same person before ghosting them. He was an asshole, he knew that...but now, for the first time in years, he wanted more.

Wanted it all.

Jodelle. The first time he'd heard her name, Baker had thought it was the most beautiful name he'd ever heard. She'd laughed the first time he'd called her that and told him that everyone used her nickname, Jody. But he refused. He'd always think of her as Jodelle.

He'd fought against her pull for months. For years, actually. And he couldn't fight it anymore. He'd hoped the connection he felt would fade. Actually, Baker was sure she'd do something to piss him off or annoy him. Something that would prove she was just like most of the other women he knew. But instead, the longer he got to know Jodelle, the more he liked her.

She was sensitive. Introspective at times. Didn't feel the need to fill a silence with idle chatter. She genuinely cared about the kids she kept her eye on. That had been proven time and time again. She was selfless, not pretentious, and Baker definitely liked how she looked in a bathing suit. She was curvy in all the places a woman *should* be curvy.

All-in-all, he hadn't found one negative thing about Jodelle since he'd met her. And that both irritated and intrigued him. No one was as saintly as she seemed to be. No way.

Even being as attracted to her as he was, he'd still been determined to stay away. She was too good for him, that was crystal clear. But after witnessing how happy Mustang and Elodie were, how happy *all* of his SEAL friends were with their women, not to mention the love in Pid's eyes when he looked at his new baby daughter...Baker's mindset had begun to change.

He tended to keep people at arm's length, men *and* women. But after an old SEAL teammate of his had come to Hawaii with a serious grudge—and used Monica Collins, the woman of one of his acquaintances, as bait—Baker did some serious soul-searching.

He came to the realization that he didn't want to be an old man with no friends. Too much of a stubborn asshole to let anyone in. After so many years, the thought of being alone no longer appealed.

And when he thought about his future, about who he might want to hang out with when he was old and gray, the only person who came to mind was Jodelle. It was crazy, they didn't know each other, not really, but Baker couldn't stop thinking about her.

Then Ashlyn Taylor, the girlfriend of another SEAL friend, was shot several months ago, and Baker envisioned Jodelle being in her place.

He panicked. It wasn't logical. Wasn't something he'd ever dwelled on in the past, his friends being hurt. But the last couple of years had proven danger comes when you least expect it, especially in regard to his SEAL friends and their women. Now he couldn't shake the image of Jodelle lying in a hospital bed, suffering from a gunshot wound. He didn't *ever* want to see that happen.

And the best way to keep her safe...was to keep her by his side.

The thought didn't freak him out. For the first time since Tabitha, Baker wanted to be in a relationship. Wanted to go to sleep with a woman at his side and wake up the same way. He wanted her to text and let him know how her day was going, and he wanted to share what was going on in his own life right back.

Jodelle wasn't Tabitha. She'd never even think about stealing from him. And plotting to kill him? No way would that happen. Baker knew that as clearly as he knew his own name.

Earlier today, when he'd wrapped his arm around her chest to keep her from interfering with the medic's evaluation of the teenager she was so worried about, Baker knew instantly that he was a goner. She fit against him absolutely perfectly. He'd never been one to go for petite women, but Jodelle changed his thoughts on that. Aside from her curves, he loved her long dark brown hair that never seemed to want to stay confined in whatever hairdo she put it in, and her golden-brown eyes that hinted at a pain he wanted to soothe. She was also the most expressive woman he'd ever met. He knew exactly what she was thinking without her having to say a word.

But it was that agony deep in her eyes that called to him most. The woman was broken inside. She was merely going through the motions of life. Every smile was subdued, every chuckle tinged with grief. Baker wanted to hold her close and tell her that she didn't have to hide from him, that he'd put her back together piece by piece—but he had to earn the right.

And he was more determined than ever to do just that.

Baker knew she'd had a son, and that he'd died. But he didn't know any of the details. Her son's death had to be what had broken her, and while Baker couldn't know exactly what she was feeling, he'd experienced loss himself.

As he'd held her back from going to Ben, Baker had made a decision. He'd been a coward for too long. Afraid to let anyone in. But no longer. He'd seen the looks Jodelle had sent his way. She was interested, but had absolutely no intention of doing anything about it, which made her different from other women. Baker knew if he didn't at least attempt to explore the connection they had, he'd regret it for the rest of his life.

So today was the first step toward healing them both. Maybe things would work out, maybe they wouldn't, but he'd be damned if he didn't at least try.

"It's nice," Jodelle said as she looked around his place.

Baker shrugged. He hadn't thought much about decor in the past. The house was functional, and that was all he needed. Tile on the floor, small kitchen and living areas. Decent-size master bedroom with a bathroom attached. An extra bedroom where he usually stored his surfboard and other miscellaneous crap he'd accumulated over the years. He had the requisite large-screen TV and a comfortable couch and oversized easy chair.

But looking around, he didn't see anything that screamed "home." No pictures on the walls. No knickknacks. It was kind of cold...which was a feat, since he lived in Hawaii.

"It's a place to sleep, that's it," he told Jodelle with a shrug. He knew she was merely being polite. The thing of it was, he had no idea how to warm the house up, how to make it a place she might want to hang out.

"Come on," he said a little more gruffly than he'd intended. "Let's get you settled so I can feed you."

"I'm fine," Jodelle said as he put his hand on the small of her back and led her over to the small table next to the kitchen. Baker couldn't remember when he'd last sat there. He usually ate standing up or on the couch while watching TV.

Ignoring her protest, Baker opened one of the cabinets in the kitchen and scanned its contents. "I can make some killer spaghetti. The pasta would probably be good for you, since it's been a while since you've eaten." He then went to the fridge and looked inside. "Or I've got some steaks I can grill." Leaning over, Baker spied a package of chicken in the back. He grabbed it and stood, looking for the expiration date.

"Baker," Jodelle said from her spot at the table.

"I was gonna say I had some chicken, but I can't read the expiration date and I don't remember when I bought this. Not gonna risk you pukin' your guts out later." He walked over to his trash can and threw away the package of chicken thighs, making a mental note to take the trash out later so it didn't stink up the house.

"*Baker*," Jodelle said again, a little more forcefully.

He turned his head to look at her.

"You don't need to make me anything. I'm still unsure about why I'm actually here. Don't get me wrong, I was happy to give you a ride, but you've probably got things to do. I should go."

Baker strode over to where she was sitting and put one hand on the table and the other on the back of her chair. She'd turned so she was sitting sideways, and she was now effectively blocked in by him. He leaned down and couldn't help but be pleased by the way her cheeks flushed and she stared at him with wide eyes.

"The only thing I've got to do right now is make sure you don't pass out from lack of sustenance. We'll talk after we eat. You want spaghetti or steak? Unfortunately, those are the best options I've got right now. If you pick my killer spaghetti, the sauce really should simmer for at least six hours to get the full effect, but we'll make do."

"Um...spaghetti."

Baker studied Jodelle for a moment. "You eat meat?" he asked.

"Yes. I mean, not a lot. I don't have anything against it, but it's so easy to get fresh fruit and veggies here. The farmers market in Waialua is awesome, and I go there a lot, so I usually fill up on salads and pineapple. Besides, it's not like I need the extra calories from heavy, meaty dishes."

"No," Baker said.

She scrunched her nose. "No? No what?"

"Don't denigrate yourself. You're perfect exactly how you are."

Jodelle chuckled, but it wasn't exactly a humorous sound. "Baker, I'm forty-eight. At this point in my life, I know what I am and what I'm not, and what I'm not is perfect. I'm about twenty...okay, probably more like thirty pounds heavier than I should be. When you're barely an inch over five feet, those extra pounds really show. And living here in Hawaii, seeing all the beautiful women in their bikinis, just hammers that home all the more."

"I've never understood the desire for women to be skin and bones," Baker said. His eyes strayed, raking down her length, stopping on her tits for a moment before scanning the rest of her body. She had on a pair of shorts, and it took everything in him not to reach out and caress the tanned skin of her thigh. "Trust me when I say, I love how you look. You okay with ground buffalo in the spaghetti sauce?"

She stared up at him for a beat. Baker could see her pulse hammering in her neck. But eventually she took a deep breath. "I haven't ever had ground buffalo. What's it taste like?"

"Beef," Baker said, slowly standing up. There was nothing he wanted more than to lean down and kiss her, but it was too soon for that.

"Then why not just get ground beef?" Jodelle asked with an adorable tilt of her head.

"Because buffalo's leaner," he told her, forcing himself to head back into the kitchen.

"And why not get lean beef?" she asked.

Baker's lips twitched. He couldn't help it. Never in a million years would he have thought he'd be standing in his kitchen having a discussion about the merits of buffalo meat over beef. "It's got selenium, an antioxidant that helps prevent oxidative stress and reduces the inflammation that a poor diet causes. It also has more iron, higher levels of vitamins, and twice as much beta-carotene."

"Well, all right then," Jodelle said with a chuckle.

Baker stared at her for a moment, fighting the sudden urge to go to her, pick her up, and carry her into his bedroom. Had he ever felt this way about a woman?

No, definitely not.

"Can I help?" she asked.

Baker didn't need help. He could make the spaghetti sauce in his sleep, but his kitchen wasn't very big, and if Jodelle helped, they'd most certainly get in each other's way... and he'd have a chance to brush up against her.

"You want to brown the meat for me?"

She immediately stood. "Of course."

Forty-five minutes later, Baker carried two plates of pasta topped with sauce to the table. He'd made it less spicy than usual, since Jodelle said she wasn't a huge fan of hot food. She stared down at the heaping plate of spaghetti and laughed.

"I can't eat all this."

"Then don't," Baker said with a shrug. "Whatever's left over, I'll eat later."

When she continued to stare down at the plate and didn't pick up her fork, Baker frowned. "What's wrong? If you changed your mind, I can still grill us some steaks."

Jodelle looked at him in surprise. "What? No. You went to all the trouble to make this, there's no way I'd change my mind now."

Baker leaned forward on his elbows from across the table. He wished he'd picked the seat next to her rather than opposite. Though, it wasn't that big of a table, and he could reach out and take her hand in his even from where he was sitting, but he forced himself to stay still. "Anything you want, Jodelle. I never want you to do anything with me just to be polite. You change your mind, about anything, at any time, I'm more than happy to accommodate you."

She stared at him for a moment, confusion and apprehension swirling in her brown eyes. "I don't understand."

Baker knew they needed to talk, but first, he really did want to feed her. She hadn't eaten all day, had been too worried about taking care of "her" kids. He regretted worrying her. He sat back and took a deep breath. "Food first, then we'll talk."

His words didn't seem to relax her, which just made him regret coming on too strong all the more. Baker had never been a subtle man. When he wanted something, he got it. Period. But this situation wasn't like wanting to be a SEAL. Or wanting to track down a terrorist. Or wanting the newest gadget. He was dealing with Jodelle, and he needed to back the fuck off or he'd scare her away, which was the absolute last thing he wanted.

"Go on," he said, attempting to lighten his tone. "Try it. Tell me what you think of the buffalo."

He watched her take a deep breath, straighten her shoulders, and nod. She picked up her fork and wound some noodles around the tines, making sure to scoop up a healthy portion of sauce in the process. He waited with bated breath as she forked the bite into her mouth and chewed.

After she swallowed, she gave him a small smile and said, "It's really good."

"Of course it is," Baker said with a touch of pride. He might not be a chef like Elodie Webber, but he could make a mean spaghetti sauce if he did say so himself.

Jodelle chuckled, then shook her head as she stared down at her plate. "Spaghetti. Is there anything less dignified to try to eat in front of someone you—" Her words stopped abruptly.

Baker hoped like hell she was about to say "someone you like." But he didn't want to embarrass her, so he did his best to deflect the conversation away from what she'd almost said.

"I'll never forget when I was in Morocco and my team and

I had been invited to a local tribe leader's home. He was as proud as he could be to serve us some local delicacies. He brought out a plate of food, and we couldn't recognize anything. But it would be rude, and quite the insult, to refuse to partake. I picked what I thought was the most inoffensive-looking item on the plate. Our host had this huge smile on his face, which I should've realized meant I should definitely *not* eat whatever it was I'd chosen. But as team leader, I had to suck it up. Our host picked up another one of the round balls and popped the whole thing in his mouth, then nodded at the object in my hand, as if to tell me to get on with it. So I mentally shrugged and copied him."

Jodelle was smiling and leaning toward him as if enthralled with the story. "And? What was it?"

Baker realized for the first time that during a meal probably wasn't the best time for this story. "Uh...maybe we should finish eating first."

"Oh no, you started this story, you can't leave me hanging. It's not gonna turn me off this amazing pasta, Baker. Continue."

"Right. Well, the thing was slightly squishy, so I could compress it with my teeth...but then it expanded again. The only thing I could do was bite into the soft sack. As soon as I did, a rush of slimy liquid filled my mouth, and it was all I could do not to spit it out right there. But as our host was nodding and smiling like I'd just given him the world, I forced myself to swallow. At least the thing in my mouth wasn't quite as big as it was before, but what remained was rubbery, almost impossible to chew. No matter how much I chomped on whatever it was, it wasn't getting any softer and it was still too fuckin' big to just choke down.

"So I did what I had to do—I shoved it into the side of my cheek, pretended to swallow, and smiled at the tribal leader. He let out a triumphant yell and grinned at me. When he turned around to grab another piece of questionable cuisine, I spit the hard whatever-it-was out of my mouth into the dirt and quickly buried it."

Baker shuddered. "It was one of the worst things I've ever eaten in my life, and trust me, I've had some bad shit."

"What was it?" Jodelle asked with a wide grin.

"Sheep's eye. I didn't find that out until later though, and it's a good thing. I probably would've thrown up right then and there if I'd known."

Jodelle shuddered dramatically.

"So...spaghetti doesn't even rank in the top one hundred of undignified things to eat in front of someone else," Baker told her with a grin of his own.

"Thanks for not feeding me eyeballs," she said, returning his smile.

"Never," he said.

The rest of the meal went by smoothly. Baker could hardly believe Jodelle was actually here in his house, eating a meal with him. He wasn't the most loquacious man in the world, but she didn't seem to mind. Even when there were long silences between them, she didn't seem nervous or uneasy. Better yet, she didn't yammer on about nothing just to fill those silences.

Eventually, Jodelle sat back in her chair with a sigh. "Uncle," she said. "I ate as much as I could."

Baker was impressed. He'd put quite the pile of noodles and sauce on her plate, and she'd managed to eat just over half. He liked that she hadn't been afraid or embarrassed to actually eat in front of him. Some women would've taken a few bites and pretended to be full.

"It was good?" he asked as he stood and reached for her plate.

"Delicious."

Baker nodded in satisfaction. A familiar thrill swelled inside him. He'd felt this way when he'd completed a mission in the past, or after riding a killer wave, or when he'd uncovered an important piece of information while researching bad guys...but never had he experienced the emotion after making a meal for someone.

They worked together to package up the leftovers and when they were done, Baker said, "It's fairly early, the traffic out there will still be awful. If you leave now, it'll take you forever to get to your house. Want to sit for a while?"

Jodelle stared at him for a second, then asked, "You know where I live?"

Baker thought about lying, about saying that he just assumed she lived closer to Waimea Bay, but he didn't want to start their relationship by being dishonest. "Yes," he said simply.

Jodelle tilted her head and stared at him. "I don't know anything about *you*," she said after a moment.

"Yes, you do," he countered. "You've known me a while now."

"Fine. I know that you're a hell of a surfer, you used to be a Navy SEAL, you have some pretty awesome friends—if the few I've met are any indication. I know you're the strong-and-silent type, you're kind of bossy, and that you're kinder than you want most people to know."

Baker nodded. "Except for that last one, you're right on."

"You don't think you're kind?" Jodelle asked.

"I know I'm not," he said as he gestured to the couch with his head. "Shall we sit?"

She immediately nodded and followed his lead to the small sitting area. She sat on one end of the couch and Baker settled on the other. He wanted to pull her into his arms and into the oversized easy chair, but that was a bit much, even for him.

"I think you've probably seen some pretty awful stuff when you were active duty," Jodelle said, continuing their conversation. "And it's made you wary of most people. But I've seen you interact with the kids. You're tough with them, you don't beat around the bush when they mess up, whether in the waves or in school, but you aren't cruel about it. You tell them what they did wrong and how to fix it. They respect you for that, you know."

Baker shrugged.

"I mean, don't get me wrong, you can be a jerk. But most of the time, at least from what I've seen, the people you call out deserve it."

Baker wanted to tell her she was wrong. That he was anything but kind. But he also wasn't an idiot. He wanted her to like him, and fessing up to all the times he'd called out people for being assholes and when he purposely went out of his way to piss someone off because they deserved it...that wouldn't do the trick.

"I'm glad you see me that way," he eventually said.

To his surprise, Jodelle laughed. "Wow, was *that* diplomatic."

Baker couldn't help but smile.

"Anyway, you know where I live...what else do you know?" she asked.

"I know that seeing you makes my day one hundred percent better. That being around you makes me feel less like a washed-up old Navy SEAL and more like a normal man. That you've got more pain deep down inside of you than anyone I've ever met, and that I've never wanted a woman more than I want you."

Jodelle blinked in surprise. "Oh, um...wow."

Baker inwardly cringed. Shit, he was no good at this. "I'm not a nice man," he continued. "But being around you makes me want to be the kind of man you see in me. I'm fifty-two. I've figured out that things go much better when I spit out what I want, rather than beating around the bush or being vague. I want to get to know you better, Jodelle. Go out. I can't stop thinking about you. It's crazy, I've never been like this before, and I want to see if the attraction we seem to have for each other is something we can build on, or if it'll burn hot and fast, then fizzle out."

She stared at him for so long, Baker had a feeling he should've at least attempted to come on less strong.

"Why now?" she asked.

Relaxing a fraction, since she hadn't outright laughed or denied there was an attraction between them, Baker said, "Because I've fucked around too long as it is. If there's anything the shit that's happened to my friends has taught me, it's that life is short. I mean, you'd think I would've already known that being a SEAL and all, but my eyes have been opened even more recently, and I've realized what an idiot I've been."

"I'm not sure I want to be in a relationship," she said.

Baker respected her even more for her honesty. "I'm not sure I do either," he told her.

Her lips twitched. "So we're two people who don't want to go out, but will attempt it anyway?"

Baker shrugged. "You're different," he said quietly. "I don't know why, but I want to find out. I always thought I would be alone for the rest of my life, and I was fine with that. I've been satisfied helping take out the assholes who think they can abuse others and do whatever they want without any consequences. But at the end of the day, I come home to this empty and soulless house, and I've realized that while people appreciate what I do...if I disappeared off the face of the earth tomorrow, no one would give a shit."

"That's not true," Jodelle said softly. "Your friends would care."

"They would," Baker agreed. "For a short while. Then they'd get back to their own lives, as they should. I'm not explaining this well. I just...I realized I want more out of my life than simply being the man people call in when they need help or want to dig up some dirt they can use to prosecute someone."

"And you think you want *me*?" Jodelle asked.

"Yes," Baker said simply.

Jodelle shook her head. "I don't think I have it in me to love anyone again, Baker."

He snorted.

"I don't," she insisted.

"You have more caring in your little finger than some people have in their entire bodies," he told her. "Take what happened to Ben today as one small example. The second you heard he was in trouble, you didn't even hesitate to try to get to him. And I know you're still thinking about him, even now."

"That's common decency, not love," she insisted.

"The hell it's not," Baker told her. "Look, I know I'm comin' on strong. I don't know any other way to be. If you don't want to explore the connection we seem to have, all you have to do is say so. I'm not one of those guys who can't take no for an answer. It'll suck, but I'll respect your feelings."

"I just don't want to lead you on. I'm a mess, Baker. Seriously."

"That wasn't an answer, Jodelle."

She sighed. "I also don't want to disappoint you."

Baker decided he was done putting distance between them. He scooted over until his leg was touching hers. He lifted his hand and palmed the side of her neck. Inwardly, he stood up and cheered when she subtly tilted her head into his hand. "You won't. I have a feeling I need to be the one worried about disappointing *you*."

He wanted to kiss her. So damn bad. But Baker forced himself to stay still. To gaze into her eyes and try to read the emotions he saw swirling there.

Then, after a long pause... "Okay."

"Okay?" Baker asked. "Okay what?"

"I was attracted to you the first time I saw you...who wouldn't be? You're a good-looking man. But I've seen lots of handsome men in my lifetime. However, the more you hung around in the mornings with my kids, the more I realized that you weren't just a hot surfer. You're confusing, kind of scary sometimes, never beat around the bush...but you're also protective, a hell of a good friend, and have the kind of honor I haven't seen in anyone else, ever. I'm lonely too. But I always thought it was penance for all the wrongs I've done in my life. I'm not sure...no, I *know* I don't deserve someone like you. But I'm too weak to say no."

"You aren't weak," Baker told her with a small frown.

She didn't reply.

"You aren't. I don't know why or how you think that of yourself, but I'm going to do everything in my power to make you see yourself the way I do. Life is hard, Tink. It beats us up, then delights in throwing curve balls when we're already down for the count. Weak would be giving in. Becoming bitter. There's a saying in the SEALs, the only easy day was yesterday...which is so fuckin' true. And yet in you, I see the same thing I saw in my SEAL teammates. A refusal to give up."

"There are times when that's exactly what I want to do," Jodelle said.

"But you don't," Baker countered. "Which makes you strong as fuck. I see you, Jodelle Spencer. And I like what I see."

She shivered and lifted a hand to grab hold of his wrist. "This is probably a mistake," she whispered.

"You want me?" he asked bluntly.

She nodded.

"Then it's not a mistake," Baker said. "I can't see the future, but I can tell you this—whatever happens between us will be good. Great. And if we mutually decide to go our separate ways, we'll do so. It won't be full of drama, it'll just happen. Okay?"

She sighed. "I'd like that. But as you said, you can't see into the future. Things happen."

"They do. But I'll never, *ever*, turn on you. You have my word on that."

"Okay."

"Okay," Baker agreed, feeling more excited and happy than he'd felt in a very long time. "You wanna watch TV? I can put in a movie. Or we could take a walk."

She looked up at him with her big brown eyes, and Baker wanted to think he saw the same excitement he was feeling reflected in her gaze.

"Are we gonna kiss to seal the deal?" she asked shyly.

"Yes. But not right now. I've moved things fast enough. You need time to absorb what's happening between us."

"Oh."

The disappointment in that one word almost made Baker lose the tenuous hold he had on his control. "We'll get there, Tink. There's no rush."

"I just..." She shook her head. "It's hard for me to believe that we've gone from casual acquaintances to...whatever we are."

"We were never really casual acquaintances, and you know it," Baker said.

She stared up at him and nodded slightly.

"A walk," Baker decided, reluctantly dropping his hand from her neck. "It'll help me keep my hands to myself."

"I like your hands on me," Jodelle admitted.

He closed his eyes and took a deep breath. Fuck. She just laid it right out. No games, no being coy.

"Baker?" she asked in concern.

His eyes opened and he stared down at her. "I like my hands on you too," he said. Then he stood. "Come on. Polo Beach isn't that far from here, it's usually not very crowded and it'll be a good place to walk off some of that pasta."

Jodelle stood with a smile and asked, "This isn't going to

be a forced march, is it? Because I'm full. And I might puke if you make me walk too fast."

Baker chuckled and wrapped his arm around Jodelle's waist. "We'll go at your pace, Tink."

"Thanks. Your legs are a lot longer than mine, and with your training, you'd outpace me in seconds."

"You think I'd leave you behind?" he asked as he steered them toward his front door.

"No. But I have a feeling you were a tough team leader. I can picture you barking at your sailors and telling them to get their shit together and get a move on."

Baker laughed because she wasn't that far off the mark. He wanted to pull her against his chest and kiss the hell out of her, but he settled for leaning down and kissing the top of her head instead. "Promise. This is a lazy after-dinner stroll. Nothing more."

"Okay. Baker?"

"Yeah?"

"This is weird. And really unexpected. But I'm not upset about it."

He beamed. "Good."

He let go of her long enough to open his door, and once it was closed and locked, Baker was thrilled when Jodelle shyly reached for his hand. It was crazy how simply holding her hand made tingles shoot up his arm. He was fifty-two, and for the first time in his life...he was almost giddy about being with a woman. He wasn't sure if he should be concerned about that or just go with the flow.

Jodelle looked up at him, smiled shyly again, then turned her attention back to the sidewalk in front of them.

Baker decided to go with the flow.

# CHAPTER THREE

Jody lay on her bed the next morning and stared up at the ceiling. Yesterday had been...interesting. The last five years of her life she'd enjoyed a kind of comfortable routine. Looking out for her kids most mornings before school started, coming home and doing some work, heading back to the beach again in the afternoon, then spending the evening at home alone, eating dinner and often working again, before heading to bed to do it all over the next day.

Yesterday had been quite a change from that routine, and she wasn't sure if she liked it or not. There was safety in doing the same thing day in and day out. Jody'd had enough surprises and change to last her a lifetime.

Yesterday had shaken her out of her comfort zone. First off, there was Ben. Something was wrong, and she desperately wanted to talk to the teenager and see if there was anything she could do to help. She didn't know a lot about the boy, just that his parents were wealthy and he was a fairly quiet but well-liked kid.

Then there was Baker.

Sighing, Jody closed her eyes as last night replayed in her head. It was hard to believe that he was actually interested in *her*. She wasn't anything special. Some days she felt as if she was barely holding her head above water. Yet Baker seemed to be completely serious when he'd told her he wanted to see where things could go between them.

He was slightly arrogant, but Jody knew if she'd rebuffed his advances in any way, he would've backed off. But she hadn't. For the first time in a long time, she was taking a risk.

Mana would've told her it was about time.

Thinking about her son, Kaimana, was still painful, but this morning, picturing her son smiling at her and giving her a high-five wasn't as debilitating as it had been in the past. She missed her goofy kid more than she could put into words. It had been just the two of them for so long, it still felt odd to wake up and not have him in the house.

Knowing if she dwelled on the loss, she'd be in a funk for the rest of the day, Jody forced her thoughts back to Baker. She liked how upfront he was. He was intense, but she definitely knew where things stood between them, which was a relief. She was too old to play dating games.

Their walk to the beach had been nice. They'd held hands and talked about the day's surfing competition—and how much they hated the resulting traffic—among other things. Baker had told her just a little about his time in the Navy, and his decision to stay here in Hawaii after retiring from the SEALs. It was comfortable, and Jody felt as if she'd known the man forever. She was still confused about how they'd gone from barely friends who saw each other a few times a week on the beach, to apparently dating, but she couldn't say she was upset about it, even if nerves still plagued her.

Baker was...it was hard to come up with the words to describe him. All Jody knew was that she liked being around him. He filled her up inside, and she'd felt utterly empty ever since Mana had died.

Refusing to let herself get morose, Jody sat up and swung her legs over the edge of the bed. She was taking a rare day off from going to the beach. This was the last day of the surfing competition and her kids would most likely be there watching, as they'd been the last few days. Tomorrow they'd get their beach back, surfing in the early morning hours before school started, and Jody would be there to keep her eye on them.

She had today to herself...which wasn't exactly her favorite thing. But she had a few graphic design jobs she wanted to work on, as well as a website she needed to build from scratch. Jody was very thankful for her job...it gave her something to focus on when the pain of losing Mana became too much, and it allowed her to stay in the house she'd shared with her son.

After showering, Jody grabbed a Pop-Tart out of the pantry and stood in her kitchen as she ate it. She knew they weren't healthy, like at all, but they'd been one of Mana's favorite things to eat, and having one for breakfast every morning made her remember her son.

She'd just finished the treat when her phone beeped with a notification. Frowning, not sure who would be contacting her so early, Jody walked over to the table where she'd left her phone the night before and picked it up.

Seeing Baker's name on the screen made butterflies swim in her belly. They'd exchanged numbers last night.

BAKER

Had a good time last night. I'm trying not to come on too strong, so I'm gonna resist the urge to come over today.

Knowing she had a goofy smile on her face, Jody leaned against her counter and used her thumbs to type a response.

JODY

You weren't kidding about not fucking around, were you?

BAKER

Nope. You'll learn that about me. When I want something, I give it my all. What are your plans for the day?

This felt nice. It had been a long time since she'd had someone to share plans with.

JODY

Nothing exciting. Doing some work.

BAKER

No beach?

JODY

You told Rome I wouldn't be there, so I'm going with that. Besides, it's Sunday. No school and the competition is still going on. My kids will be too busy trying to soak up the rad vibes from their favorite surfers to get into trouble.

BAKER

But tomorrow you'll be there?

JODY

Yeah. Why?

BAKER

Just making sure I'll get to see you soon.

Goose bumps broke out on Jody's arms. Man, this guy was lethal. Then she frowned. He could tear what was left of her heart out of her chest and stomp it into bits. Second thoughts raced through her. Maybe this wasn't a good idea.

BAKER

No rush and no pressure, Tink. Just being real.

It was as if he could sense her freaking out and did what

he could to try to alleviate that. She took a deep breath and replied.

JODY

I can't pretend this isn't making me nervous…but I did wake up with a smile on my face for the first time in years.

BAKER

Good. Expect a call from Elodie today.

Jody blinked in confusion. She knew who Elodie was. She was married to one of Baker's Navy SEAL friends. She'd met a few of them over the last year or so, but had no idea why the other woman would be calling her.

JODY

Elodie? Why?

But instead of three dots appearing at the bottom of the text screen to indicate Baker was replying to her question, her phone rang in her hand, scaring the shit out of Jody. She laughed at herself before clicking on the icon to answer.

"Hi," Jody said a little shyly.

"I hate fuckin' texting," Baker said in lieu of a greeting. "And I'd much rather hear your voice in my ear anyway. Good morning, Tink."

The last three words were said a little softer and gentler than the others.

"Morning," Jody told him.

"Elodie will be in touch because I talked to Mustang this morning and happened to mention that I'd spent the evening with you. He's gonna share that with his wife, and I have no doubt she'll get super excited and call me, wanting your number so she can welcome you into the fold…so to speak."

Jody wasn't sure what to say about that. "Um…okay."

"It's how she is," Baker said gently. "How all the women

are. They're curious about you, and they're gonna want to get to know you. If you want me to tell them to back off, I will."

"No!" Jody said quickly. "I mean, I'm curious about them too, if I'm being honest. The few times I've met some of them, they seemed nice."

"They *are* nice," Baker reassured her. "They're also nosey as hell, so if they ask you anything you aren't comfortable answering, don't. They won't get upset."

"Maybe I'll grill Elodie about *you*," Jody teased.

"Go for it," Baker said.

Jody shook her head. Figured the man wouldn't be afraid of what his friends had to say about him. But that also comforted her.

"But seriously, Jodelle, you don't want to go there with Elodie or any of the other women yet, just say the word. I'll tell them to back off, that we're still getting to know each other and they can just wait until we're more solid before inviting you to their sleepovers."

Jody laughed. "They have sleepovers?"

"Yeah. Usually at Kenna and Aleck's penthouse. The view is awesome from up there. Anyway, Aleck makes himself scarce and the girls do their thing. And before you ask, the guys are all more than all right with the tradition because it beats the women getting dressed up and going to a bar to get drunk. Much safer."

A longing swept through Jody, along with sorrow. She couldn't help but remember some of the sleepovers Mana had when he was younger. The sound of boys giggling had long since faded from her house, but the memories were as vivid as if they'd just happened yesterday.

"Tink?" Baker asked.

"Sorry, I'm here," Jody said.

"Fuck. Didn't mean to make you sad."

How this man could read her moods through a phone line was beyond her, but Jody didn't dwell. "I'm not sad, exactly.

It's just been a long time since I've thought about sleepovers."

"Heads-up, Tink...I'm gonna want to hear all about your boy at some point."

Jody closed her eyes. She wasn't sure what to say. Mana's death wasn't a secret, and she wasn't surprised Baker knew about him.

"Because straight-up, sucks hard that he died," Baker said. "I wish I'd known him. With how amazing his mom is, I know he would've been a hell of a man."

Two tears fell from Jody's eyes as she blinked at Baker's words. It had been a long time since someone had come right out and talked about Mana. Most people avoided talking about him at all costs. She knew it was because they assumed talking about Mana would upset her, but by avoiding the topic, it almost felt as if they were doing their best to erase him altogether. But not Baker. "I wish he could've known you too," she said after a long moment.

"You want me to tell Elodie to give us...you...some time?" Baker asked.

Jody swallowed and wiped her face. She'd experienced just about every emotion possible this morning, and it wasn't even nine o'clock yet. She'd felt numb for so long, and while she wasn't a huge fan of these wild mood swings, she couldn't deny that she felt more alive than she had in a very long time. She felt as if she was slowly thawing after spending years encased in ice. The jury was still out on whether or not that was a good thing.

"No. I think I'd like to talk to her," Jody told Baker.

"Okay. I hate to admit this...but I don't know what it is you do for a living."

Grateful for the change of topic to something less deep, Jody chuckled. "I'm a graphic designer. I do everything from making logos, to designing T-shirts, to putting together websites."

"And you can do that from home?"

"Yeah, luckily. My hours are my own, so I can fit in work when I need to. There are times someone has a rush job they need completed, but generally I pick and choose how much to work and when."

"I like that your schedule is flexible, Tink."

She couldn't help but smile at that. Again, Baker didn't hesitate to tell her what he was thinking, which she was really starting to enjoy. "Me too. What about you, Baker?"

"What *about* me?"

"What do you do? I know you're retired from the Navy and you used to be a SEAL, but what do you do now?"

"I'll tell you when I see you again," Baker told her after a pause.

Jody frowned. That sounded a bit ominous. "That sounds kind of scary," she told him.

"It's not. It's just hard to explain. And I'd rather not have you misconstrue anything I tell you. If I'm face-to-face with you while we have that talk, I can nip any misgivings you might have in the bud."

"Am I *going* to have misgivings?" she asked.

"It's possible."

Shit. Jody didn't like the sound of that.

"But if you do, I'll make sure you don't by the time we're done talking."

She couldn't help but laugh at his conceit.

"I like that," he said softly.

"What?"

"Hearing you laugh. Gonna make it my mission in life to hear that every day."

A weird feeling settled over Jody then. She couldn't remember the last time anyone had looked out for *her*. Concerned about what she was thinking or feeling. Or wanted to make sure she was eating, resting, laughing...just happy.

"Jodelle?" Baker asked when several seconds went by without her saying anything.

"I'm here. I just...it's been years since anyone's cared about what I was doing or thinking."

"I care. I'm gonna let you go so you can get some work done before Elodie interrupts you. Don't be surprised if you're agreeing to host a Tupperware party or some shit for her and the other women without a clue how she talked you into it."

Jody smiled. "Okay."

"I mean it. The woman's got some sneaky skills. But, Tink, if you aren't ready or comfortable, don't be afraid to say no. It's not going to turn Elodie off. You tell her you need time or space, she'll give it to you."

"All right."

"You good?" he asked.

"Yeah, Baker, I think I am."

"I'll be checking in today to make sure you stay that way. You okay with that?"

"By checking in, do you mean peeking in my windows at random times of the day or showing up at my door?"

It was Baker's turn to chuckle, and Jody loved hearing it. She had a feeling he didn't laugh all that much either. "I was thinking more like sending a text now and then. Maybe calling you tonight."

"I'm okay with that," Jody told him. "But for the record, I wouldn't have minded if you said you were planning on popping over either."

It was Baker's turn to be silent for a beat. "Fuck. Killin' me. Love that you don't play games, Tink. I'll touch base later. Have a good day."

"Okay." Jody realized that she hadn't asked him what he was doing today, but it was too late now. "You too."

"Bye."

"Bye." Jody clicked off the phone, but didn't move from

her position leaning against her counter. She realized after a minute or two that she was still smiling.

Eventually, she headed into her bedroom and the small desk in the corner. Her house had two bedrooms, but even after all this time, she couldn't bring herself to turn the second room into an office. That was Mana's room. Would always be his. She'd given most of his clothes to charity and packed up his belongings, but still, seeing the bare double bed and the stickers Mana'd put on the drawers of his dresser was enough to make her break down, even all these years later. She'd thought about transforming the room into an office, but...she honestly couldn't imagine changing anything about it.

So the room sat empty, and she did her work on the small desk in the corner of her bedroom. If she wanted a change, she brought her laptop out to the living area and worked on her table or on the couch.

Jody wished she had some sort of glorious view to gaze at while working, like the waves rolling to the shore from the ocean, but her house was small and tucked behind an even larger one, so all she could see was the neighbor's house out of her bedroom windows and trees out of the larger windows in the living room. She did have a fairly good-size backyard, which was a blessing. The fruit trees were a bonus as well.

The lack of a view was probably a good thing, since it made it easier to concentrate. But today she was having a harder than normal time keeping her mind on what she was doing...thanks to Baker. A part of her thought maybe she was hallucinating, that the handsome man hadn't actually declared his intent to "stop fucking around" when it came to a relationship with her. But all she had to do was glance at her text messages to reassure herself that she really *had* spent yesterday afternoon and evening with him. And that he seemed to be into her.

It was weird. She was a middle-aged, divorced, messed-up-in-the-head woman still drowning in grief. So much so, sometimes she barely got through the day. Not to mention, she carried too many extra pounds on her slight frame and found it easier to get along with a bunch of teenagers than people her own age. What in the world did Baker see in her?

Jody wasn't convinced a relationship between them would work out, but she couldn't deny that for the first time in years, she wanted to try. She was tired of being sad all the time.

Taking a deep breath, she forced herself to put everything out of her head except the graphics she needed to work on. Her client needed a large cling that would be placed on a hotel elevator at a conference. It needed to be eye-catching and easy to read at a glance. And he'd given her carte blanche to create what she thought would work best.

Three hours later, Jody leaned back in her chair and stared in satisfaction at the screen in front of her. She loved what she'd designed, and just hoped her client would as well.

Focused as she was, her ringing phone scared her so badly, she almost fell out of her chair. Chuckling, and thinking it was kind of sad that she hadn't heard her phone ring in so long it could actually made her jump in fright twice in one morning, Jody answered.

"Hello?"

"Hi. This is Elodie. Is this Jodelle?"

"Yeah, but please call me Jody. Everyone does."

"Everyone but Baker," the woman said with a laugh.

"True. I've told him that no one calls me that, but he doesn't seem to care."

"That sounds like Baker. How are you?"

"I'm good."

"I'm sorry we missed you at the surf thing yesterday. Baker was nice enough to get a friend to let us hang out in his backyard so we'd have a bird's-eye view of the action without dealing with the horrific parking. I don't know how you do it."

"Do what?" Jody asked, somewhat amused at Elodie's slight rambling. If she didn't know better, she'd think the other woman was nervous, but that was crazy. If anything, *she* should be the nervous one, not Elodie.

"Live up there with that traffic all the time."

"Well, yeah, it's not fun, but it's not as bad all the time as it is when there are surf competitions. And is the traffic on the H1 any better?"

Elodie laughed. "Good point. So...you have to know... we're all really curious about you."

Jody scrunched her nose. "I'm really not all that interesting."

"Wrong," Elodie said without hesitation. "Look, I've known Baker for a while now. He actually saved my life. And that man does not suffer fools. He's super picky about who he gives his time to, and you are *definitely* included in that rare club."

"He saved your life?" Jody asked.

"Yup. And I'll tell you all about it—and how he also had a hand in saving the lives of all my friends—if you'll meet me for lunch one day."

Jody couldn't help but laugh. God, she'd laughed more today than she had in a very long time.

"What? Was that funny?" Elodie asked.

"It's just that Baker warned me you'd have me agreeing to host a Tupperware party or something by the time we finished our talk."

Elodie chuckled. "So? Wanna have lunch? I was thinking that maybe we could meet halfway. Just south of the Dole Plantation on H2 is a place called Sunset Smokehouse that Scott says is fabulous. But if that's not okay, we can go somewhere else."

"I've been there, the barbeque is awesome," Jody told her.

"Cool. And I'm gonna push my luck here, but how do you feel about some of the others coming too?"

"The others?" Jody asked.

"Monica, Lexie, Ashlyn. You've met Mo, and you waved at Lexie when she was up meeting with Baker once, and Ashlyn is actually protective of the man...if you can believe that. It's kind of crazy, but true. Kenna and Carly want to meet you too, but they magnanimously said they could wait until you came down for one of our sleepovers."

Truthfully, Jody was a little freaked out, but she had to laugh yet again. "Baker told me about your sleepovers too."

"Good. Because we totally want you to come to one. Soon."

"Um...forgive me if this sounds bitchy, I don't mean it to... but you don't know me. And Baker and I literally just agreed to give this dating thing a try last night. It hasn't even been a day, so I don't understand how you and your friends can be so...excited about meeting me."

"Here's the thing, Jody...Baker's the shit. He's done more for all of us than you can possibly even imagine. I'd do *anything* for that man, and I don't mean that in a weird way. But he'll never ask. He exists in a bubble. He's happy to help others, but never reaches out for himself. He's been interested in you for a long while now. And if Baker's interested, that means you're a hell of a person. When Scott, my husband, wants something, nothing keeps him from getting it. And while I might not know Baker all *that* well, I do know that he's a lot like my husband."

"Yeah, I'd have to agree that it sounds like it."

Elodie chuckled again, and Jody found herself smiling in response.

"So, you'll come to lunch?"

"Yeah, I'd like that."

"Good. How about this weekend?"

"Oh, um...okay."

"Saturday? One o'clock okay? And as much as it pains me, don't let Baker talk you into letting him come along. Girls only."

"It pains you?" Jody asked.

"Baker is mysterious. None of us have really hung out with him much. He kind of just appears, then he's gone a minute later. So yeah, I'd love to actually sit down and chat with the man when the shit *isn't* hitting the fan, but first, I just want to get to know you."

Jody wasn't feeling all warm and fuzzy about the shit-hitting-the-fan thing, but she didn't dwell on it. "Sounds like a plan. Saturday at the Sunset Smokehouse. One o'clock."

"It'll be fun. Promise," Elodie said.

Jody wasn't so sure about that. She was already having second thoughts. But all she said was, "I'm looking forward to meeting some of Baker's friends."

"You've got my number, so you can call or shoot me a text if something comes up. I'm looking forward to meeting you," Elodie said.

"Same."

"Okay, talk to you later."

"Bye." Jody clicked the connection off and immediately added Elodie's number to her contact list. It was kind of sad how few people she had in her address book, and it actually felt good to be adding someone new.

Without thinking about it, Jody opened her text messages and began typing out a note to Baker.

JODY

Elodie called. No Tupperware party planned, but we're going to lunch on Sat.

Not even a minute after she'd hit send, three dots appeared as Baker replied. It was so like him not to make her wait to get a response.

BAKER

You okay about that?

JODY

Sort of.

BAKER

Explain.

JODY

Elodie said Monica, Lexie, and Ashlyn would be there too. I've met Monica and she seemed shy, but nice. I saw Lexie one time, as well, but she said Ashlyn was protective of you.

BAKER

You need me to call Elodie and tell her that it's too much, too fast? I don't want you to feel ganged up on.

It didn't escape Jody's notice that Baker didn't address the protective thing, but maybe text wasn't the best place to talk about that anyway.

JODY

No. I'm a big girl, Baker. I can deal.

BAKER

All right, but if you can't, it's okay.

JODY

I kind of feel like I need to make friendship bracelets to distribute on Sat.

BAKER

LOL

JODY

OMG, did you just say LOL?

BAKER

You've got eyes, Tink. Looks like I did.

JODY

I just didn't see you as a text-speak kind of guy.

BAKER

I'm not.

JODY

And yet you typed LOL.

BAKER

It was either that or tell you what a kook I think you are, and how much I fucking love that you can be that way. And I'm thinking it's probably a bit too early to be calling you a kook and telling you that I love anything about you. So...I settled with LOL.

Jody swallowed hard and goose bumps once more broke out on her arms. God, this man.

BAKER

And now I've told you anyway. And freaked you out. Sorry.

JODY

No! Okay maybe a little, but in a good way. It's been a very long time since I've been anything but Mana's mom, or Miss Jody, or the graphic designer someone hired.

BAKER

You're all that and more to me. You done with work today?

JODY

No. I got one project done, but have two more to start, and I need to check my emails and see what projects I want to line up next.

BAKER

Then I'll leave you to it.

JODY

Okay.

BAKER

Elodie and the others are good women. You
have nothing to worry about. I'll call later.

JODY

Sounds good.

When three dots didn't pop up on the screen, Jody
figured their conversation was over. She took a deep breath,
shook her head at how crazy her life seemed now, compared
to twenty-four hours ago, then stood up to head into the
kitchen and grab some lunch before getting back to work.

# CHAPTER FOUR

The next morning, Baker left for Waimea Bay earlier than usual. He was already a morning person, but now he was anxious to see Jodelle. He had no idea what it was about her that drew him so easily, but he was done fighting her pull.

The parking area was crowded, even this early, but Baker wasn't surprised to see Jodelle's colorful VW van already there. He climbed out of his Subaru Crosstrek—a smaller-size SUV, but one of the best-rated cars for hauling around surfboards—pulled up his wet suit, grabbed his surfboard from the rack on the roof, and headed for where Jodelle always set up while she kept an eye on her kids.

He'd done some research yesterday, and while a part of him felt guilty for prying into her personal life, Baker justified it because the last thing he wanted to do was say something that would upset her.

He'd known her son had passed about five years ago, but that was the extent of his knowledge on the topic. It wasn't hard to find out the details about how Kaimana had died. It was tragic and heartbreaking, and it gave Baker a greater understanding into why she got up at the crack of dawn every day to watch the high schoolers surf.

"Hey," he said as he got close, not wanting to startle her by walking up on her without warning.

Jodelle turned and smiled at him—and just like that, Baker's cock twitched. Fuck. When was the last time he'd lost control over his body? Never. It just proved this was the woman for him, and Baker would do whatever he could to not fuck things up between them.

"Morning," she said. She had a travel cup between her hands, and when Baker got close he could smell the scent of chocolate.

"Coffee?" he asked, already knowing the answer.

"No. Hot chocolate," Jodelle said. "It was..." She stopped, shrugged, and said, "I like it."

"What were you going to say?" Baker asked.

"Nothing," Jodelle lied.

Baker propped his board against a nearby tree, then walked closer. She was sitting on top of a picnic table, her feet propped on the seat, giving her a clear view of the ocean in front of her. The waves were still fairly small; later in the day they'd swell into the monsters the North Shore was known for this time of year.

Baker leaned into her and shook his head. "What were you gonna say about your hot chocolate, Tink?" he repeated.

For a moment, he didn't think she was going to reply. Then she said softly, "Just that it was one of Mana's favorite drinks and we always shared a cup in the morning before he headed out to surf."

"Don't be afraid to talk about your son with me," Baker ordered. "You don't have to watch what you say. Hearing you talk about him won't make me uncomfortable. Something reminds you of him, I want to know. Sucks, but the only way I'm gonna learn more about him is through you. Of course, if that makes you uneasy or causes you pain, then by all means, we can avoid it. But I just want you to know that you don't have to feel weird about bringing him up around me."

Jodelle's eyes filled with tears, and she swallowed before nodding but otherwise remained silent.

Baker was a little disappointed. Even though he wasn't much of a sharer himself, he still wanted her to talk to him about what she was feeling, but he'd give her time. She'd learn that he never said something he didn't mean.

He leaned in, kissed her on the forehead, then pulled back. He glanced out at the water and said, "Looks like there's a lot of people in the lineup this morning. Who's out there?"

A lineup was the area in the water, away from the swell, where surfers waited their turn at catching a wave. Baker knew Jodelle was familiar with surfing lingo when she answered without hesitation.

"Everyone. Felipe, Rome, Brent, Lani, Kal..." Her voice trailed off again.

"Not Ben?"

"No," she said softly, her lips drawn down into a frown.

It wasn't in his nature to wade into a situation when he wasn't asked to, but since Jodelle was obviously worried, it was time for him to get involved. "I'll see what I can find out."

She tilted her head and studied him intently. Just when he thought she was going to ask the questions he could see lurking behind her eyes, she merely said, "Thanks."

There came a time in any serious relationship when a SEAL had to decide how much he was going to share with his partner. Baker had known some men who shared literally nothing. There were many details they couldn't talk about, even if they wanted to, but he knew for a fact that some SEALs *did* talk to their wives about what they'd done and seen.

Baker had never been tempted to tell anyone about the things he'd done in the past, and what he still did. Not even his friends knew the extent to which he was still involved in the top-secret world of national security. Now, for the first time, he felt the urge to explain to someone else exactly what he did for a living. But telling Jodelle could potentially put her in danger, and that was the absolute last thing he'd ever do. She'd been through enough hell in her life, Baker wouldn't add to it.

Still, he had a feeling he'd open up to this woman more than he had to anyone else in his life...and he was all right with that.

"How well do you know Ben?" he asked.

Jodelle shrugged, took a sip of her hot chocolate, then said, "As well as I know the other kids, I suppose. He first started coming out in the mornings to surf a couple years ago. He's always been quiet, respectful. He had an ear infection at the end of the last school year, but he still came out here in the mornings. He sat with me and we'd chat. Never about anything super personal, but still...I like him, Baker. He's a good kid. But something's wrong. I feel it."

Baker nodded and repeated, "I'll see what I can learn."

"And you'll tell me?"

Baker frowned in surprise. "Of course."

"Oh...okay. I guess I just thought since you're so secretive, that you might get info and then keep it to yourself."

Baker wasn't surprised Jodelle thought he was secretive. He was. He leaned toward her, thrilled when she didn't lean away. He lifted a hand and curled it around the side of her neck, his thumb brushing against her cheek. She sat frozen beside him, looking up at him with wide eyes.

"This is not the time or place for the conversation I want to have with you about what I do, but I'll give you some of it. Though, there's a lot of things I can't talk about, Tink."

"I know," she said before he could continue. "You were a SEAL. I get it."

"That's part of it. But I'm still working for the government. When they need information, they call me. I'm good at what I do, and what I do is gather intel."

She stared up at him without blinking.

"I will not share that part of my life with you. Not in detail. And it's not because I'm a dick, or because I don't want you to know. But because I don't want it to *ever* touch you. If we're going to do this," Baker said, using his free hand to gesture between them, "you need to understand and accept that."

"I do," she said without hesitation.

Baker took a moment to inhale a deep breath. God, this woman. She had no idea how much her trust in that regard meant to him. He could be doing illegal or immoral searches, but he had a feeling that hadn't even crossed her mind.

"Means the world to me, Tink," he told her. "But while I won't share what I'm working on for the government, I'd never keep information to myself about anything that affects you."

"Like Ben," she said.

"Like Ben," he confirmed.

"Okay."

Baker waited. When she didn't say anything else, he raised a brow. "That's it?"

"Um...yeah?"

"I really want to kiss you right now," he told her after a long pause.

Jodelle's breathing sped up, and her lips quirked in a small smile. "I'm all right with that, even if I'm not sure why you feel that way right this second."

"And that's part of why I want it," Baker retorted. "But I don't have the time or privacy to kiss you like I want to right now. And I have a feeling once I start, it's gonna be hard to stop. Besides...it's too soon."

"There's a schedule for this kind of thing?" she asked.

Baker chuckled softly. "No. But the last thing I want is

you thinking I just want to get into your pants. You're gonna be worth the wait, Tink."

"Um, maybe you shouldn't have high expectations when it comes to that, Baker," Jodelle said, breaking eye contact with him for the first time.

He moved his hand from her neck to under her chin, and tilted her head up so she had no choice but to meet his gaze once more. "Explain," he ordered.

"Apparently, I'm not all that good in bed," she told him.

Baker was speechless for a moment—then he threw his head back and laughed. When he got himself under control and looked down at Jodelle, he saw she was frowning and shooting daggers at him with her eyes.

"I'm sorry, Tink, but that's a load of crap."

"You don't know that."

"I do," he insisted.

"No, you don't. I think I'd remember if you and I shared a bed before."

"Jodelle, there's no fuckin' way you're anything but out of this world when it comes to sex."

She looked adorably confused...and pissed. Baker knew he was a dick for being turned on by that, but there it was.

"Seriously," she said. "I'd tell you to ask my ex, but he's dead, so you can't. But trust me, he told me so often how shitty sex was with me, I had little choice but to believe him."

"Wrong," Baker said, all humor gone from his eyes. "You're the most sensual woman I've ever met. If sex between you and your ex was bad, it was all on *him*, Tink, not you."

"He had affairs," Jodelle admitted softly. "Said since he wasn't getting what he needed from me, he had to get it from someone else. He also told me it was my fault it took so long to conceive Kaimana."

"That douche was a fuckin' idiot as *well* as an asshole," Baker returned immediately. "And if he wasn't dead, I'd definitely be having some words with the man. I think you know that I've been into you for a good while, and if you didn't, you do now. Trust me when I say, you were meant for loving. From your body, to your lips, to the way you rub your thumb and forefinger together when you're nervous...like now," Baker said with a smile, flicking his glance down to her hand, which was doing exactly what he'd just described. "Besides, between the two of us, I think I'm the one who has to be worried about his performance in the bedroom. It's been over a decade since I've been with a woman."

Baker hadn't meant to admit that, but he'd do anything to make Jodelle feel more comfortable with him. He wasn't ashamed of the fact that he hadn't been laid in so long; it was by choice. He simply hadn't felt the need or desire to be intimate with anyone. Until now.

"I just—" Jodelle started, but Baker put a finger over her lips and she stopped mid-sentence.

"No. Trust me."

She smiled under his finger, and Baker slid his hand back around her neck.

"I'll try," she told him.

Baker knew it was impossible to hide his erection since he was wearing a skintight wet suit, but he didn't even care. If Jodelle knew how much he wanted her, all the better. He leaned forward and kissed her forehead once more, lingering, inhaling the slight scent of plumeria and knowing if he fucked things up between them, he'd lose something precious.

Taking a deep breath, Baker pulled back. He wanted nothing more than to stay right where he was, but if he was going to figure out what was going on with Ben Miller, he needed to start with the people who knew him best. And some of those people were out in the water surfing...so that's where Baker was headed.

"Gonna go and catch some waves," he said, liking the unfocused look on Jodelle's face. Liked knowing he affected her that way.

"Okay."

"How much time do they have until it's time to head to school?" he asked.

Jodelle looked down at her wrist. "About forty minutes."

It wasn't much, but it would have to do. "Okay. See you soon."

She smiled at him. "I'm thinking your days of going to high school have long since passed, Baker. You don't need to leave the water when they do. In fact, you usually stay in long after."

He did. One, because he liked it when he didn't have to wait in line to catch a wave, but also because he'd been trying to keep his distance from Jodelle. But no more.

"I know," was all he said. "I'll see you in about forty minutes."

She gave him a shy smile. "Okay."

Baker forced himself to turn and grab his board. Not able to help himself, he looked back once when he was on his way to the water, and smirked when he saw Jodelle's attention glued to his ass.

Baker wasn't a vain man. He kept in shape because it had become routine to work out when he'd been active duty, but he couldn't deny that he liked how she looked at him. With a small chuckle, he ran into the ocean and began to paddle out past the impact zone toward the surfers.

Everyone greeted him warmly and there were several minutes of talk about the surf competition and speculation about how big the waves were going to be later that afternoon. After Kal caught a big wave, Baker paddled over to Brent. He would've preferred to talk to the kids after he'd done some research on Ben and his family, but he wasn't going to waste this opportunity.

"Haven't seen Ben around. What's up with that?"

"Don't know," Brent said. "Ever since he's been interested in the new girl, we haven't seen him much."

"The new girl?" he asked. Jodelle hadn't said anything about Ben having a girlfriend, and she was usually up on all the high school gossip since she hung out with the kids so much. But maybe it was a new thing, and with the competition breaking up the usual routine, she hadn't heard about Ben's love interest yet.

"Yeah, her name's Tressa Dixon. She's super-cute. Petite, but too shy for me. She's also in the school band. That's about all I know," Brent said.

"Are you guys talking about Tressa and Ben?" Lani asked as she paddled closer.

"Yeah. Baker was asking if we'd seen Ben lately, and I said that he's been hanging out with Tressa," Brent said.

"She bad news?" Baker asked.

"Tressa? Not that I know of," Lani said. "But I go to Waialua High and they attend Kahuku High on the north side. I heard from Parker Dunn—he's a senior at Waialua—that there's gonna be another big party at the Miller place this weekend, if you're looking for Ben."

"Another?" Baker asked.

Lani nodded. "Yeah, there're parties at Ben's house all the time. His dad is super generous and cool and doesn't mind when people come over to hang out. Anyway, Parker goes out with Nora, who's a junior at Kahuku, and she said Tressa's gorgeous. She's also a junior, has long black hair, big brown eyes, and apparently all the guys have the hots for her. But she keeps to herself, doesn't talk to anyone much...except for Ben. That pisses Alex Flores off, who's another senior at Kahuku, and he said he's gonna beat the shit out of Ben when he sees him—which, as everyone knows, will be at the next party at his house, since everyone goes to them."

"So he's lying low?" Baker asked. That would make sense. If he'd gotten word that someone wanted to beat him up, he might be reluctant to show his face at his usual hangouts.

"Not really," Lani said. "Ben's pissed on Tressa's behalf.

Because everyone knows Alex's a douchebag and he has a tendency to smack his girlfriends around. He's said some shit to Tressa in the halls, which hasn't gone over well with Ben."

Baker shook his head. Jesus, he definitely didn't miss high school drama. But he was glad to hear that Ben seemed to be protective of this girl.

"Alex is just being a jerk. Besides, it doesn't matter. I've heard Tressa's a virgin," Rome said. He'd approached their group a minute or so earlier and heard Lani's last comment.

"I heard that too," Brent agreed.

"Does it fucking matter?" Baker asked a little more hotly than he'd intended.

"Well, yeah," Lani said, as if Baker was the slowest person on the planet. "It means there's no way she's gonna give out to an asshole like Alex. And since he and his dickhead friends only go for the slutty girls, eventually he'll get tired of picking on Tressa and move on."

Baker wasn't so sure, but then again, it had been a long time since he'd been sixteen and in high school. "So what's up with the party then?" he asked. "If this Alex guy is threatening to beat him up, and he harasses his girlfriend, why's Ben having a big party? Seems to me that's an invitation for trouble."

And just like that, the previously chatty kids got quiet.

After a nervous pause, Brent shouted, "Party wave!" and the other kids immediately began paddling toward the large wave big enough for several people to surf at the same time.

Well, shit.

Baker sat on his board and nodded at a few more kids hanging out, waiting for another wave, thinking over the gossip he'd just learned.

Ben had a new love interest, who was a virgin, and shy, and someone wanted to beat him up over her, and there was a big party at his house this coming weekend. That last part didn't add up, which made Baker uncomfortable. Not to mention, his expertise was definitely not with teenagers and their angst. Give him a psycho terrorist any day over this kind of crap.

But since Jodelle was worried about Ben, he'd do what he could to figure out what the hell was going on, if only to ease her mind. Baker had a feeling the kid was simply engrossed in a potential new relationship and whatever was going on with the guys who were gunning for him, and that's probably why he hadn't been surfing in a while and was acting weird.

If it was a simple case of teen drama, however, why had Lani, Brent, and Rome avoided his question about the party at Ben's house? It was possible they were just afraid of getting in trouble. Where there were parties, there was usually alcohol and possibly drugs.

Even more alarming...why were there several changes of clothes and a *pillow* in Ben's car the other day?

Baker's intuition was screaming at him that there was more to Ben's current problems than just girlfriend drama and bully trouble.

Sighing, he watched as the kids Ben usually surfed with started to head to shore. Now he *knew* they were avoiding him. They didn't usually voluntarily head in before Jodelle came to the edge of the water to let them know it was time to get ready for school.

By the time Baker made it to shore himself, Ben's friends had already rinsed off in the showers and were heading to their cars.

"Well, that was different," Jodelle remarked when he walked up to where she was standing next to the picnic table.

"What was?" he asked, already guessing the answer.

"Instead of dragging their feet, they actually all seemed in a hurry to get to school. Weird, huh?"

"Yeah, weird," Baker agreed, but inside his curiosity had been piqued. Something was definitely up, it was no longer just Jodelle who was worried. He also had a feeling he had his work cut out for him. He was an adult. The kids weren't going to confide in him, and it wasn't as if he could use his usual techniques for getting information from a reluctant informant.

Jodelle leaned over to pick up her cooler, but Baker took it from her. His surfboard was once more leaning against a tree, and he reached for her hand with his free one. "I'll walk you to your car," he said.

"I think it's safe enough for me to make it there on my own," she teased.

Baker shrugged. "Probably. But if there's a one percent possibility of you being hurt or attacked, I'm not going to take the chance. Besides, it gives me another minute or so of being with you."

"How can I complain about that?" Jodelle asked.

"You can't."

They headed for the parking lot and her colorful VW van in the back. "Why don't you park closer?" he asked.

Jodelle shrugged. "Habit, I guess. I don't get a ton of exercise since I sit at my computer for work almost all day. So I figure the extra steps won't hurt me. And it lets others who might not be able to walk as far have the closer spots."

His Jodelle was kind.

Baker didn't even freak out at the "his" thought.

All too soon they arrived at her vehicle. She took the cooler from him and slid open the back door, placing it inside on the floor.

"I'm shocked you don't have lights and peace signs all over the inside," Baker teased. "Isn't that a requirement to drive one of these things?"

Jodelle laughed. "Probably, but I never did like being predictable. And before you ask, I've got the seats at my house in the garage, but I took them out because it was easier to haul stuff around."

"Stuff?" Baker asked.

He saw Jodelle's cheeks turn pink, and he was instantly intrigued. He thought he'd pegged this woman, but every time he was around her, he found out more and more things he didn't already know.

"Yeah. Sometimes I drive one of the kids home when their ride falls through. The last thing I want is them hitch-hiking...and I needed the room for their surfboards in the back. Other times, when I'm not slammed with work, I go out and collect trash. People are so rude, throwing bottles and cans out their windows as they go. It's handy to have the room for the bags I collect."

Baker wasn't surprised she went out of her way to be considerate. It was just who she was. He'd seen it time and time again in the last year or so. He'd thought her kindness was restricted to making snacks for the teenage surfers, but he was obviously wrong.

"When I think I might need to transport more than one person, though, I put in the seat. I don't like to have anyone sit in the back without a seat belt."

"How do you get the seat in?"

"Um...I don't understand the question," Jodelle said with a small frown.

"You're tiny, Tink. Do you ask your neighbors for help with putting the seat back in and taking it out?"

"My neighbors are either older or they're at work," Jodelle said.

Baker stared down at her.

"Fine. It's not pretty, and there's lots of swearing and grunting, but I manage," Jodelle admitted a little defensively.

Baker hated the thought of her wrestling the seat for the van by herself. "Next time, let me know and I'll come help you."

"It's not a big deal, Baker. I'm used to it."

He leaned into her until she'd backed into the side of her

van. "Next time you need to put it in or take it out, let me know, and I'll come help you," he repeated.

"Uh...okay."

"I mean it, Jodelle."

"I said okay," she protested.

"But did you *mean* it?" he asked, cocking one brow up.

"Yes?"

Baker couldn't help but chuckle. "Right. This is who I am. I'm not being sexist or an asshole. The seat has to be as big as you are. I just want to help you."

"All right," Jodelle said, sounding a little more sure of herself. "But here's the thing—I've had to learn to do a lot of stuff by myself. You can't always be there when I need help."

"I can try," he countered.

Jodelle shook her head. "Whatever," she mumbled.

Baker leaned in and nuzzled the skin on her neck just below her ear.

"Um...Baker?"

"Yeah?"

"What are you doing?"

"Smelling you."

She laughed a little self-consciously. "It's warm this morning, I'm sure that can't be pleasant."

Baker lifted his head. "Plumeria," he said.

When Jodelle licked her lips, it was all Baker could do not to take them right then and there.

"It's my perfume."

"You put on perfume to come to the beach?" Baker asked, trying to understand.

She shrugged. "It's a habit. When Mana was young, he used to sit on the counter and watch me get ready in the morning. It was kind of our thing. He always wanted to spray me with my perfume. Spritzing myself in the morning is another one of the little rituals that remind me of him."

Baker lifted a hand and brushed it over her head. "That's sweet. Glad you have that memory, Tink."

"Me too," she said softly.

"And for the record...it smells fuckin' awesome on you."

She smiled shyly. "Thanks."

"You're welcome. You have a busy day ahead of you?"

"About normal, why?"

"Just wondering if you're gonna get a wild hair to head out and clean up the island, save the whales, protest against plastic straws, or find a random tourist and give them a private tour of Oahu or something today."

Jodelle giggled. "Not today. Got too much stuff to do. But —just because I'm curious—what would you do if I said I was going to do any of that?"

"I'd see if I could wrangle an invitation to come with you," Baker told her honestly.

"Really?"

"Yeah. Why are you so surprised?"

"My ex never wanted to do anything like that with me. Always told me I was a do-gooder in a tone that I could tell meant he thought it was ridiculous."

"It's not ridiculous," Baker told her without hesitation. "And fuck him."

Jodelle smiled. "Yeah." Then she sobered. "Did anyone have any insight into what's up with Ben?"

Baker sighed and backed up a fraction, giving her some space. She didn't move from her spot against the side of her van. "Not really. But I'm gonna look into it."

Her shoulders sagged. Baker wanted to tell her about the party, but he had a feeling if she knew, she might take it upon herself to go and see what she could find out. And with Baker's unease about the shindig, that was the last place he wanted her near. So he downplayed what he'd learned from the kids.

"I appreciate you trying to talk to them," she said. "I'll see if I can get anyone to open up to me this afternoon. They usually don't hang around on the beach though, they're too anxious to get in the water and catch some waves."

"Not sure you'll have much luck with that then, since the waves are supposed to be bitchin' this afternoon," Baker said.

She smiled.

"What?"

"You saying bitchin' is kinda funny."

"Why?"

"I don't know, it just is."

Baker couldn't help but smile at her. "I'm a surfer, babe. Gotta speak the lingo."

Her smile widened.

"Come here," he ordered, reaching out and giving her a small tug toward him. She came without hesitation, putting her arms around him and hugging him tightly.

Being this close to her made Baker's dick twitch, but she didn't seem to mind. Jodelle held onto him for several glorious minutes, until she sighed and pulled back.

"Thanks."

"For what?"

"It's been a long time since I've gotten a hug. Mana was a touchy-feely kind of kid. Every time he left the house, he gave his mom a hug. I miss having that connection with someone."

"For the record, anytime you need a hug, I'm there for you. But I feel as if I should warn you..."

"About what?" she asked, scrunching her forehead adorably when he didn't immediately continue.

"You should probably brace yourself...because Elodie and the others...they're huggers."

Jodelle chuckled. "Yeah?"

"Uh-huh. Thought it was annoying at first, but I've gotten used to them. But *nothing* beats having you in my arms, Tink."

Her cheeks pinkened again. He fucking loved that he

could make her blush. He had a feeling she'd be doing that a lot as their relationship progressed. He wasn't a man to temper his words...especially in bed.

"It's getting late. You need to get home, get a healthy breakfast in you, and get to work so you can be ready to come back this afternoon."

"Will I see you later?"

He liked that she seemed eager to see him again. "I'm not sure. I need to see how the day plays out. But I'll definitely call tonight if I can't get here to see you."

"Okay. Baker?"

"Yeah, Tink?"

"I think I like this. Us. I'm still not sure what changed, but I'm glad it did."

He'd make sure in the not-so-distant future that she not only *thought* she liked what was happening between them, but fucking loved it. "What changed is that I got my head out of my ass. And I like it too. I'll talk to you later. Be safe."

"I will."

He brushed his fingers against her cheek once more, then stepped back. She climbed into the driver's seat—and *climbed* was the word for it, since she was so short—gave him a small wave, then backed out and headed for the road.

Baker walked back to the beach and grabbed his board, returning to his own vehicle and securing the board to the roof rack. After he sat down behind the wheel, he lifted his hand to his nose and inhaled. He could still smell the slight scent of plumeria on his skin from where he'd held onto her neck. He'd never be able to smell it again and not think of her...which was perfectly all right with him.

He hadn't gotten nearly enough of a workout that morning. Hell, he hadn't even surfed a wave, so he'd need to work out when he got home. But he'd do it thinking about the Ben Miller situation. Baker didn't know if this Tressa person had anything to do with whatever was going on with the boy.

Maybe it was all the bully Alex causing the issues. Or maybe there wasn't anything wrong at all, and the kid's priorities had simply switched from surfing to girls. It wasn't outside the realm of possibility.

But then again, Ben's friends had acted awful suspiciously this morning, which made Baker uneasy. He had some digging to do, and if there was something hinky going on, he'd figure out what it was, if only to give Jodelle some peace of mind. If there was anyone who needed a life filled with easy, it was her. She'd had enough hardship in her forty-eight years. He'd do what he could to make sure from here on out she had nothing but goodness.

# CHAPTER FIVE

Jody bolted up in her bed and listened hard. Knowing exactly what she heard, as she'd heard it more times than she could count, she threw back her blanket, leaped out of bed, and ran to her door. She whipped it open and practically threw herself at Mana's bedroom door. She jerked it open, ready to scold Mana for getting home so late after curfew.

But instead of seeing her son standing in his room, looking sheepish and smiling at her, all she saw was darkness. The room was empty and cold.

The sound of Mana's keys thumping down on his dresser was nothing more than a dream. Her imagination.

Stumbling backward, Jody's chest heaved with a sob. Every time she thought she was finally coming to terms with the fact that her beloved son was never coming back, her mind had to go and play a cruel trick on her.

She spun and staggered back to her bed. Without thinking about what she was doing, Jody reached for her phone.

The last thing she'd heard before falling asleep was Baker's deep voice in her ear. She'd seen him twice that week, both times in the mornings before he headed out to surf with the teenagers, but he'd called her every night. It was now Friday...well, Saturday, since it was well past midnight, and today she'd be going to have lunch with Elodie, Monica, and Ashlyn. Lexie had something come up and she couldn't make it.

Jody was excited, but also nervous. Baker had reassured her that she had nothing to be nervous about and everything would go smoothly.

Then for some reason, maybe it was her nerves getting the best of her, but she'd dreamed about Mana for the first time in quite a while. She used to dream about him all the time, and when they'd faded away, it was both a blessing and a curse. She missed her son, desperately, and while dreaming about him was painful, at least she got to "see" him again.

Tonight, she'd woken with the sound of her son's keys hitting the top of his dresser. It had been so clear. So real. And it had happened before. In fact, for a while after Mana died, she heard him all the time. Entering the house, flushing the toilet, talking on the phone in his room. Heard him so often, she'd begun to think she was going crazy.

The phone rang through the speaker in her empty room. Just as Jody was coming fully awake, and realizing it wasn't a good idea to be calling Baker at—she looked over at the clock —three twenty-four in the morning, he answered.

"What's wrong, Jodelle?"

Amazingly, he sounded completely awake and alert. It was too late to hang up and pretend she hadn't called now.

"I...nothing," she said.

"Talk to me. Now," Baker said sternly. "You've got two seconds before I'm in my car headed to your place."

"I had a nightmare," Jody whispered, feeling silly that she'd woken him up.

"What?"

"A nightmare. Or hallucination. I don't know what you'd call it. I'm sorry, I didn't mean to worry you. I'm fine. As fine as I *can* be. I'll let you go back to sleep. I don't know why I called you."

"Don't hang up," Baker ordered, sounding much more relaxed than a second ago. "What was it about?"

"What it's always about," Jody said with a sigh.

"Mana," Baker guessed.

"Yeah."

"Tell me about it."

Surprising herself, Jody did just that. She *needed* to talk to someone. Feel not so alone for once. "It happens every so often. It's the same every time. I'm asleep, and I swear I hear the sound of his keys hitting his dresser. It was a habit for him. Whenever he got home, he'd go straight to his room and dump them on top of his dresser. He learned that from me. I always put my keys in the same place when I get home, otherwise I lose them. Mana had to help me search for them so often, we finally made a pact to always put them in the same place the second we got home. Mine are in a bowl on the kitchen counter. His was on his dresser."

Jody closed her eyes and smiled sadly, remembering how hard it had been for both of them to get in the habit of putting their keys in the designated place.

"So you heard that tonight?"

"Yeah," Jody said softly. "My brain tells me that his death was a horrible dream. That he's home. I'm out of my bed before I even really wake up. I run to his room, ready to scold him for getting home after curfew, but all I see is that empty space. I go from being ecstatic to devastated in the space of a heartbeat. It still hurts, Baker. So damn much."

"Are you cold?" Baker asked.

Jody wasn't sure why he was asking for a moment, then she realized that her entire body was shaking. Even her teeth were chattering. He must've heard it in her voice.

"Freezing," she told him.

"Where are you?"

"Lying on my bed."

"Get under the covers."

Baker was being bossy again, but Jody wasn't quite herself, so she didn't really mind. She bent her legs and pushed them under the sheet, pulling up the blanket as she lay down.

"Are you under them?"

"Yes," she whispered.

"Close your eyes."

"Baker, I'm sure you have better things to do, I'll just—"

"Hush," he told her, not unkindly.

Jody hushed.

"I don't know what your beliefs are about God, Heaven, or what happens when we die, but I'll tell you what I think."

Jody nodded. He couldn't see her do so, but he apparently didn't need to in order to keep talking.

"You aren't hallucinating. And you aren't crazy. You and your son share a unique bond. You were close, very close, and I believe his soul is still here...watching over you. You dreaming about him, or hearing things like his keys hitting the wood of his dresser, is his way of letting you know that he's near. That he's protecting you.

"I also believe that when we're born, we're tasked with learning something about life. That might be love, that might be friendship, it might be what it's like to be a parent, or to struggle through adversity and learn how to deal with it. When we die, the life we've led is reviewed...if we learned what we were supposed to, we move on to another life, another chance to learn something new. If we didn't learn our lesson, we get a second chance to learn what we were supposed to in the next life."

"You're talking about reincarnation?" Jody asked.

"Yeah. I also think that souls reincarnate together. So the people you love the most appear in your next life in some way. As your friend, child, spouse, a teacher who touches you in some way. I think souls are linked...which means Mana's waiting for you, Jodelle. Those dreams are his way of letting you know that he's out there, watching over you, waiting until you can be reunited and start over together at some point in the future."

Jody thought about Baker's words. Some people would immediately dismiss them as being hokey or way too out there...but she liked the thought of being with Mana again in the hopefully distant future. Though, one thing bothered her about what Baker said. "I'm not sure my boy had time to learn whatever lesson he was supposed to learn," she admitted.

"What were his best traits?" Baker asked.

Jody didn't even have to think about that. "He was one of the kindest people I've ever met. He literally made friends with everyone. He was always bugging me to stop so he could hop out of the car and give a homeless person money. Once, he even took off his own shoes when he saw a homeless man wasn't wearing any. He helped younger kids learn how to surf, and I swear I never heard him say a bad word about anyone."

"I'm thinking maybe whatever higher power is out there had other plans for your son," Baker said quietly. "Maybe it wasn't his job to learn a lesson in this life, but to *be* a lesson for others. To teach others how to be accepting, nonjudgmental, and kind."

Tears welled up in Jody's eyes. She liked that. A lot. Not the part where Mana had to die way too young, but that maybe, just maybe, others had learned compassion from his example.

"The way I see it," Baker said, "is that you shouldn't be afraid of your dreams, or of hearing Mana puttering around in the house. Embrace it, find joy that his soul is still out there and waiting until you can be reunited."

The tears spilled over onto her cheeks. "I want to, but I miss him so much, Baker."

"I know you do, Tink. I'm sorry I never got to meet him."

"Me too. He would've liked you," Jody said. Then something else struck her about what Baker had said earlier. "So... souls reincarnate together?"

"I believe they do," Baker said.

"Do you think *we* knew each other in a past life?"

"Yes." Baker didn't hesitate even a heartbeat before answering.

"So I could've been your teacher or father?"

"Possibly, but I'm thinking not."

When he didn't continue, Jody asked, "Why not?"

"It's probably too early for this conversation," Baker said, avoiding an answer in a way that wasn't normal for him.

"I'm sorry I called so late...or early," Jody said.

"I don't mean that. It's just...we're still getting to know each other. I don't want you to freak out."

"Baker, I called you in the middle of the night to tell you that I heard my dead son throw his keys onto his dresser...if anyone should be freaking out, it's probably you," Jody said dryly. Amazingly, she felt a hundred times calmer than she did when she'd picked up the phone. Usually after an incident like this one, she'd fall into a depression so deep, it would take several days to crawl back out. But after talking with Baker, and hearing his thoughts on the afterlife, she already felt better.

"You need me, you call. I don't give a shit what time it is," Baker said firmly. "Got it?"

"Yeah. And while I can't think of any situation where you'd need *me*, the same goes for you."

"Sometimes hearing a soft voice, one that isn't asking you for anything other than simply to talk, is the most precious gift you can receive," Baker said.

"Baker," she whispered, both loving and hating his words.

"Soul mates," he said quietly. "Sometimes there's one person out there who's it for you. Who's been with you life after life. It's fuckin' hard to find them, especially when there are lessons to be learned in each of the lives we're given. But I think in every life, you cross paths, and if your eyes are open to the possibility, you rejoice in having found the other half of your soul. You grab onto that person and hold on with all your worth. No matter what obstacles are put in your way, you hold the fuck on...and in return, are rewarded with a love so strong, so pure, nothing can tear you apart."

Jody swallowed hard. Never in a million years would she have thought she'd be having a conversation like this, in the middle of the night, with Baker Rawlins. She wasn't sure she completely believed what he was saying, but a warmth deep down inside her seemed to grow with every word he spoke.

Under his tough exterior, his gruff and sometimes scary countenance, he was a romantic. The dichotomy was a total turn-on.

"I know that sounds crazy," Baker went on. "And it's taken me way too fuckin' long to get my head out of my ass, but I truly believe you're that person for me, Jodelle. The second we met, something inside me clicked. I resisted our connection, feeling like after the life I've led, I was meant to be alone, but I can't deny it anymore. That doesn't mean we're rushing things though. You need time to believe what we have is real, and I'm going to give you all the time you require. So we're still taking this one day at a time. Baby steps, Tink."

"Okay," Jody said.

"You still cold?" Baker asked.

Jody thought about it for a second, then said, "No."

"Good. You want to sleep or keep talking?"

"You said you were heading down to Honolulu to check on a friend tomorrow morning," Jody said.

"Yup."

"You need to get some sleep so you can do that," Jody told him.

"Much rather talk to you, make sure you're good. Won't be able to sleep anyway if I'm worried about you," Baker said.

Jody snuggled into her blankets a little more, turning onto her side and curling her knees up so she was in a ball. "Will you tell me about the friend you're going to visit?"

"Of course. But before I do...you nervous about tomorrow...or rather, today?"

Jody realized Baker did that all the time. Turned the conversation around so they were talking about her and what she was doing. She didn't mind, and it felt good that he was interested, but she wanted to talk about him sometimes too. "Yes, but in a good way."

"What does that mean?"

"I haven't been out with girlfriends in a long time. I grew apart from my old ones after I got married and had Kaimana. Then when I got divorced, it was all I could do to take care of myself and my son. I felt as if I was barely keeping my head above water. As Mana grew up, I got heavily involved in my work, trying to make enough to give my son everything he needed and wanted. When he died, just getting up every morning was a challenge. And when I finally did start to heal, I was busy with my work again, and going to the beach in the mornings and afternoons to watch over the kids. So I'm nervous, but also excited. I'm intrigued by your friends' women and I want them to like me."

"They already do," Baker said.

"They don't know me," she protested.

"Doesn't matter. They know you're with me, and not being conceited or anything, but they like me, Tink, and they know that I'm no idiot. If I like you, that means you're awesome. So you have nothing to worry about when it comes to them liking you. If anything, I need to be worried they're gonna want to take up all your free time, and I'll be left out in the cold."

Jody laughed at that. "Um, not gonna happen, Baker."

"I'm glad. They're good people," he told her gently. "They know what it's like to be scared. What it's like to feel like you're completely alone in the world. Remember what I said about souls reincarnating together? These are your people, Jodelle. That sounds ridiculous, but I swear it's true. All you have to do is be the person you already are. You know why Mana was as kind and considerate as he was, don't you?"

"Why?" Jody whispered, almost overcome with emotion once more.

"Because he learned it from his mom. I've seen you with those kids at the beach. And with others. Those sandwiches you make aren't just for the teens you keep your eye on. They're for anyone who looks hungry. And don't think I haven't noticed the bag of flip-flops you keep in your van in case you run across someone who can't afford to replace their own worn-out shoes."

Jody closed her eyes and took a deep breath.

"The friend I'm going to see tomorrow? His name's Theo. He lives in Barbers Point near Food For All, where Elodie, Lexie, and Ashlyn work. He's in his mid-forties, used to be homeless, and he saved Lexie's life. He's got something wrong mentally, but he's the most talented artist I've ever seen, and somehow, even though we're complete opposites...we're friends."

Jody smiled, not surprised that Baker had taken Theo under his wing. She asked Baker about Theo, about Food For All, how he got into surfing and other easy topics. Before she knew it, another hour had passed.

When she yawned for the tenth time in five minutes, Baker asked gently, "You think you can sleep now, Tink?"

Jody's eyes felt heavy and she was more relaxed than she'd been in a very long time. "Yeah."

"Good. Like this, Jodelle."

"What?"

"Talking to you when you're all soft and sleepy. It'll be a dream come true when I get the chance to do it in person."

"What?"

"Talk you down after you have a bad night. I'll like it a hell of a lot more when I get to hold you while I'm doing it."

Jody had not a doubt in the world that she'd like that better too.

Baker didn't give her a chance to respond. "Have a good time tomorrow. Drive safe. Will you let me know when you get home?"

Again, that warmth spread through her. The idea that someone cared where she was and if she got home all right. "Will you let me know when you get home from visiting Theo? I'm gonna worry since I kept you up."

"Yeah, Tink. I'll let you know. Gonna want you to meet Theo at some point too. He's gonna be extremely curious about you."

"You're going to tell him about me?" she couldn't help but ask.

"Of course."

"It's only been a week since we decided to be more than friends," Jody hedged, reminding him of something she knew he was well aware.

"Soul mates," Baker said simply. "Go to sleep, Tink. I'll talk to you tomorrow. You can tell me all about how great lunch went and when your sleepover with the girls is planned."

Jody chuckled. "I'm not sure we'll go from meeting for the first time to BFFs planning a pajama sleepover."

"Don't underestimate the power of Elodie and her posse," Baker said with a laugh. "Have fun tomorrow. Sleep well."

"You too."

"Night."

"Good night," she said, then clicked off the phone. She lay there in a ball for a moment before rolling over, placing her phone on the table next to her bed, then rolling back to her other side. She closed her eyes and whispered out loud, "Good night, Mana. Love you."

Feeling a million times better than she had when she'd woken up earlier, Jody closed her eyes and immediately fell into a deep, dreamless sleep.

# CHAPTER SIX

Jody pulled into the parking lot at the Sunset Smokehouse and couldn't help but grin when she saw the three women standing at the entrance, talking. She recognized Monica from the one time she'd met her, and just assumed the other two were Elodie and Ashlyn.

She was relieved to see that she'd chosen correctly on what to wear. Jody had decided to go casual, but not too casual. She had on a cotton sundress she'd picked up on a whim while shopping in Honolulu about two years ago. It had cap sleeves, an empire waist, and came down to her knees. It was black with purple and yellow flowers. It was brighter than what she usually wore, but Jody loved the way it fit her perfectly, and she actually felt pretty when she wore it.

She'd completed the look with a pair of black wedges with a beaded sparkly flower at the toes. Mana had always made fun of them for being too girly, but he'd admitted once that he thought they were cute. Jody thought about him every time she wore them...which was why she hadn't put them on since the day he'd died. But today, after thinking about what Baker had said last night, it seemed right to bring him along with her to hopefully meet her new friends.

Before getting out of the car, she pulled out her phone and typed in a quick text, letting Baker know she'd arrived at the restaurant safely. He hadn't asked her to, had only asked that she let him know when she got home, but he'd sent her a note earlier reassuring her that he'd arrived in Barbers Point without any issues, and that while he was tired, he wasn't *too* tired. It was considerate, as she'd been worried about him. Now she wanted to return the favor.

JODY

I'm here. The girls are waiting for me at the entrance, but I wanted to let you know I arrived all right.

BAKER

Appreciate it. Have fun.

His text was short and to the point, but Jody wasn't offended. He was probably doing his thing with his friend and it was nice that he'd immediately responded. She put her phone into her purse, took a deep breath, and climbed out of her van.

The three women were all watching as she walked toward them. They probably hadn't missed her colorful VW pull into the lot.

"Hi," Jody said when she got close. "I'm Jody."

The three women were all smiling. The black-haired woman stepped forward when Jody got close and said, "I'm Elodie. It's so nice to finally meet you."

Then she shocked the shit out of Jody by opening her arms and giving her a long, heartfelt hug.

Monica said, "It's good to see you again, Jody," and also hugged her.

And lastly, the tall woman who had to be Ashlyn greeted her and did the same.

Baker hadn't been kidding, these women *were* huggers...

and it felt awesome. Jody couldn't keep the goofy smile off her face.

"I can't believe you're actually here! We didn't think Baker was ever gonna get his head out of his butt and ask you out," Elodie said with a smile.

Ashlyn still wore a friendly smile as well, but Jody knew instinctively that she was going to be the toughest one out of the bunch to impress. Jody remembered Elodie telling her on the phone that Ashlyn was protective of Baker. Instead of being irritated by that, it made Jody feel good. She liked that someone had his back, because it was dawning on her that he was the kind of man who always looked after others.

They all walked inside and Jody inhaled deeply. It smelled so good...she couldn't wait to dig into the delicious-smelling smoked beef. They went through the line and Jody got beef brisket, as did Elodie. Monica got pulled pork and Ashlyn ordered the pork spare ribs. They got a large order of potato salad to share and some spicy pinto beans. Once they found a seat, a server brought over a basket of Hawaiian sweet rolls.

"I can't believe I never knew this place existed," Ashlyn said after they'd all started eating. "Texas barbeque is my absolute favorite."

"It's so good," Jody agreed. "They also cater and have takeout...although it might be a bit far from Barbers Point for you to pick up."

"I'm sure Slate wouldn't mind coming up here. I mean, look at this...it's totally worth the drive." She held up one of her spare ribs. Her fingers were covered in sauce and there was even some on one of her cheeks. Everyone laughed.

"Very true," Jody said.

"I'm sure Baker would drive down here and get you guys some too, right?" Elodie asked with a gleam in her eye.

Jody knew she was blushing, but she gave the other woman a small smile. "Probably."

"So...you guys are finally together?" Elodie asked bluntly.

Jody was impressed she'd waited this long to bring up Baker. But she couldn't blame her...she was well aware that this visit was about the other women not only getting to know her, but getting the deets on their new relationship. "I guess," she said.

"Wait—you guess?" Ashlyn asked. "Elodie said you guys were dating."

"I mean, I guess we are, but he's been busy, as have I, and we haven't actually gone out on a date yet," Jody said.

Elodie blew out a breath and sat back in the booth with a small huff. "That guy," she said with a shake of her head.

"I pegged Baker as the kind of man who didn't mess around...it's kind of disappointing to know that's not the case," Monica said.

Jody didn't like the others thinking anything bad about him. "He told me he thinks I'm his soul mate," she blurted.

Elodie and Monica smiled at hearing that.

"That's more like it," Elodie said.

"I can see him saying something like that," Monica mused.

"And you? What do you think?" Ashlyn asked.

It was a good thing Jody had the food to distract her, because otherwise she had a feeling she'd be quaking in her shoes. She swallowed the bite of beans she'd just put in her mouth as Ashlyn asked her question, then met the other woman's gaze.

"I think Baker's the best thing to happen to me in a very long time. He makes me feel safe, he makes me laugh, and he's the first person to ask me how I'm doing—and mean it— in years. I also think I'm not nearly good enough for him. He deserves someone who doesn't wake up sad, then goes to sleep the same way at the end of most days. Someone who's not so...broken. But I already know I'm going to do everything in my power to be the kind of woman who deserves him. I have no clue if I can do that or not, but I'm gonna try.

I also think that he's got to be just as amazing as I think he is, if the three of you have his back."

Throughout her little speech, Ashlyn's expression lost some of its reserve, and by the time she was done speaking, Elodie had tears in her eyes. She reached for Jody's hand and squeezed. "He saved my life," she said softly.

"And mine," Monica added.

Jody's gaze went to Ashlyn.

"He didn't save mine. But he felt so damn guilty that he didn't somehow have the ability to know what was going to happen in the future, and that he wasn't at my friend James's house the moment his asshole home health aide went apeshit and shot me, that he was sitting on the beach in the middle of the night, stressing over it. Which isn't safe, and I told him so. I also told him his guilt complex was ridiculous, but he's the kind of man who hates when his friends are hurting, and hates even more when he can't help."

"Um...wow...okay," Jody said, trying to wrap her mind around everything Ashlyn had just said. "You were *shot*? Are you okay now?"

Ashlyn's expression relaxed even more. "I'm good," she said quietly.

"And the guy who shot you?"

"Is dead," she said flatly.

"Okay."

"Has Baker told you anything about us?" Elodie asked.

"Not really. Just that you were all awesome and that he thought you were strong as hell," Jody said.

"Figures. So, my deal is that I was on the run from a mob guy who wanted to kill me because, as his chef, I refused to put poison in the food to kill one of his guests. I hid out on a cargo ship for a while, but terrorists hijacked it. I met Scott, came to Hawaii, thought I was safe, but the mob guy's hitman found me and left me in the middle of the ocean to die a slow, horrible death."

Jody's eyes widened and she gasped. Her food forgotten, all she could do was stare at Elodie. "Holy crap!"

"Yeah. But Baker went to New York, met with the new mob boss who'd taken over after the asshole who wanted me dead was killed, and they 'talked shit out.' Baker reassured me that I was safe."

"Seriously?"

"Yeah," Elodie said.

"Then one of Baker's old SEAL teammates came to Hawaii and kidnapped me, using me as bait so he could lure Baker out and kill him. Baker didn't hesitate to put himself in danger to deal with that jerk, either," Monica said.

"Oh my God. One of his *teammates?*" Jody asked in disbelief.

"Yeah. I guess as team leader, Baker gave him a bad review or whatever it's called, and since the guy was crazy—and totally deserved that review—he stewed about it for years and years and then made his move. But don't worry, he burned up in lava on the Big Island...just as he'd intended for Baker."

Jody could barely believe what she was hearing. "One of his teammates tried to kill him. With lava."

"Yeah," Monica said solemnly. "But obviously, he didn't succeed."

Jody looked down at her plate, not really seeing the delicious barbeque anymore. "What in the *world* does he see in me?" she whispered. "I'm so boring compared to what he's used to."

"I think Baker deserves boring," Ashlyn said.

Jody looked up and met her eyes.

"And I don't mean that in a derogatory way," she said quickly. "Baker goes to great lengths to help our guys however they need it. Research for missions, when shit goes sideways for their women, and however else he can help. He needs someone who brings him some normalcy. I think he probably welcomes boring, considering everything that's happened in the last couple years."

Jody wasn't sure she agreed.

"Has he told you what he does for a living?" Elodie asked.

Jody shook her head. "No. Why? What does he do?"

"Well, darn. I was hoping *you'd* be able to tell *us*," Elodie said with a smile. "I mean, we know he has some amazing connections...the man flew to New York and was able to meet with a mob boss, for goodness sake. But none of us know exactly what his job is."

"Does it matter?" Jody asked.

For once, all three women seemed to be speechless.

Finally, Ashlyn chuckled. "No, it absolutely doesn't matter. We love Baker because he's a fabulous human. He's also helped all of us, and our men, when we've needed it the most. It doesn't matter at all what he does."

Jody was relieved to hear that, because she felt the same way. The more she learned about Baker, the more in awe of him she was. "Well, I don't have any mob bosses after me, that I know of at least, and I don't think I'm in any danger of being kidnapped anytime soon. I'm a normal graphic designer who sits at home most of the day in front of my computer, a former mother, and someone who spends my mornings and afternoons at the beach looking after the high school surfers who congregate there. If he's good with boring, he's hit the jackpot."

"Former mother?" Monica asked. "I'm not sure there's such a thing."

"My son died," Jody said bluntly.

She saw the surprise in Monica's eyes, then the pain when her words sank in.

"I'm so sorry," she said, reaching across the table and touching Jody's hand. "I had my first child, Charlotte, just over a month ago, and I seriously can't think of anything worse than losing her."

"There *is* nothing worse," Jody agreed.

She expected that to be the end of the conversation, but to her surprise, Ashlyn asked, "What was his name?"

"Kaimana."

"That's a beautiful name," Elodie said gently.

"It means 'power of the ocean,'" Jody said with a small smile. "Which is appropriate because from the moment he learned how to swim, he loved being in the water. He was a great surfer. There was nowhere he felt more comfortable than on a board in the surf."

"Which is why you hang out there now?" Monica asked.

It felt a little weird talking about Mana, but in a good way. It had been so very long since anyone had asked about her son, so between Baker and these women, he was in her thoughts even more than usual. "Yes and no. He died one morning while surfing. A riptide came out of nowhere and started dragging people out to sea. A younger surfer panicked and tried to swim back to shore, rather than staying with his surfboard, and Mana went after him, giving him his own board when he saw the boy struggling to stay afloat. He began to tow the boy on his board parallel to shore, to try to get out of the rip, and he was succeeding. But a huge wave washed over them, and Mana was stuck in the whitewash. He hit his head, got disoriented, and drowned."

Silence settled over the table, and Jody immediately regretted her overshare. She hadn't meant to bring the mood down. "I go to the beach and watch over the kids because if someone had been there the morning my son died, they could've called for help. Maybe Mana wouldn't have drowned."

"You're their guardian angel," Elodie said quietly.

Jody shrugged. "I don't know about that. I just don't want another mom to suffer like I am."

"Tell us about him?" Monica asked.

Jody looked at her in surprise. And when she glanced at the other two women, they both nodded and smiled.

"I... What do you want to know?"

"Whatever you want to tell us. Your son sounds as if he was amazing," Ashlyn said.

"He was."

"How old was he?" Elodie asked.

"Seventeen. He was a junior in high school."

"I bet he was a ladies' man," Monica said.

"Not really. He was more into surfing than girls," Jody said with a smile. "Although I did convince him to go to a dance not too long before he died. And he even admitted afterward that he had a good time."

For the next thirty minutes, she continued to answer the other women's questions and talked about her son. When the talk naturally turned to Monica's daughter, and the way her husband was completely overprotective of her, Jody couldn't help but close her eyes and savor the unusual feelings coursing through her.

"Jody? You okay?" Elodie asked.

She opened her eyes and nodded. "I'm good. Really good. I want to thank you all for letting me talk about Mana."

"Why wouldn't we?" Monica asked.

"Most people feel uncomfortable even mentioning him. They think if they don't bring him up, I won't be sad. But I'm *always* sad. Talking about him, remembering some of the good times, actually makes me feel good for a short period of time."

"He was a living, breathing person who deserves to be remembered," Monica said.

"Exactly, so thank you for giving me that," Jody said.

"Anytime you want to talk about him, you go right on ahead. It won't make us uncomfortable in the least," Elodie assured her.

"This is so weird," Jody said as she wiped away the tears that had managed to escape.

"What is?"

"In the last week, I've gone from a lonely middle-aged woman who'd kept to herself for the last five years, to having a fabulous man interested in me, talking about my son constantly—when I rarely mention him out loud, because I'm afraid of making others uneasy—and sitting in a restaurant with three women I really, *really* want to be friends with."

"We're already friends," Ashlyn assured her, without missing a beat.

"Not only that, there are three other women who'll be jealous as hell that we got to spend time with you today and they didn't," Elodie said with a grin.

"Oh, I'm sure Kenna will have a sleepover planned immediately after hearing about lunch," Monica said with a chuckle.

"Baker's told me about these legendary sleepovers," Jody said.

"They're the shit," Elodie said. "Wait until you see the view from Kenna's balcony. It's to die for. She's bubbly and gorgeous, but you can't even be mad at her because she's the nicest person ever who shares her killer view."

"I think I'm probably too old for a sleepover," Jody said a little self-consciously. "I'm what, twenty years older than you guys? I was married before some of you were even born."

"So?" Elodie asked. "Age is nothing but a number. Besides, we could probably all use your wise advice on things like being a mom—and of course we want to hear *all* about whether Baker's a good kisser or not."

Everyone laughed.

"Of course he is," Ashlyn said. "He's *Baker*."

Everyone looked at Jody with expectant looks on their faces.

Jody shrugged and said, "If you're waiting on *me* to tell you how he kisses, I'm afraid I'm going to disappoint. Unless you want to know how he can make my legs weak with the touch of his lips on my forehead."

Everyone gawked at her for a moment, before Monica said, "He's going slow."

Jody nodded.

"He knows not to rush things when he's going after something important," Ashlyn agreed.

"And for the record, that's you," Elodie finished.

"And just to warn you...the others like to talk about sex," Ashlyn added. "They aren't pushy about it, but they don't hold back. If that makes you uncomfortable, that's cool, you don't have to join in, but I wanted to give you a heads-up before we have the next sleepover."

"I don't mind talking about sex in general, but I'm not going to talk about Baker," Jody said firmly. She didn't want to alienate these women when she felt like she'd just gained their respect and friendship, but the last thing she wanted was to gossip. "I'm certain that he values his privacy, and I don't want to go behind his back and break his trust."

All three of the other women beamed at her.

"I love that for him," Ashlyn said softly.

"I love *you* for him," Elodie corrected.

"I think you're exactly what he needs," Monica agreed. "Thank you for coming to meet with us today. Thank you for being you. And thank you for not getting offended by our questions."

"Thank *you* for letting me in," Jody countered. "I knew when I saw you on the beach that day that you were someone special," she told Monica.

"Don't make me cry," she complained as she blinked quickly.

The rest of the meal was fairly uneventful compared to the emotional topics they'd already covered. Jody learned more about Lexie, Kenna, and Carly, and made a promise to come down to visit both Food For All and to go to dinner at Duke's one day. Elodie said she could stay at her house if it turned into a late night, and that started an argument about who Jody might stay with, as both Monica and Ashlyn invited her to crash at their places too.

It felt good to be wanted, but Jody ended the argument by saying that Baker would probably insist on taking her back home up to the North Shore, no matter *what* time dinner ended...and that she trusted him to make sure she got home safely.

Feeling stuffed and happy, Jody followed the others out of the restaurant into a beautiful Hawaiian afternoon. She exchanged numbers with Ashlyn and Monica, and even put Lexie's, Kenna's, and Carly's numbers into her address book on Elodie's insistence. Seeing all the names in her previously scarcely populated contact list made Jody smile.

Ashlyn gave her a hug, as did Monica, then Elodie held her tightly for a long moment. "Thanks for coming," she murmured. When she pulled back, she kept her hands on Jody's arms. "I know it was probably weird, but we all truly do want the best for Baker. He's a good man. Mysterious and a little scary at times, but we'd all do anything for him. We're happy he finally got up the nerve to go after what he so obviously wanted."

Jody blushed at that. "Me too. I thought he was pretty incredible for a long time myself."

"Drive safe," Monica told her. "Maybe, if it's okay, the next time we have lunch or something, I can bring Charlotte?"

"I'd love to meet her," Jody said honestly. She loved babies and rarely got the chance to be around them. "I'm happy to come down to Honolulu or Barbers Point too."

"It's kind of far," Elodie mused.

Jody smiled. "It's not *that* far. I mean, it takes an entire day to drive across Texas...coming down to the city is nothing in comparison."

"Very true," Elodie said. "I guess I'm just spoiled now. I think anything above twenty minutes takes for-ev-ver," she said, drawing out the last word dramatically.

Everyone laughed.

"You guys drive safe," Jody told them.

"We will. You too," Ashlyn said. They all waved and Jody headed to her van. Seeing it made her smile. The other women had all gushed over her car, and loved the fact that she had a hula girl on her dash. Jody insisted she couldn't have a classic VW van and *not* have a hula girl.

The second she got into her car, she rolled down the windows to get some fresh air and dug her phone out of her purse. She saw Baker had texted, telling her that he'd made it home. She typed out a quick response.

JODY

Lunch is over and I'm about to head back home.

BAKER

All good?

JODY

You have amazing friends.

BAKER

I take it that means things went well?

JODY

You'd be right. There was only one problem.

Jody was feeling damn good after the successful lunch. And brave.

BAKER

What? Do I need to call the guys and tell them to have their women back off? Or apologize?

The warm feeling within her grew at his immediate concern.

JODY

No.

BAKER

Then what's wrong?

JODY

The girls wanted to know if you were a good kisser. And I had to admit that I had no idea.

It took a full minute for the three dots to appear on the screen, just enough time for Jody to wish she hadn't been *quite* so brave. She was just about to tell him to forget what she'd said and proceed to die of embarrassment when his response appeared on the screen.

BAKER

We'll remedy that the next time I see you.

JODY

I didn't mean to pressure you.

BAKER

You didn't.

JODY

It took you three years to respond to my stupid comment.

BAKER

It wasn't stupid. And it took so long because I haven't had a spontaneous woody like I got when I read your words since I was fourteen years old. I was trying to regain control.

Jody breathed a sigh of relief.

JODY

I know you said you wanted to wait.

BAKER

I wanted to wait for you to be comfortable with where we're going. I already know where I want us to go. And after last night, and you not freaking about my talk of soul mates, and then not only texting me when you got to the restaurant, but letting me know you were about to be on your way home, I'm thinking we're good.

JODY

We're good.

BAKER

Then the next time I see you, you'll have something to report back to your girls.

JODY

I don't kiss and tell.

BAKER

You want to tell them I'm the best kisser you've ever had, I'm okay with that.

Jody laughed out loud. If anyone was watching her, they'd think she was looney...sitting in her car, laughing by herself. She didn't care.

> **JODY**
>
> You that sure of yourself?

**BAKER**

No. I'm that sure of you, Tink. You're gonna blow my mind, I have absolutely no doubts. Drive safe going home.

> **JODY**
>
> I will. You have a good visit with Theo?

**BAKER**

Yes. I'll tell you about it later.

> **JODY**
>
> Okay.

**BAKER**

Glad you had a good time.

> **JODY**
>
> Me too.

**BAKER**

They schedule that sleepover?

> **JODY**
>
> Ha! Not yet, but it was mentioned.

**BAKER**

Told you. Okay, really letting you go now. Talk to you soon.

> **JODY**
>
> Later.

She put the phone back in her purse and smiled. Had she ever felt this way when she was dating Kaimana's father? No. Not even close. Maybe there was something to Baker's soul mate theory. It was a scary thought, but a good one. Jody was still scared that things wouldn't work out, but she was going to do everything in her power to give this relationship a chance.

There was no rule book that said people in their forties and fifties couldn't find love. She may not have been looking for another relationship, but she wasn't dumb enough to turn her back on a man like Baker.

She smiled all the way back up north to her house.

# CHAPTER SEVEN

Baker sat across from Jodelle that evening in her house and mentally grinned. She'd called when she'd arrived home and asked if he wanted to come over for dinner. Baker wasn't an idiot, he accepted her invitation in two-point-one seconds. It was obvious she was nervous when he'd arrived. He couldn't figure out if it was because he said they were going to kiss or if it was something else.

When she'd gotten up the courage to ask him about fifteen minutes after he arrived if he was going to kiss her, he'd said, "Yes. But not when you're so worked up about it. Relax, Tink." His words hadn't completely relieved the tension in the air, but at least she'd seemed to unwind a little.

Baker liked her small house. It wasn't fancy, but she'd made it a home. Everywhere he looked there were pictures of her son. From baby pictures to one that had to have been taken not long before he was killed. He was wearing a suit and tie and was towering over Jodelle, his arm around her shoulders, and they were both laughing. It was beautiful and heartbreaking at the same time.

But he loved that she hadn't hidden her son away. He was as much a part of her life now as he was when he was alive.

Jodelle had baked a casserole and pulled it out after he'd arrived. Now they were sitting at her small table, eating.

They talked a bit about his visit with Theo, and Baker explained the formerly homeless man's role in Lexie's drama, and how she'd rented a studio apartment for him near the new location of Food For All in Barbers Point. He'd added that while the man now had a place to stay, he sometimes still liked to sleep on the streets. It was what he knew and what he was comfortable with.

"You respect him," Jodelle said.

"Of course I do. He's a good man."

"There's no 'of course' about it. Many people would, and probably do, look down on him because he sleeps on the street sometimes and has some sort of mental deficiency."

"I'm not one of them," Baker said firmly.

Jodelle smiled. "I'd love to meet him someday."

"And he wants to meet you," Baker told her.

"Cool."

It *was* cool. Baker couldn't help but be relieved that Jodelle didn't even blink after hearing about his friendship with Theo. "This is amazing," he praised as he shoveled another forkful of the casserole into his mouth.

"Thanks. This was Mana's favorite meal." Then she wrinkled her nose and said, "Sorry."

"For what?" Baker asked.

"For constantly bringing him up."

Baker put down his fork, leaned over and put his hand under Jodelle's chin, and turned her face so he could see her eyes. "I've said this before, and I'll keep saying it until you *hear* me. Don't ever apologize for talking about Mana. He was part of your life, a wonderful part—and he still is. You don't have to be sorry for bringing him up."

"Sometimes people feel awkward when I do," she told him honestly. "They think I should've moved on by now."

"It's only been five years," Baker said gently. "And them feeling awkward is *their* issue, not yours."

She rewarded him with a small smile. "I guess talking about him to the girls at lunch has made me think about him more than usual today. You know how he died?" Jodelle asked.

Baker took the chance to rub his thumb over the incredibly smooth skin of her cheek before dropping his hand. She had a few wrinkles in her face, but to him, they were badges of honor. Jodelle hadn't lived an easy life, especially in the last five years, but the fact that she was still so kind said a lot about her resilience and strength. And he liked that a hell of a lot.

"Yeah. I did some research to spare you talking about the details," Baker told her.

"That's probably a good thing. I don't mind talking about Mana, but not about that day," Jodelle said.

"He was a hero," Baker said gently.

"I know. And the only thing that makes me feel even a little bit better about what happened is that I know Mana would be proud of what he'd done. He'd prefer that he died, rather than that kid."

"You know, that's how I felt every time I went on a mission as a SEAL. That if my death could save even one person, it'd be worth it," Baker said.

Jodelle lifted her gaze to meet his. "I'm glad you didn't die," she whispered.

It took everything Baker had not to push back his chair, pick up Jodelle, carry her to her bedroom and ravish her. He settled for saying, "Me too. If only to be here right this second, eating this fabulous meal, sitting next to the most beautiful woman I've ever laid eyes on."

She blushed and dropped her gaze from his, concentrating on the plate in front of her. "You don't have to flatter me."

"I don't flatter anyone," he said in a tone that was probably a bit too hard for the conversation at hand. "I say shit like it is. You're gorgeous, Jodelle."

Her cheeks turned pink. "Baker, the last time I wore makeup was around nineteen ninety-nine. I've got too many wrinkles from being out in the sun so much. I'm more round than svelte, and my height leaves a lot to be desired."

"And I'm a washed-up Navy SEAL with more wrinkles than good sense. The muscles I used to be so proud of are starting to sag, and I frown far more than I smile. People take one look at me and cross the street because they're scared. We are *more* than our outer shells, Jodelle, but I am not blowin' smoke up your ass when I say you're beautiful. You think I want someone younger? Someone who takes a year to cake a bunch of shit on her face before she'll step out of the house? Someone who refuses to spontaneously go for a swim because it'll ruin their makeup? In case you're confused, the answer to those questions is *no*.

"I want you. Not someone *like* you, but you, Tink. I like your curves, a hell of a lot. And your size is perfect. You fit against my body as if you were made for me...and we already know my thoughts on that. When I tell you that you're gorgeous, I want you to believe me."

"I...It's hard to believe something you've never heard in your entire life," Jodelle said after a minute.

"You telling me Kaimana never told his mom how pretty she was?" Baker asked skeptically.

Jodelle shrugged. "He was a kid."

"Maybe. But he wasn't stupid. I never met him, but from all that you've told me, I know that without a shadow of a doubt."

"No, he wasn't stupid," Jodelle agreed.

"Are we really arguing about your beauty?" Baker asked under his breath as he shook his head.

Jodelle's lips twitched.

"Guess that's better than arguing about other, more stupid

shit," Baker said as he forked a large helping of the cheesy, meaty, Tater Tot casserole into his mouth. After he swallowed, he said, "We need to talk about what it is I do."

That got Jodelle's attention. She nodded. "Okay."

"Not right now, after we eat. We'll settle on your couch and have our talk. If you're okay with what I tell you, maybe we'll find a movie or show to watch and chill."

Jodelle's gaze met his head on. "If I'm okay with what you tell me?" she asked.

"Yeah."

"Is it bad?"

Baker shrugged. "Depends."

When he didn't elaborate, Jodelle asked, "On what?"

"On if you're the kind of person who sees the world as black and white, or if you're okay with gray."

Jodelle studied him for an uncomfortably long moment. "All right," she finally said, then turned back to her plate.

Baker wanted to ask her what that meant, but he was the one who said they'd talk after they ate. It didn't take long to finish their meal and put the dishes in the dishwasher. When Jodelle turned to him and bit her bottom lip as if uncertain, Baker asked, "You comfortable?"

"Um...what?"

He nodded to her. "What do you usually wear to lounge around your house at night? I'm guessing it's not tight shorts and a frilly blouse. As much as I love seeing your legs, Tink, I want you to be comfortable."

"I wanted to look nice for our first date," she admitted.

"This isn't a date," Baker corrected.

"It's not? Funny, we had food, you want to hang out and watch a movie. Sounds like a date to me," she sassed.

Baker chuckled. "Right, you have a point. But in my eyes, a date is when I take you out so I can show you off and make other men jealous. Then we drive out to a beach and sit and watch the sunset as we make out. I bring you home, ask if I can come inside, then we can't keep our hands or mouths off each other and we end up in bed, where we make slow, sweet love all night long."

"Um...wow," Jodelle said as she shifted back and forth on her feet. "You sound like you're quite the expert."

"I'm not," he countered. "You remember that I said I haven't had sex in a decade, right? But when I think about taking you on a date, that's what I envision."

"Then what's this?" she asked, gesturing her hands to indicate them and the house in general.

"Me getting to know my woman," Baker said. "Making her comfortable in my presence without the pressure of sex. Talking about what I do so there are no secrets between us. Making sure we can proceed without any misunderstandings or surprises. Getting that first kiss out of the way, so she can tell her friends that her boyfriend isn't a slouch in the kissing department and to prove that we're more than compatible."

Jodelle stared at him with wide eyes. It was cute as fuck, but Baker wanted to get what he needed to say out of the way, so they could move on to the more pleasurable parts of the evening...namely, him holding her while they snuggled on the couch. He didn't even get weirded out about the fact he'd never, in his entire life, had the desire to fucking *snuggle* with a woman, and now he couldn't think about anything he wanted more.

"Oh," she said, and even that was fucking adorable.

"So, since this isn't a date, and we've already covered that you don't need to do a damn thing to impress me. I'm already impressed and think you're beautiful. Go put on a pair of sweats or leggings and a T-shirt or something, then come back out here and we can find something to watch on TV and relax."

Jodelle smiled. It should've relieved Baker...but instead, something about the expression made him tense up.

"Okay. I'll go change into what I usually wear when I'm alone, puttering around my house at night."

"Good."

"For the record?" she said.

When she didn't continue, Baker raised a brow. "Yeah?"

"I'm not scared of what you're going to tell me. It's obvious *you're* nervous about it, and you being nervous reassures me that you don't do what you do lightly, and that you care about what I'm gonna think. If you didn't, you'd just blurt it out and tell me to deal with it. So...I'm ready to get this talk over too."

With those parting words, she turned and headed for the hallway and her bedroom.

"Fuck," Baker said under his breath as he palmed his cock and did his best to adjust. But there was no getting comfortable when he was as hard as he was. It had been a very long time since he'd dated, and it had never been like this. Baker had always been wound tight, worried about saying the wrong thing and pissing off his dates. It was nice to be with a woman who was older and didn't read shit into every little thing he said.

And Jodelle was right, he was nervous about what she'd think of his work. It was a potential deal breaker. He wasn't going to stop, and she'd have to be all right with it if they were going to have any kind of relationship. He lived in a gray world where right and wrong were often blurred. He did what he did for the good of his country, and for the people he cared about, but it wasn't always legal. Jodelle would have to keep what he told her to herself. If she couldn't, there wasn't a chance in hell of a relationship working out. Soul mates or not.

And that was what had Baker on edge. Why he'd done his best to ignore his attraction to her. But that was no longer an option. After everything that had happened with his friends' women, he was done playing it safe. He'd lay everything on the line tonight, and either Jodelle would accept him as he was, or she wouldn't.

Baker had been so far inside his head that he didn't realize Jodelle had re-entered the room. When she cleared her throat, he jerked his chin up—and stared at her in disbelief. "You're fuckin' kidding me, right?" he asked gruffly.

Jodelle giggled. "You said to get comfortable. To put on what I usually wear at night."

"Fuck me," Baker mumbled, already stalking toward her.

Jodelle had been smiling, but when she saw what had to be an intense look on his face, her grin slowly faded and she began to back away.

Smart, but it was too late. She was already in his sights.

Her back hit the wall and Baker immediately caged her in. He rested his forearm on the wall above her head and leaned in close. He lowered his head and buried his nose in the crook of her neck. She tilted her head to the side, giving him room, as her hands came up and gripped the shirt at his waist.

"Baker?" she asked.

"You smell delicious," he murmured, and his warm breath against her skin made her shiver. "Sweet and irresistible."

"Thanks," she whispered.

"You really wear this to bed?" he asked.

"Yeah. I don't like to be hot when I'm sleeping."

Baker held onto his control by a thread. She wore a pair of thin boy shorts that didn't hide any-fucking-thing, and a tank top that clung to her curves like a second skin. She was definitely doing her best to push him.

Baker lifted his head and let his gaze roam down her body. Her tits were magnificent, he'd always thought so, but seeing them molded by the tight tank made his mouth water. He could see her nipples harden right in front of his eyes as he stared at her. It was taking every ounce of control he'd learned as a SEAL to stay right where he was and not pull the material down so he could get his lips on her bare skin.

Forcing himself to look away from her nipples, he saw that she had a small pooch of a belly, but instead of being turned off, all he could think about was how soft she'd feel against his hardness.

Her thighs were thick, and once again, his thoughts turned to sex, how her legs were going to cradle him as they tightened around his head and shoulders when he went down on her. He couldn't see her ass, since it was against the wall, but Baker had ogled it plenty in the past. He already knew it was as luscious as the rest of her. Jodelle's feet were tiny, and her slender ankles didn't look as if they could hold up all the deliciousness that was her body.

"You know you're killing me, right?" he said after his eyes had made the journey back up her body.

"Just following directions," she said with a smirk. "But if it makes you feel any better, those blankets on the back of the couch aren't for decoration. I like to burrow under them while I'm watching TV."

"Thank fuck for that," Baker breathed, thinking he might just get through the night if he could cover her body with a blanket.

Jodelle laughed again. "If you really want me to, I can go find some sweats or something."

"No." The word escaped without Baker having to think about it.

She smiled lazily.

"You're always gonna keep me on my toes, aren't you?" he asked, leaning back down to inhale her sweet scent. Plumeria and Jodelle. There was nothing like it in the world.

"I wouldn't want to be boring," she told him.

"Never that. Come on, let's get you settled under one of those blankets," Baker said. He twined his fingers with hers and pulled her away from the wall and headed for her couch.

"Are you all right? You're walking funny," Jodelle said, the confusion easy to hear in her voice.

Baker looked at her in disbelief yet again. "Seriously?"

"Um...yeah?"

"Tink, I'm so hard it's actually fuckin' painful to walk," he told her, gesturing to his dick with his head.

Her cheeks got so red, Baker couldn't help but laugh.

"What did you expect, parading out here practically naked?"

"I'm not naked!" she protested immediately.

"Tink, that tank top might as well be painted on, and those shorts? They're not hiding one damn thing from me."

"I...well..." She sighed. "Okay, I'd hoped that after you told me whatever it is you're all worked up about...maybe I could convince you to do more than watch a movie."

Baker sat on the couch and pulled Jodelle down with him. She let out a small squeak in surprise as he hauled her onto his lap. He grabbed a fuzzy blanket from the back of the couch and wrapped it around them both. Then he settled into the corner of the extremely comfortable sofa, with one arm around Jodelle's back and the other draped over her blanket-covered thighs.

"Guess I'm sitting here," she said dryly. "Am I...hurting you?" she asked as she shifted in his lap.

"Want you near me so I can read your reaction when we talk," Baker told her honestly. "And you sitting on my dick could never hurt me. Is it bothering *you*?"

"Um...no."

"Good. Ignore it."

She chuckled. "Not sure that's possible, Baker."

"It'll go down...maybe," he said. "You should know something about me."

When he didn't continue, she said, "What?"

"I'm stubborn. And old and set in my ways. And I'm old fashioned."

A look of horror settled on Jodelle's face. "Oh my God,

please tell me you aren't about to say you won't have sex unless you're married."

Baker blinked in surprise, then threw his head back and laughed so hard, he had tears in his eyes. When he had himself somewhat under control, he looked back down at Jodelle, pleased to see she wasn't upset with him for laughing. "Fuck no," he said with a shake of his head. "But I'm also not the kind of man to jump into bed with someone just because I can. At my age, I want it to mean something. And with you, it's gonna mean more than something, it's gonna mean everything. I want us both to know without a doubt that when we make love, it's because we're *in* love."

"Oh, okay...but..."

"But what?" he asked when she didn't continue. "Be honest with me, Tink. You have been so far tonight, and I like that you don't play games."

"What if we don't fall in love? What if we like each other a lot, and really, really want each other, but aren't sure about the whole love thing?"

"Then we aren't doing it," he said.

Jodelle sighed. "That's kind of crazy, Baker."

"It's not. Look, I'm fifty-two, you're forty-eight. We aren't getting any younger, but I don't *need* to be with someone to be happy. I've been on my own for a while now, you have too. I can give myself orgasms, as can you. I'm not going to settle for a half-assed relationship, and I don't want you to either. I like you, a hell of a lot, and yes, I can see myself falling in love with you, but I don't like the thought of having sex just for the sake of sex. I want more. I want it all."

Baker stared at Jodelle, praying this wasn't the end of them before they even got started.

"I...You're right."

"I know."

Jodelle rolled her eyes. "And kind of a pain in the ass."

"Yup. I just think that sex between two people should be

more than getting off. And I want to enjoy getting to know you before we act on our attraction. Trust me, it'll make things that much better in the long run."

"If you say so."

"I do. But that doesn't mean we can't...play."

Her eyes lit up.

"You like that," Baker said confidently.

"Why wouldn't I?" she asked. "I'm going out with the hottest former-SEAL hot-shot surfer the North Shore has ever seen."

Baker chuckled. "Let's not get crazy, Tink."

"Whatever. So...let's get this done so we can move on. What did you want to tell me?"

Baker wasn't sure he was ready. But Jodelle was right. He needed to stop beating around the bush and get this done.

"You know I was a SEAL," he started. When Jodelle nodded, he went on. "When I retired, I found that I was bored out of my skull...so I talked to my former commander and offered my assistance on information gathering before missions. He took me up on it."

"And?" Jodelle asked when he stopped to gather his thoughts.

"And it turns out, I'm really good at finding information. Over the years, I've collected a lot of contacts, both in the States and outside of it. I have dirt on people who definitely don't want that dirt being disclosed, so they're willing to tell me what I want to know in exchange for my silence. And I'm not afraid to use the intel I have for that purpose. In return, I do favors for them too. Pass along shit I learn about things that might interest them. I live in a give-and-take world, a dark one that's full of bad shit."

Baker held his breath as Jodelle absorbed what he was telling her.

"So...you're a contractor for the government?"

Snorting, Baker shrugged. "Yeah, something like that."

"You find out information about bad guys, so that the good guys can go out and do their thing."

"Pretty much."

"Okay."

Baker frowned. "Okay? Okay what?"

"Okay. You told me what you do for a living. Is that it?"

"I don't think you understand, Tink. I'm not above blackmailing people to get info. I rub elbows with some pretty horrible men and women. I ignore the illegal and immoral shit they do in order to get the goods on others who are even worse."

"Like the mob boss you met with to sort out Elodie's situation?" Jodelle asked.

"Exactly."

She nodded, but didn't say anything else.

"I don't think you're getting this," Baker said in frustration.

"No, I am," Jodelle countered calmly. "I just don't care."

Baker stared at her in bewilderment.

"I'm not an idiot. I know how the world works. And to answer your earlier question...apparently I'm okay with gray. I'm not naïve either. Sometimes you have to get dirty in order to save others. Take child pornography, for instance. I know a lot of times the detectives who look into that shit have to ignore the people on the lower rungs of that disgusting ladder, let them get away in order to nab the guy higher in the food chain. It sucks, but in the long run, it's the right thing to do. To take out the ring leaders, they have to let the little guys go."

She raised a hand and wrapped it around the back of Baker's neck, then leaned in. "I'll tell you this, if I was ever kidnapped and held for ransom by some crazy mob guy, I'd have absolutely no problem whatsoever if you went to that guy's brother or cousin or whoever, and made a deal in order to find me. I know that two wrongs shouldn't make a right, but if you save my life in the process, they absolutely do."

"You aren't gonna be kidnapped," Baker growled. He'd underestimated his Jodelle, and he wouldn't do it again. He should've known she wouldn't even blink at hearing about the shit he was involved in. Even if she didn't know exactly what that shit was, she knew it was still shit, and she didn't care.

"I know, I'm just saying," she said a little petulantly.

"I'm serious. The shit I do doesn't touch you. Not ever. I won't involve you, I won't talk about it, I won't share."

"Fine."

"If someone even thinks about using you to try to get to me, I'll fuckin' destroy them."

"I said okay, Baker."

He stared at her, still trying to wrap his mind around the fact that she'd reduced what he did to being a "contractor." Fucking hell. She was made for him—and he'd bend over backward to make her his.

"I'm gonna kiss you now," he warned.

"It's about time," Jodelle said with a gleam in her eye.

"This is your one shot to end this," Baker told her. "If you have any concerns or second thoughts about what we're doing, say something now. Otherwise, I'm not letting you go."

"Ever?"

He wanted to say no, not ever, but that would be a bit too controlling, even for him. But she didn't give him a chance to answer her question.

"I accept you, Baker Rawlins, exactly as you are. You're a good person, even though you just did your best to convince me otherwise. Are you perfect? No. But that's okay because I'm not either. I say and do stupid stuff all the time. I have regrets, I think you know about what, but I'm trying not to let them paralyze me. I want to move forward, I want to be happy again. And in the last week, I've been happier than I've been in five years. I'm actually glad you have the kind of connections you do. Yes, they can be dangerous, but at the same time, it's comforting to know that if something happens—to me, to you, to your friends, to their women, to some SEAL team overseas doing their damnedest to keep us all safe—you can call on those connections to help."

And with that, Baker was done warning her. He cupped the back of her head, his other hand gripping her waist as he leaned in.

Jodelle met him halfway.

Their lips touched, and there was nothing tentative or gentle about their first kiss. Baker closed his eyes and inhaled as he devoured her. Jodelle didn't sit passively in his arms either. Her hands gripped his biceps and she dug her nails into his skin as he kissed her as if his life depended on it.

Their tongues dueled as they learned the taste and feel of one another. Baker swore his toes fucking curled. It was ridiculous, but he knew without a doubt that this would be the last woman he ever kissed.

He lifted his head, pleased as fuck when Jodelle whimpered and did her best to keep the connection. He waited until her eyes opened and she was looking at him before he said, "My soul's been waiting to find yours for over five decades. Didn't fully trust that I had until two seconds ago."

"Baker," she whispered, but he didn't give her a chance to say anything more. He dropped his head again, and this time did his best to give her gentle instead of out-of-control passion.

How long they sat on her couch kissing, Baker couldn't say. It could've been a minute or an hour, since time seemed to stand still. All he knew was that he was lost in the touch and feel of her. He memorized the little noises she made in the back of her throat. Took note of how she liked it when he nipped her lower lip, then soothed the small hurt with his tongue. How she shivered in delight when he nibbled her ear and arched against him when he sucked on the tiny bit of flesh.

Kissing Jodelle was more satisfying than actual sex with other women had been. He could literally kiss the woman in his arms all night and be completely content. But when Jodelle's hands started wandering under his shirt, Baker knew they had to stop.

Reluctantly, he pulled his lips from hers once more. He stared down at her, memorizing the way her lips were swollen from his kisses and the dreamy look in her eyes. He'd shifted at some point so they were lying on the couch, Jodelle under him, Baker caging her in. Even lost in pleasure, he'd known how much smaller she was than him and hadn't crushed her with his body weight. His cock was as hard as steel and impossible to hide, pressing against her inner thigh. The only thing keeping him from pushing inside her body was the small scrap of material between the legs of her boy shorts and his jeans.

"Um...wow," she said as she stared up at him.

"Yeah."

"I can honestly say that I'm not gonna have any problem letting the girls know that my man can *kiss*."

Baker barked out a laugh. Then he abruptly sat upright, taking Jodelle with him. He settled back into the corner of the couch, got Jodelle situated again on his lap, and wrapped the blanket around them once more. Then he reached over and picked up the remote control sitting on the table next to the couch.

"Anything you want to watch?" he asked.

Jodelle stared at him for a beat, then shook her head as she smiled. "Figures I'd hook up with the one man who actually backs up his words with action. We're really gonna sit here and watch TV?"

"Yup."

She sighed, then snuggled into him, scrunching down

until she could rest her head on his shoulder. "Okay, but don't blame me if your legs fall asleep."

There wasn't a chance in hell of that happening, so Baker simply grunted in response.

"And I don't care what we watch. As long as I can do it here in your lap, I'm happy."

Baker had a feeling that was a completely accurate statement.

"Okay, Tink. I'll find something."

"Baker?"

"Yeah?"

"I like having you here. And as much as I hate to admit it...I'm glad the pressure of sex is off the table for now. Believe it or not, my bold move tonight with coming out here in my pajamas...I'm not sure I'm ready to go further yet."

"I know," Baker said. And he did. His Jodelle might put on a good act of being confident in her sexuality, but the fact that she had no idea how pretty she was belied that. He had no problem going slow. She was worth the effort and time.

Jodelle fell asleep within twenty minutes of the football game he'd put on. Baker sat on her couch with his arms around her and wouldn't have been able to say who won the game if his life depended on it. All his concentration was on Jodelle. The way she breathed, shifted in her sleep, and twitched her nose when the crowd on the television got too loud. He memorized every little thing, until he knew she was fully imprinted on his mind and heart.

When the game finally ended, Baker stood with Jodelle in his arms. She stirred.

"What time is it?"

"Late," he told her as he walked toward her room. He leaned over and gently placed her on the covers. "Scoot in," he ordered.

Still half asleep, she did as requested, allowing Baker to pull the sheet and blanket up and over her. Then he went into the other room, found her phone, and brought it back with him. He put it on the table next to her bed.

"You need to get up in the morning for anything?"

"I have some work I need to get done, but I usually try to sleep in on Sunday."

"Sounds good. I have a feeling you work too hard."

"On Monday, I was gonna go to the beach," she said. "I want to see if Ben shows up and if I can get him to talk to me."

"You care if I join you?" Baker asked.

"No, I'd like that."

Once again, Baker appreciated that she didn't play games. "Okay. I'll call you to make sure you're up. That work?"

"Perfect," she said.

"I'm gonna see what I can find out about him too."

At that, Jodelle's eyes opened all the way. "I'm not sure your connections will have anything on a senior in high school who probably hasn't ever done anything wrong in his life."

"I don't either. But if there's anything to find, I'll find it." He didn't mention the parties at Ben's house, and how his friends had been uncomfortable talking about them.

"I know you will," Jodelle said with a sigh. "But I hope there's nothing."

"Me too, Tink. Me too. Try not to worry about it."

She huffed out a breath. "Telling me not to worry about one of my kids is like telling me not to breathe."

"I know. Which is why I'm on this."

One of her hands lifted and she speared it into his hair. "Your hair's long."

"Yeah. I'm too lazy to get it cut."

"I like it. I can tangle my fingers in it," she told him.

"I noticed," Baker said with a smile. And he had. When they'd made out earlier, she'd thrust both hands into his hair and held on tight as he ravished her. Or was it when she'd ravished *him*?

"Drive safe."

"It's not that far," Baker said with a smile.

"I know. Still."

"I will. You want me to text when I get home?"

"Yes. I'll probably be asleep, but when I wake up in the middle of the night I can look at my phone and know that you made it all right. Heads-up, if there's no text, I'm calling in the cavalry."

"*When* you wake up in the middle of the night?" he asked.

"Yeah. I always wake up at least once. I think it's from getting up to check if Mana had made it home yet."

Baker didn't like that for her and made a mental vow to do what he could to break her of the habit. He couldn't bring her son back, but maybe he could make her comfortable enough with her memories, and her current life, that she didn't feel the need to wake up. "All right, I'll text."

"I had a good time on our non-date tonight, Baker."

"Me too," he said with a smile. Then he leaned down and kissed her forehead gently, inhaling deeply one last time before he drew back.

"I like how you keep smelling me."

"Good. Because it's not something I'm gonna stop doing anytime soon."

"Go," she ordered. "I'm sure you have some motorcycle club president to blackmail tomorrow and you need your sleep so you can be on top of your game."

Baker chuckled even as he shook his head. "Sleep well, Tink."

"You too, Baker."

"I'll talk to you soon."

"Good."

"Night."

"Good night."

With that, Baker forced himself to back away and head for the door.

"Baker?"

He resisted the urge to go back to the side of the bed. He'd made it to the doorway, which was a minor miracle, so he wasn't going to test his control any more tonight. "Yeah?"

"There's a key under the fifth flower pot from the front door. The purple one with the yellow flowers. That was Mana's favorite. You can lock the door with it and put it back."

Warmth spread through him. He was well aware she wasn't giving him a key to her place, but he liked that she trusted him with knowing where it was. "Okay. Thanks for letting me lock you in. Wasn't keen on just having the knob locked."

"Mana always said the same thing. It's why he insisted on having the hidden key outside. He didn't like to carry it on his keyring, in case someone stole them. He always said someone could take his car and it wouldn't be a big deal. But knowing that same person could get into the house was a hard no."

Baker couldn't say a single word—because his throat closed up. He fucking hated that he hadn't had a chance to meet Kaimana Spencer. He would've been a hell of a man. *Was* a hell of a man.

"Good night, Baker."

"Night," he managed to say, before turning and walking down the hall. He grabbed his keys from the bowl on the counter—the same bowl Jodelle's keys were in, where she always put them when she came home—and headed out. He found the flower pot and palmed the key. After locking the front door, he stared for a long moment at the key in his hand. Then he closed his eyes, lifted his head, and said a silent prayer to Kaimana. Vowing to do right by his mom and to take care of her the way the boy would want him to.

He slid the key back under the pot before making his way

to his car. He had some things he needed to do—he'd gotten behind in the last week, since he'd spent a lot of time thinking about and talking to Jodelle—but he definitely had time to go surfing Monday morning.

Smiling at the thought of seeing Jodelle again so soon, Baker felt lighter than he had in years. And he had a little spitfire to thank for it.

# CHAPTER EIGHT

"You're disappointed," Baker said Monday morning after he'd greeted Jody.

"Well, yeah. I was hoping Ben would be here and I could talk to him," Jody said.

"I'm sorry, Tink."

"Me too."

"I started looking into him Saturday night," Baker told her.

Jody frowned. She was sitting at her usual place on the picnic table, feet on the seat, so she could watch the kids out in the surf. "But you left kinda late."

"Yup."

"Baker, you need to make sure you're getting enough sleep."

He chuckled. "Worried about me?" he asked.

Jody frowned harder. "As a matter of fact, yeah. You got a problem with that?"

"Fuck no. It's been a long time since anyone's given a shit if I get enough sleep or not. Usually all they care about is whether I've been able to find them the intel they need."

"Well, I'm not 'them,', whoever they are. And you can't be off making deals with nefarious people if you're tired."

Baker chuckled. "Right. Anyway, I should've looked him up a week ago, but I got sidetracked. Decided to stop putting it off. Partly because after all you've told me about Ben in the last week, I'm worried about him too. But also because I know if I don't find out what I can, it's likely you'll head off on a reconnaissance mission of your own."

"He's a kid," Jody told him softly. "I know there could be lots of reasons why he changed up his routine and no longer comes to the beach before school...but I have a bad feeling about it."

"Yeah."

"So? What did you find out?"

"No time to talk now. I've got some waves to catch and I want your full attention when we do chat. And I know you don't like to be distracted while you watch your kids. So I'll call later. Give you a chance to get some work done."

"Is it bad?" she couldn't help but ask.

Baker's lips pressed together. "It's not bad...specifically. But that doesn't mean it's good either. It's...unusual. And part of the reason why I'm getting pretty interested in talking to Ben too."

"Shoot," Jody said.

Baker grinned.

"What?"

"That your version of a swear word?"

"I was a mom," she protested. "Couldn't exactly go around swearing like a sailor."

"Are a mom," Baker countered.

"What?"

"You *are* a mom," he repeated.

"Baker," Jody said in a whisper, almost overcome with emotion.

"Mana's death doesn't strip that title from you, Jodelle.

Besides...look at you. You're here at the ass crack of dawn watching over a bunch of children you didn't give birth to. You feed them, make sure they get to school on time. You're worried about Ben. I've never met anyone who is more of a mother than you are."

Now she *was* crying.

Baker put a hand on the side of her neck and leaned in. "Don't cry, Tink."

"I can't help it," she told him. "You're being too sweet this morning."

"Better get used to it," he said. "Because I'm thinking you need more sweet in your life."

"You need to go surf," she told him.

"I will. Once I know you're good."

"I'm good," Jody said without hesitation. And amazingly, she was.

"Okay. How much time does everyone have?"

Since Baker hadn't dropped his hand, and she didn't want to do anything that would make him stop touching her one second before he needed to, Jody picked her arm up and looked at her watch. "About an hour."

"I'll do my best to corral them when it's time."

Jody smiled at him. "Thanks." There had been times when it was impossible to get the kids in from the surf, especially when the waves were good. This morning she didn't think that would be a problem as they seemed kind of messy, which in surfer speak meant they were irregular and unpredictable. Not ideal conditions for surfing.

Then Baker leaned down and kissed her lips. It wasn't a long, passionate kiss like the ones they shared before, but it was no less intense.

He pulled back way before Jody was ready and studied her for a long moment. She had no idea what he was looking for, or what he saw when he nodded in satisfaction.

"Doesn't bode well for me," Baker said mysteriously.

"What doesn't?" Jody asked.

"That the smell of plumeria gets me hard. I can just see in the future, I'll be minding my own business, walk by a plumeria plant, and boom—erection."

Jody giggled.

Baker grinned at her. "Like the smile better than the tears," he said, caressing her cheek with a thumb before dropping his hand and backing away.

"Be careful out there," Jody couldn't help but warn.

"I will. See you in a bit."

Jody watched as he grabbed his board where he'd stuck it in the sand and jogged toward the ocean. She sighed. Baker really was a good-looking man. She could totally picture him decked out in top-secret SEAL gear, slipping into the ocean to plant a bomb on a boat or sneak around in the waves gathering intel on the bad guys. Okay, so she had no clue what it was SEALs really did in the water. All she had to go on was movies like *Under Siege* and *The Rock*.

A shout sounded from the area where the kids were lined up to wait for a wave, and Jody tensed. But then she realized they were just greeting Baker. It was pretty impressive that the high schoolers actually liked it when he surfed with them. They didn't hang with other adults in the water, and it was obvious Baker had earned their respect. It was just one more reason Jody was falling for him.

She supposed she should be worried about how fast things were moving with them, how they'd gone from barely speaking to each other to almost being connected at the hip. But Jody had known Baker for quite a while now. She knew the kind of man he was simply by watching him interact with people around him. A good one. The kind of man any woman would do anything to have at her side. And while Jody had been on her own a long time, she couldn't deny having Baker around was...pretty wonderful.

As she watched the surfers and the sun slowly moved

higher in the sky, her thoughts turned to Ben. Worry hit her once more. She racked her brain to come up with other reasons why he'd been sleeping in his car in the middle of the afternoon, and had been so tired that he'd ignored the onset of heat exhaustion. Maybe he'd just stayed up too late the night before and was totally beat. The possibility that he'd gotten involved in the wrong crowd and had started taking drugs or drinking could be another reason.

Jody shook her head. No. Ben wasn't like that. She'd often thought he reminded her a lot of Mana. He was always respectful and she truly didn't feel as if he would turn to drugs, no matter what was going on in his life.

But she couldn't help but worry about those clothes, the pillow, and the tons of fast-food wrappers she'd seen in his car while he was being seen by a paramedic. She was even more sure now that he'd been living in his car, and that scared the crap out of her.

Ben sleeping in his vehicle made no sense, he had a family and a home here on the north end of the island. There was absolutely no reason for him to be homeless.

Unless his parents had moved and he refused to go to another school. Or maybe something had happened to his folks and he was on his own. Or he could've had a fight with his parents.

Resolve hardened inside Jody. She had to find him. She didn't know why he was sleeping in his car, but if she and Mana had a fight and he left home, not even one night would've gone by before she'd hunted him down. The fact that his parents didn't seem to be looking for him worried her. If they were, surely they'd have come to the beach at some point, since it was one of his regular hangouts.

True, she didn't know the dynamics of his family, but something just didn't feel right. He needed someone to give a shit about what was going on with him—and that would be her.

She had one project she had to finish this morning for a client, but everything else could wait. She'd head out and see if she could find Ben.

He should be at school, but if she couldn't find his car there, she'd check all the other parking lots at popular surfing spots, and even the touristy beaches. He had to be somewhere, and the sooner she found him and talked to him, the better Jody would feel.

Something relaxed inside her now that she had a plan. She wouldn't mention it to Baker because she knew he'd want to go with her. And while she wouldn't mind that, she also knew that he had work of his own he needed to accomplish. Besides, it wasn't as if she was doing anything dangerous. She was simply looking for a teenager who may or may not need a helping hand getting back on track.

Fifty minutes later, the kids started paddling back to the shore. Jody was ready for them by the time they walked up the sand toward her. She stood to grab her cooler and handed out sandwiches as they strolled past her, making a point to greet each and every one of her kids, letting them know in her own small way that she cared about them.

"Here, take two, Rome. Water looked kinda gnarly this morning. Is that a new wet suit, Felipe? I like it. I made this one especially for you, Brent. No meat, just eggs and cheese. Good luck on your math test today, Lani! Did you grow another inch since I last saw you, Kal? I swear you're getting taller by the day!"

They smiled and joked with her as they rinsed the saltwater off in the outdoor showers. They ate Jody's breakfast sandwiches as they headed for the bathrooms to change out of their wet suits and into their clothes for school.

An arm snaked around her waist, and Jody jumped until she realized it was Baker.

"You're good with them," he observed.

She shrugged. "They're good kids."

"Not everyone would think so. They'd look at them and think they were beach bums. That they're not gonna go anywhere in this world because all they want to do is surf."

"Well, those people would be wrong. Lani's in advanced-placement math. I think that's why she's such a great surfer, she can somehow calculate angles and trajectories of the waves and know which ones will be good and which ones she should pass on. Rome wants to be an engineer. Brent wants to work with sea turtles. And Kal is a genius when it comes to cars. They're good kids, Baker, and anyone who only sees them as lazy beach bums is an idiot."

"There's that mama bear coming out again," Baker said into her ear.

Jody shivered. She loved being in his arms like this. Being held against him. She didn't have a chance to answer, as the kids began to exit the bathrooms. They all waved at her as they headed for the parking lot.

"Drive safe!" Jody called out.

"We will!" they all yelled back.

Jody looked up and back at the man behind her. "Want a breakfast sandwich?"

"Yup."

Baker loosened his hold on her and Jody reached into her cooler. "I made you one with all the trimmings. The kids don't usually like all the stuff on it, they stick to the basics." She pulled out the sandwich she'd made just for him. It was kind of silly, but if the way to a man's heart was through his stomach, she would work that angle.

She handed him a sandwich that was in a reusable silicon pouch. "And don't give me any crap about the reusable bag. There's way too much plastic in our oceans and dumps as it is. I don't want to contribute to the problem."

"I wasn't going to say anything," Baker promised as he pulled out the sandwich. Jody took the container and threw it back into her cooler. She turned as Baker lifted the top piece of bread to see what he was about to eat.

"It's kind of a southwest omelet inside a sandwich. Egg, bacon, green pepper, tomato, slices of provolone and pepper jack cheese, lettuce, and a slice of ham for good measure. There's also some salsa in there to give it a jolt of flavor."

Baker looked up at her then, and Jody couldn't read his expression.

"Are you serious?" he finally asked.

"Um...yes?"

Then he took a huge bite of the sandwich, closed his eyes, and groaned as he chewed.

Jody bit her lip as she watched. Even eating, the man was ridiculously sexy.

The second he swallowed, Baker said, "Marry me."

Jody laughed. "I take it the sandwich doesn't suck?"

"No, it fuckin' does not," Baker told her. "It's amazing. And totally hits the spot after being in the waves this morning."

"I'm glad."

"You eat?" Baker asked.

Jody shrugged. "I'll grab something when I get home." There was no way she was going to admit to Baker, looking as fit and fabulous as he did standing in front of her in the skintight wet suit, that she ate a Pop-Tart every morning.

He took a step closer and held out his sandwich. "Here, have a bite."

"It's okay," she said with a small shake of her head.

"Humor me," Baker said in a tone of voice she didn't understand.

So she did. She took hold of his wrist to hold his hand steady, then leaned forward and took a much smaller bite than he had. The flavors from the combination of ingredients hit her taste buds, and she smiled as she chewed.

"Thanks," she said once she'd swallowed.

Baker took another bite, then held the sandwich back out to her. They didn't speak as they shared the meal, but it was still the most intimate moment Jody had shared with another human being in years.

After he popped the last piece of sandwich into his mouth and licked his fingers, Baker reached for her and pulled her against him. Jody could feel every inch of his hard body against hers. The dampness of his wet suit seeped into her T-shirt, but she didn't care. She was already wet from him holding her earlier anyway.

"There will never be a time I eat in front of my woman when she's not also eating," Baker said.

"Baker, I made that sandwich for *you*."

"Don't care. I mean, I care that you went out of your way to make me the best fuckin' sandwich I've ever eaten, but I will still not stuff my face and leave you hungry. Ever."

"I wasn't hungry," Jody said softly.

"Not happening, Tink."

She stared at him for a moment, and saw that he wasn't going to back down about this. "Next time I'll make two," she finally told him.

"Appreciate that. Here's the thing...you may not have had anyone looking out for you in the last five years, but you do now."

Jody liked that. A lot. Not because she needed looking after; she didn't, not really. But because Baker was acknowledging that Mana had done what he could to take care of his mom.

"You sleep all right this weekend?" he asked.

Jody nodded.

"You wake up at all?"

"No."

"Good. After I do some more digging on Ben and his family, I have to go down to the Naval base," Baker said.

"Okay," Jody told him, not sure why he was telling her.

"Thought I'd stop by Leonard's Bakery and grab some malasadas on my way home. You interested?"

"In malasadas? Duh," Jody said with a smile.

Baker returned it. "Didn't get it before."

Jody waited for him to say more, but when he didn't, she asked, "Didn't get what?"

"Why Mustang and the others go so far out of their way to do shit for their women. But I get it now. I'd do just about anything to see that smile on your face."

Jody melted into him. "You don't have to buy me stuff to make me smile, Baker. You do that just by being you."

"Glad to hear it, but I like spoiling you. When's the last time you had Leonard's malasadas?"

"God...years?"

"So it's all right for me to come by when I get back later?" he asked.

"Yes."

Baker's expression softened. "No hesitation. You didn't ask when I thought I might be back or anything."

"Baker, you want to come over, no matter when it is, you've got an open invitation. If I need to do some work, I'll tell you. I'm assuming since you're half a century old, you can entertain yourself until I'm done. Then we can talk, eat, watch TV, or whatever."

"The same goes for you, Tink. Open invitation for you to come to my place."

Jody smiled. "Thanks."

"Although your place is nicer."

"Baker, it's practically the same as yours."

"Nope. Yours smells like you."

Jody rolled her eyes.

"And it has your computer, which I'm assuming has the programs and shit you need to do your graphic stuff."

That was true.

"Besides, Mana's there, so it's more like a home."

He wasn't wrong. Mana *was* there. Not physically, but in spirit. She'd felt that more and more since her conversation with Baker about reincarnation. Not to mention everywhere she turned, Jody could see his face in all the pictures she had.

"You're gonna make me cry again," she warned.

"Don't want that. How about you kiss me and we get on our way. I have research to do on Ben, a meeting to attend, and malasadas to buy," Baker said.

Jody immediately went up on her tiptoes and tipped her head back. Baker's hand pressed against the small of her back, steadying her as his head dropped.

Their kiss this time was deeper than earlier, but not quite as carnal as it had been on her couch a few nights ago. Jody was finding that she liked all the different kinds of kisses Baker gave her.

She pulled back way before she was ready, but she didn't think a public beach was the time or place to drag her new boyfriend down to the sand and have her wicked way with him.

"Like that look in your eyes, Tink, but we both have shit to do."

"Darn," she whispered.

Baker laughed, then he sobered. "I'm gonna take care of you," he said.

"Can I take care of you back?" she asked.

"Abso-fucking-lutely."

"All right then."

"All right then," Baker echoed.

Jody licked her lips, tasting salt, sandwich, and Baker. "Drive safe going down to Honolulu today."

"I will. I'll text you when I leave, when I get there, and when I'm on my way home."

"You don't have to," she said, worried that he might start thinking it was a pain in the ass and he didn't like having to tell her where he was all the time.

"I know I don't. You gonna worry?"

Jody bit her lip. She totally would.

"Right. So I'll text," he said, not needing her to say the words.

"Okay."

Baker leaned down and kissed her hard and fast with closed lips. Then pulled back. "Come on, I'll walk you to your van."

"I can make it on my own," she couldn't help but point out.

"I know."

Right. She guessed this was one more way he wanted to "take care of her." She was all right with that. He grabbed her cooler and wrapped his arm around her waist as they began to walk to the parking lot. As she climbed into the driver's seat and rolled down her window, he put her cooler in the back, pulling the sliding door shut. "Talk to you soon," he said.

Jody nodded.

Baker reached out and gently palmed the back of her head. He pulled her in for another short kiss, then let her go, sliding his hand through her hair as he did. Then he gave her a chin lift and stepped back.

That chin lift. Lord. It was such a guy thing to do. Her thighs tightened. It was silly to get so turned on by something as small as that, but there it was.

"You gonna go, or sit there staring at me all day?" he quipped.

"I'm going, I'm going," Jody said. "Baker?"

"Yeah, Tink?"

"Thanks." She wasn't sure what she was thanking him for. Maybe for being so good with the kids. Maybe for being appreciative of her making him the sandwich. Maybe for being the kind of man who didn't think anything of telling a woman that he was going to take care of her. Maybe it was all of it, wrapped up in one intoxicating package.

But typical Baker, he didn't question her. All he said was, "You're worth it."

Yeah, it was safe to say Jody was falling hard and fast for this man.

She waved at him like a dork, then pulled out of the parking spot and headed home. As much as she loved being with Baker, she needed to finish the urgent job she was working on, then head out to find Ben. She hadn't forgotten about the young man. She prayed that nothing was wrong. That she'd find his car at school and her worry would be appeased.

But deep inside, she suspected that wouldn't be the case.

Looking in her rearview mirror, she saw Baker still standing where she'd left him. He hadn't immediately gone back to get his surfboard, he stayed where he was, watching her until he couldn't see her anymore.

Another shiver went through her body. Yeah, Baker may have tried to convince her he wasn't really a good guy while explaining what he did for a living—but he was wrong.

# CHAPTER NINE

It was eleven-thirty and Jody hadn't found Ben. She was frustrated. She'd gone to his high school first and hadn't found his car in the lot. She knew she probably looked suspicious as hell, driving around the parking lot slowly, but she didn't care.

Next, she'd driven down the coast, stopping at all the beaches. She prayed that Ben was simply skipping school to surf, but she hadn't been able to find his car at any of the good surf spots. Her belly had started grumbling a while ago, so she'd stopped to grab a shrimp taco from one of the many food trucks along Kamehameha Highway. She'd just finished eating and was tossing her trash when her phone rang.

Baker had texted earlier, saying he was leaving for the Naval base. Then he'd let her know that he'd arrived. His meeting must not have gone on for too long if he was calling her now.

"Hi," Jody said as she answered. "Your meeting over?"

"No. But we're taking a break for lunch and since I didn't have a chance earlier to let you know what I found out about Ben, I wanted to do that now."

"Are you going to be able to eat something if you talk to me?"

Baker chuckled. "Yeah, Tink. Already grabbed something. Feels good, you looking out for me."

"Someone has to," Jody retorted, feeling like a pile of mush at his praise.

"Right. So, our boy has good grades. Almost straight A's. Hasn't ever been in trouble, no suspensions or detentions. He's not in a whole lot of extra-curricular activities though, which seems off to me. Most kids his age are working on building up their resumes, so to speak, so they look good for college. But it seems Ben doesn't care so much about that."

"Not all high schoolers want to go to college," Jody felt obligated to point out. "They might want to go into the military or work a trade. Lord knows the world needs mechanics, linemen, and plumbers."

"Not arguing with you, Tink, but after looking into his parents, that doesn't seem like a road Ben would go down."

"What's wrong with his parents?" Jody asked in concern.

"Nothing's wrong with them. It's just that they're loaded. Well, his stepdad is."

"His stepdad?"

"Yeah. His biological father died when Ben was a baby. His mom struggled when he was young, lived in a shitty apartment down in Honolulu and struggled with her mental health. She did a stint or two in the psychiatric ward of the hospital and a neighbor watched Ben while she was in. Looks like she did the best she could by him though. Worked two jobs trying to keep a roof over their heads and food in their bellies."

"Oh, Baker, that's awful."

"Not that unusual," Baker said.

That might be true, but it still didn't make Jody feel good.

"Anyway, her life changed when she met Al Rowden. He stopped at the gas station where Ben's mom was working and apparently he liked what he saw. They were married less than five months after they met. Al moved Emma and Ben into his house up here, got her a job as an admin at a doctor's office, and things changed for the better for Ben and his mom."

"That's good, isn't it?"

"I think it was," Baker agreed. "Al Rowden is a judge for the Hawaii Juvenile Justice department. He makes good money, has reasonable hours, and is well respected. He's responsible for hearing cases against offenders under the age of eighteen and deciding the punishment for their actions."

"Why do I get the feeling that you're going to tell me something I'm not going to like?" Jody said.

"Because you're smart," Baker said. "Here's the thing. On the surface, I can't find anything that points to Rowden being on the take or a bad judge. He seems to be tough but fair. Many former kids he's dealt with have nothing but good things to say about him helping them see the light and giving them a chance to get back on the straight and narrow."

"But?" Jody asked.

"I can barely find anyone who's spoken out *against* him. Which is weird. I mean, you'd think there would be plenty of people pissed they were sentenced to do time, or probation, or community service. But there's not. It's mostly praise."

"That's not normal," Jody said unnecessarily. "I mean, even I've got some bad reviews out there about the work I've done. I don't agree with them, but they exist."

"Jodelle, the bad reviews about you are bullshit. Most of your clients would know that."

"You've read them?"

"Yes. And again, they're bullshit. I looked at the website you designed for that one woman about her fuckin' chickens, and it was beautiful. Easy to navigate and not one of the links was broken. Her complaints were ridiculous."

"Thanks," Jody said. "That job took four extra months because she kept changing her mind about what she wanted and sending me different pictures. She was definitely difficult to work with and even harder to please."

"Right. You should've dumped her ass halfway through and made her find someone else to put up with her shit."

"Then she *really* would've had something to complain about," Jody argued. "When I take a job, I want to finish it."

"Because you're you," Baker said. "Anyway, you're right, the fact that there aren't more than a tiny handful of complaints about Judge Rowden is fuckin' suspicious in and of itself."

"What about Ben's mom? Is she still working?"

"No. She quit about a year and a half ago. And in the last year, she's been hospitalized twice. She went almost a decade without having any issues, and suddenly now she's relapsing? It doesn't make sense," Baker said.

"Hospitalized for mental issues?" Jody asked.

"Yeah. Involuntary too. Her husband brought her in both times, said she was suicidal and seeing little green men. Claimed she was a danger to herself and her son. She stayed the maximum seventy-two hours the second time, then she requested a longer stay and ended up in the hospital thirty days."

Jody wasn't sure what to make of that. So she settled for asking, "What does that have to do with Ben?"

"I don't know," Baker said. "But the hair on the back of my neck is standing up."

Jody knew that wasn't a good thing. Baker continued speaking.

"Ben's grades have been slipping in the last few months. He was a straight-A student, but lately he's been skipping school and not turning in assignments. The last grading period, he had four C's, a D, and a B. I'm thinking everything is not okay at home and it's showing in his grades."

"I'm thinking you're right. I didn't see his car in the parking lot at the high school this morning," Jody said.

"You were at the high school?" Baker asked.

Jody bit her lip. She hadn't told him of her plan to look for Ben, not because she was trying to hide it, but because she hadn't wanted him to worry about her while he had other things to do. "Yeah. I need to find him, Baker."

"You still out looking?"

"Yes."

"Wish you'd told me, Tink."

"I didn't want to bother you."

"You are *never* a bother," Baker said sternly. "You feel even the slightest bit nauseous, I want to know. You feel like taking a drive around the island, I want to know. You want to picket the beaches with 'end the use of plastic' and 'save the turtles' signs, I want to know. Doesn't mean I'll try to stop you, I just fuckin' want to know where you are so I can do what I need to do if shit goes sideways."

"Baker—"

"No," he interrupted before she could continue. "I'm a paranoid son of a bitch. Can't be anything else after all the shit I've seen and done. I know the evil that's out there, Jodelle, and I can't stand the thought of it touching you. I've seen my friends' women kidnapped, beaten, left for dead in the middle of the ocean, and too much other shit. I will do everything possible to keep that from happening to you, and, God forbid it does, I'll rain hell down on anyone who dares to put their fuckin' hands on you. But I can't get to you, can't keep you safe, if you don't *talk to me* and tell me what your plans are."

That was a lot, and Jody couldn't say that it didn't make happy tingles shoot through her, but it also gave her cause for concern. "I've been on my own a long time, Baker. I can take care of myself."

"That's what Carly said before she was stuffed into the trunk of a car and taken out to the middle of the ocean," Baker said.

Jody closed her eyes. He had a point. "I wasn't trying to deceive you," she said again.

"I know, Tink. I just...shit, I can't handle if it something happens to you."

"Nothing's going to happen to me," she told him. "I'm just driving around trying to find Ben. He has to be here somewhere. His car was a mess. I'm more and more sure he's been living in it."

"Yeah, if things are bad at home, that's not a bad assumption," Baker said.

Jody sighed in relief that Baker wasn't going to continue to harangue her.

"Where have you looked so far?" he asked.

She told him about the beaches and some of the popular hangout spots she'd heard the other high schoolers talking about.

"Try looking at grocery stores and other more populated spots. He might think he'll stand out too much at the beaches. If he goes to a lot where people are constantly coming and going, no one will think twice about seeing his car there for hours on end, because they won't be there that long."

"Good point," Jody said.

"He's probably smart enough not to go to the usual places. While it's likely he might be somewhere crowded, it's equally possible that he'd want some space to think where there aren't a lot of people around. Maybe he's hiking, hiding out during the day so someone doesn't ask what a teenager is doing out and about and not in school."

"Okay."

"Call me if you find him," Baker ordered.

"I will."

"Don't care what I'm doing, I'll take your call," he continued. "His stepdad has a lot of power on this island, and if Ben feels as if his back is against the wall and there's nothing anyone can do to help him, he's not going to want to be found."

"I know," Jody whispered.

"From what I can tell, he's close with his mom. Not so much with his stepdad. Never took his name, kept his mom's maiden name. You find him, that's your way in. Ask about his mom."

Jody didn't like the feeling she got when she thought about needing to find a way in with Ben, but Baker was right. And he obviously knew a lot more about trying to get someone to talk than she did. She didn't want to speculate about how he'd gained that knowledge. "Right."

"Jodelle?"

"Yeah?"

"You'll find him. And he'll trust you because you're *you*. Just be careful."

His faith in her felt good. "I will."

"I should be home around three or so."

"Is that including the time it'll take to get malasadas? Because Leonard's is always busy," Jody asked.

"It's including the time it'll take to get malasadas, because there won't be a wait for me. When I tell you I have connections, Tink, I mean I have connections—and they aren't all nefarious mobsters either. Some of them are with owners of kick-ass restaurants who always have a seat for me if I want it...or piping-hot, fresh-from-the-fryer malasadas when I stop by."

"Do I want to know what you did in order to be able to jump the line at freaking Leonard's?" Jody asked.

"Yes, you want to know, but no, I'm not telling you. My work and you day-to-day don't exist together, told you that."

"I don't want to sit down and have a chat with a terrorist you're letting live because he's feeding you info on another terrorist who's even worse, but I think a local owner of a restaurant is a different story," Jody retorted.

"And that's why you're the way you are, and I'm the way I am. No one is immune to shit that happens in the world. No one."

"Fine. But is it wrong that I'm not upset that you being the way you are means I get hot and fresh malasadas without having to wait an extra hour to get them?"

"No."

"Okay. Then I'll look forward to seeing you later with my treats then."

Baker laughed, and Jody relaxed. She didn't like upsetting him, and she knew she'd done just that by not telling him she was heading out to look for Ben. She should've. It wasn't as if he'd reprimanded her for her actions, just for not telling him what she was doing. And his reasons were more than solid. He wasn't being controlling. He wasn't trying to be an asshole. He was just worried about her. She could live with that. Especially when she hadn't had anyone give her safety a second thought since Mana had died.

"I hope I find him," Jody said quietly.

"You will," Baker said. "Keep me updated."

"Okay. Have a good rest of your meeting."

Baker chuckled. "Not the kind of meeting that's good, Tink."

"So it's bad?"

"No. It's just a meeting about intel I've gathered to help keep the men and women who protect our country safe."

"Right. Then go and impart all the knowledge so that can happen."

After a beat, he replied, "I waited too long."

"Pardon?" Jody asked.

"Should've gotten my head out of my ass way before now. Missed out on the awesomeness that is you for too long, Tink."

"I could've gotten up the nerve to ask *you* out," she told him.

"Probably good you didn't because I likely would've said no, hurt your feelings, and then you wouldn't be giving me the time of day now. I need to head out. Be smart out there, Tink. You even think for one second that something is wrong, or you aren't safe, you back off. Okay?"

"He's a kid, Baker."

"He's almost a foot taller than you and a hundred pounds heavier. He might be a kid but that doesn't mean he's not dealing with some serious shit and probably has some anger inside about it all. I'm not asking you not to help him, just to back off if necessary, until I can help you figure out how to do that."

"Got it. I promise," Jody said.

"I appreciate it. I was serious when I said I'd rain hell down on anyone who hurts you. That includes seventeen-year-old boys."

Jody frowned. "You'd hurt Ben?"

Baker paused, then said, "I know I should say no, because that's what you want to hear, but I can't. I *will* assess the situation carefully though. If it warrants me putting my hands on someone to keep you safe, I'll do it. But there are other ways I can rain hell on someone that don't include getting physical."

Jody wasn't sure what Baker was telling her, but she did appreciate his honesty. "Because of your connections?" she asked.

"Because of my connections," he agreed. "I don't go around beating the hell out of people, Jodelle."

"I didn't think you did," she told him honestly.

"Shit, we should be having this conversation face-to-face," Baker muttered. "I'm not an asshole. I don't like violence and prefer to make my point in more subtle and lasting ways. By hitting people where it hurts the most— their bank account. Money talks, Tink, and I'm very good at making the stuff that people value disappear.

With that said, I'm okay with violence when it's warranted."

"Like with Monica and the lava thing?"

He sighed. "She told you about that?"

"Yeah."

"Then yes, like that. All I'm saying is that I don't like the thought of anyone putting their hands on you. No matter how old they are or what gender. And I'll do what I need to in order to make it clear that shit won't be tolerated."

"Okay, Baker."

"Are you agreeing with me because you're shocked and just want to get me off the phone to rethink our relationship, or are you agreeing with me because you know it's what a man does when he cares about his woman?"

"The latter."

"Good. Because I care about you, Jodelle. And I'll do what's necessary to make you happy *and* keep you safe."

"Can I do the same for you?"

"Yes. As long as it doesn't include getting physical with anyone or putting yourself in danger."

"That doesn't seem fair," Jody cajoled.

"Nope," Baker agreed.

She sighed. "You really *are* kind of a pain in the ass."

"Yup. But I'm a pain in the ass who gives a shit about you and wants you to stay exactly how you are. And someone hurting you would change you and piss me off. So yeah, that's not gonna happen."

Jody couldn't help but chuckle. "You're a caveman too."

"I've been called worse," Baker said. "And now I really have to go. You get something for lunch?"

"Just had a shrimp taco from a food truck."

"Good. Be careful, Tink. Let me know if you find Ben."

"I will."

"Later."

"Bye, Baker."

Jody hung up the phone and sat in her car in the small pull-off on the side of the road for a long minute. That conversation had been both good and somewhat worrisome. She wasn't scared of Baker, more concerned about the fate of someone who dared do something to her that Baker didn't like. People were jerks all the time, she'd gotten very good at ignoring ignorant and asshole-ish behavior, refusing to let others bring her down. But she was thinking she wasn't going to have to worry about anyone being mean to her more than once when Baker was around.

Deciding she'd deal with his overprotective tendencies when they actually reared their head, Jody looked down at her phone and the map of the north side of the island. Baker's suggestions were good ones. If she was a teenager who was trying to stay hidden, she'd try to blend in as well. She'd been wrong in looking for him at all the normal places she thought kids went to hang out. She needed to look in out-of-the-way places, or crowded parking lots where he thought he could blend in.

Jody had no idea what was wrong in Ben's home life, but she was determined to find out. She wanted him to know he had a friend and that he could count on her to help.

More determined than ever, she pulled out onto the highway. Ben was out there somewhere, and she was going to find him.

# CHAPTER TEN

It took another hour, but when Jody pulled into the Kaʻena Point Trail parking lot, she recognized Ben's older-model Kia immediately. There were about a dozen cars there, but Ben's was the only one she was concerned about. Jody parked directly behind and took a deep breath before she got out.

She peered inside his car, and saw that he wasn't there. Her shoulders slumped. Now what? There weren't too many places he could be. Either down on Mokulēʻia Rock Beach or he'd walked the trail to the northwestern tip of Oahu, called Kaʻena Point. Looking down at her flip-flops, Jody sighed. She hadn't worn the right shoes for a hike, but now that she'd almost found Ben, she wasn't giving up.

Jody locked her van and prayed it wouldn't get broken into while she was gone. Too many cars had their windows broken, people's belongings stolen, while parked at touristy spots.

She set off on the two-and-a-half mile, fairly level dirt roadway, smiling at the few people she saw on her way. The ocean crashing to her right made her sigh. She loved living in Hawaii. Some people had suggested that maybe she'd heal faster if she moved back to the mainland, got away from the memories of Mana, but memories were the main reason Jody wanted to stay.

Yes, it hurt thinking about her son, but she didn't *want* to forget him. And the way to be closest to him was to be near the things he loved most...especially the sea.

The sun was warm, and Jody wished she'd grabbed a hat before she'd left the house this morning. The breeze coming from the ocean helped keep her from overheating, but she knew she'd still probably be sunburnt when she got home. She prayed she'd find Ben after all this.

Eventually, she got to the end of the point—and sighed in relief when she saw a lone person sitting off to one side on a large lava rock.

Ben.

"This is one of the best spots on the island to watch for whales," Jody said quietly, standing about ten feet behind him.

He turned his head to look at her, and Jody couldn't read the expression on his face.

"Long time no see," she said after he'd turned back around to stare out at the waves crashing on the coastline.

Taking a chance, she walked forward and took a seat next to him. "You're a hard person to find."

"Aren't you going to give me shit about not being in school?" he asked.

"Nope," Jody said, pulling her legs up, putting her feet flat on the rock in front of her and wrapping her arms around her knees.

He looked at her out of the corner of his eye. "Why not?"

"Because I don't know why you're here and not there. It would be presumptuous of me to scold you for something I know nothing about."

Ben looked surprised and huffed out a breath.

"I think you could've found a shadier place to hang out though," Jody told him. "You know, so you don't have a relapse and get heat stroke again."

"I'm fine," Ben said.

"*You* might be, but I'm old," Jody teased.

"No offense, but I didn't exactly invite you to come out here."

"No, you didn't," she agreed. "But when you're worried about a friend, you don't let things like not wearing the right shoes or the lack of a hat hold you back."

Ben didn't say anything for at least three full minutes. Jody gave him time to process that she was here and actually cared about him before saying, "I'm worried about you, Ben. This isn't like you. You're a good student. Responsible. Skipping school and sleeping in your car instead of hanging out with the surfers...something's wrong...and I want to help."

"I'm not going home," he said forcefully.

"Okay," Jody agreed easily.

He looked over at her with a frown.

"What? If you don't want to go home, there has to be a good reason. So we'll figure out something else."

"Why are you being so cool about this? It's weird. Most people would be telling me that I'm not old enough to not want to live at home."

"I'm not most people," Jody said simply. "Talk to me, Ben."

He shook his head and looked back out at the water.

Jody hadn't thought it would be easy to get him to tell her what was going on, but that didn't mean she wasn't going to try. Her main goal at this point was to make sure the boy was safe and healthy. And by the looks of him, he was definitely living rough. She'd seen the food wrappers and trash in his car when she'd looked inside before starting her hike. His clothes were filthy and he didn't smell all that great. She figured it was because his clothes hadn't been washed in several days, if not a week or more. He could shower at one of the many public beach facilities, but washing his clothes would be more difficult.

"I'm not here to bust your chops," Jody said softly. "I've been worried about you. I haven't seen you in the mornings and after what happened at the surf competition..." Her voice trailed off. "I don't know what's going on, but I want to help," she repeated.

"You can't," Ben said, his shoulders slumped.

"Try me."

The teenager sighed.

Jody didn't take offense. Kids his age were naturally overly dramatic. The smallest thing could depress them, just as it could hype them up for days. She remembered that from when Mana was alive. But Jody also knew it was a hormonal thing. A phase. They grew out of it. She just had to be patient.

"You ever been between a rock and a hard place, Miss Jody?"

At least he was using her name now. "Yes."

"Then you know that it's not a fun place to be."

"I do," she said. "I also know that given enough time, things often work out."

Ben looked down at his hands. "My car's pretty much out of gas and I don't have any money to fill it up. I haven't eaten in a day. I smell awful, so I refuse to see the girl I like. Which is depressing because she's really awesome. Things aren't good at school, and they're worse at home. I'm stuck. I can't go forward, but I can't go back and change some of the things I've done. I wish I could."

"You're right, you can't go back. I think you know that I, more than most people, wish that was possible," Jody said.

"I knew him, you know," Ben said softly. "Your son. Mana."

Jody was surprised, but did her best to hide it. "You did?"

"Yeah. He was an instructor at a surf school I took when I was in the fifth grade."

"I remember that. He loved it," Jody said with a small smile.

"He was a really good teacher," Ben said. "And not only that, but when I saw him outside the clinic, he was nice to me, unlike the other kids, who pretended I didn't exist. He helped me with my stance on the board and taught me exactly what to look for when picking a wave to ride. He was patient and funny, and didn't care if his friends gave him shit for working with a grom."

Jody smiled wider. She hadn't heard that surfing term, for a young and inexperienced surfer, in years. "That was Mana," she said simply.

"I'm sorry he died," Ben said.

"Me too, Ben. Me too," Jody told him. "How about this... you come home with me. We'll get you cleaned up, your clothes washed, get a healthy meal inside you...then you can reassess what your next steps are. You can stay with me for as long as you want. I'd much prefer that to you sleeping in your car. It's not safe, Ben."

He chuckled, but it wasn't exactly a humorous sound. "Not safe. Yeah, I know. Why are you going out of your way to help me?" he asked.

"Because you need it. And I like you."

"You gonna call my mom if I go with you?"

"Do you *want* me to call her?"

"No."

"Then I won't. But I feel like I have to say this...she's your mom. She's probably worried sick about you. I know if Mana was living in his car and I didn't know where he was, I'd be a basket case. I don't know what's going on, and I hope you'll eventually feel comfortable enough to tell me, but my offer of assistance doesn't come with any strings."

"There are strings with everything, Miss Jody. Everyone has an ulterior motive."

"Not me," she said firmly.

Ben didn't reply, and Jody let him have some time to think about her offer. While she was waiting, her phone rang. She pulled it out of her pocket. It was Baker.

"Baker's calling me. Is it okay if I answer? He knows I was looking for you and is probably worried."

Ben shrugged.

Jody took that as a yes and clicked on Baker's name. "Hey."

"You find him yet?"

"Actually, yeah, I did."

"Good news, Tink."

"Yup."

"Where was he?"

"At Ka'ena Point."

Baker didn't say anything for a beat. Then he asked, "How'd you find him all the way out there? Or was he in the parking lot?"

"His car was in the lot, but he's sitting out at the end of the trail."

"You walk all the way out there?"

"It's not that far, Baker."

"It's two and a half miles, Jodelle. That's not exactly a short stroll."

"The trail's pretty level. It wasn't that bad."

"Where are you now?" Baker asked.

"Still out here at the point with Ben. He's mulling over my offer to come back to my house."

When he didn't respond, Jody asked, "Baker? You still there?"

"I'm here. You invited him to come home with you?"

"Yes." Her eyes went to Ben, and she saw that he was staring at her. "He needs a friend, and that's me. He hasn't eaten a decent meal in who the heck knows how long and he needs a safe place to sleep and regroup."

"He tell you what's up?"

144

"No."

"Wait—you said you're still out at the point? You wearing a hat or have sunscreen on?"

Jody couldn't help but smile. "No. But I'm okay."

"Shit. You're probably wearing flip-flops too, aren't you?"

"How'd you know?"

"Tink, it's what you always wear. Fuck. I'm too far away to come get you."

"You don't need to come get me. I'm fine, Baker."

"You're hatless, baking in the sun, and you've already walked two and a half miles in what amounts to fuckin' bare feet. You aren't *fine*."

"I am," she insisted, even though his concern felt good.

"And you still have to walk back to your car."

"Baker, stop. It's all good."

"It's not. I should've left the base after we talked earlier and gone with you to look for Ben. I'm sorry."

"Tell him I'll make sure you're okay getting back," Ben said.

Jody's gaze whipped up to Ben's.

"I heard him," Baker said. "Tell him I'd appreciate that."

"Um...Baker can hear you, he said he'd appreciate that," Jody said.

Ben nodded. "I can hear him too. Hope that's okay. Your speaker is turned up pretty loud," he told her.

"Then you can hear that he's overly protective," Jody said wryly.

"You guys dating?" Ben asked.

"Yeah," Jody said.

"Cool."

"Put the phone on speaker, Tink," Baker ordered.

"Why? He can already hear you."

"Just do it, please."

"Fine," Jody said on a sigh. She clicked the button. "There. Done."

"Ben?"

"Yes, sir?"

"I don't know what's going on with you, but I advise you to accept Jodelle's assistance."

"I shouldn't," Ben said.

"You should. You having issues with your stepdad?"

"How do you know Al?" Ben asked, sitting up with a jolt.

"I don't. But from what I've found out, he doesn't give me happy-go-lucky vibes," Baker said.

"He's a respected judge. Everyone loves him," Ben said quietly.

"I don't respect people because of their job titles," Baker replied calmly. "I respect them based on their actions. I've got a friend who was previously homeless who I'd go to for help before I'd go to most other so-called respectable people on this island. I've got one question...no, two. First...will going home with Jodelle put her in danger?"

Ben swallowed hard, and Jody's heart started thumping harder in her chest.

"I...I don't know."

"Thank you for being honest. Second question...is there any shade out there at the point?"

He'd clearly startled the boy with his question. "Um...not really."

"Right. Then I'd appreciate it if you started heading back to the parking area so Jodelle can get out of the sun. Jodelle?"

"I'm here," she said.

"I'm done with my meeting and Leonard is working on preparing me a box of malasadas as we speak. By the time you get back to your home, I should be there. If I'm not, wait for me before going inside."

"Before going inside my house?" Jody asked in confusion.

"Yeah."

"Why?"

"Because you aren't alone. No offense, Ben."

"Baker! Ben's not going to hurt me."

"We already had this conversation, Tink," he said.

"He's right," Ben interrupted. "We'll wait outside, Baker."

"Appreciate it. Take your time going back to your cars. Don't overdo it."

Jody would've rolled her eyes, but Baker had managed to do something she hadn't. Ben had pretty much agreed to go back to her house. He'd said "*We'll* wait outside."

"I don't have enough gas to get back to Miss Jody's place," Ben said.

Baker was silent for a moment, then he said, "I'll take care of it. Leave the keys under the mat in the back passenger-side floor."

"All right."

Jeez, Ben didn't even hesitate. Jody was amazed. Baker had some pretty damn good persuasive powers. She'd have to keep that in mind for the future. Stay on her toes. Otherwise she'd be agreeing to everything he said, no matter *what* it was.

As soon as she had that thought though, she dismissed it as inconsequential. Baker would never ask her to do something that would hurt her, mentally or physically.

"How about you get started back for the parking lot so you can both get out of the sun and Jodelle can take care of you," Baker said.

"I'm seventeen. I don't need taking care of," Ben retorted.

"Wrong. You'll learn this over time, but we all need someone to take care of us," Baker said. "And when you find that someone, you do everything in your power to nurture and protect that person's good heart. Understand?"

"Yes, sir."

"Good. Jodelle?"

She wanted to say something snarky about him finally remembering she was there, but she was feeling too emotional about what he'd just said. "Yeah?"

"You did good."

His praise made her feel all warm and fuzzy.

"Now get your ass out of the sun and make sure you drink lots of water when you get back to your van. I know you've got a cooler full of cold water in there, don't you?"

Jody smiled. "Of course I do."

"Good. Text me when you get back to the car."

"I will."

"See you soon."

"Bye."

Jody clicked off the phone, and to break the somewhat awkward silence between her and Ben, she said, "He's kind of uber protective."

"As he should be," Ben said, then he stood and held out his hand. "Come on, we need to get out of the sun and back to your van so you can drink that water."

Jody wanted to roll her eyes, but she liked that he was echoing Baker's words. Wanting to make sure she was safe. Proving he was the decent kid she thought he was. She still had no idea what Ben was hiding or running from, but at least he'd agreed to come home with her.

As Ben pulled her to her feet, making sure she was steady before dropping her hand, Jody's mind spun with everything she needed to do if she was going to have a houseguest. She had some food in the house, but if Ben stayed longer than a day or so, she should go to the grocery store and stock up. He was a growing kid, and if he was anything like Mana had been, he'd eat a lot. He'd also need some soap and shampoo; her girly stuff wouldn't cut it. She needed to get clean sheets on Mana's bed...

No. It wasn't his bed anymore.

"Miss Jody?" Ben asked as they walked slowly back down the dirt trail.

"Yeah?"

"Thanks for trying to find me."

"You're welcome."

"I didn't think anyone would even notice I was gone. Well...besides maybe Tressa."

"I noticed," Jody said unnecessarily. "And I'm certain Tressa has too."

Then she promptly tripped over a rock in the middle of the path.

"Careful," Ben warned as he grabbed her arm to steady her.

It was safe to say that Ben Miller was definitely a good kid. Jody vowed to get to the bottom of whatever was bothering him. Between her and Baker, she had no doubt that they could figure it out and get Ben back to his normal routine.

# CHAPTER ELEVEN

Baker pulled up to Jodelle's small house less than ten minutes after she'd texted to let him know she and Ben had arrived home.

He parked behind her van, shut off his engine, and immediately climbed out. He made a beeline for Jodelle, who was standing next to Ben. He gave the kid a chin lift, but his attention was all on the woman at his side.

Her cheeks were pink, obviously from the sun she'd gotten today. Her feet were filthy, coated in dirt from the path to Ka'ena Point. The hair at her temples and behind her ears was wet from sweat, but still he'd never seen a woman more beautiful. Putting a finger under her chin, he asked, "You good?"

"Of course I am," she told him with a smile. "But I'd be better if you gave me those malasadas you were supposed to pick up."

Hearing her teasing made Baker relax for the first time since he'd gotten the call that she'd found Ben. He leaned forward and gave her a brief kiss, letting her know without words that he was relieved she was all right. Then he turned, keeping his arm around Jodelle, and held out a hand to Ben. "Good to see you."

Ben nodded and shook Baker's hand.

The boy looked rough. Baker hadn't been all that keen on Jodelle inviting him to her house, but now that he saw him, he knew she'd done the right thing. Ben clearly wasn't doing well on his own. As much as he probably would argue that point, the teenager was hurting. And living out of his car had obviously been harder than he thought it would be.

"Called a friend. He'll fill up your car and bring it by sometime tonight," Baker said.

Ben swallowed hard. "Thanks."

"No problem. But I'm not helping you out of the goodness of my heart," Baker told him.

Jodelle stiffened against him and tried to pull away, but Baker refused to let her.

"What do you want then?"

"I want you to graduate. I want you to remember this moment and do what you can to help others the way you're being helped today. Life isn't easy. It's fuckin' hard. But I want you to find the strength to get past whatever shit's eating at you, and let it make you even stronger."

"Baker, don't swear," Jodelle scolded.

"Tink, I swear all the time," Baker said.

"I know. And I usually don't care, but Ben's a kid, he doesn't need to hear that kind of language."

Baker met Ben's gaze and saw the teenager was just as amused at Jodelle's words as he was. "He's not a kid, and I'm guessing nothing I say will faze him."

"Maybe, but still," Jodelle said.

Because she was so damn adorable, Baker said, "I'll do my best to curb it."

"Thanks."

"I can do all that," Ben told Baker quietly. "But I haven't

been living out of my car because I'm throwing a temper tantrum," he warned.

"Didn't think you were," Baker said. "You're a good man. Have a good head on your shoulders. But problems shared are more easily solved."

Ben looked skeptical, but Baker decided not to push right now. The kid would feel better after he got clean, filled his belly, and had a good night's sleep. One that wasn't in the back seat of his car and where he wasn't worried someone might find him and possibly do him harm.

"You want to grab the box from Leonard's Bakery from my front seat?" Baker asked Jodelle.

Her eyes lit up. "Yes!"

Baker dropped his arm and she immediately headed for the passenger side of his car. He knew he only had thirty seconds or so before Jodelle was back, so he spoke fast. He looked Ben in the eye and said, "Do *not* hurt her. I can tolerate a lot of shit, but not her getting hurt. Understand?"

"Yes, sir," Ben said immediately. "I'll leave as soon as my car gets here."

Fuck, that wasn't what Baker meant. "You leave, that'll *definitely* hurt her," he said. "She'll worry."

"I..." Ben looked confused and scared. "My stepdad's not a good man."

"I figured as much. We'll deal with that. I just need you to give me the intel necessary to keep her safe."

"These smell so good!" Jodelle enthused as she approached with the Leonard's Bakery box in hand, the lid open an inch and her nose buried inside.

"You're a goof," Baker said with a smile.

"They're malasadas," Jodelle said. "Everyone's a goof over malasadas. Come on, Ben, let's get you inside so you can shower and help me eat these." She smiled at the teenager, then headed for the front door.

"I'm trying to keep other people safe too," Ben said in a tone low enough that Jodelle wouldn't hear.

Baker nodded. He understood that, and his admiration for the teenager rose a notch. "I know this is new, and you don't really know me outside of surfing, but you'll discover that I'm perfectly capable of having your back and keeping shit from spreading. While you're learning that, I'd appreciate if you kept where you're sleeping on the down low."

"Yeah, sure," Ben said.

"Good. Whenever you're ready, I'm here to listen. I just hope you get ready sooner rather than later," he finished.

"You guys coming?" Jodelle called from the open front door.

Baker turned and headed for his woman. Things had changed. His timetable for wooing Jodelle had just been moved up. He couldn't say he was upset about that; the more he hung out with the woman, the more he wanted her. Not just in the bedroom either. In his life. Under his skin. Intertwined with his psyche so much he couldn't ever shake her loose.

Baker walked into Jodelle's house and grinned when he heard her oohing and ahhing over the malasadas. He threw his keys in the bowl on her counter and felt satisfaction blossom inside when he saw her keys already there.

"I'm sorry, but I couldn't wait," Jodelle said, her words muffled because she was talking with her mouth full of fluffy pastry. "They're so good!"

Baker laughed. "Jeez, woman, not sure you need to eat a couple tablespoons of sugar right after being out in the sun all day."

Jodelle rolled her eyes at him. "Whatever." Then she turned to Ben. "Shower first, or malasada?"

He looked uncomfortable. "I should shower, but I don't have anything to put on."

Jodelle put down the pastry and wiped her hand on her

shorts, making Baker smirk. "I've got some of Mana's things you can wear until we get your stuff washed and dried."

"Oh, I couldn't, Miss Jody."

"You can," she said firmly. Her tone gentled as she said, "After Mana died, I gave away most of his clothes to charity. But there was a box I couldn't part with. It was all his favorite shirts, sweats, and jeans. Now I'm thinking there was a reason I couldn't give them away. They might be a bit musty, and they might not fit perfectly, although you seem to be about the same size as he was. You'll feel much better if you change, Ben."

"I don't want to cause you any pain," the teenager admitted. "If seeing me in his clothes will hurt you, I'll wait."

Baker saw Jodelle's lips quiver, but she got control over her emotions and said, "I think it'll be more painful to sit here and smell you in those clothes, bud." She winked. "The box is in the closet in...the guest room. Help yourself. Seriously. It'll make me happy to put his clothes to such good use."

"If you're sure," Ben said hesitantly.

"I'm sure," Jodelle confirmed. "There's hand soap in the bathroom. It's not shampoo or body wash, but it'll do until we can get something more appropriate. I think there's also a new toothbrush in a drawer, and toothpaste too. Take your time."

"If I take too long there might not be any malasadas left for me," Ben quipped.

She beamed. "True. So you better get going then."

Ben and Jodelle smiled at each other.

"Thank you, Miss Jody," he said.

"You're welcome," she returned.

Then Ben turned and walked down the hall as if he'd been there all his life.

Baker didn't even wait for the boy to be out of sight before he was pulling Jodelle back into his arms. She came without hesitation, burrowing into him and pressing her face against his chest. They didn't say anything for a full minute. It wasn't until the bathroom door shut behind Ben that Jodelle looked up at him.

"Something's really wrong," she whispered, her brow furrowed in concern.

Only then did Baker realize her enthusiastic and happy demeanor since they'd gotten home had been a clever façade. She was worried sick about Ben and now that he wasn't around, she was letting her guard down. With him.

"We're gonna figure out what it is and fix it."

And just like that, some of the stress went out of her. She melted against him even more. "Yeah. Mr. I-have-connections can fix it."

"Damn straight," he said with a small smile. Then he sobered and ran a finger over her pink cheek. "This hurt?"

"No."

"Your feet?"

"Dirty, but no blisters."

"Good. Why don't you go shower too?"

"You saying I smell?" she teased.

"Never. But I *will* say that I prefer your plumeria perfume."

Jodelle laughed. "You're obsessed with that stuff."

"Nope. I'm obsessed with *you*," Baker said honestly.

"You aren't gonna eat all the good malasadas while I'm gone, are you?" she asked with a tilt of her head.

Baker chuckled. "No."

"Okay. Baker?"

"Yeah, Tink?"

"I'm glad you're here."

He nodded. "No other place I'd be. Go. Get comfortable. And I'm talking sweats and a T-shirt, not your pajamas."

She rolled her eyes. "No way would I wear that in front of

Ben," she said with a small shake of her head. "Only the man I've got the hots for and want to try to entice."

"No trying about it, Tink," Baker told her.

She smiled. "Kiss me before I go?"

He didn't hesitate. He leaned down and took her lips with his. It wasn't a chaste kiss like earlier. It was deep, possessive, and he tried to let her know exactly how much he cared about her, how worried he'd been for her today.

When he pulled back, she said, "Wow."

Baker smirked. "Go shower, Jodelle. Give a man a break. The last thing I want to do is make small talk with Ben with a fuckin' hard-on."

Her hips pressed against his, as if she needed to confirm what he was saying wasn't a lie. When she felt his erection against her belly, she smiled. "That feels painful."

"There's pain and then there's pain."

"Spoken like a true soldier."

"Sailor—and yup," Baker said.

She smiled again, then backed away. She reached for the malasada she'd taken a bite out of earlier and held it up with a grin. "Sustenance for my shower."

Baker merely shook his head. His woman had a sweet tooth. It was fucking adorable.

She took another large bite, then turned and headed down the hall.

The second she was out of sight, Baker's shoulders tensed. Shit. He was torn between being thrilled he was getting to spend more time with Jodelle and stressed about the unknown threat that seemed to be hovering over Ben. Baker was a man who didn't like not having the information he needed to make smart decisions. Until Ben felt comfortable sharing with him, he was flying blind. And that was how people got hurt.

But Ben wasn't a terrorist or a killer, and while Baker was worried about what had driven him to live out of his car, he didn't think it was a life-or-death situation. At least he hoped not. He wasn't naïve enough to think bad shit couldn't infiltrate his piece of paradise—he had plenty of experience to the contrary—but he prayed it wouldn't be anything like what had happened to his friends' women. That kind of thing touching Jodelle, after everything else she'd been through in her life, made him want to lock her in the house and throw away the key.

But that wouldn't make her happy. It would kill the light that was shining so bright inside her, even after the pain of losing her son. So the next best thing was getting to the bottom of whatever shit Ben was trying to deal with on his own and help him fix it, allowing Jodelle to relax once again.

* * *

Hours later, Ben was clean, full from the three hamburgers he'd eaten, his car was on the street outside the house, his clothes were in the dryer, and he was lounging half-asleep on one end of the couch while Baker and Jodelle were snuggled together on the other end.

Jodelle looked up at Baker and said, "It's getting late. You're probably tired after your meetings and stuff today. You should head home."

"Not going home. I'm staying here," Baker told her.

Jodelle frowned and sat up against him. "What?"

"I'm staying."

"But...um...we aren't...shoot. Baker, we've only been dating like a week."

"I'm sleeping on the couch, Tink. Relax."

"Oh, but—"

"I'm staying," he said firmly. Baker could sense Ben's eyes on him, but he kept his gaze locked on Jodelle. "I'm guessing I can trust Ben, but I wouldn't be the man I am if I left you alone in your house with a guy twice as tall and heavy as you."

"Baker, he's not going to hurt me."

He shrugged, not swayed in the least. "I'm thinking he's not, no."

"So you don't have to stay."

He didn't respond, just met her gaze as they had a silent battle of wills. One she was going to lose, but Baker respected her for engaging in it anyway.

"He's right," Ben said from the other end of the couch. "Again."

Jodelle turned toward him. "Are you going to hurt me?" she asked a little forcefully.

"No."

"See?" she said, turning back to Baker.

"He's protecting you, as he should," Ben said. "I can say the words until I'm blue in the face, but actions speak louder. People lie all the time, Miss Jody. Say things they know the other person wants to hear, then they go ahead and do whatever they want anyway. Baker staying here is the smart thing to do."

Jodelle sighed. "Well, I trust you, Ben."

"Thanks. But he's still right," the teenager said.

Jodelle looked back up at Baker. "The couch isn't that comfortable. It doesn't even pull out."

"It'll be fine. Believe me, I've slept in worse places in my life."

Her forehead wrinkled once more. "Not sure that's making me feel any better," she said. "Now all I can think of is you lying on some cold, wet ground, shivering, as gunfire shoots over your head," she mumbled.

Baker couldn't help but chuckle. He wished he could reassure her that had never happened, but he couldn't.

"I can sleep out here," Ben volunteered.

"No," both Baker and Jodelle said at the same time. She grinned at him.

"You need to catch up on your sleep," Baker told the boy.

"You've got tomorrow to get your bearings, but then you need to get back to school."

Ben frowned and looked down at his lap.

"We can go surfing if you want," Baker offered. "Maybe mid-morning. Nothing clears your head better than catchin' a good wave."

"I don't have my board," Ben said, still talking to his hands.

"I've got an extra at my place," Baker told him. "Know it's not the same as having your own, but it's better than nothing."

Baker held his breath, then relaxed a fraction when Ben finally nodded.

"Good. It *is* getting late, and you've probably got shit—Er...jobs you need to catch up on tomorrow, Tink," Baker said. "You've been practically snoring in my arms, so don't say that you aren't tired."

"I wasn't snoring," Jodelle protested.

"If you say so," he teased.

"I...are you sure you'll be okay out here? Wait, do you have your overnight stuff?"

Baker chuckled. "My overnight stuff?"

"Yeah, pajamas, clothes for tomorrow, toothbrush, things like that?"

"Tink, I sleep in my boxers, and I think I can put on the same thing I wore today long enough to go to my place in the morning to get something clean."

"But what about a toothbrush?" she pressed.

"You have another extra?"

She bit her lip. "Yes." Then said quickly, "It's because I always get a free one when I go to the dentist, but I don't like the ones they give out. I like to buy my own. So I throw the freebies in a drawer...just in case."

"Wasn't questioning why you had extra brushes, Tink, but I'm relieved to hear you aren't collecting them because you spontaneously invite people to stay the night at your house on a regular basis," Baker said.

Ben laughed from next to them, and Baker was thrilled to hear that the kid had loosened up enough to find humor in something, but he kept his gaze locked on Jodelle's.

"I don't. I think this is the first time since Mana died that anyone's stayed the night. I just...I don't want you to be uncomfortable."

"I won't be. Promise."

"Okay. But I still say there's no need."

"And I say there is," Baker retorted.

"And I agree," Ben piped up.

"All right, all right. I'm outnumbered, I get it. Jeez!" Jodelle said as she let out a breath.

Ben got up from his place on the couch and stood a little awkwardly in the middle of the room. "I'll just go on to bed then. Thanks again for everything, Miss Jody."

"Of course, honey. I'm glad to have you here, and you're welcome to stay as long as you want. Even if that's months. I mean it, Ben."

Baker saw tears glisten in the teenager's eyes before he lowered his head. "Thanks," he repeated quietly.

"See you in the morning," Jodelle said, and it was obvious to Baker that she'd seen the tears too and was offering a few more words so he wasn't embarrassed by his emotions.

Ben nodded and headed out of the living room.

Baker waited until the door to the guest room had shut once more before asking Jodelle, "You okay?"

She frowned up at him. "Why wouldn't I be?"

"Because Mana's room is occupied by someone other than him for the first time since he passed."

Jodelle closed her eyes for a moment, then opened them. "Yes. I thought it would be hard, and I had a little moment when I was making the bed earlier, but I got over it. This is the right thing to do, and I know Mana would be thrilled Ben's here. He knew him."

It took Baker a second to understand what she meant. "Mana knew Ben?"

"Yeah. Ben told me earlier. Said that Mana was his instructor in a surf clinic thing. And something I heard once hit me when I was putting the sheets on the bed. Someone was trying to comfort me, and she said that everything happens for a reason. And when I heard that, I was so angry. I couldn't imagine what the hell the reason might be for my child *dying*. It made no sense and felt like some trite shit people spout when they don't know what else to say.

"But...I'm starting to understand how true the saying is. I mean, I wish I still had my son, but if Mana hadn't died, then maybe the kid he saved wouldn't have survived, so there's that. And other little things too. I wouldn't have started hanging out at the beach in the mornings, wouldn't have met you, wouldn't be here with you right now. I wouldn't have met Ben either, and noticed something was up with him. I wouldn't have gone looking for him, and he'd be stranded out there at Ka'ena Point with no gas, hungry, probably scared. He definitely wouldn't be here now, and I wouldn't have ever known he knew Mana, or the impact my son had on his life.

"So...while I still wish my son was here, I'm finally starting to open my eyes to some of the good things that have happened because of his death. Does that make me a bad person?"

"No," Baker said, prouder of her right that moment than he could put into words. "I think it's a healthy way of looking at life."

"Mana would want me to look after Ben. Give him his bed, clothes, a safe place to regroup until he can figure out what's what."

"I agree," Baker said. "You okay with me staying?"

"Yeah. But would it be too forward of me to say that I wish you weren't sleeping on the couch?"

Baker's muscles tightened. "Shit, woman."

"Too soon?"

"Yes...and no. I feel the same, but I'm making a point. One I'm pretty sure Ben has no problem with."

"I'm thinking you could probably protect me better if you were right next to me," Jodelle said a little coyly.

"Fuck..."

Jodelle licked her lips and grinned up at him. "Okay, okay. I'm sorry. I'll stop. But, just saying, Baker. I'm a grown woman. Not a kid. And it's obvious that I like you...at least, I think it is. I know we haven't been together all that long, but it feels as if I've known you forever. I know you're a trustworthy man. You aren't going to fuck me then dump me the next day. So if you've got some preconceived idea that you have to wait a month or two, or whatever, before we consummate this relationship...you need to maybe rethink that."

Baker shifted them both until Jodelle was on her back, her dark brown hair spread over the cushion under her, and he was lying between her legs. "Consummate?" he asked with a grin.

She rolled her eyes. "Yeah."

"Then no, Tink, I have no timeline in mind for our *consummation*, but I really wanted to give you the time to get to know me—the me that most people don't get to see—before we went there. I'm not an easy man, and I need you to understand that before you give me your body."

"I don't want easy. Easy's boring."

"You say that now, but don't think I missed how you argued with me over something as simple as me wanting to protect you by staying the night," he retorted.

"I think *you* missed how good that made me feel. That you cared enough to want to protect me."

Baker stilled as he stared down at her. She was right—he *had* missed it.

"And not only that, but you respected me enough to not even for one second think you'd be sleeping in my bed tonight. Yeah, you're hardheaded, stubborn, and overprotective, but I've been on my own for years, Baker. I had to raise a son by myself; that's not easy, not by any stretch. I was responsible for not only him, but myself for nearly my entire adult life. I can take you not being an easy man, if it comes with also knowing you care enough not to leave me alone in my house with someone else, even if that someone else would no sooner hurt or steal from me than my own son would."

"I've done a lot of shit in my life," Baker warned.

Jodelle rolled her eyes. "Of course you have, you were a SEAL."

He hadn't done that stuff just as a SEAL. He continued to do things he wasn't exactly proud of, but those actions had been for the greater good. "I'm trying to give you one final out here," he told her.

"I don't want one," Jodelle said firmly. "Baker, from the first day I met you, I wanted you. You give off pretty intense vibes, but somehow, I knew you wouldn't hurt me. Or the kids you surf with every day. And the more I saw you, the more that was proven time and time again. Even when you were trying to be a hard-ass with Monica the day you met her, you were doing so because you wanted to protect your friend."

"Looks like you left some stuff out when you told me about your lunch with the girls," Baker said wryly.

Jodelle smiled at him. "I was there that day, remember? And when Monica freaked out after seeing your tattoo, you went out of your way to make sure she didn't get hurt. You talked to her, soothed her. I couldn't hear what you were saying from where I was sitting, but I *could* see that you hated the fact she was scared of you.

"That's the man I want. The man I dream about when I'm alone in my bed at night. The man I have no problem with sleeping on my couch and using his connections to buy me fresh malasadas. But...half my life is over. I'm not willing to sit around and play some stupid dating game until some arbitrary amount of time has passed that someone, somewhere, feels is adequate before sex happens."

Baker studied her for a long moment. "Right. Tonight, I'm on the couch. Tomorrow, I'm in your bed. From there, we'll take things as they come."

Jodelle beamed up at him. "Sounds good to me."

"It's a good thing you don't like easy, Tink, because I have a feeling you're gonna get irritated with me a lot," he warned her.

"Probably," she said, still smiling. Then her hands slid under his T-shirt, her warm palms running up his back. "But I have a feeling the make-up sex will be unforgettable."

"Shit," Baker swore as he felt his cock jerk to attention. She had to feel it too, because she shifted under him, arching slightly so he was notched more firmly right between her legs.

She pressed against his back, trying to get him to lower his body. When he stayed propped up above her, she pouted. "Baker."

"Yeah?"

"Kiss me," she pleaded.

He couldn't resist.

They made out on her couch for several long minutes, until Baker knew he had to stop or he'd lose control. His hand was under her shirt, and he had her bra cup pulled down and her breast in his hand. Her nipple was rock hard, stabbing into his palm as he sucked and licked at the skin right under her ear. Her head was turned, giving him access, and one of her hands was gripping his ass as she rocked slowly against him.

The other began fumbling with the fastener of his belt.

Baker took a deep breath, slid her bra back into place, and removed his hand from under her shirt. He grabbed the hand that was trying to undo his belt and brought it up to his mouth. He kissed the palm and waited for Jodelle to look at him.

She was breathing hard, and he could see the top of her chest was flushed with arousal. Baker desperately wanted to see if the rest of her also turned red.

"Can't wait to experience everything with you," Baker told her.

"Me too," she replied breathily.

"But more than that, looking forward to simply holding you while I sleep. Falling asleep with your plumeria smell in my nose, knowing that somehow, after everything I've done, I still found my soul mate."

Jodelle's eyes immediately filled with tears.

"No crying, woman," Baker scolded. "This is a happy moment."

She took a deep breath. "It's also a frustrating one," she replied when she'd gotten control over her emotions.

"Yup. But we're old and wise, we'll get through it," Baker said.

She grinned briefly, then said, "I've never slept in anyone's arms."

"Seriously? You were married," Baker said.

"He didn't like to cuddle. Said I made him feel claustrophobic."

"He was a fuckin' idiot," Baker told her.

"Think I'm gonna like cuddling with you," she said.

Baker regretted saying he would sleep on the couch. He wanted to show her how great it could be to sleep with someone. Just sleep. "And I think you should probably enjoy your last night sleeping alone."

"It's gonna be a long one."

"Longest night ever," Baker agreed. "But what do they say? Anticipation makes everything better?"

"Whoever 'they' is, they're an idiot too," Jodelle complained.

Baker laughed. "I'm thinking you're right." Then he did what might've been the hardest thing he'd had to do in a very long time, and climbed off Jodelle's soft, welcoming body. He pulled her upright, then tugged her so she was standing in front of him. "Get some sleep, Tink."

"You think I can sleep *now*?"

"You better. I don't want you comatose tomorrow night."

She grinned, then wrinkled her nose. "Now I'm wondering how cool it is to sleep with you with Ben down the hall."

"As much as I want between your legs, I'm looking forward to just holding you, Tink. Besides, Ben's not an idiot. He's also not five."

"I know, but still."

"We'll play it by ear. If we need to, we'll go to my place."

"Really? You'd let him stay in my house by himself?"

"Not tonight. Not tomorrow. But in a while, once he's proven we can trust him? Yeah. If you're more comfortable making love with me when he's not around, and I know you're not going to kick him out anytime soon, then that's what we'll do. But for the record, I'm not gonna need to jump you every single night like a twenty-year-old. I'm too old for that shit. Sometimes, there's more intimacy in lying in someone's arms than there is in fucking."

Jodelle squeezed him. "I'm one hundred percent all right with that," she whispered.

Baker couldn't help but kiss her again. Then he pressed his lips to her forehead and simply held her.

"I'll grab an extra pillow and a blanket," she said.

"I want yours."

"My what?"

"Pillow," Baker told her.

Jodelle blushed again, but nodded.

"Wanna smell you when I'm sleeping," Baker added, even though she didn't ask for an explanation.

It was a fucking miracle he hadn't scared her off yet. He was moving a million miles an hour, but she hadn't even blinked. Another thing that proved she was perfect for him. Then again, she'd admitted she was interested from the first moment she saw him. The same had gone for him, although like an idiot, he'd hesitated to make a move. Baker had a feeling he'd be kicking himself for not seeing where this could lead a long time ago. He'd missed out on at least a couple years of having Jodelle by his side, in his bed, and under his skin.

He might be moving fast now, but he had a lot of time to make up for, and he wasn't willing to waste one more day getting to where they both wanted to be.

Baker let Jodelle go so she could get him a pillow from her bed. He stayed where he was, afraid if he followed, he wouldn't be sleeping on the couch. He also did his best not to look like he was going to pounce on her when she returned.

"Good night," she said softly.

"Night, Tink."

"See you in the morning."

Baker nodded, clenching his teeth to try to keep control. Jodelle stared at him for a beat, then turned and walked back toward her bedroom.

It took five full minutes of standing where she'd left him, listening to her puttering around in her room, for Baker to relax enough to move. Then he went to the front door, made sure it was locked, and checked the windows as well. Once he was satisfied the house was as secure as it could be, he sat back down on the couch. He lifted the pillow Jodelle had given him to his face and inhaled deeply.

Grimacing at the way his cock immediately came to life at the scent of plumeria, Baker sighed. It was going to be a long night, but strangely, he was more satisfied than he could remember being in a long time. It felt right being under the same roof as Jodelle, even if he wasn't by her side. He was where he was supposed to be, he had no doubt.

It had taken fifty-two years for him to get here, but now that he was, Baker wasn't going anywhere.

# CHAPTER TWELVE

Jody hadn't slept well. She kept dreaming about Baker. She woke several times, well aware he was just steps from her bedroom door. All she had to do was tell him she had a bad dream, and he'd be in her bed. She knew it, but she refused to play those games with him. Baker was...different. Very different than her ex, who didn't care about anyone but himself. Different from the few men she'd dated over the years. He seemed to get her on a level that no one else had before. She could talk to him about Mana without Baker getting weirded out or annoyed that she couldn't just accept that her son was dead.

Kaimana would always be a part of her. She refused to forget about him or take down his pictures.

A noise coming from her son's room made Jody sit straight up in bed. Was that...?

For a split second, when she heard the floorboard in his room creak, joy careened through her. But the happiness was short-lived. Mana was gone, and what she was hearing wasn't her son, but Ben.

Jody flopped back down in bed and stared at the ceiling, dissecting the emotions inside her at the moment. Was she upset? She didn't think so. Her lack of sleep made her think for a second that she was hearing Mana, but knowing that Ben was there made her feel...comforted. She knew down to the marrow of her bones that Mana would be happy she was helping him. Even though Jody didn't know what had gone so wrong in Ben's life, it was enough at the moment to give him a safe place to sleep, food to eat, and unconditional friendship.

She heard the water in the bathroom turn on and sat up again, hurrying into her own attached bathroom to get ready for the day. She wanted to make a big breakfast for Ben...and for Baker. It wasn't often she missed breakfast at the beach with her surf kids, but she could make a rare exception this morning.

Looking in the mirror, Jody saw that she had a smile on her face. It felt great to not wake up alone. She'd gotten used to it, but that didn't mean she liked it. Throwing her hair up in a messy bun, she put on a pair of leggings and an oversized T-shirt. Then she hurried out of her room, hoping to have breakfast started before Ben was done with his shower.

She was concentrating so hard on getting to the kitchen and thinking through what food she had in the house, that she wasn't paying attention when she exited the hallway into the living area.

Her breath whooshed out of her as she literally bounced off Baker. She would've fallen on her ass if he hadn't caught her around the waist.

He pulled her close, until she was plastered to his body, and chuckled deep in his throat. The sound made goose bumps spring up on Jody's arms. Looking into his jade-green eyes, she couldn't catch her breath for a second. Dang, even first thing in the morning, Baker was hot. His hair was mussed, almost sticking straight up. He had a crease on one chiseled cheek from the pillow he'd used, and the jeans he wore sat low on his hips because he hadn't buttoned them yet.

Jody had seen him plenty of times in a wet suit, which left nothing to her imagination, but seeing him like this...clearly having just woken up, pants barely on, chest bare under her hands...was completely different. More intimate.

"Morning, Tink," he said in a low, rumbly voice that immediately made wetness leak from between her legs. Good Lord, the man was lethal.

"Hi," she managed.

His own eyes roamed down her body leisurely, and by the feel of his erection against her stomach, he liked what he saw.

"Sleep well?"

She shrugged.

Baker frowned. "No? What's wrong?"

"Nothing's wrong," she said, caressing his chest with her thumbs unconsciously. "I've been alone in this house for so long, I think my subconscious knew there were people here again. It'll take a bit of getting used to, that's all."

Baker relaxed a bit and nodded. "I get that. I woke up several times myself. Got up to check the house, make sure all was good. Habit. I'm sorry if you heard me walking around and that's what woke you."

"You do that a lot?" she asked.

"Yeah. Byproduct of my past," he said with a shrug, as if it wasn't a big deal he couldn't sleep through the night without feeling as if he needed to get up and check for boogeymen. Aware that she wasn't all that happy about what he'd said, Baker lifted a hand and buried his fingers in her hair, loosening the bun. "It's fine. I usually go right back to sleep afterward. God, I love your hair."

Blinking at the abrupt change of topic, Jody didn't complain when Baker leaned down and inhaled deeply.

"You're so weird," she told him, secretly loving that he liked the way she smelled.

"Probably," he muttered without lifting his head.

Then he shocked the shit out of her by slowly swaying them back and forth.

"What are you doing?"

"Dancing," Baker said.

Jody's heart melted. She turned into a big pile of goo right there in her living room. She swallowed hard and closed her eyes, letting Baker lead them in a slow dance.

Several minutes passed while they shuffled back and forth in each other's arms—until Ben's confused voice broke the spell they were apparently under.

"What's going on?"

Jody jerked her head to the side to see Ben standing there, staring at them in confusion.

"We're dancing," Baker repeated, not seeming embarrassed or concerned in the least.

"It's," Ben looked down at the watch on his wrist, "seven-thirty in the morning."

"Yup," Baker said.

"Okay...whatever," he muttered. "I thought I'd head out."

Jody pulled out of Baker's arms upon hearing that. "What? Where? I haven't made breakfast."

Ben looked away. "I've taken enough, Miss Jody. I don't wanna be a mooch."

"Benjamin Miller, you are not a mooch," she said heatedly. She turned to face Ben, hands on her hips as she frowned at her houseguest. "If you're going to go surfing today with Baker, you need sustenance. I'm guessing you haven't had a good breakfast in a while. If you don't want to be a *mooch*, you can help me, but you aren't leaving until I've fed you."

Ben's lips twitched slightly. He looked at Baker. "She's kind of bossy."

"Yup," Baker said with a smile, wrapping his arms around Jody from behind.

"I *am* bossy," Jody said. "You can stir the waffle mix while I make the bacon."

"Guess I'm staying," Ben sighed.

"You got your wet suit?" Baker asked.

"Yeah. I brought it in last night," Ben told him.

"Good."

"I need to clean my car out...throw away the trash and stuff," he said hesitantly, as if embarrassed.

"You can do that after you eat," Jody said. "You sleep okay?"

"Yes."

"Good."

"Miss Jody?"

"Yeah, Ben?"

"I...I appreciate you letting me stay here last night."

Jody pulled out of Baker's grasp and walked over to the teenager. He wasn't quite as tall as Baker, but he was close. She lifted a hand and placed it gently on Ben's cheek. "As I told you last night, you can stay here as long as you want."

"Thanks," he whispered.

Jody took a deep breath and dropped her hand. "Right, before I turn into a pile of mush, we have breakfast to make while Baker showers."

"I'm going to the beach to surf," Baker reminded her.

"And?" Jody asked, turning to face him. "You want your stinkiness to contaminate the ocean and kill the turtles?"

Baker choked back a laugh. Jody knew she was being extra bossy and ridiculous, but she wanted some time alone with Ben. Baker seemed to make him nervous, and she wanted her houseguest to relax as much as possible.

As if he understood, Baker nodded. "All right, but I'm using your en suite bathroom."

A shiver ran through Jody at the thought of Baker naked in her shower. "Okay, but if you come out smelling like my perfume, I'm really gonna wonder about you."

Baker chuckled. "Like to smell it on *you*, Tink, not bathe in it." Then he lifted his chin at Ben and turned to head for her bedroom.

When she heard the door shut, she turned to Ben. "Now that he's gone...don't tell him, but I think we need a malasada as a breakfast appetizer."

Ben chuckled. "You're a nut."

"Yup," Jody said with a smile, thrilled to see the grin on Ben's face.

By the time Baker got out of the shower—Jody had the feeling he'd purposely taken an extra-long time in there— breakfast was ready. Before sitting, she reached into the pantry and pulled out a strawberry Pop-Tart and put it next to her plate.

"Waffles, bacon, and malasadas not enough?" Baker asked, the amusement easy to hear in his tone.

Jody was determined not to be embarrassed about her ritual. "Mana always had a Pop-Tart for breakfast. I mean, literally every single day. A strawberry one. Except... Except *that* morning." She took a deep breath. "I know it's silly, but..." Her voice trailed off.

Baker leaned over and wrapped his hand gently around the back of her neck and pulled her closer. "You want to eat a Pop-Tart every morning, you eat a Pop-Tart every morning. Nothing silly about that," he said softly as he rested his fore-head against hers. They sat like that for a heartbeat before Jody nodded.

She didn't think Baker would make fun of her, or tell her with an eye roll that Mana hadn't died because he didn't eat a Pop-Tart that morning five years ago. Deep down, she knew that. But it didn't keep her from indulging in her son's favorite snack every morning because it made her feel closer to him.

The waffles were delicious, and Jody was thrilled when Ben ate several. Baker did a good job of eating his fair share as well. A trip to the grocery store was definitely going to be in order sooner rather than later.

Ben seemed to relax even more as they ate. Baker kept the talk light and easy and didn't press the teenager to share his troubles. By the time they were ready to head out to surf, he seemed almost like the kid Jody had met a couple years ago on the beach.

"Is there anything particular you two like to eat? I'm going to the store while you're frolicking in the ocean this morning," Jody said.

"Whatever you get is fine," Ben said softly, obviously uncomfortable at the reminder that she was feeding him. He headed toward the door.

Baker reached for his wallet and pulled out a credit card and held it out to her.

"Um...what's that for?" she asked him.

"For food."

"Oh, I'm good. Thanks though."

Baker didn't drop his hand. He motioned to the card with his chin. "Take it, Jodelle."

"Really, it's not necessary."

In response, Baker stepped toward her. He didn't touch her, but he definitely had her attention. "You're not paying for food you're gonna cook for me," he said.

Jody pressed her lips together and tried not to get irritated. This was the kind of man Baker was. She knew it, even enjoyed the way he wanted to look out for her. Hell, he'd just told her last night that a relationship with him wouldn't be easy. But she didn't want him thinking she was angling for a sugar daddy or something. "I know we haven't talked about this, but I make good money at what I do, Baker. I don't need —or *want*—you to pay for every little thing as if I need your money. I don't."

"I know you don't," he said, not sounding irritated in the least. "I'm glad you're not hurting when it comes to money, but what you just said goes for me too. I'm not looking to live off you."

"Are we at an impasse then?" she couldn't help but ask.

"No. We're new, we're talking shit out," Baker said.

Okay, that was nice. She took a moment to calm herself before speaking. "I usually go to the grocery store once a week, but I haven't gone in a while. Now Ben's here. He's a teenager, and he eats a lot. At least I'm assuming he does, based on my experience with Mana. He's had a tough road lately, and I want to make this a safe place for him, and that means having good food for him to eat for as long as he stays. Not to mention, I want to impress my new boyfriend by cooking for him. It's been a long time since I've had the opportunity to make something that's not a single serving. I *like* cooking. I want to cook for you both, and in order to do that, I need food. Food that I can buy with the money I've earned."

"I get all that, and it means a lot to me, because I can't cook all that well and I like to eat," Baker said. "Seeing you happy in your kitchen, cooking a meal for us, is something I'm looking forward to. Especially knowing you enjoy it. That said, you're not cooking or buying groceries just for yourself. You're doing it for three people. I want to contribute. And Ben's a kid, he shouldn't have to pay for his meals. I'm not hurting when it comes to money either, Tink, and I want this to be a give-and-take relationship, not one-sided."

"How is it one-sided if I buy food that I'm gonna eat?" Jody asked.

"Because I won't be much assistance preparing that food," Baker said reasonably.

Jody could understand his argument. But she wasn't ready to give in quite yet. "I don't want our relationship to be about ticking things off on a piece of paper, recording who pays for what, making sure it's all fifty-fifty."

"Neither do I. You want to go out and get us tacos from a

food truck for dinner, I'm all for it. You forget something and run to the store on the fly to pick it up, I'm not gonna think twice. We get to a point down the line that we want this thing between us to be permanent, I'm hoping you'll be open to combining our bank accounts. Then it won't matter who pays for what because it'll be *our* money, and not yours or mine. Then we won't have to have this kind of conversation at all. Our talks about money will be about whether we want to spend five thousand bucks flying to the mainland for vacation, or what kind of mortgage we can afford if we decide to upgrade either one of our houses."

Jody swallowed hard. She liked that. A lot. "Okay."

"Okay?" Baker asked.

Jody nodded.

He held up his credit card, and Jody took it without another word.

"I have a question."

Baker rolled his eyes with a smirk, but said, "Shoot."

"I've never used anyone else's card before. Are they going to ask for my signature? Or ID? If I end up sitting in the back office at the grocery store because I'm being arrested for fraud, I'm not going to be happy."

Baker burst out laughing, and Jody was once again mesmerized by the sound. He pulled her against him then, as he was wont to do. "Four-five-three-two. That's my pin. You put it in when you swipe the card and you'll be good. Cashiers don't even touch the cards anymore, Tink. Even so, they give you shit, you call me and I'll take care of it."

"You aren't gonna send one of your *connections* to rough up the cashier if I call, are you?" she asked with a small smile.

"Smart-ass. No. I'll simply tell them you have approval to use my card. Now, we done? Have a feeling we're missing the good waves."

"Whatever, Baker."

He grinned down at her and said, "Like this, Tink. A lot."

She knew what he meant. "Me too."

He kissed her briefly, then turned to shoo her toward the door.

They both stopped short at seeing Ben standing there.

Jody was embarrassed that she hadn't realized he was still inside. She'd been so into what she and Baker were talking about that it hadn't even crossed her mind the teenager could hear their entire pseudo argument.

"Um..." she started.

But Baker talked over any apology she might have made.

"Your woman has a problem with something, you talk it out. And don't stop until you understand where she's coming from, and she gets where you're coming from, and you come to some sort of understanding together."

Ben nodded.

God. Baker was incredible.

"You're awesome," Jody said, not able to keep the words back.

"You got something good, you do whatever it takes to *keep* it good," Baker said. "Never had it before, so you better bet I'm gonna work my ass off to keep you happy, Tink."

She liked that too.

But since Ben's eyes were on them, and it was obvious Baker wanted to get some surfing in before he did whatever it was he had to do today, she simply nodded. "Right, on that note, I have Baker's credit card and I need to get to the store. So...I'll ask again, anything particular you guys want?"

"You buy it, I'll eat it. Except for broccoli. Won't eat that," Baker said.

Jody looked at him in surprise. "But broccoli's good for you."

"And it's gross. Those little pieces of green get between my teeth, and it's like eating a weed plucked from the ground."

Jody couldn't help but giggle at the imagery Baker's words evoked.

"You like broccoli?" Baker asked Ben.

He smirked and shrugged. "Yeah."

"Shit. I'm outnumbered," Baker muttered.

"You don't like it, I won't make you eat it. You're an adult," Jody reassured him.

"I don't like green beans. Does that mean you won't make me eat those?" Ben asked.

"They're good for you. And you're a kid. You need to eat greens so your brain can grow," Jody retorted.

"Damn. It was worth a shot," Ben said, but Jody saw his smile before he turned for the door.

She didn't know if he was kidding or not, but she totally wasn't going to make him eat green beans if he truly didn't like them.

Baker cupped Jody's cheeks in his hands after Ben left and tipped her face up to his. "Be careful going to the store."

"I will. You going home to get the boards before you go to the beach?"

Baker smirked. "Can't surf without them."

"Right. Do you think he'll open up to you?"

"Don't know, but I'm guessing it'll take time. He has to learn to trust us. He'll get there, Tink. I know it."

"I hope so."

"You okay with us coming back after we surf, or do you have shit you need quiet to do?"

"If I say I need some time?"

"Then I'll take Ben back to my place until you're done."

Baker was *such* a good guy.

"How long do you think you're going to be surfing?"

"How long do you need to get your shit done?"

Jody thought about the jobs she had waiting for her and said with a scrunch of her forehead. "Maybe until around three? Is that too long?"

"Not at all. It'll be nice to be able to stay out in the water for a while."

"What about your work? Do you have things you need to do? Bad guys you need to catch?"

Baker shook his head and smiled. "I'm good for today."

"Okay."

"Okay."

Then Baker leaned down and kissed her. It was a long, slow, easy kiss, and when he pulled back, Jody immediately wanted more. "Love your big heart, Jodelle. Loved it back even when I didn't know you. Just knew you were a good woman who went out of her way to take care of teenagers that weren't even hers. See you this afternoon."

She was still thinking about Baker's words thirty minutes later as she walked through the grocery store. And when she was putting away the groceries she'd bought after getting home. And she could still hear them as she headed for her bedroom and her computer to get some work done, so she'd be free later to hang out with Baker and Ben.

Her life had changed a lot in a short period of time, but she was ready. A few years ago—hell, even a few months ago —Jody wasn't sure she would've been as open as she was now to getting into a relationship with Baker.

She stopped in front of the second bedroom in her house and stared inside. For the first time in five years, it looked lived in. The bed was made. Ben's laundered clothes were sitting neatly in a small stack near an open duffle bag on the floor. Jody saw deodorant and a comb sitting on the dresser.

Amazingly, instead of making her sad, it felt right.

"Miss you, Kaimana," Jody whispered. She didn't get a response, but she felt her son's approval in her heart. Then, feeling lighter than she had in years, Jody turned and headed for her room. She had work to do.

# CHAPTER THIRTEEN

Jody, Ben, and Baker had fallen into an easy routine over the last week and a half. Ben was back at school, and the three of them would go to the beach in the mornings for surfing, then when Ben went to class, Jody went home to work, and Baker either went to his own place or headed down to Honolulu to the Naval base.

Then he'd come back to her place in the afternoons, and the three of them would eat a big dinner Jody made. Ben would either do homework or they'd all watch TV until it was time for bed.

Baker had slept in Jody's bed every night. They hadn't done anything more than make out and sleep, but Jody didn't feel an urgent need to rush things. Nor was she freaked out that, after all their sex talk, he hadn't made a move toward changing the nature of their relationship. She was...comfortable.

That wasn't to say she didn't get horny and didn't sometimes touch herself during the day when she was alone. She absolutely did. But she liked the intimacy of being with Baker without the pressure of sex getting in the way.

She also loved sleeping with him. Adored falling asleep in

his arms and waking up the same way. Outside of bed, he was constantly touching her, but not in an aggressive or overly suggestive way. He rested his hand on her belly or under the hem of her shirt, his open palm on the small of her back. Wrapped his hand around her neck and kept her close. And his kisses made her feel as if she was the most precious thing in the world.

Yes, it was safe to say, she was enjoying having Baker in her life. He was overprotective, even borderline paranoid at times, but when he got too over-the-top, she thought about all that he'd seen and done in his lifetime, and she let it go. There was a reason he was the way he was, and honestly, Jody liked that he cared enough to remain hypervigilant.

They were working slowly to encourage Ben to open up to them about why he'd moved out of his parents' house and begun living in his car, but so far he hadn't said much. Baker had done more research on Al Rowden, but on the surface, he was exactly what he seemed to be—a well-respected and popular juvenile judge.

Emma, Ben's mom, was more of an enigma, and even Baker hadn't been able to get access to the files on her from when she was hospitalized. He had a friend named Tex who he said could probably get them, but the man was currently helping another friend with an issue, so Baker was reluctant to bother him.

They'd talked about it more than once and had agreed to back off until Ben was ready to share. He was safe, going to school, and seemed to be relaxing. That was what they considered most important.

"What are you thinking about so hard?" Baker asked.

They were in bed, reluctant to get up and start the day, and her head was tucked against Baker's chest, his arms around her. They were as close as two people could be. Jody could feel his morning erection against her thigh, but he didn't pressure her to do anything about it. He'd told her more than once that having an erection was his normal state when he was around her, especially when he woke up with Jody in his arms, her scent all over his skin.

"Honestly?" she asked.

"Always," Baker said.

"I was thinking about how nice this is. Having you here."

"Yeah," Baker agreed, pulling her even closer.

"And trust," Jody blurted.

"What?"

"Trust. I think that's what I'm supposed to learn in this life. You know how you said you believe we're supposed to learn something in each life we live? Well, that's what I think I'm supposed to learn."

"You have a hard time trusting?" Baker asked.

Jody shrugged. "I didn't think so, but I've been pondering it since we had that discussion. I go to the beach to watch the kids surf in the mornings because I don't trust that they'll be safe. I think my relationship with my ex suffered not only because he was a jerk, but because I didn't trust him—and I wasn't wrong to feel that way. He wasn't trustworthy in the least. I haven't been in another relationship since because I think deep down, I didn't trust anyone to have my back. Not to turn on me, tell me I needed to move on from Mana's death. I don't even have friends, because I don't trust that they'd understand my grief.

"Then I realized that wanting Ben to trust me, trust *us*, with whatever is going on...it's hypocritical. Why should he trust *me* when I don't trust others? It's hard to put yourself out there like that. To open yourself up to hurt and pain if the person you're trusting betrays you. Mana trusted everyone and everything. He was open and honest with just about every person he met. I want to be more like him, but I don't know how. I mean, with some things, I have no problem. Like trusting Ben not to hurt me or steal from me while he's staying here. But in other ways, like emotionally, I have a harder time. Do you think it's ever too late to learn what you're supposed to in a lifetime?"

"No," Baker said immediately. "It's never too late."

"I hope not. And maybe I won't have to worry about it... because I'm starting to think I can trust *you*, Baker."

His arms tightened. "You can. And I know saying the words doesn't make it so, but no matter how long it takes, I'll prove to you that you can one hundred percent trust me. With your heart, your innermost thoughts, your memories of Mana, your beliefs...and of course, physically."

"Your job scares me a little," Jody admitted softly.

He tensed against her.

She went on. "I mean, I'm proud of what you do, and I have no doubt that you're making a difference in the world. I know you said you're really good at it, and that it'll never touch me, but what if it does? What if someone uses me to get to you? But what truly scares me the most is that it might take you away from me. That you'll get arrested or killed. I know that's not fair, and you can't prevent every little thing... but I can't handle losing someone else I care about. It'll break me. Especially considering how deeply I'm falling for you."

Baker rolled until Jody was on her back and he was hovering over her. She had no choice but to meet his gaze. "I think you know better than most that there are no guarantees in life."

Jody nodded. "Which is why I'm scared to trust that what we have is gonna last. Or that you aren't going to get hurt or end up in jail."

"What can I say to make you feel better about where we're going?" Baker asked.

"I don't know."

Baker looked frustrated, which was extremely rare—and it hurt Jody's heart. "I didn't start this conversation to upset you."

"I know you didn't. And I never want you to hold back

when you've got a concern. I'm not a Boy Scout. You know that by now."

Jody nodded.

"I swear to you that I'm good at what I do. I cover my tracks and there's no way anyone will be able to bring charges on me. For anything. Not only because I'm a fuckin' ghost when it comes to finding information, but because I've got people very high on the food chain who will have my back if the shit hits the fan."

Jody wanted to ask who those people were, but she knew Baker wouldn't tell her. It was probably better she didn't know. "You get mad though," she said softly.

"What?"

"When you think people might hurt me. You get mad," she repeated. "I worry that you'll do something to someone that you can't take back. I don't want to be the cause of you getting in trouble."

"You know I'd never hurt you, no matter how mad I get, right?"

"Yes. But that's not what I'm talking about. It's lashing out at *other* people that I'm worried about."

"So you trust me not to hurt you, but you can't trust that I won't hurt other people who have done you wrong?"

Jody bit her lip. She knew it was ridiculous, but she couldn't help it. "My trust button is broken."

"It's not broken," Baker insisted. "And it's not that you don't trust me; you're worried about me. You're worried about your own heart and what opening it up will do to you if I do something stupid."

Jody didn't respond, just stared up at him.

"Right. I give you my word, Jodelle, that no matter how pissed I am at someone, I will not do *anything* that will take me away from you. That doesn't mean I won't make them pay in my own way...but I won't do something the police can't ignore. Like beat the shit out of someone or kill them. Does that make you feel better?"

Surprisingly, it did. Jody had a feeling when Baker Rawlins gave his word on something, nothing would make him break it. She was a little worried about the whole "pay in my own way" thing, but maybe that was a concern to talk about at another time.

"Yes," she said softly.

"Good. And as far as the trust thing goes...you'll get there."

"You sound so sure."

"I am. Because you're you. I don't trust easily either, but I don't think that's my lesson for this life."

Jody stared up at him, intrigued. "No? What do you think you need to learn?"

"Love."

Her heart started beating faster.

Baker went on, "My parents were older when they had me. I was kind of a surprise baby, and I'm not sure they really even wanted kids. They weren't abusive, but they were more into their own lives than into raising a child. They were in their sixties by the time I graduated high school, and I think they were relieved I went into the Navy when I was eighteen and left the house."

"Were they proud of you?"

"Yes."

His answer came without hesitation, which Jody liked. "Good."

"They're both gone now, but I spent so much of my time feeling alone growing up, I just got used to it. *Too* used to it. I didn't let anyone in, was determined to become a SEAL, and then my focus was on missions. I had some girlfriends, but never felt all that upset when they broke up with me. Had a bad experience with a woman I *thought* I loved. Turned out she was just with me for money. Had actually planned to kill me to get my Navy life insurance. Needless to say, that turned me off love altogether.

"It wasn't until I started gettin' to know my friends' women, and seeing how their husbands reacted when they were in danger, that I started to understand love. Mustang, Midas, Aleck, Pid, Jag, and Slate would do literally anything for their women. *Anything*.

"Then I met *you*, and I tried to keep my admiration for you separate from any deeper feelings, but realized I was failing spectacularly. The thought of you in any of the situations Elodie, Lexie, and the others found themselves in makes me literally break out in hives. And witnessing the love you had, *have*, for your son makes me understand the emotion that much more."

Jody wasn't sure what to say, especially about the woman who was crazy enough to want to kill Baker for money, so she simply squeezed his sides, where she was already holding onto him tightly.

Baker smiled. "I'm not saying I love you yet. It's too early for that, and it would freak you out. But if I could love anyone, it'd be you, Jodelle."

"Baker," she whispered.

He leaned down and kissed her gently. "We're both kinda fucked up," he said.

Jody couldn't help but laugh at that. He wasn't wrong. "Yeah."

"But together, I'm thinking maybe we can get unfucked."

"I hope so."

"You can trust me," he said seriously. "I know those are just words to you right now, but I'm telling you, one hundred percent honestly, you can. I'll treat you with care, always come for you if you need me, and you can share your innermost thoughts with me. I won't betray you, and if you give me your trust, I'll spend every day of the rest of my life proving to you that you haven't made a mistake in doing so."

He didn't give her a chance to respond before saying, "I want to take you out tonight. On a date."

"Okay. Although don't you think it's a little weird that we're going on our first date when we've been sleeping together for over a week?"

"I've had to share you with Ben. Not that I don't like the kid. I do. But I want you to myself, at least for a few hours."

"I'd like that too."

"Good. You gonna be done with your work by the time Ben gets home from school?"

"Yes." She had no idea what she needed to get done today, but she'd make sure she was finished by four. Then something else struck her. "You think it's okay for Ben to be in the house by himself now?"

"Thought it was okay even back on that first day," Baker told her.

Jody frowned. "But you said—"

"I know what I said, but I was making a point. A point he got loud and clear. You aren't alone, and you've got a champion. Not only that, but there's no way he'll do anything to fuck up the situation he's got going. Safe place to sleep, food in his belly...he knows what that kind of security means now, and he's appreciative."

That made Jody feel good. She nodded.

"It's getting late. We need to get up if Ben and I are gonna get to the beach and get some wave time in."

"Okay."

"You good?"

"As good as I can be after our deep and intense conversation, yeah."

"You aren't, we can lie here as long as it takes for you to *become* good," he said.

Jody's heart melted once more. "I'm good, Baker. Promise."

"Okay. You need to talk this shit out more, give me a yell."

Yes, it was official—Baker was the best man she knew.

"All right. Is this date tonight the dress-up kind, or more of a shorts and flip-flops thing?" she asked.

"Are there any five-star restaurants up here in the North Shore?" Baker asked.

"Um, no, but we could go to Honolulu."

"Nope. Not driving all the way down there twice today. Besides, I'm not the kind of man who likes that shit. That a problem?"

"No. I prefer being casual."

"Fuckin' perfect. Okay, now I'm really getting up."

"I'll go and make breakfast sandwiches for the surf kids while you're changing."

"Okay. I'll finish them up when I'm done and you can have your turn."

Just another way Baker was amazing. "Sounds good."

He stared down at her but didn't make a move to get up.

"Baker?"

"I'm lucky as hell," he said quietly. "I know it. Don't deserve you, but gonna go out of my way to be the man you can trust, Tink." Then he kissed her deeply, before climbing out of bed and headed for the bathroom.

Jody lay on the bed staring at the ceiling for a long moment. Then she climbed out of bed with a smile.

# CHAPTER FOURTEEN

It was four-thirty and Baker wasn't home yet. He called to say that, unfortunately, a meeting he had with an admiral had gone later than expected and he wasn't going to be there at four. Jody had reassured him it was okay and told him not to speed home.

She'd made a casserole for Ben to eat for dinner and had just given him instructions on when to take it out of the oven. He was leaning against the counter in the kitchen and Jody was opposite him, leaning against the sink.

"Can I ask you something?" Ben asked.

"Of course. You can ask me anything," Jody told him.

"How did you and Baker know you wanted to go out?"

Jody blinked in surprise, but did her best to keep her expression neutral. "Well, I guess it was a gradual thing. I've known him for a while, and I saw how good he was with all of you. He was respectful to me, and of course, I was physically attracted to him as well."

Ben nodded as if nothing she said was a surprise. When he didn't say anything else, Jody asked, "How are things going with that girl you like?"

"Tressa?"

"Yeah. Pretty name."

"Uh-huh. She's as gorgeous as her name too. She's new to the area though, and shy. She has long black hair and pretty brown eyes, and she's petite like you. I don't get to see her much, since we're in different classes, but we've talked a bit at lunch. There's this guy...he's an asshole, and he's been bugging her."

"Bugging her how?" Jody asked.

"Just up in her face all the time. Giving her compliments and asking her out. Being pushy about it. She's told him she's not interested, but Alex won't give up."

"You want to protect her."

"Yeah," Ben admitted. "But I shouldn't bring attention to her. Alex doesn't like me. Like, *really* doesn't like me, and if I throw down for her, it could make him even more of an asshole toward her than he already is."

"That seems like a tricky situation. Do you think this Alex guy would listen to you if you tried to talk to him rationally and calmly?"

"No."

The answer was swift and to the point.

"Why not?"

"Alex and I have history. We used to be close, but we went in different directions. He thinks I'm a pussy and I think he's a douchebag. So yeah, he's not gonna listen to me."

"I'm sorry."

Ben shrugged. "But he's not getting the hint that Tressa's not interested, and I'm worried for her."

"Is that all?"

"Is what all?"

"You're just worried about her?" Jody asked.

"No. I like her. She's sweet. That shy thing she's got going on is cute as hell. Not only that, but she's *nice*. I want to ask her out, but I don't want to bring any more trouble down on her than she already has."

"Here's the thing," Jody said. "You're not exactly a troll, Ben. You're tall, dark, and handsome, and I'm guessing you haven't gone unnoticed to her either. And I'm thinking that she'd probably really like to have a champion. She's in a new school, is probably still trying to find friends, and if this Alex guy really is harassing her as badly as you say, she's probably really nervous being around him."

"He hates me, and the feeling's mutual," Ben said. "If I start talking to her, it might not be good."

"What if you got her number and texted her? Start with baby steps," Jody suggested.

Ben didn't nod or say anything.

"I'm sorry," Jody told him. "I'm not that good at advice in situations like this. Mana wasn't all that into girls so I don't have experience in giving teenage boys dating advice. But, if it was me, and I was Tressa, I'd totally be all right with risking the wrath of Alex if it meant having someone like you in my corner. If you do ask her out, and things escalate with him, are you going to leave her hanging?"

"No," Ben said in a somewhat defensive tone.

"Right. Then my advice is to go for it. Life is short, Ben. I've learned that the hard way. You don't know what Alex is going to do, but whatever he does is on *him*. The only person you can control is yourself."

"That's very true. And it sucks," Ben said.

"Can I ask *you* something?" Jody asked.

"Sure."

"Have you told your parents where you are?"

Ben scowled.

Jody hurried on to say, "You haven't said what happened to make you leave your house, but obviously it was something big. And no matter what was said or what happened, you can stay with me. I'm just thinking that by now, your folks have to be worried sick about you."

"They aren't," Ben said curtly.

"Ben," Jody said gently. "If Mana and I had a fight and he left and never came back, no matter what happened, I'd be freaking out."

"You're nothing like my mom," Ben told her. "And Al definitely doesn't care what I do, as long as I'm out of his hair."

"Your mom...she's..." Jody searched for the word she wanted to use that wouldn't sound too harsh, but would still get her point across. "She's fragile?"

"Yeah, she is," Ben agreed.

Jody waited for him to say something else, but when he didn't, she sighed. "You should call her at least," she finally said.

"She doesn't answer the phone," Ben said. "She doesn't even have a cell of her own. She does whatever Al tells her to without question. I can't call the house and *not* talk to Al. And trust me, he doesn't want to hear from me, and he definitely doesn't want me talking to my mom."

Jody didn't like the sound of that. At all. "He works during the day, right? Maybe you could go by the house to see your mom when he's not there?"

"I appreciate your concern, Miss Jody, but the bottom line is that it wasn't my choice to leave the house. Al kicked me out. My mom was there, and she didn't say a word to contradict him when he told me to get the fuck out."

Jody's heart broke for the man-child in front of her. "Time has a way of changing people's minds," she said gently.

Ben snorted. "Not Al's. But it's fine," he said firmly, standing up straighter and meeting her gaze. "I don't want to be there anyway. It's not...a good place to be."

Jody had what seemed like a hundred questions, but instead of asking them, she said, "If you ever want to talk about it, I'm here. I know you don't know me all that well, but like I said before, I'm a great listener."

"Thanks," Ben said. "I appreciate you letting me stay here.

I'm trying to find a job so I can make money and find a place of my own, so I can get out of your hair."

Jody shook her head. "No."

"No?" Ben asked in confusion.

"Don't get a job. You only get to be a kid once. And being an adult isn't always fun. You can stay here as long as you want. I mean that, Ben. No strings. You will *always* have a safe place here in my home."

It was obvious Ben was doing everything in his power to keep his composure. He finally nodded. "Thanks. I still want to find a job so I can have some money. I want to help out with things like groceries. It's not cool that I'm living here and not contributing."

Jody wanted to disagree. Insist that Baker was right—as a child, he shouldn't have to pay for anything. But he'd obviously soaked in some of Baker's alpha-ness and she didn't want to belittle that by disagreeing. "All right, but it'll have to be part time. There's school, and I don't want you staying out too late. You've got homework, and you need to make sure you get enough sleep. Not to mention if you and Tressa work out, you'll want time to take her on dates."

Ben's lips twitched. "So you want me to find a job where I can work from like six to eight at night?"

"That'd work," Jody told him with a grin.

He rolled his eyes. "Not sure such a job exists."

"I'm really glad you're here, Ben," she told him, feeling emotional.

"Me too, Miss Jody."

"And I was serious about listening if you ever want to talk."

"I know."

Jody wanted to beg him to tell her what had happened to make his stepdad kick him out of his house, but she knew she had to let Ben make that choice. She couldn't force him to talk to her.

The sound of the front door opening made them both turn in that direction, and upon seeing Baker, Jody did her best to put her worried thoughts aside.

He took one look at the two of them and frowned. "What's wrong?"

"Nothing's wrong," Jody insisted brightly.

Baker turned his eyes to Ben, eyebrow raised in question. "Ben?"

"We're good. Was just asking Miss Jody for her advice."

Baker stared at him for a moment before nodding. "Okay, but if you need to talk, I'm here too. You about ready, Tink?"

Jody blinked at his abrupt change of topic. "Yeah. What's the hurry?"

"The hurry is that I had to be in a fuckin'—Sorry...frickin' annoying meeting for longer than I wanted to be, knowing my girl was waiting on me to get home so I could take her out for our first date. I want to get on that, enjoy my time with you."

Jody smiled gently. "Okay, Baker."

"Curfew's ten o'clock," Ben said.

Jody whipped her head around to stare at him, barking out a laugh. "Um, what?"

"Don't want you kids staying out too late and being all wild and crazy," he joked.

"Twelve," Baker said.

Jody turned to look at *him* now. "What's going on, exactly?" she asked.

"We're negotiating," Baker said with a grin.

"Eleven," Ben shot back.

"Eleven-thirty, and we'll sit in the driveway making out for twenty more minutes before we come in."

"Deal," Ben said with a laugh.

"Oh my God, this isn't happening," Jody mock-complained, enjoying the banter between them. Baker walked forward and snagged her around the waist, pulling her close.

"Why are you always dragging me into you?" she groused, not meaning a word of it.

"Because you're too slow in greeting me," Baker said. "Kiss me, woman."

Jody rolled her eyes and looked at Ben. "I hope you aren't taking notes. This is *not* how you should be treating any woman you date."

"Yes, it is. Showing her that he gives a shit is never a bad thing. Now, kiss me, Tink, so we can get the hell out of here and go on our date."

"You haven't told me where we're going," she said, dragging out the anticipation. She wanted his lips on hers more than she wanted to breathe, but it was fun to tease him.

"You're right, I haven't. That's because it's a surprise," Baker said.

"I don't know if I like surprises," she hedged.

"You'll like this one." Then Baker was apparently done waiting for her to kiss him, because he slipped his hand under her hair and grasped her neck, pulling her even closer.

The kiss he gave her wasn't exactly what she wanted, but Ben was standing there, watching in amusement. When Baker finally lifted his head, he said without taking his gaze from hers, "That's how it's done, Ben."

"Noted, Baker," he said with another loud laugh.

Jody rolled her eyes but didn't struggle to get out of Baker's grip.

"I...thank you for trusting me to be here by myself," Ben said a little hesitantly.

Baker let go of Jody's neck, turning her and wrapping his arm around her shoulders so they were both facing him. "You're welcome. You're a good kid, Ben. Don't know what's up with you, and I hope you'll eventually share. But when you're ready, you're ready. In the meantime, you've proven to me and Jodelle that you're trustworthy."

Jody nodded in agreement.

"Thanks," he said softly.

"Okay, we're going," Baker announced.

"Make sure the door is locked behind us. And if you smell smoke, get out of the house, then call 9-1-1. The casserole should be done in another twenty minutes or so, don't let it burn. It's your turn for dishes tonight, but be sure to rinse them off before putting them in the dishwasher. And I know it's not a school day tomorrow, but don't stay up too late."

"Tink, he's good," Baker said, urging her toward the door with his hand on the small of her back.

"I just want to make sure he—"

"Have fun," Ben interrupted with a smile and a wave. "I'll be good. Just gonna eat, do the dishes, then watch the boob tube for a while. I'll probably be asleep when you get home, so don't feel the need to make out in the car in the driveway, you can totally do that in here on the couch."

"Oh, jeez," Jody said with a shake of her head.

"Appreciate that," Baker told him. "Later."

"Call if you need anything," Jody added as Baker led her out the door.

Instead of starting the car when they got inside, Baker turned to her and put a hand on her cheek. "You two looked pretty intense. Everything okay?"

"Ben's interested in a girl and wanted my advice. I also suggested he might call his mom and let her know he was all right, and he shared that he didn't leave home voluntarily. His stepdad kicked him out, and his mom didn't say or do anything to stop that from happening. Also says that his stepdad won't let him talk to her. But Ben's not feeling very charitable toward either of them at the moment, so I doubt he's gonna try anytime soon to reassure her that he's okay." She paused for a moment. "Why would his mom let that happen, Baker?"

"I don't know, Tink."

"How could a mother let her only son be kicked out when

she knows he has nowhere to go and no money to buy food or anything?"

Baker didn't answer, but his thumb brushed gently against her cheek.

"He wants to get a job. Feels as if he should help pay for food and stuff, but there's no need for that. And he'll have to worry about rent, food, and bills soon enough."

"You actually upset that he's not a mooch?" Baker asked.

"No!" Jody said forcefully. Then she sighed. "I just hate that he can't enjoy being a kid a little longer."

"I might be able to find him something."

Jody's gaze whipped up to his. "Um, no offense, but I'm not sure I'm okay with him doing what you do."

Instead of getting upset, Baker merely smiled. "You can trust me, Jodelle."

She closed her eyes for a moment, then nodded and opened them. "Sorry."

"Don't be. I know a guy who manages some food trucks. Their hours are reasonable, and I'm thinking he could find a place for Ben. He wouldn't have to drive down to the city to work and his schedule would probably be flexible. Hours on the weekends and after school, but not too late, that kind of thing."

Jody reached up and wrapped her fingers around the wrist of the hand that was against her cheek. "That would be amazing."

He nodded. "Anything else worrying you?"

"I worry about everything," she said with a small smile. "But you've covered the most recent stuff."

"Good." Then he leaned toward her, kissed her gently, and sat back. "Because I've got a date with my girl."

\* \* \*

Four hours later, way before the curfew Ben had given them, Baker pulled back into Jody's driveway.

"Looks like the house is still standing," he quipped.

All Jody could do was smile. The night had been amazing. Baker had surprised her with a picnic on the beach. Complete with a tablecloth, real dishes, and candles. Apparently, Baker had conspired with Kenna and Carly and brought an entire meal from Duke's down at Waikiki for them to eat. The food hadn't been hot, but it was still delicious. They'd laughed and talked about nothing and everything, enjoying the beautiful sunset and each other's company.

After they'd cleaned up and packed away the picnic supplies, they'd taken a long walk on the beach, complete with lots of stops to make out. It was a laid-back night, and Jody had never had a date as wonderful as this one.

"I had a good time tonight," Jody said. She wanted to make sure Baker knew what he'd planned had been perfect.

"Me too," he told her with a small smile. "I'm sorry the dinner wasn't at an actual restaurant, I—"

"No!" Jody exclaimed, interrupting him. "You aren't allowed to apologize for the best date I've ever been on. I don't need fancy, Baker. I just need you."

"You've got me," he said in a deep, rumbly voice.

Jody had never felt as connected with someone as she did right that second.

Baker leaned forward and kissed her. They'd shared plenty of kisses throughout the evening, but somehow this one seemed more intimate.

"You know, it'd be easier to make out in your van than in here," Baker said with a chuckle after he'd pulled back.

Jody giggled. "There *is* a bed in the back of it," she said.

Baker's eyes widened, and Jody couldn't help but giggle.

"You're fuckin' with me," he accused.

Jody nodded. "Yeah. There's no bed. It's full of boxes and other random shit. We do have a perfectly good bed that we've both been sleeping in for the last week on the other side of that door," she said, gesturing to her front door.

"I've never slept as well as I have recently," Baker said. "There's something about holding you in my arms that makes me sleep like a fuckin' baby."

Jody smiled. "Yeah?"

"Yeah. And while I'm looking forward to getting inside you, I have no need to rush," Baker said.

"Me either, but..."

"But what?"

"We *are* going to eventually get there, right?"

"Fuck yeah, we are," Baker said with such fervor, Jody shivered in delight.

"Okay."

"Okay," he agreed with a nod. "But I told you once that I wanted to wait to make love until we both were sure where things were going between us. That hasn't changed. Now, how about we get inside before Ben really does think we're sitting here making out."

Jody laughed. "Yeah, we wouldn't want him to get any ideas."

Baker chuckled. "Think he's already got those ideas, Tink."

She wrinkled her nose.

Baker was still laughing when he climbed out of the car. Jody met him at the front and he immediately reached for her hand. He'd been touching her nonstop all night. Holding her hand, putting his hand on the small of her back as they walked, resting his warm palm on her thigh as they ate. It was nice. Really nice.

Ben was nowhere in sight when they entered the house. Jody couldn't help but smile as Baker threw his keys in the bowl on the counter where her keys were resting. The kitchen was clean, there were no dishes in the sink, and the slight scent of the casserole she'd made still lingered in the air. Ben had also folded the blankets that were on the couch and placed them neatly in a stack at the end of the cushions.

"Wow," she said softly. "I'm impressed."

"You want to watch TV?" Baker asked.

Jody shook her head.

Without dropping her hand, Baker led her to the master. "Go ahead and change and climb in. I'll go check to make sure everything's secure."

Jody nodded. The first time Baker insisted on checking to make sure everything was locked up, Jody had assured him that she hadn't opened any windows and had already double checked the lock on the front door. He'd explained that he wouldn't be able to sleep if he didn't see for himself that everything was secure. She hadn't protested further. It was just a part of who Baker was.

Not able to help herself, after he left, she headed for Ben's door and tapped lightly. If he was asleep, she didn't want to wake him, but just as Baker couldn't sleep if he didn't check the house, she couldn't go to bed without making sure Ben was safe and secure in his room.

"I'm up," Ben said from inside.

Jody opened the door and poked her head inside. Ben was sitting on the bed, a book open on his lap, the lamp on the nightstand the only illumination. For a second, she saw Mana instead of Ben. He loved to read, and many nights she had to tell him to put the book down and go to sleep so he wouldn't be a zombie the next morning.

"Everything go okay tonight?" she asked.

"Yeah. The casserole was awesome. I put the leftovers in the fridge. I'm thinking about having some for breakfast."

Jody smiled. "I'm glad."

"You have a good time?" he asked.

"Uh-huh. Baker had his friends get us takeout from Duke's and he set up a picnic on the beach. We ate, talked, walked, and it was perfect."

"Hula pie?" Ben asked.

"Can you eat Duke's and *not* have hula pie?" Jody returned. He smiled.

"I just wanted to make sure you were good. I'll see you in the morning, Ben," Jody told him. "Don't stay up too late reading."

"I won't. Miss Jody?" he asked as she began to shut the door.

"Yeah?"

"I sent Tressa a text tonight."

"Oh yeah? How'd you get her number?"

"I asked a buddy of mine to ask a friend who's in the band with her to get it for me."

"And?" she asked.

Ben grinned. "It was good," he said.

"I'm glad."

"I invited her to come watch me surf sometime," Ben said.

"Cool. I'd love to meet her."

"That's why I did it. I told her she wouldn't be sitting on the shore alone, that you're cool and would keep her company. And if she had any questions about surfing, she could ask you."

Jody felt her heart swell. She wasn't sure she was cool by any stretch of the imagination, but it was kind of Ben to say so. "I'm looking forward to spending some time with her."

"I also invited her to eat lunch with me on Monday," Ben continued.

Jody nodded, proud of him.

"I warned her that it would probably piss Alex off. She said that she didn't care about him. Said he was a jerk, and she'd eat with whoever she wanted to."

"She sounds brave."

"Yeah," Ben agreed. "But that doesn't mean I want Alex up in her face."

"I don't suppose you do."

"We shared schedules, and while we aren't in any classes together since she's a junior and I'm a senior, I think I can swing it so I can walk her to and from her classes to make sure Alex doesn't harass her."

"That's awesome."

"Yeah. I just wanted to thank you for encouraging me to talk to her. I'm not sure it's the best thing to do with everything else I have going on, but you're right. Life is short, and I'd kick myself in the ass if I lost my chance to get to know Tressa."

Jody didn't like his "everything else I have going on" comment, but she let it go for now. She just hoped he'd talk to her when he felt comfortable enough. "Happy for you, Ben."

"Wouldn't be able to do anything if it wasn't for you, Miss Jody."

"Yes, you would. I know you would've figured things out in your own time. But I'm glad you're letting me help you."

Ben nodded, and Jody knew he was done talking for the night. "Sleep well, Ben."

"I will. You too. Will you tell Baker that if he wants to check out that new surf spot tomorrow, I'm game?"

"Of course. Good night."

"Good night, Miss Jody."

Jody shut the door quietly and closed her eyes for a second. She was overwhelmed with feelings. Sorrow that she didn't get a chance to share this kind of closeness with her own son. Happiness that she was sharing it now with Ben. Worry about what was really going on with his mom and stepdad. Excitement that it seemed as if this Tressa girl liked Ben back.

Uneasiness that everything in her life seemed to be going smoothly.

It was her experience that just when she got comfortable,

life would deal her a harsh blow. And the very last thing she wanted was something going wrong just when it seemed as if her life was on an upward trajectory.

An arm wrapped around her waist, and Jody immediately leaned back into Baker.

"He good?" Baker whispered.

Jody nodded.

Baker steered her away from Ben's door and into the master bedroom. He shut the door and turned her to face him. He studied her face for a moment before nodding in satisfaction. Then his lips quirked upward and he said, "You didn't get changed."

"I needed to check on Ben. He said he texted that girl he liked and they're planning on eating lunch together, and he's going to walk her to and from her classes, and he even invited her to watch him surf."

"Sounds serious," Baker teased.

"For a teenager, it is," Jody assured him. Then she put her cheek on his chest and wrapped her arms around him tightly in a hug. "I'm afraid something's gonna happen that will burst my happy bubble," she admitted.

"It will," Baker said calmly.

Frowning, Jody looked up at him. "That wasn't a nice thing to say."

He shrugged. "Shit happens, Jodelle. And I'm not saying that flippantly. It's how you deal with that shit that matters."

She put her cheek back on his chest. Jody could hear his heart thumping under her ear. "I don't want any more shit to happen to me."

"If it does, we'll deal with it together," he said simply.

God, Jody liked that. Nothing would have made her son's death any easier, but if she'd had someone like Baker at her side to help her deal, she had a feeling it wouldn't have been quite so gut-wrenching.

"Go on, get changed. I'd rather cuddle horizontally," he said.

Jody smiled. She looked up at him once more without letting her arms drop from around him. "Baker?"

"Yeah, Tink?"

"I'm so glad you're here."

"No place I'd rather be," he returned. Then he kissed her forehead, and turned her to face the bathroom and gave her a playful shove. "Get a move on, woman."

"What am I? Eight?"

"You complaining about me wanting you to hurry up so we can make out in your bed?" he asked.

No way in hell would she ever complain about that. So she just gave him a smile and, as requested, got a move on.

After she'd changed and done her bedtime routine, Jody came back into the room and smiled at seeing Baker sitting in her bed. The covers were at his waist and he was shirtless. The smattering of hair on his chest was sexy as hell. As were the tattoos that practically covered every inch of his exposed skin. From the ones on his arms, to his back and chest, he'd explained them all to her. And every single one had some sort of meaning. Some were sweet, like the heart with his parents' initials in it, and others were somewhat dark, like the skull with the number twenty-two, a reminder of a bad day when he was a SEAL. But they were all part of who Baker was, and Jody wouldn't change one thing about him.

He smiled at her, and Jody's knees almost buckled. She could spend every night for the rest of her life walking into her bedroom and seeing Baker there, smiling at her, and die a happy woman.

She padded over to the other side of the bed and climbed under the covers. Baker held up his arm and Jody snuggled into him. He grunted in protest when she put her cold feet on his calves, but he didn't pull away, which made Jody smile.

"You wanna watch TV?" he asked.

She shrugged. "I want to do whatever *you* want to do," she told him.

"You care if I watch the news for a bit before we make out?"

"No."

"You sure? Because if you do, it's not a big deal."

Jody looked up at Baker. She put a hand on his cheek, feeling his short black beard liberally speckled with gray under her palm. It was soft, something she hadn't expected before he'd kissed her for the first time. "If I cared, I'd tell you," she said seriously.

In response, he put his hand over hers and leaned down. Jody stretched upward so he could reach her lips.

"There's nowhere I'd rather be than right here with you," he said softly after he'd kissed her.

Jody melted, nodding into his shoulder as his arm tightened around her. He clicked the remote for her small TV and she closed her eyes. She supposed with his job, he needed to stay up-to-date on what was happening in the world, but she couldn't care less about the news.

She tried to stay awake so she could enjoy more of his amazing kisses, but she fell asleep with the sound of Baker's heart beating under her cheek and the feel of his arm around her shoulders, keeping her close.

# CHAPTER FIFTEEN

"I have to leave for a while," Baker told Jodelle a week later over breakfast. He and Ben had convinced Jodelle that none of the kids would be surfing on such a dreary, rainy morning, so she'd made huge omelets for the three of them. Baker's was a meat-lovers, and Ben had asked for southwestern. Jodelle's was decidedly smaller than the ones she'd made for him and Ben, but she had her usual Pop-Tart to help fill her up.

She put down her fork and stared at him with wide eyes. Baker could see the questions in her gaze, but he also knew she wouldn't verbalize them. She knew he couldn't tell her any details about where he was going or what he'd be doing.

"When?" she asked softly.

"Today. Found out last night. Didn't want to ruin our night. I shouldn't be gone more than a week," he told her. "I might be back sooner."

"Okay," Jodelle said in a somewhat shaky voice.

Baker hated hearing her distress, but knew this was going to happen sooner or later. If they had a chance in hell of making a relationship work, they had to get through this first trip. He turned to Ben. "Gonna need you to keep an eye on Jodelle for me."

Ben sat up straighter. "Of course."

"Glad things are going well with your girl, but I'd appreciate it if you could get home before dark. Jodelle also has a tendency to forget to look after herself while she's looking after others, so if you could be on the watch for that too, it would be great."

"I'm sitting right here," she complained, but Baker didn't take his gaze from Ben's.

"I've noticed. I'll do my best to make sure she eats something in the morning besides her Pop-Tart. If it's okay with you, maybe I can see if Tressa wants to come over for dinner? She can reassure her parents that Miss Jody will be here and it's not like we'll be alone or anything."

Baker nodded in approval. "I'm sure both Tressa and Jodelle would like that."

Jodelle let out a loud, annoyed sigh. "Seriously, I'm right here. I can hear you talking about me as if I'm not."

Baker switched his gaze to her then and put his hand on her thigh. His plan had been to wait to make love with her until they were both one hundred percent sure their relationship was going to move forward. But since *he'd* already gotten there two seconds after he'd walked through her door for the first time, it was getting harder and harder to resist.

Sleeping beside her was better than anything he could've imagined. And while he wasn't a man who needed sex, the decade since he'd been with a woman serving as proof of that, keeping himself from moving things forward had become almost impossible recently. He didn't want to leave her, but maybe having some time away from her delectable scent, holding her in his arms, and feeling her hands caress him even in her sleep would be a good thing.

His thumb stroked her inner thigh, trying to soothe her, even as Baker turned back to Ben. "We haven't pushed for more information about what happened with your folks, but I need you to promise me that whatever it is, it's not going to blow up in Jodelle's face while I'm gone."

Baker wasn't thrilled when Ben dropped his eyes and wouldn't meet his gaze.

"As you know, I haven't been back to my house. Haven't even talked to my mom. I doubt either of them cares where I am or what I'm doing. But on the slim chance they do, I promise I'll do whatever needs to be done to keep Miss Jody out of it."

Baker pressed his lips together firmly. He didn't like that answer. "Don't get me wrong, I want Jodelle protected, but not at your expense," he told the boy.

"I'm used to it." Ben sat up straighter and looked Baker in the eye. "Feels like my entire life I've been protecting my mom. Being here, having Miss Jody treat me as if I'm her son, when I know it has to hurt her sometimes, and seeing how you are with her, has shown me that being protective can be a good thing...but the person you're protecting has to earn it."

"Ben," Jodelle said sadly.

Baker squeezed her thigh and nodded at the teenager. "That's very true. If the person you're protecting doesn't appreciate and treasure your efforts, it makes it twice as hard to find the motivation to keep doing it."

Ben nodded. "I'll keep Miss Jody safe, because she's done more for me in the last few weeks than my own flesh and blood has in years."

"We've given you space and time," Baker said. "But I'm thinking the time's a comin' when we're gonna need to know what's going on."

"I don't want to drag either of you into it," he said honestly.

"Maybe you haven't figured it out, but I can take care of myself. And Jodelle. And *you*, Ben." When he didn't respond, Baker went on. "Whatever you think is so big you can't share, you're wrong. I'm thinking whatever's eatin' at you has to do with your stepfather."

Ben's breath hitched, but he still didn't respond.

Baker knew he'd guessed right. "His connections are child's play compared to mine," he told him. "I might look like a surf bum to you, but trust me, I'm anything but. When I tell you I know people, I *know* people."

"He's a judge," Ben said softly.

"And I'm a former Navy SEAL with friends in low *and* high places. People who will do anything I ask them to because of what I've done for them. And one thing I don't like is someone who mistreats women and children. Especially women who are in a vulnerable spot, trying to raise their son and working their ass off to put food on the table. You understand what I'm saying?"

"They've been married for years, Baker. My mom stopped worrying about buying food and anything else the day she married Al," Ben said.

"I realize that, but that doesn't mean she hasn't struggled." Baker knew he was pushing hard, but he wasn't feeling comfortable with the situation and the thought of leaving right now wasn't sitting well at all. "We'll talk when I get back," he told Ben firmly.

"Okay," the teenager whispered.

Baker was going to have to be content that he'd agreed, even if he had to wait a week to hear what was going on. "In the meantime, I'm trusting you to have Jodelle's back."

"I won't let you down," Ben said firmly.

Baker turned to Jodelle then. "I know you've been on your own for a while, Tink, but I'm gonna worry about you while I'm gone, so I'm asking that you not find other homeless men or women to invite home and maybe curb your inclination to save the world for a week or so."

Jodelle rolled her eyes. "So *now* I'm a part of this conversation?"

Baker grinned. "You've always been a part of it. If I wanted to talk to Ben without you hearing, I would've done so."

She eyed him. "You're annoying."

"I know."

Jodelle blew out a breath. "I'm not going to invite anyone to stay at the house," she told him.

"Thank you."

"But...and I know you aren't going to like this...I'm not going to sit around wringing my hands and playing the helpless damsel in distress if someone comes after Ben. He's a kid, and I'm the adult. They'll have to go through me to get to him."

Ben did his best to cover his snort of laughter.

Baker grinned at her.

"You guys are so frustrating. I'm definitely gonna need Tressa to come over to counterbalance the overabundance of testosterone in this house."

"I'll talk to her tonight and see if we can work something out," Ben said with a smile.

"Ask her what her favorite kind of food is, and I'll see if I can come up with something that'll wow her," Jodelle said.

Baker squeezed her leg again, trying to let her know how much he appreciated her willingness to go with the flow.

She looked at him and nodded, as if she totally understood his nonverbal communication.

They finished up their breakfast and when Ben was about to walk out the door to go to school, Baker stopped him. Jodelle had already said bye to him before she went to jump into the shower.

"I meant what I said earlier," Baker told Ben. "I don't want you getting hurt protecting Jodelle. The shit hits the fan, you call 9-1-1. Get help. Understand?"

Ben swallowed hard. Then nodded.

Which again, didn't make Baker feel any better. If shit

was bad enough that the kid didn't protest calling the police for assistance, it was even worse than Baker thought. He regretted not pushing harder, sooner. Not digging deeper into Judge Rowden. He was one hundred percent certain he was the threat. Not Ben's mother.

"You'll be careful?" Ben asked tentatively.

His concern felt good. "Always am," Baker returned.

Ben nodded. "See you when you get back then."

"Yup. Take care of yourself, and Jodelle."

"I will. Later, Baker."

"Later." Baker stood in the doorway and watched until Ben had pulled away from the house, then he shut the door, locked it, and headed for the kitchen. He was sipping a cup of coffee when Jodelle reappeared.

"He get off okay?"

"Yeah."

"He needs to talk to us. Tell us what's wrong."

"He will." Baker put his coffee cup down on the counter and said, "Come here."

Jodelle immediately came toward him. She didn't stop until she was plastered against his front. Baker loved how she felt against him. They fit together perfectly. He put one hand on the small of her back and the other he wrapped around her nape. He rested his forehead on hers and said, "Gonna miss you."

"Me too," she whispered. "Please be careful. Whatever you're doing, I know it'll be dangerous. I can't lose you too."

"You won't. Trust me, Jodelle. I'm coming back."

"I'm trying, but I'm scared."

Baker hated that, but it showed that his woman wasn't stupid. He wasn't heading out on a fishing trip with buddies. He was wading into the bowels of evil in the hopes of getting information he needed to pass along to the people who could act on it.

"I know you are. I'm sorry." He wasn't sure what else to say.

Jodelle took a deep breath and straightened. "Don't be. It's good. I'm good. You go do your thing and I'll be here when you're done."

"For the first time in my life, I've got something to look forward to when I get home."

She smiled. "I could up those stakes."

Baker tilted his head and raised a brow.

"We've waited long enough, Baker. I want you. You want me. When you get back, I'm not going to be content to fall asleep in your arms every night. I want more."

Baker's dick lengthened. "You want my cock?" he asked bluntly.

"Yes," Jodelle said with only a tinge of pink entering her cheeks.

"It's yours," he said without hesitation.

She smiled. "Good. Maybe that'll be incentive for you to hurry home."

Home. Fuck, he liked that. Baker hadn't been back to his house except to grab clothes here and there in weeks. He'd pretty much moved into Jodelle's house, and she hadn't complained in the least. In fact, she'd moved some of her things around to give him space in a dresser and in her closet. His toiletries were on her bathroom counter, his shampoo in her shower. She'd welcomed him into her home without a second thought, and that said more than anything else that she'd already accepted their relationship. There was no way, if she didn't want him there, that she would've been so accommodating.

"Yeah, Tink, it definitely is. You should know, when I packed last night, I stole your pillowcase."

She blinked in surprise. "I wondered why you'd changed my pillowcase, but not any of the rest of the bedding."

"Want you to smell me when I'm away, just as much as I

want to have your scent while I'm gone." It was a silly thing to do, but when he was knee deep in filth, he needed something clean and good to remind him why he did what he did. And having the pillowcase that Jodelle rested her head on every night would do just that.

Out of the blue, her eyes filled with tears, and Baker mentally swore. He yanked her close, holding her tight.

"Please, please come back to me," she whispered against his chest.

"I will." There wasn't much else Baker could say.

They stood that way for several minutes, until Jodelle finally pulled away. She wiped her cheeks and gave him a wobbly smile. "You need to get going, I'm sure. The world needs saving."

Baker took her cheeks in his hands and tilted her face up to his. Then he kissed her with all the emotion he had in his heart for her. He loved this woman, so much it was almost scary. Intellectually, he knew she'd likely be fine while he was gone, but there was always the chance that something could happen when he wasn't here to protect her.

Jodelle melted against him and it was a full minute before he forced himself to lift his lips from hers.

"Gonna talk to the guys. Ask them to keep their eye out for you."

"That's not necessary," she protested.

"It is to me. Mustang's gonna want you to check in every day, so be sure to do that, otherwise you'll have a SEAL team up here ready to storm the house and rescue you from bad guys."

She chuckled. "Thanks for the heads-up. I'll text him."

"Appreciate it."

They stared at each other for a heartbeat, then she said, "You need to go now, Baker. Dragging this out is killing me."

He nodded. She was right. Taking a deep breath, he

stepped back, losing touch with her downright physically painful.

"Be careful," she whispered.

"Always. I'll be back before you know it."

"I hope so."

Baker so wanted to tell her that he loved her, but he held back. He needed her trust. Needed her to break through that wall she had when it came to truly having faith in him. It was good that she recognized the issues she had in that arena, and it made him all the more determined to gain that trust.

He lifted his chin, then forced himself to move toward the front door. He grabbed his keys along the way, then his bag, which he'd put by the door after Jodelle had gotten in the shower. He turned, memorizing the sight of her bravely smiling at him, before heading out the door.

He'd always known that Jodelle was special, but it was hitting home exactly how important she was to him. For the first time since he'd gotten out of the Navy, Baker thought about retiring. At least phasing out the face-to-face "visits" he made with contacts. He could continue researching information and making deals remotely. That would lessen the stress on Jodelle. He was thinking long term when it came to their relationship, without any qualms.

She was it for him.

Period.

If things didn't work out between them, he'd be alone for the rest of his life. He was that sure she was meant for him. It had taken him decades to find the other half of his soul, and he'd do whatever it took to protect that. Protect *her*.

Feeling good about his decision, Baker turned his thoughts to his upcoming trip. It wasn't going to be a walk in the park, he'd have to be on his A-game. He never trusted the people he did deals with, and working with a terrorist to learn information about another, more dangerous man wasn't exactly high on his list of people to associate with. But in the long run, any deal he made this week would save lives, which was the goal.

After he pulled into a parking space on the Naval base, Baker took the time to pull out his phone and send a message to Mustang. As expected, his friend had no problem keeping an eye on Jodelle. He even said he'd have Elodie call and maybe set up another lunch date.

His time was running out, and Baker had a plane to catch, but he took the time to send a quick text to Jodelle.

BAKER

> Just wanted to send a note before I left to let you know how proud I am of you. You're a hell of a woman, and I still have to pinch myself that you're with me.

Three dots immediately started dancing at the bottom of the text string. She never left him hanging. Had never been coy. It was one of a thousand things he loved about her.

JODELLE

> See, you've got it all wrong. I'm the lucky one. Be safe saving the world, Baker. I'll be holding my breath until I hear you're back.

The urge to say he loved her was almost overwhelming, but Baker resisted. He wouldn't do that the first time over text.

BAKER

> We're both lucky then.

JODELLE

> I can live with that.

BAKER

Stay strong, Tink. Be safe. If possible, see if you can get ahead in your jobs, because I have a feeling when I get home, I'm not gonna wanna let you out of bed long enough to work.

JODELLE

I'll see what I can do. :) I did promise you something special if you got back in one piece, after all.

BAKER

When I get back in one piece, we're both gonna get something special. Talk to you soon.

JODELLE

I'll be thinking about you every minute you're gone.

BAKER

Ditto.

When the three dots didn't appear, Baker took a deep breath and turned off his phone. He climbed out of his car and headed for the large administrative building. He was going to debrief with the rear admiral in charge of the base before getting on a military bird. The upcoming week was going to be long and hard, but his reward would be waiting when he got home. A reward that he didn't deserve, but was going to hold onto with all his strength anyway.

# CHAPTER SIXTEEN

Jody didn't think she'd be able to concentrate after Baker left, but surprisingly, she found that once she sat down in front of her computer each morning, she had a focus she never would've thought possible. She realized it was because she wanted to do just as Baker had suggested...get ahead with her projects so when he returned, she could concentrate on just him for a few days.

She texted Mustang every day, letting him know that she and Ben were doing fine, and she'd heard from Elodie and the rest of the women daily as well. Elodie had opened a group chat and it was fun to read all the banter going back and forth between the women.

Jody thanked Kenna and Carly for the Duke's food, which had started a day-long conversation about hula pie and if it was better fresh or a couple days old. The consensus had been that it didn't matter. Duke's hula pie was amazing no matter what.

They'd wanted to set up another lunch, but with all the work Jody was trying to get done, she said she didn't think she'd be able to make it. Everyone had understood, but

Kenna had warned that she wanted to have a sleepover, *soon*, and she wasn't going to take no for an answer.

Ben's relationship with Tressa was progressing slowly, from what he told her, and Jody encouraged him to do what Baker had suggested, invite her over for dinner. He had—and tonight was the night.

Jody had put a pot roast in the Crockpot and made a cheesy broccoli casserole. Since Ben had said he liked it, Jody figured now was the time to make a dish with the vegetable Baker hated.

Ben was nervous, which Jody thought was pretty cute. He'd left a while ago to pick up Tressa, and she expected them back anytime now.

Ten minutes later, she heard Ben's car pull into her driveway and smiled in the direction of the front door.

They walked in—and despite Ben's description, Jody was still taken aback by how pretty Tressa was. She had long, straight black hair and dark eyes. Her skin was flawless, and she was only a couple inches taller than Jody. She wore a pair of dark jeans and a white short-sleeve blouse. She looked casual, but also as if she'd put in the effort to look nice for her date.

"Hi," Jody said, walking toward her. "I'm Jody. I'm so glad you could come over."

"Miss Jody, this is Tressa. Tressa, this is the woman I've told you so much about. You know, the one who makes awesome breakfast sandwiches and who cracks the whip to make sure we all get out of the ocean and to school on time."

Tressa smiled shyly and said, "It's nice to meet you, Miss Jody."

"I hope you're hungry," she said warmly. "Without Baker, my boyfriend, being here to help us, we've got a lot of food to eat."

"It smells delicious. Can I help do anything?"

Jody internally nodded approvingly. Tressa was pretty, polite, and it was easy to see Ben was completely besotted. "I'm good. Why don't you guys go hang out on the back deck while I finish up?" She wanted to give the teenagers some privacy, because there definitely wasn't anywhere in the small house they could go to talk without her overhearing, and Ben's room was absolutely not an option. He might not be her biological son, but she wasn't going to give him carte blanche to seduce Tressa under her roof.

While she made a salad, Jody kept one eye on the teenagers on the other side of the sliding-glass door that led out to her small backyard. The deck wasn't much of a deck, really, just some boards nailed together and two beach chairs. But she thought it was adorable how Ben held Tressa's hand as they quietly talked.

When the casserole was finished, Jody called the pair back inside and they all loaded up their plates before taking them to the table.

"So...how'd you end up in Hawaii?" Jody asked Tressa once they were all eating.

"My dad's Japanese and my mom's American. My mom was working over in Tokyo when she met my dad, and they fell in love. We've been splitting our time between Japan and California for years, but my dad got the opportunity to work here in Honolulu and so...here we are."

"And you live up here at the North Shore?" Jody asked.

Tressa nodded. "My mom isn't a huge fan of cities. I think living in Tokyo cured her of ever wanting to permanently live in one. My dad wanted to make her happy so he found a house up here to rent. He drives down to the city every day."

"That's tough," Jody said.

Tressa shrugged. "He says he doesn't mind. He leaves really early, like four in the morning, so he misses the worst of the traffic, and that also means that most days he's home by the time I get out of school."

"That's great, at least."

"Yeah."

"And you're in band?" Jody asked. She was aware that she was carrying the conversation, but Tressa didn't seem uncomfortable with her questions and Ben was content to observe.

The girl nodded. "I play the trombone."

"Cool!"

Tressa smiled. "Yeah, in sixth grade when we had to pick instruments, I didn't want to be like all the other girls and pick the clarinet or flute. The trombone seemed unique." She shrugged.

"She's really good too," Ben chimed in. "She made second chair, ahead of almost all the other guys."

"Do you have a favorite subject in school?" Jody asked.

The rest of dinner went by smoothly, with Tressa answering all of Jody's questions and Ben interjecting here and there to praise something Tressa had said or done. It was more than obvious he was head over heels for the girl, and Jody couldn't be happier for him.

After they ate, Ben volunteered to do the dishes, and while Jody took a seat in the living area, she watched as the teens laughed and flirted while they filled the dishwasher.

They watched two episodes of a true crime show on television, and got into a spirited discussion about how stupid some people were and the best ways to get away with a crime. By the time Ben had to take Tressa home to meet her curfew, Jody was one hundred percent supportive of the relationship.

Tressa was shy, as Ben had said, but the longer she'd been there, the more she'd loosened up. She was funny, and she couldn't keep her eyes off Ben. They were cute together, and Jody loved that for him.

"I'll be back soon," Ben said as he led Tressa to the door. He had his hand on the small of her back, like Baker always did with Jody when they walked somewhere.

"Drive safe," she warned.

"I will."

Jody was sitting on the couch when Ben returned thirty minutes later. She tilted her head back and watched him lock the front door after he entered. He came into the living room and plopped down on the couch next to her.

Jody smiled. "She's cute."

"I know."

"And really nice."

"Yup."

"You like her a lot."

Ben nodded. "She's different from most of the girls at school. She doesn't seem to care about being popular. She's got her own style, and she's funny when you get to know her."

"You need to treat her with care," Jody advised.

Ben looked at her with a frown. "What do you mean?"

"Just that. Look, this isn't my place, but I can't *not* say it. That girl thinks the world of you. She couldn't take her eyes off you all night. I have a feeling she'd do anything you asked. So, you need to be careful about that. She's shy, and I have a feeling she hasn't had many boyfriends." Jody knew she was beating around the bush, but she felt awkward saying what she really wanted to say.

"I know all this, Miss Jody," Ben said.

"All I'm saying is that I don't think you should rush anything...physically, I mean. She seems a little naïve, and not ready for sex."

Ben sat up straighter and Jody could tell she'd irritated him. "I know that."

Jody nodded. "You have plenty of time for that, Ben. I'm just suggesting you two enjoy being together without the pressure."

"I'm not a virgin," he said...sounding almost angry.

Jody swallowed hard. Yeah, she probably shouldn't've have started this conversation. "Okay."

"On my fourteenth birthday, Al brought some girl home,

left us alone, and the next thing I knew she had her hand on my dick and was undoing my pants."

"Ben..." Jody started, really not wanting to hear the story about how he lost his virginity, but he ignored her protest.

"She pushed me to my back, put a condom on me, and we did it right there on the damn couch. After, she taught me how to remove the rubber, kissed me on the cheek and left. I was still kind of dazed and feeling almost proud of myself, like an idiot." He shook his head. "I decided that I was hot shit, and I wanted to get her number so I could see her again. I foolishly thought that sex meant we were dating or some bullshit, so I followed her. I saw Al giving her money in the doorway before she left."

"Oh my God," Jody breathed, not liking Ben's stepdad at all right then.

"Yeah. He hired a prostitute to make me a man—his words, not mine. I was too young to understand what was happening. He *stole* that from me, and I'll never forgive him for it," Ben said in a low, tortured voice. "There's no way I'd ever rush Tressa into something she's not ready for. And I know, Miss Jody, that she's not ready for sex. I like being with her. I kissed her goodbye tonight, and I swear that was her first kiss. And...I like going slow. I want her to know I respect her enough not to pressure her."

Jody could hear shades of Baker in Ben's words and tone. He hadn't been around him all that long, but his positive influence was rubbing off regardless.

"I'm trying not to be offended that you even think I'd be that kind of guy," Ben said.

"I don't. I just...you're important to me, and I didn't want you to do something either one of you would regret. I didn't mean to hurt your feelings."

Ben was silent for a while, then he said, "I appreciate it. In the last few weeks, you've been more of a mom to me than my own has been in years."

That made Jody feel good and sad at the same time. She opened her mouth to reply, but a loud knock on the front door made her jump in surprise. Looking at her watch, she saw it was past nine at night. Way too late for anyone to be there to see her.

"You expecting anyone?" she asked Ben.

He shook his head.

Jody got up and went to the door. She looked through the peephole and frowned. There was a man at her door, and she could see a woman standing about eight feet behind him, on the walkway leading up to the small porch.

"Benjamin! It's time to come home!" the man shouted.

Jody glanced at Ben in surprise. The look on the teenager's face made Jody's heart hurt. He was scared.

No. Terrified.

"It's Al," Ben said softly.

Well. Jody had some things she wanted to say to Ben's stepfather. The story about how he'd hired a woman to take his stepson's virginity fresh in her mind, she unlocked the door and jerked it open. She stood in the doorway, making sure the man knew he wasn't invited inside. She might be small, but no way was Ben leaving with this guy. No freaking way.

"Can I help you?" she asked a little belligerently.

Al Rowden looked down his nose at her. "Yeah. My son has had his fun, made his point, and now it's time for him to come home."

"First of all, he's not your son," Jody told him. "Secondly, you think it was *fun* for him to sleep in his car and have to scrounge for food?"

Al smirked, as if Ben's struggle amused him. "He needed to learn a lesson."

"What lesson was that?"

"That he's not as smart as he thinks he is, and that he needs to listen to his parents."

Jody shook her head at the level of assholery coming from this jerk. "He's not going anywhere."

"Pack your shit, Ben. You're coming home," Al said, looking over Jody's head.

"Did you hear me? He's not going with you. He's fine here. Better, in fact." Jody glanced at Ben's mom. Emma. She was looking at the concrete under her feet as if it was the most interesting thing she'd ever seen. She wasn't even trying to see her son, to make sure he was all right. Her lack of emotion disturbed Jody more than she wanted to admit.

Al took a step forward, and Jody spread her arms out, blocking his entrance. "You aren't welcome here. And if you take one more step, I'm calling the police."

Al sneered. "You think you can keep me out?"

"Probably not. You're bigger and heavier than I am," Jody said in a voice more calm than she felt inside. "But I'm not surprised you're trying to use your size to intimidate me. That seems like something you'd do."

He glared at her. "You don't know anything about me," he said.

"I know enough," Jody insisted.

"Ben's been talking, I see," Al said. Then he looked at Ben over her shoulder. "No one likes a tattletale."

Jody didn't dare take her eyes off the man in front of her, but she had a feeling Al was threatening Ben in some way. "It's late. You need to go," she insisted. Her heart was beating a million miles an hour. She had no idea what she was going to do if he pushed his way inside her house and tried to manhandle Ben to get him to leave. But there was no way she was letting Ben go without a fight. She might be small, but she was a scrapper. And she had a loud voice. If she screamed loud and long enough, one of her neighbors would definitely call the cops.

But to her surprise, Al took a step backward. His hands were clenched, but he didn't make a move toward her. "Fine.

But don't think the police won't hear about how you kidnapped my son."

"It's not kidnapping when he *wants* to be here after you kicked him out of his home," Jody said, not bothering to correct the man about calling Ben his son.

"You think he'll tell the police that?" Al asked with a small laugh. "He knows better."

Jody didn't like the way Al sounded so sure. She turned her attention to Ben's mom. "Why'd it take you three weeks to come for him?" she asked. "He was living in his *car*. He had heat exhaustion because he was sleeping in it with the sun beating down on him. He wasn't going to school. Wasn't eating properly. From what I understand, you worked your butt off to make sure your little boy had food on his plate when he was young. What changed?"

The woman looked up, and for a moment, Jody saw anguish in her expression. But then it was wiped clean and the blank look returned. She didn't speak.

"The little shit's been coddled and spoiled for too long. Learning what the real world's like is good for him. He should've been left to learn that lesson, not taken in so he could mooch off someone else," Al said, stepping to the side, blocking Jody's view of Ben's mom.

"He's your son," Jody said, still aiming her words at the other woman. "I'd give anything to have one more day, hour, *minute* with mine. But you're throwing yours away...for what? Why?"

"We're leaving," Al said abruptly, turning and stepping down from the porch. He took Emma's arm and jerked roughly, spinning her around. He looked back at Jody. "But this isn't over. He can't hide behind you twenty-four hours a day."

"Is that a threat?" Jody seethed, genuinely shocked.

"Of course not," Al said with a smirk, then he yanked his

wife closer to side as he marched her toward a Mercedes sitting at the curb.

Jody felt Ben come up beside her, and they both watched as his mom and stepdad drove off. Then she closed the door, locked it, and took a deep breath.

"I'm sorry," Ben said, but Jody held up a hand, stopping him from saying anything else.

"You have *nothing* to apologize for," she said firmly. She gently cupped his cheek. "You're an amazing man, Ben. I can't pretend to know what your life was like in that house, but if that little chat was any indication, it obviously wasn't fun."

"You've made him mad," Ben said, his voice shaking.

"I don't care," Jody said.

"You should."

"I'm not afraid of him."

"He can make your life miserable," he warned.

Jody studied the boy in front of her. He sounded completely freaked out. "What's he got on you?" she asked softly.

Ben's eyes closed, and for a second Jody thought he was finally going to speak his truth. But when he opened his eyes and met her gaze, she knew he'd gotten his emotions under control, and the moment was lost. "It doesn't matter. I should leave."

Jody moved her hand to his shoulder, squeezed tightly, and said, "No."

"The last thing I want to do is make shit harder for you."

"I can handle that jerkface," Jody said. "And when Baker gets back, he'll make sure your stepdad doesn't bother you again."

It took a moment, but Ben's shoulders finally relaxed a fraction. "Jerkface?" he repeated with a small forced smile.

"Yeah, I would've used a bad word, but since I got on Baker for swearing in front of you, I didn't figure it was appropriate."

"I think when talking about Al Rowden, it's absolutely appropriate," Ben said.

"You're probably right."

"About what you said to my mom," Ben added. "I didn't notice the change in her until it was too late. She lost herself...and in doing so, she lost me."

"I'm so sorry, Ben," Jody said quietly, stepping into his personal space and wrapping her arms around him. She hugged him fiercely, pleased when he returned her embrace. Then she stepped back.

"I'm sorry about your son," Ben replied.

"Me too. But having you here has done me a lot of good. For the record, I *like* having you here, Ben. You aren't a burden, and you have plenty of time to learn how to be an adult. For now, your only worries should be your grades and treating Tressa right."

"I *wish* that was all I was worried about," Ben said quietly.

"Me too," Jody whispered.

He took a deep breath. "When's Baker getting home again?"

"I'm not sure. He said he thought he'd be gone about a week. So hopefully only a few more days."

"What's he doing?"

They were still standing in her foyer, but since Ben was actually talking to her, Jody didn't want to risk him clamming up by asking him to move back to the couch. "He works with the government. He's an information seeker of sorts."

Jody didn't know exactly *what* it was that Baker did, but she didn't think telling Ben he worked with extremely dangerous people was smart right now. Though, as Ben stared at her, it was as if he could see right through her vague words.

"Maybe I'll talk to him when he gets back."

"I think that's a wonderful idea," Jody agreed. She wouldn't be upset if Ben opened up to Baker and not her. The teenager seemed to really admire the man, and who wouldn't? He was an admirable guy, that was for sure.

"I think I'm gonna stay up for a bit and watch TV, but you can go on to bed if you want," Ben said.

Jody narrowed her eyes. "If you step one foot outside this house, Ben Miller, I'm gonna lose my mind."

His lips quirked upward. "I'm not going to leave," he told her.

Jody raised a brow.

"I'm not. Promise. I have no desire to go back to that house. Ever. If I have to wear the same ten outfits I took with me when I left for the rest of my life, I will. If my mom ever gets her head out of her ass, she'll have to come see *me*. I just...the night's been so good, perfect. I got to kiss my girl for the first time, then *he* had to ruin it."

"No one can ruin memories, Ben," Jody told him. "Those are all yours."

He nodded. "I need to think. He's gonna try something, Miss Jody, and I have to be ready when he does," Ben said.

She didn't like the sound of that. "Baker will help when he gets back," she assured him.

"Yeah," Ben said.

Jody felt as if she'd said all she could for tonight. She'd do what she could in the morning to try to reassure him once more. "All right. I'll turn in. But if you need anything, I'm just down the hall."

"Thanks, Miss Jody." Then he shook his head. "I can't believe you stood in front of him with your arms out...as if that would keep him from getting by you."

"You might be taller and bigger, Ben, but you're still a kid. Over my dead body was he going to get to you," she promised.

Ben swallowed hard and looked down at his feet as he took a deep breath.

Jody gave him time to gain his composure. "You aren't

Mana. I know that, but that doesn't mean I'm not going to protect you with everything I have. I know he could've pushed past me, but I was willing to risk being hurt in order to stand up for you, Ben."

"I wish *you* were my mom," Ben whispered.

It was Jody's turn to have to swallow hard to prevent herself from bursting into tears. When she felt she had herself under control, she said, "I might not be your biological mother, but as far as I'm concerned, from this moment on, you're my adopted son. You need something, anything, you come to me. Water, food, a roof over your head, a shoulder to lean on, girl advice, or just a place to chill where you don't have to think...my door will always stay open for you."

"Thanks," Ben said. He stepped toward her, hugged her hard once more, then turned and went back to the living area.

Jody took a deep breath, then headed for the hallway leading to her room. "Good night, Ben. Don't stay up too late."

"I won't," he said as he sat down and picked up the remote. "I'll check the doors and windows before I go to bed, so don't worry."

Yes, it was safe to say Ben was soaking in all of Baker's goodness. "Okay. Thanks."

"Good night, Miss Jody."

"Good night, Ben."

Jody got ready for bed, crawled under her covers, and pulled the pillow Baker used into her arms. She buried her head in it and finally let go of the tears she'd held back. She cried because she'd actually been terrified of what Al might do. Cried for Ben. For Emma Rowden, who had no idea what she'd thrown away...or maybe she did. Cried because she was worried about Baker.

When her tears dried up, Jody felt as if she'd been through the wringer. She had no idea what was up with Ben's stepdad, but it wasn't good. Ben was terrified of the man. He had some hold over his stepson, that was clear, and Jody desperately wished she knew what it could be.

She hoped Baker would be able to figure it out. Maybe with his connections, he could sever whatever hold Al had on Ben and the teenager could live his life without the black cloud of worry that seemed to be hovering over him for months. It had disappeared for a while tonight, when he'd been with Tressa, but now it was back.

The thought that Ben might back off his pursuit of Tressa to try to protect her ran through Jody's head. The more she thought about it, the more she suspected that was exactly what he was going to do. She made a mental note to talk to him tomorrow. It would crush Tressa if Ben tried to break up with her now. She'd think it was because of something she'd done tonight, or because she wasn't a good kisser, or some other nonsense, not because Ben was trying to be noble.

Lying there, unable to sleep, thinking about Ben and how to help him, was overwhelming and made Jody miss Baker all the more. He'd know exactly what to do in this kind of situation. If he'd been there tonight, there was no way Al would've said all those horrible things. Jody was proud of how she'd handled the guy, but she wished Baker had been here all the same.

It was scary how she'd been muddling through life, feeling almost disconnected for the last five years, and now suddenly in the last month her life seemed to go from gray to Technicolor in a nanosecond. It was uncomfortable and kind of scary, but Jody couldn't deny that she'd much rather have this life...with Ben and Baker and all the uncertainty that went along with both...instead of drowning in grief and missing Mana with every breath.

As if thinking about her son somehow conjured him, the dull clank of keys hitting his dresser sounded almost loud in her room. Sitting up, Jody tilted her head. Was she dreaming once again?

Then she heard footsteps on the hardwood floor in the other room. Ben.

Jody lay back down and smiled. Ben wasn't Kaimana, but having him here felt right. "Miss you, Mana," she whispered.

Jody swore she felt a brush against her cheek after she said the words.

Her son's soul *was* here. Watching over her. For the first time in ages, she felt comfort when she thought about her son, rather than an overwhelming grief.

She curled onto her side once more and cuddled Baker's pillow against her chest. He'd be home soon, but until then, she'd be all right. She and Ben would figure things out as best they could, and when Baker was back, Ben would talk to him and he'd do what was necessary to handle Al Rowden.

Jody fell asleep with Baker's scent in her nostrils and the hope that he'd be home soon.

# CHAPTER SEVENTEEN

Jody jerked open the door and watched as Baker pulled in behind her van in the driveway. He'd called about an hour and a half ago, letting her know he was home, had a few things to do on base, then was headed straight for her house.

She'd been watching impatiently for him ever since. Earlier, Ben had run out to grab food from Aji Limo Truck, a food truck that was permanently parked near Shark's Cove, a popular snorkeling spot on the North Shore. He'd considered taking a job there, but had decided to concentrate on school and Tressa instead, and Jody approved.

She'd been almost too excited to eat, but had managed to choke down a delicious poke bowl. Ben had also gotten extra for Baker, in case he was hungry when he got home.

Jody couldn't wait for Baker to come to her. She met him at the driver's side of his car and the second he stepped out, she threw her arms around him.

"Hey, Tink."

"I'm so glad you're home," she mumbled against his chest.

Baker's arms tightened around her as he whispered, "Best homecoming I've ever had," against her ear.

Shivers raced down Jody's spine. She was perfectly fine

being on her own, had been for a very long time, but being in Baker's arms right this second was one of the best feelings she'd ever experienced.

Pulling back, she kept her hands on his biceps as her gaze went from his head down to his toes then back up, checking to make sure he really was in one piece.

"I'm good," he said, obviously knowing what she was doing.

"Are you tired? Hungry? Did you get any sleep on the plane? I don't know how long your flight was, but you look exhausted. What do you need from me?"

"You're doing it," Baker said with a pleased smile.

Jody shook her head. "I'm not doing anything," she protested.

"You couldn't wait the extra five seconds it would've taken me to get to you," Baker said. "You're eyeballing me as if you can see through my clothes to inspect for any boo-boos. And the first thing you did was try to take care of me by offering food and rest. You're doing everything, Jodelle."

His words made tears spring to her eyes. "Shoot," she said, pressing back into him. "I promised myself I wouldn't cry."

Baker chuckled, and she felt the rumble under her cheek. "As long as they're happy tears, I'm good," he told her.

"Welcome back," Ben said from the doorway.

Jody felt Baker's chin lift—then his whole body tensed. He said just loud enough for her ears, "There a reason Ben looks completely fuckin' petrified?"

Jody sighed. She hadn't wanted to get into this the second Baker got back, but maybe it was for the best. "Something happened two nights ago," she told him.

Baker's muscles coiled even tighter against her. "What?"

"His stepdad and mom came by. Tried to take him home."

Baker frowned. "What the fuck? How'd they know where he was? Better yet, if someone told him he was living at Miss Jody's house, how'd he know where *you* lived?"

"I don't know. I handled it, but Ben's terrified of his step-dad. I think he's holding something over his head."

"Blackmail?" Baker bit out.

"I don't know that I'd go that far, but there were defi-nitely some things said that weren't good."

"He touch you?" Baker asked.

Jody immediately shook her head. "No."

"He touch Ben?"

"No. I wouldn't let him in the house."

Baker didn't look mollified by her response. "He talk to you? Ben, that is?"

"He told me some things before his stepdad made an appearance that made me really not like the man, but there's a lot more he's not saying. I think he's trying to protect me from whatever it is. He wanted to leave after his stepdad left. To keep me safe."

"I'll talk to him," Baker said.

"Okay. I'm sorry."

"About what?"

"That you have to deal with this two-point-three seconds after you got home."

"Don't care if it's two-point-three seconds or three days, Jodelle. Something's happening that puts not only a kid I respect and like at risk, but my woman too? The sooner that shit gets dealt with the better. Thank you for not hiding the fact that asshole came by from me."

"Why would I?" Jody asked with a tilt of her head.

He stared down at her for a beat, then said, "I haven't kissed you yet."

"No, you haven't, but seriously, Baker, why would I keep something like that from you? I know the kind of man you are. And you promised you wouldn't lose your mind and do something stupid that would take you away from me—in this case, like storm to his house and challenge Al to a duel. Besides, Ben needs to talk to someone, and if it's not going to be me because he wants to shield me from the shit in his life, it should be you. I know you're strong enough to not only take whatever he wants to tell you, but you'll have the wisdom to advise him on what he should do next."

Jody's voice lowered even more. "And with the connections you say you have, I'm hoping you can use some of them to teach Al a lesson...namely, that it's not cool to kick your stepson out of his house to 'teach him a lesson,' knowing he'll be living rough and out of his car and most likely going hungry."

In response, Baker looked up at Ben and said loudly, "I'm gonna kiss Jodelle now. There's gonna be tongue, and it's gonna be long, deep, and hard. So I suggest you go back in the house. We'll be inside in a bit."

Ben smirked. "I'm going," he called out. "But I'm not sure Miss Jody's neighbors will appreciate an X-rated show in her driveway."

"Not gonna be X. Maybe R though," Baker told him. "And she's welcoming her boyfriend back from a dangerous trip... I'm sure they'll understand."

The smile on Ben's face never wavered. He gave them a chin lift, emulating Baker yet again, then turned and went inside the house.

"Baker," Jody said when he looked back down at her with an expression so intense, she couldn't even start to interpret it.

"All my life, I've dealt with people doing everything in their power to deceive me," he said, his voice low and rumbly, almost like a growl. "They lie about every fuckin' little thing, from what they had for breakfast to more important shit, like who they're colluding with to try to fuckin' kill me and my countrymen and women. You? I haven't even taken two steps out of my car and you're spilling the beans about Al Rowden paying you a visit, giving me a heads-up that Ben has some serious shit he needs to share, and you're doing so while trusting me not to lose my shit. That means something to me, Jodelle. Means the world."

"Baker," she whispered.

"I'm gonna sort this shit," he vowed. "Might not be tonight. Might not be tomorrow. But I'm gonna make sure Rowden knows you're off limits. He doesn't talk to you. Doesn't show up at your house. Doesn't even fuckin' *look* at you. It'll be Ben's choice if he wants the same, but if he does, then I'll send that message too. And it's good that you aren't spooked by the fact I might call in some markers to deal with this."

"I'm not," Jody said. "If Al's as big an asshole as I'm guessing he might be, he deserves everything he gets."

Baker shifted, putting his finger under Jody's chin and tilting her head back at the same time he lowered his own. Jody met him halfway, going up on her tiptoes and moving a hand to the back of his head. She tangled her fingers into his hair and immediately opened to him as their lips met.

His beard was a bit longer than it'd been a week ago when he left, but Jody didn't mind in the least. She was consumed with need for this man. She went from zero to five hundred in a matter of heartbeats. Their tongues twined together as they relearned the taste and feel of each other. Jody could feel Baker's erection hard against her belly, and she shamelessly rubbed against him. Wanting more. Needing to be closer.

When Baker finally pulled back, Jody's leg was hiked up on the outside of his thigh and her nails were digging into his scalp. One of his hands was under her shirt on the small of her back, holding her tightly against him, and the other had shifted to her nape, holding her still for his assault on her mouth. An assault she wanted more of. A small whimper left her throat as he stared down at her.

"Want to make you mine tonight," he said.

"I'm already yours," Jody said without thought. "But if you're taking about sex, yes. Please, yes."

Baker took a deep breath, then smiled.

"What?" she asked.

"Plumeria. Fuckin' missed that."

Jody melted into him. She lowered her leg and forced herself to unclench her hand from his hair. "I missed you so much, Baker."

"Anything else happen while I was gone other than Rowden being a dick?"

"I got a bunch of new jobs to do, including a contract to completely redesign a large sportswear company's website. Which is gonna take a long time, but they're paying me a huge chunk of change, so it'll totally be worth it. Tressa and Ben are now boyfriend/girlfriend. She came over for dinner the same night Al came by, but Ben had already taken her home by the time he showed, which is a good thing. My surf kids are all doing great. Apparently Kenna's planning a sleepover to happen sooner rather than later, and if the group chat I got added to is any indication, that could even be in the next week or so. Truthfully, I'm really nervous to go, but also excited, which I know is crazy. Anyway...Ben picked up some poke bowls for dinner. I've already eaten, but there are two inside for you."

Baker was smiling now. "Sounds good, Tink. I'm starving."

"Then why are we still standing out here?" she asked.

"Because I'm enjoying my welcome home from my woman. Would take having you in my arms over food any day."

Jody shook her head. "Well, how about we go inside, you let me feed you, then you can have a chat with Ben and we'll go to bed."

"Sounds like a plan. Missed you, Tink."

"I missed you too," Jody whispered.

"Thank you for not playing games. Or hiding anything from me. And I'm sorry I wasn't here to have your back with Rowden."

"You're welcome. And nothing to be sorry about. I'm not helpless, and while the encounter wasn't fun, I was fully prepared to scream my head off if he tried anything. My neighbors would've called the police in a heartbeat."

"Good to know. Come on, let's get inside so I can eat and get to talking with Ben. Can't wait to fall asleep with you in my arms again."

"Same," Jody agreed.

Baker let go of her long enough to open the back door of his car and grab his duffle bag, then he put his arm right back around her waist and led them to the door.

Jody brought his bag to her bedroom while Baker greeted Ben with a manly hug and some slaps on the back. As Baker ate, he didn't talk much about where he'd gone or what he'd been doing, but he did say that it rained almost the entire time and he was glad to get back to Oahu and the sunshine.

After Baker ate and put the takeout containers in the recycle bin, Jody said, "I'm going go and get a head start on that website project I've got. You guys can hang out here. And I'll have my headphones on, so if you need to say bad words, don't feel guilty because I can't hear anything with my music in my ears."

Baker's face got soft. "Thanks, Tink."

"Of course. Ben, you need anything?"

"No, I'm good, Miss Jody."

"All right. If I don't see you before you head to bed, sleep well. You going surfing in the morning?"

Jody wasn't surprised when the young man looked at Baker.

"I haven't been in the waves for a week. I know I'm in for some surfing tomorrow."

Ben nodded. "Me too."

"Good. Make sure you get all your homework done," Jody said.

"I will."

"Okay. Good night." Then she took a deep breath and added, "I'm so glad you're here, Ben. You've made the last week much less lonely. And you've been a huge help, with the yard work and other chores you do."

Ben pressed his lips together and nodded. "It's nice to be appreciated. Good night, Miss Jody."

Taking that as her cue, Jody turned and headed for her bedroom. She so wanted to eavesdrop and find out once and for all how big of a jerk Ben's stepdad was, but she didn't want to lose either Ben's or Baker's trust if they discovered she was listening. So she sat down in front of her computer, picked up her headphones, clicked on the app to bring up her favorite playlist, and pressed play. Then she got to work.

# CHAPTER EIGHTEEN

"How bad was it?" Baker asked Ben the second he heard the door close behind Jodelle.

Ben sighed and said, "Bad."

Baker nodded. He was afraid of that. He had a feeling Jodelle had downplayed what had happened with Rowden. "Let's sit. You can tell me about it."

They sat on the couch and, for the next ten minutes, Baker did his best not to lose his shit as Ben described what Rowden had said, and how Jodelle had put her fucking arms out, as if that would keep the asswipe from getting into the house. He wasn't surprised Jodelle had thrown down for Ben. No way was anyone going to take him from her house if she had anything to say about it.

"What did she think she was going to do if he pushed her?" Baker asked with a shake of his head.

"I asked her the same thing. She told me she would've jumped on his back like a fucking monkey and screamed her head off."

"Good Lord," Baker said, but he couldn't help it when a small chuckle escaped. It wasn't funny. Not at all. But the image of her doing just that was somewhat humorous even if the situation wasn't.

He sobered. "Talk to me, Ben," Baker said. "I've done some research into Rowden and while nothing about the man makes me feel all warm and fuzzy, I didn't find anything concrete. I need information if I'm going to help you."

Ben looked down at his hands clenched together in his lap. "I don't think you *can* help," he admitted. "Al's very good at tying up loose ends. At making sure no one says anything bad about him."

"I noticed he has nothing but praise when it comes to his job," Baker said.

Ben nodded. "Yeah...because he lets off the kids who work with him, and the ones who don't get the worst punishments."

"How does he keep people quiet? I'm guessing blackmail?" Baker asked, wondering about the "work with him" comment.

Ben sighed. "To explain, I have to go back."

Baker nodded and braced as Ben began to speak.

"When my mom first married Al, things were good. We didn't have to struggle anymore. We moved into the big house up here at the North Shore. I was happy to get out of the city and away from the kids who picked on me because my clothes were worn. I stopped being hungry, and even my mom was happy. But after Al got her that job as a receptionist at the doctor's office, he started getting mean. He'd yell at her, and she cried a lot. Then she fell one day and hurt her back. I was never told *how* she fell...but I think Al pushed her. Anyway, she got a prescription for codeine. When that didn't seem to dull her pain much, her doctor changed it to oxycodone."

"Shit," Baker said.

Ben nodded. "Yeah. During that time, I still thought Al was pretty nice, even though he yelled a lot. I was twelve and I craved his acceptance and attention. I liked when he was nice to me more than when he yelled at me, of course. While my mom was stuck in her room, whacked out on painkillers... Al taught me how to break into cars. I was just a stupid kid, so I thought it was fun and exciting, and it seemed fairly harmless at the time. We'd go out to the crowded beaches and other tourist hot spots and he'd drop me off at one end of the parking lot and wait for me at the other. Some cars were always unlocked, those were easy, but others I had to use different tools, depending on the car, or even break a back window. I brought back cameras, purses, and other stuff. Al would bring everything to a guy he knew and get cash in return. He gave me some, and I thought that was so cool.

"Then he started recruiting my friends...including my best friend Alex. Again, at first it was exciting. Like a game. We'd spread out in a parking lot and grab as much stuff as we could, competing with each other. Al taught us which stuff would bring in the most money. But as time went on...it got less fun. I was almost caught several times, and instead of making it more exciting, that scared the shit out of me. A few times, my friends *did* get caught, and they went to court. Al let them off with a warning and some bullshit community service, which he always supervised.

"Shortly after turning fourteen, I refused to do it anymore. Al wasn't happy, but since Alex and my friends were still willing to continue, he didn't give me too much shit."

"What did he do with all the money?" Baker asked. This was unlike anything he'd expected—and worse, since it involved kids. But he had a feeling Ben wasn't done.

"He used most of it to buy drugs. He bought MDMA for my friends. Started throwing parties at our house where he hands out ecstasy like candy. The kids stay up all night dancing and drinking alcohol that Al conveniently leaves around. He never serves it to kids directly, but it's available for anyone who wants it. *Everyone* goes. He has a rental property too, and he throws even more parties there, so our neighbors don't get suspicious over all the frequent gatherings.

"At the parties, he recruits more kids into his operation. And once he lures people in, he makes sure they stay by taking video of them breaking into cars, and getting drunk and high at the rental, which has hidden cameras everywhere —he *never* tapes at the parties in our house. He's too careful for that. If someone wants out, he blackmails them with the videos and threatens to turn the evidence over and they'll end up in court. He's already done it a few times, and he made sure those kids spent time in juvey. The only way to get out is when the kids graduate and leave."

"Jesus, Ben."

"I know. He's got a ton of videos of me, Baker. I was his little protégé," he said bitterly. "I did everything he asked me to do and didn't care that he was recording. At first, I was actually proud that I was good at getting in and out of cars without being caught. After I stopped, I thought of telling someone what he was doing, regardless of the videos." He sighed heavily. "But I couldn't. Because of my mom.

"By that time, she was hooked on oxy. She was fired from her job because her boss figured out she'd stolen a few prescription pads. She was desperate for drugs, and Al's little side business kept her supplied. He's been drugging her for years, Baker." Ben shook his head. "She's so out of it, most days she has no idea what's going on. She has no friends and she's so dependent on Al for the pain meds that she does whatever he tells her to without complaint.

"He needs the money from the robberies to support his gambling habit too," Ben went on. "He's in so far over his head that I know he would've lost our house by now if it wasn't for the money he gets from kids stealing. They think it's all risqué and exciting. They get drugs and a chance to party without fear of repercussions, and Al gets money to continue gambling."

"And you're stuck," Baker said, feeling sick. "If you turn in your stepdad, your mom will be left hanging. She has no job, no way of supporting herself thanks to Rowden, not to mention a substance abuse problem that would be hard to kick, even if she was strong—which, no offense, it doesn't sound like she is. Not only that, but if word got out about what was going on, a lot of your friends and other kids would be in trouble, possibly have to do some time in juvenile detention, or even regular jail if they're old enough."

Ben nodded. His head was still down and it looked as if the weight of the world was on his shoulders. "I did that shit too," he said. "Nearly every week for two years. He's got me on video. I'd go down right along with him. He promised me that. Said he'd tell everyone that it was my idea in the first place."

"Tell me this, Ben—you're a pretty tall guy right now. Built. What were you like as a twelve-year-old?" Baker asked.

"Scrawny," Ben said without hesitation. "It wasn't until I started working out and surfing regular, and hitting puberty, that I started to grow into my body."

"Right. And the videos Rowden has? I'm assuming they're from when you were twelve to fourteen?"

"Yeah."

"I get that you're trying to protect everyone. Your mom, the kids at school, yourself. But trust me, if Rowden pulls out those videos to try to convince the cops or a judge that you were the mastermind behind everything, *no one* would believe him."

Ben looked up at Baker. "Why wouldn't they?"

"Because you were a kid," he said. "And this was a man who'd saved you and your mother from a life of extreme poverty. You looked up to him and respected him, and he took advantage of that. Everyone will immediately realize that you were an easy mark."

Ben shook his head. "I just want it to stop."

"I know you do, and you're taking the first step right now to make that happen. Why'd you get kicked out of the house?" Baker could see that Ben wanted to believe him. Wanted to have hope, but he wasn't quite there yet.

"It's gotten harder to recruit kids," Ben said. "There are cameras everywhere now, especially after the break-ins became so frequent. It's almost impossible to go to a parking lot at a tourist spot and break into cars without being caught on security cameras. He wants me to recruit for him. Wanted me to talk to some of the younger kids who surf with us and persuade them to attend the next party. I refused. He got pissed. Told me if I wasn't going to cooperate, I wasn't welcome in his house.

"My mom just sat there, with the same blank stare she's had on her face for years. Didn't stick up for me or anything. So I left. He cornered me on the way out and said if I told anyone, he'd kick Mom out too. He'd drop her off on a street corner in Honolulu with nothing. Said she'd turn to prostitution within a day to get the drugs she needed. And I...I believed him."

Baker's heart broke for Ben. But at the same time, a fire was brewing in his belly. Al Rowden was a menace to society. He'd blackmailed his own stepson and ruined who knew how many other young lives as well. He should've dug even harder to find information when something seemed off about the guy.

"First off, I don't blame you for staying silent about everything," Baker said.

Ben looked at him in surprise. He could see the fear in the boy's eyes. "You don't?"

"No. Rowden's a piece of shit. But he's a smart piece of shit. You were trying to protect everyone around you all by yourself. It's a fuckin' awful position to be in, and honestly, I admire how you stood up to him and got out of that toxic situation."

"I left my mom there though," Ben said in a small voice.

"This is gonna hurt to hear...but she's an adult," Baker said gently. "It was her choice to stay. Her choice to let him do what he did."

"He probably blackmailed her too," Ben said.

Baker nodded. "Yeah, I think you're right. Maybe even showed her the videos of you breaking into cars and threatened to turn you in if she didn't toe the line. He probably encouraged her to steal the prescription pads too."

Ben shuddered at those words.

"Regardless...I'm not a parent, but I'm guessing if you asked Jodelle what *she'd* do if she was in that situation, if she found out a man was teaching her son how to be a thief, she'd lose her fuckin' mind and haul you, and herself, out of that situation faster than you could even blink. She'd probably go to the cops herself, not giving him a chance to spread his filth. And even if he did, she'd fight like hell to make sure her son was living clean and safe."

Ben chuckled, but it wasn't a humorous sound. "She'd *so* do that. But my mom isn't as strong as Miss Jody."

"No, she's not. But she should've been. For you. From what I've been able to find out, she worked hard to keep a roof over your head when you were younger. She could've done it. Could've fought for you—but she didn't," Baker said quietly.

"No, she didn't," Ben agreed. Then he looked Baker in the eye and said, "Now that you know, I can leave. Al's not gonna take me being here well. He's gonna threaten Miss Jody, and the last thing I want is for anything to happen to her. I stayed long enough for you to get back, so I could try to keep her safe, and now that you're here, I'll go."

"You aren't going anywhere," he retorted.

Ben blinked in surprise.

"First, if you think Jodelle is gonna let you leave, you're delusional. The woman in the other room has unofficially adopted you. Not only that, but you've been good for her. For five years, she's been grieving, missing her son something awful. You being here has made some of that sorrow fade. You aren't a replacement for Kaimana, but she needs you as much as you need her."

"I don't want Al causing her trouble. You didn't see him, Baker. He was *so* pissed. He retreated so he could regroup, but I know he's planning something, and I'm scared to death it's going to involve Miss Jody."

"Not gonna happen," Baker said. "Now that I know exactly what to look for, I'm gonna dig deep and expose him for what he is—an abusive husband, a drug dealer, a child abuser, a gambling addict, and a fuckin' judge on the take. He's *done*, Ben. Might not be tomorrow, but it's gonna be soon. I give you my word on that."

"How?"

Baker smiled coldly. "I'm calling in some markers. And I'm gonna find the kids he recruited. I'll track them down at their universities, in the military, at their workplaces. By the time I've had a chat with them, they'll agree to testify against Rowden. I fuckin' guarantee it."

"But—"

"No buts," Baker interrupted. "There will be no blowback on you or your mother. We'll get her into a treatment center. No lie, Ben, it's not going to be easy for her. She doesn't have a lot of inner strength, so I'm not all that sure she'll be able to kick her habit. But I'll get her away from Rowden so she at least has a shot. And yeah, you participated in his shit, but again, you were a kid. Once you were old enough, you stopped. You been recruiting for him?"

"Fuck no," Ben said. "I left, remember?"

"Since you told me that less than a minute ago, yeah, I remember. I'm just making a point. You stopped, refused to cooperate with him, left the house with nowhere to go, living homeless in your car in order to stay away from him. That's gonna make an impression. A good one, Ben."

"And Miss Jody? He *really* wasn't happy with her, Baker."

"She'll be good."

Ben stared at him for a long moment, then, "I'm suddenly thinking you're kind of scary."

"You'd be thinking right. But not to the people I care about. And news flash, you're one of those people, Ben. You're a good kid. You did what was right when the odds were stacked against you. You're gonna go on to do great things. Don't know what those things are, just that I'll be proud to stand up years from now and say I know you."

Ben swallowed hard, and it was easy to see he was trying to hold back his emotions. Then he asked, "You're gonna call in markers? Um...I'm not sure I wanna stop my asshole step-father from forcing kids to do illegal shit, by doing *other* illegal shit in order to make that happen."

"I'll tell you what I told Jodelle. I was a Navy SEAL. I met a lot of people in my line of work. Both good and bad. I might walk the line of good versus evil, but I always do it for decent people like my Jodelle. So she can live a happy life. And for kids like you and your friends. For your Tressa...who I'm gonna want to meet at some point. The world is a safer place because of what I do, Ben. Because of who I know and what I know about them. Some people would say I'm no different than your stepfather, but they'd be wrong. I only use the shit I know against the people who would rain terror down on others."

Ben stared at him for a long time, then nodded. "I can live with that."

"Good. Thank you for being honest with me. I won't let you or your mother down."

"I love her because she's my mom...but I don't *love* her anymore, if that makes sense," Ben said softly. "She lost that when she chose drugs over me."

"Your choice, Ben," Baker said.

"I want her to get help, but for herself. Not for me or for our relationship. I hope she can kick the addiction. But like you said, I'm not holding out much hope."

"I'm guessing that Jodelle will want you to stay regardless of what happens with your mom, if that's something you want too. And after you go to college or move out, she'll expect you to come back here for Thanksgiving and Christmas and every other holiday. When you have kids someday, if you choose to go that route, hopefully she'll get the honor of having some sort of grandmotherly role in their lives."

"She will," Ben said without hesitation.

"Good. Now, you have homework?"

Ben's lips twitched. "You playing Dad now?"

"Fuck no," Baker said. "Just making sure you graduate because it would cause Jodelle pain if you didn't."

"I've got some math shit to do."

"Then you best get on that."

"Yeah." Ben was silent for a moment, then said quietly. "He scares me."

"I'm getting that, and I think you'd be stupid *not* to be scared of that asshole. He's caused you a lot of grief over the years. You've had the burden of your mom, your friends, and your own future on your shoulders for a long time. I'm gonna help you get free of that. Your job is to stay away from Rowden. Do not talk to him. Do not engage with him. You see him, you go the other way. He comes back here when I'm not around, do not open the door. Do not let *Jodelle* open the door. Call the police, then call me. We'll deal with him. Understand?"

"Yes, sir."

Baker was glad to see that Ben looked a little less stressed than he had when they'd first sat down.

"Thanks, Baker."

"You're welcome. Thank you for telling me everything so

I can protect you and Jodelle. Hard to do that when I don't know what I'm up against."

Ben nodded, then stood. He went into the kitchen, grabbed a can of soda, picked up his backpack that was sitting in the foyer, where he'd probably dropped it when he'd gotten home from school, and wandered down the hall toward his room.

Baker sat where he was for another five minutes. His mind was spinning with all he'd learned. He'd known Rowden was an ass, but the depth of his assholery was almost stunning. Baker would have to be careful with his next steps. Rowden might be a motherfucker, but he wasn't stupid. He wouldn't have been able to keep up his ruse as a good guy all these years if he was. Not to mention, in Baker's first dive into the guy's life, he hadn't found any evidence of his gambling habit or his drug purchase history. True, MDMA and oxycodone weren't exactly meth and cocaine, but they were bad enough.

Standing, Baker checked the front door to make sure it was locked. Then he went to each of the windows and did the same thing. It felt great to be home, but now it was even more important to make sure the house was locked up tight.

He stood in the doorway of the bedroom and watched Jodelle's body sway back and forth to the music in her ears as she clicked on her mouse and studied the computer screen. *This* was why he'd done what he did when he was a SEAL. This was why he *still* did what he did. Why he went to the bowels of the Earth to meet with terrorists, drug dealers, and mobsters. To keep people like Jodelle safe from their brand of evil ever touching her.

Baker stepped into the room and closed the door behind him. Then he headed for the bathroom. He turned on the light, knowing it would catch Jodelle's attention in a way that wouldn't scare her. She immediately turned and took the headphones off.

"Hey," she said softly. "Your talk done?"

Baker nodded. "I'm gonna take a shower real fast. You wanna get ready for bed while I'm doing that?"

"Yeah, sure."

Thankful that she didn't press for more info about his chat with Ben right that second, Baker went into the bathroom. He saw that Jodelle had unpacked his bag for him. His toiletries were once more sitting next to hers on the counter, the sight making him smile.

He took a fast shower, the desire to hold Jodelle spurring him on. He was finished and wearing nothing but a clean pair of boxers when he wandered back into the bedroom. Jodelle was in bed, the covers pulled up to her waist as she sat against a pillow, waiting for him. He clicked off the light, plunging the room into darkness, and pulled her close.

"I'm guessing that any plans we might have had to move our physical relationship forward are now on hold?" she asked quietly, obviously sensing his troubled mood.

"Yeah, Tink. That okay?"

"Of course. Was it really bad?"

Baker shouldn't be surprised she took their change of plans so easily. He sighed. "Yeah." Then he took the next fifteen minutes to share what Ben had told him. There was no way he was keeping this shit from her. She needed to know exactly how bad Rowden was so the next time, she wouldn't fucking open the door to him. Knowledge was power, and keeping her in the dark would be a stupid thing to do. So he shared.

By the time he was done, Jodelle was stiff as a board in his arms.

"What a fucking *asshole*!" she hissed fervently.

Baker was surprised by the ferociousness of her words. If she was swearing, she was definitely not happy. He tightened his arms around her. "Yeah."

"Did he tell you about the virginity thing?" she asked.

"What virginity thing?"

It was her turn to share for the next few minutes, and when she was done, Baker hated Rowden even more than he had before...which was saying something, because he really hated the fucker.

"He's goin' down," Baker said.

"Good. Soon, I hope."

He couldn't help but smile. "As soon as I can make it happen. In the meantime, as I told Ben, you need to stay away from him. Do not open the fuckin' door if he's on the other side ever again."

"I won't. But in my defense, I didn't know all the stuff you told me tonight. I thought he was a jerk, but I didn't think he was as much of a jerk as he apparently is."

"Now you know," Baker said.

"Yeah. Now I know."

They lay quietly in each other's arms for a few minutes before Jodelle spoke once more. "I'm sorry."

"For what?" Baker asked.

"That your homecoming, after what was probably an intense week already, had to be so depressing."

"It's not depressing. I'm home. I've got my woman in my arms. I've got the info I need to end the shit going on in Ben's life...I'm good."

Jodelle snuggled into him, hitching a leg over his thigh and nuzzling her nose into his neck. She felt fucking amazing in his arms, and Baker was more than content at the moment.

"She's an idiot."

"Who?" Baker asked.

"Ben's mom. She let this happen right under her nose and she didn't protect her son."

"Yup."

"If Mana was alive, if we were married, and if you started treating me and him like that, there's no way I would've stayed. No matter how much I loved you. I wouldn't have put up with any of that, for my son's sake."

"That's a lot of ifs, Tink, but I understand. I told Ben the same thing."

"You did?" she asked.

"Yeah."

"He's hurting," Jodelle said.

"Yup."

"I'll do whatever I can to try to make him hurt less," she said.

"You already have."

Baker felt her smile against his shoulder. "God, I'm glad you're home," she said after a while.

"Me too, Tink. You sure I can have a raincheck on the making-you-mine thing?" he asked.

"I'm already yours," she said quietly.

Warmth spread throughout Baker's body. "Damn straight you are," he returned.

"I want to make love with you, but there's no timetable, like you've already told me. Tonight's been tough. You're tired. You aren't here in my bed because I'm worried Ben's gonna assault me. You aren't here because I feel sorry for you. You're here because I want you here. If I didn't, you'd still be on the couch or at your own house. You'll hopefully be in my bed tomorrow, and the night after that, and the night after *that*. I don't need or want sex every night. I think the passion ship has sailed. What I *do* want, is intimacy. Letting me hold you when you've had a shitty day and being open with me about what's bothering you. And I want you to do the same for me.

"At the end of the day, I don't want to have sex or make love for the sake of doing either. I want it to mean something. If you'd ignored the fact that you aren't in the mood and tried to initiate sex tonight anyway, it would've been a disappointment for me. Just let me hold you, Baker. I know you're a guy, but sometimes men need to be held just as much as women."

Baker tightened his arm around her. She was right. Of course she was. "When we make love, it's gonna mean everything."

"I know. You told me that you wouldn't have sex with me unless we both loved each other." She looked up at him. "I think we both know where we stand even without saying the words. Now, close your eyes, think of something other than abusive assholes and slimy trolls who live under bridges who want information in order for you to pass, and sleep."

Her words soothed his soul in a way he'd never experienced before. He'd never met a woman more giving than his Jodelle. But Baker couldn't help chuckling. "Um...what? Trolls?"

"That's how I picture the people you deal with for your job."

She wasn't exactly wrong. "I'm not gonna be doing that forever," he said.

"Good."

That was it. One word.

Fuck, he loved this woman.

"You gonna be able to sleep?" he asked.

"You're home. You're holding me. Ben's here and safe. I've got a whole new group of potential friends and a big-paying job. Yeah, Baker, I'm gonna sleep just fine."

He smiled.

She lifted her head, and Baker lowered his. It was dark, but somehow he still managed to find her lips on the first try. He kissed her long, slow, and deep. It was lazy and intimate, and possibly the best kiss he'd ever had.

"Good night, Tink."

"Night, Baker," she replied and wiggled against him until she was comfortable.

He heard her deep breaths and felt them against his bare skin not even two minutes later.

If he was anywhere else, Baker might've stayed up long into the night thinking about everything he'd heard from Ben. Plotting and planning. But with Jodelle beside him, he was able to block all the shit swirling in his head and be thankful for what he had. Tomorrow was soon enough to plan Operation Take Down Al Rowden. For now, he was going to enjoy being in a soft bed with the scent of plumeria in his nose and the woman he loved in his arms.

# CHAPTER NINETEEN

Jody was a little worried about Baker. If she thought he was focused before, that was nothing compared to how he was now. Four days had passed since Ben had shared about his stepfather. Baker spent most of the daylight hours at his own house. The first morning, he'd warned her once again if Al showed up, not to open the door and to call him immediately.

Honestly, Jody hadn't wanted him to leave, but he'd said that he needed his computer. The one at his house. He mumbled something about his setup being more secure than hers, and how he needed to upgrade her internet connection.

When she'd asked if he was supposed to go to the Naval base to debrief, or whatever it was called, he'd just smiled and joked that there were these nifty things called phones. And video chats. Figuring Baker knew what he was doing, and it was unlikely he was going to get fired, she let it slide.

The topic of sex hadn't come up since the other night. He went with her to the beach when she watched her kids surf, but he seemed tense. Hyperalert. He'd surfed that first morning after he'd returned from his mission, but ever since then, he'd sat with her on the picnic table, held her hand, and kept watch.

He was tense. Very tense. Not that Jody could blame him. She desperately wanted to do something to help him relax, to take some of the burden he was obviously shouldering, but didn't know what. She wasn't a computer guru like he obviously was. And she definitely didn't have useful connections. All she could do was feed him and hold him tightly when they slept.

Tonight, when he returned to her house, Jody was determined to help him think about something other than what an asshole Al Rowden was.

"Where's Ben?" he asked as soon as he walked through the door.

Baker had skipped sitting at the beach with her that morning, saying he wasn't at a place where he could take a break and that he'd see her at home. Hearing him call her house "home" felt really good. And she figured that if Baker thought she was in danger, he'd never let her stay by herself during the day or sit at the beach without him, so she was able to go about her normal routine...albeit while worried about the stress Baker was under, and of course, worried for Ben as well.

"He's at Tressa's house. Her parents invited him over for dinner. I told him he had to be back by ten."

Baker nodded distractedly as he leaned in to kiss her lightly.

Jody clung to his T-shirt, not letting him go when he straightened and would've headed into the living room.

He raised an eyebrow, but immediately wrapped an arm around her.

"How'd today go?" she asked.

"That fucker's days are numbered," he said succinctly.

"What does that mean?" she asked. "You aren't secretly plotting with one of your contacts to make sure Al has some sort of "accident" are you?"

Baker frowned. "As much as that would please me, no. I

promised that I wouldn't do anything that would take me away from you, and that includes conspiring to commit murder. There's only a one percent chance anyone would be able to link that kind of shit back to me, but even one percent is too high of a risk because it would hurt you, and I gave you a promise."

"Baker," Jody whispered.

"His days being numbered means, I'm finding people who are more than willing to testify against him. People he fucked. Some who know they did wrong, feel bad about it, and want to clear their conscience. Others who got caught up in Rowden's schemes, didn't toe the line, and were hung out to dry by that asshole. There are also rumblings in legal circles that something isn't right with the good judge. I've planted some seeds, sprinkled a word here and there, and I'm setting into motion a full-scale investigation into Rowden. And of course, I've made some inquiries with a few people involved in the drug trade here on the island. Made it clear that it would be a good idea to deny Rowden the next time he comes calling with his dirty money."

"Holy shit," Jody breathed. "He's been doing what he's doing for a long time. Can you really end his whole empire of evilness in four days?"

"No." Then Baker smirked. "It might take a week."

Jody pressed herself against him and wrapped her arms around his neck. "Wow."

"Moving fast on this because I don't like that he made his play when I wasn't around. He underestimated you, and I doubt he'll do it again. He's regrouping and planning something, Ben and I agree on that, and I want his attention on other things—sooner rather than later."

"Smart," Jody said.

"Also, because Ben doesn't need that asswipe hanging over his head. He needs to be clear of him once and for all."

"And his mom?" Jody asked.

Baker sighed. "She's made her bed, she's gonna have to lie in it. If she's smart, she'll take this chance to get rid of him. If not..." Baker shrugged.

"That sucks for Ben."

"It does. But it seems to me he's come to terms with how his mom is. Hate that for him, but he's a smart young man. He'll be all right. Especially since he has you."

Jody stared up at Baker. When she got divorced, she felt free. Was relieved to be on her own with Kaimana. She couldn't regret her marriage, because it gave her Mana, but she'd had no intention of ever getting married again. And when her son died, it was as if a door had slammed shut around her heart. She hadn't been willing to risk ever getting close to someone again, it hurt too much. But somehow Baker had picked that lock. She was still scared of losing him, but she was even more terrified of him deciding she wasn't worth the effort.

She loved him. Period. With everything she had.

"We've got the house to ourselves for," Jody looked at the watch on her wrist, "the next four hours."

Baker's body tightened against hers. "Yeah?" he asked.

"Uh-huh. I've got beef stew in the Crockpot, but it could probably use another hour at least."

"So...you want to watch TV?" Baker asked.

She could see the twinkle in his eye. Still, she wanted to be as clear as possible. "No. I want you. In my bed. Naked. Inside me."

Baker's pupils dilated and he inhaled deeply.

"That is...if you're ready," Jody added, suddenly feeling a little shy. It was ridiculous. After all this time, after sleeping in his arms every night. After all the kisses, make-out sessions, and talk about sex, she should be more confident. In charge of what she wanted.

Without a word, Baker reached for her hand, spun around and headed for the hallway with Jody stumbling behind him.

But he didn't let her fall, he steadied her and kept walking.

Jody couldn't keep the smile from her face. It was hard to believe this was happening. That she and Baker were finally going to make love.

He pulled her to the edge of the bed and, without a word, lowered his head and began to kiss her. This was no slow, seductive kiss. It was hard and deep. And even as his tongue pushed into her mouth and twined with hers, his hands went to the clasp of the shorts she was wearing.

His impatience was contagious. Jody lifted the hem of his shirt. Baker's lips left hers long enough for her to pull the material over his head, then he picked back up where he'd left off. Jody moaned. It was hard to concentrate when she felt drunk off his kisses.

Her shorts fell to her ankles, and the cool air between her legs made her gasp and pull back. Looking down, she saw she was naked from the waist down. Baker had pushed her panties down with her shorts, and she hadn't even noticed. Even as she was still registering that surprising fact, he was pulling her own shirt up and over her head.

Not wanting to be the only one naked, Jody fumbled with his belt and cargo pants. Baker reached behind her, unhooked her bra, and it fell down her arms as she pushed the material of his pants down his legs. He shoved his boxers down impatiently, and as soon as he was naked, Baker wrapped an arm around Jody's waist and hauled her against him.

She gasped once more at the feel of his hard body, at the warm flesh against her own, and the sound was swallowed as Baker once again devoured her mouth. Jody's fingernails scored down his back as he put his hand on her ass and yanked her against his erection. She felt a smear of wetness against her belly—and then she was flying through the air.

Jody bounced on her back in the middle of the bed, and

then Baker was there. He hovered over her, breathing hard as his gaze raced over her body.

"Look at you. So fuckin' beautiful," he murmured.

Jody bit her lip, smiling up at him.

He brushed the backs of his fingers over her cheek. Then they continued over her collarbone, along the crest of her breast, where he paused for a moment to run his fingers around her nipple, making it harden. Then he scooted up onto his knees and continued his downward trail with his hand, caressing her belly, making Jody suck it in and laugh as his touch tickled her.

Baker smiled—then his gaze went between her legs. He shifted over her, putting his knees inside her legs and widening his stance, pushing her thighs outward.

Jody spread her legs, feeling only a little self-conscious. It was hard to feel anything but turned way the hell on, what with the way Baker was looking at her. As if she was the most beautiful thing he'd ever seen.

Not only that, but he was hard. *So* hard. His cock was long. Not overly thick, but longer than anyone she'd ever been with. The mushroomed head was a dark pink, the veins along the shaft standing out in sharp relief, and a drop of precome beaded at the tip even as she drank him in. Jody licked her lips in anticipation.

"Fucking hell," Baker said, before he suddenly scooted back farther and practically fell on top of her. His lips latched around her nipple, and Jody grunted even as she arched her back, trying to get closer. One hand went to the small of her back, encouraging her arch, and the other latched onto her other breast. Pinching and playing with the nipple as he worshiped the one in his mouth.

Jody whimpered as he sucked hard, not sure if what he was doing hurt because it was legitimately painful or because it just felt too damn good. A second later, when he released her nipple with a loud pop, she decided it felt good. Better than anything she'd experienced in a very long time. A hand went to his head and she gripped his hair in her fist, trying to force him back down to her chest.

He easily resisted her pull with a smirk. "You like that?"

"Of course," Jody said with a small eye roll. Then she leaned up and took one of *his* nipples into her mouth. It was his turn to groan. The hand at her back helped her stay where she was, in a half-sit, as she played and teased him.

She sucked hard, as he'd done to her, and was rewarded with a soft, "Holy fuck," from Baker.

She let go and lay back down with a satisfied smirk of her own. "You like that?" she purposely mimicked.

"Fuck, Tink," Baker said.

Jody took that as a yes. Then they were kissing. Ravenously. Their hands roamed, and Jody tore her mouth from his to inhale sharply when his hand slipped between her legs. His thumb found her clit without any fumbling and she rocked her hips toward him.

Without a word, Baker slid down her body. He kissed the underside of one breast, then her belly. Then he roughly pushed her legs farther apart and gazed down at her pussy.

Jody wasn't in the least embarrassed. This felt perfect. Natural. As if she'd waited forever to be right where she was. She shoved both hands into Baker's longish hair and smiled down at him.

He returned the grin, then lowered his head.

Jody immediately arched her back sharply and moaned.

Baker didn't tease. Didn't playfully lick her. He went straight to her clit, as if certain that's what she'd like. And why shouldn't he be so confident? He was fifty-two. The man obviously wasn't a virgin.

Jody suddenly remembered that he hadn't been with a woman in ten years. It seemed hard to believe, especially when he was so damn good at what he was doing. But she quickly forgot about anything other than how he was making her feel—which was on the verge after just seconds. One of his hands caressed her inner thigh, then played with her folds as he continued to lick and tease her clit.

Her belly tightened as she began to thrust her hips. She was going to come, and come hard. She would've been embarrassed about how fast he'd gotten her off, but this was Baker. Just looking at the man turned her on.

He hummed a growling moan, and the vibrations against her clit only ramped up her excitement. He had two fingers inside her now, and Jody was humping against his face and hand.

"Right there...more...I'm almost...!" She was babbling. But then she couldn't say *anything* as she went flying over the edge. Jody curled up into Baker, gripping his hair hard, holding him against her as she shook with the force of her orgasm.

He lifted his head, and the sight of his beard wet with her juices was both startling and a ferocious turn-on. He wiped his face on her thigh, even as he kept his fingers moving gently in and out of her body. He scooted up, and Jody couldn't do anything but pant and stare at him.

Baker's fingers finally left her body, and she sighed as she melted into the mattress. He scooted between her legs. The hand that had been inside her went to his cock as he stroked himself.

Suddenly feeling energetic, and wanting to return the amazing feelings he'd just given her, Jody sat up. She climbed to her knees, put a hand on Baker's chest, and pushed him backward. He fell to his back willingly and smiled as Jody crawled up his body.

"My turn," she said huskily.

"Don't make me come," Baker said. "I want to be inside you when that happens."

Jody shivered at that. This man was so sexy. Made *her* feel so sexy. "Okay," she told him, then lowered her head.

* * *

Baker inhaled sharply at the feel of Jodelle's tongue. He tightened his belly as she licked his abs, then proceeded to lick and kiss every one of the tattoos on his chest. It was as if she was seeing them for the first time ever, when she'd seen his chest bare countless times, including almost daily at the beach before they got together. But having her on her hands and knees above him, her nipples brushing against his skin, her seductive plumeria scent in his beard and on his tongue... it was almost too much.

"Stop teasing and suck me," he ordered.

In response, Jodelle's lips quirked upward and a hand snaked between them to wrap around his cock.

"I will," she said, even as she began to slowly slide her hand up and down his dick.

Baker couldn't talk. Her hand felt so good. So different from his own. Even though he'd gotten himself off at least once a day since he'd basically moved in with her, it felt as if it had been years since he'd come. Her touch was both torture and the most pleasurable thing he'd felt in his entire life.

Then he was gasping for air as she slid down and licked the head of his cock. Seeing her dark hair hanging around her shoulders, kissing his thighs and dick, the twinkle in her eyes, the rosy blush from her earlier orgasm on her chest, and that tongue of hers sticking out of her mouth as she licked him, Baker literally thought his heart was going to beat out of his chest.

"This is a bad idea," he muttered. He had no idea how he was going to keep from exploding.

"I think it's a great idea," Jodelle countered as her head lowered farther.

Baker literally held his breath as he watched. Her hand cradled his balls and the other gripped the base of his cock as she held him steady. He groaned deep in his throat when her warm mouth engulfed his dick.

"Holy fuck!" he swore as he shoved one hand in her hair. He didn't push her down. Didn't force her to take more of him. He just needed to hold onto something so he didn't shatter into a million pieces. And he couldn't think of anyone better to hold onto than Jodelle.

The next few minutes were literally torture as Jodelle sucked his cock. She really got into it, bobbing her head up and down, hollowing her cheeks, letting saliva ease her way. Baker knew he was leaking precome nonstop, but that didn't seem to faze the woman between his legs.

She rose on her knees to get a better angle to suck him, and Baker did his best to memorize every second of this moment. She wasn't shy. Wasn't reticent in the least. Her technique wasn't perfect or practiced, as if she'd done this to dozens of men, which just made him love her all the more. But it was obvious by her hungry moans that Jodelle enjoyed what she was doing. She wasn't blowing him out of obligation or just returning the favor after he'd eaten her out.

He endured the pleasure/pain as long as he could, until he couldn't stand it another second. His dick throbbed and his balls actually hurt before he tightened his hand in her hair. When she lifted her head to look at him in question, the thinnest strand of saliva connected her mouth to the mushroomed head of his cock. It was so damn sexy, he almost came right then and there.

Baker was done. He needed to be inside her. Right fucking now.

He sat up, keeping his hand in Jodelle's hair, and she fell to her back laughing. Baker had never been so glad that they'd had a talk about birth control one evening while cuddling in bed. She'd told him she was on the pill to regulate her cycle, and when he'd assured her that he'd still use a condom, she actually asked him not to because she was allergic to latex, which most condoms were made of.

If any other woman had told him that, first, Baker would've used any means necessary to confirm that story—up to and including hacking her medical records. Then he'd have gone out of his way to find latex-free condoms anyway. He didn't trust easily, and though he hadn't had sex in years, the last thing he'd wanted back then was a woman he didn't love getting pregnant with his child.

But this was Jodelle. He trusted her with everything in him.

Balancing himself on an elbow next to her head, he kept one hand in her hair so she had no choice but to keep her eyes on him. Baker used his other hand to make sure she was still wet and could take him without pain. The second his finger touched her clit, Jodelle jerked and widened her legs. He gently pushed his finger inside her, satisfied with how easily he was able to slide in and out.

"I'm ready," she told him.

"Want to make sure."

"Baker," she whined as he continued to finger fuck her.

He grinned. "Yeah?"

One of her own hands snuck between them and caressed his length.

"Shit, you don't fight fair," he breathed.

"Inside me. I'm ready. Make love to me," she ordered.

With that, Baker was done being noble. Done waiting. He'd searched his whole life for this woman, he wasn't going to wait a second longer. He gripped his cock at the base and brushed the head between her soaking-wet pussy lips, up and over her clit.

She whimpered and thrust her hips upward. On the next pass, Baker notched himself at her entrance and slowly began to push inside. He gritted his teeth, tightened his hold around his cock, doing everything in his power to hold back his orgasm.

It didn't help that Jody tightened her inner muscles and squeezed him as he entered.

He stopped. "Am I hurting you?"

"Noooooooo," she moaned. "More! Please!"

Baker did as she asked, pushing until his balls brushed against her ass and their pubic hair meshed together. Looking down, he couldn't see where he ended and she began.

"You feel so good," she whispered.

"Give me a second," he pleaded as he closed his eyes and did his best to cling to his control.

He felt Jodelle's hands caressing his chest, then sliding down his biceps before stopping there and holding on tight. Her legs came up and squeezed his hips as she crossed her feet at the ankles just above his ass. "You take as much time as you need," she said. "I'm good right where you are."

Baker opened his eyes and chuckled.

The movement made her moan. "Okay, I lied. I need you to move, Baker. Please!"

Seeing her need somehow made his own fade a bit. Baker wanted to please her more than he wanted to get off. He slid his hips back a fraction, then thrust inside her again.

That got him another moan.

He did it once more.

This time he got a squeak.

Before he knew what was happening, Baker was pounding in and out of Jodelle as if his life depended on it. Every time his balls hit her ass, they both groaned in ecstasy.

"Yes. More. Harder!"

Her tits bounced on her chest with every thrust, and Baker couldn't take his eyes off her. She was the most beautiful thing he'd ever seen. And she was his. All fucking *his*. No one else would see her like this ever again. No one else would feel her cunt squeezing their dick. No one else would hear the sounds she made as he took her.

Pleasing her was now Baker's sole purpose in life. He'd kill for the honor of making Jodelle his forever.

Feeling overwhelmed by his thoughts, Baker paused the next time he was all the way inside Jodelle and rolled them so she was on top. She blinked in surprise, bracing herself with her hands on his chest.

"Your turn," he told her.

She grinned and swiveled her hips. Then she arched her back and ground herself down on his cock. Tentatively, she rose a few inches, then dropped back down. "Oh, that feels good!" she said, almost as if surprised.

Baker had the thought that maybe she hadn't made love this way before, but forgot all about that when she began to fuck him in earnest. Her tits really bounced now, and he couldn't take his eyes from them. Jodelle's head fell back as she rode him, doing her best to chase her orgasm.

Baker wasn't getting the friction he needed to get off, but he didn't give a shit. He'd lay here and let her have her way for as long as she wanted. The view was hardly a turnoff.

When her hand snaked between her legs and she began to flick her clit, Baker knew he'd been premature in thinking he could lay there all night and not orgasm.

Then Jodelle stopped moving. Instead, she bore down as she got closer and closer to exploding, her fingers racing over her clit. Her inner muscles clenched around his cock so hard, Baker's eyes rolled back in his head. Fuck, she was magnificent.

Her muscles tightened, the fingernails on the hand braced on his chest dug into his skin, and she curled into him as she went over the edge once more. Baker could only watch in fascination and awe as she gave that to him. He could feel her pussy contracting madly around his cock, and her juices leaked out of her, soaking his balls.

When her eyes opened a fraction, she met his gaze head on. "Wow," she said.

"You're so damn beautiful," Baker told her.

She blushed.

He rolled them again, until she was on her back once more. Then Baker began to move. Slowly and gently. In and out. She was soaking wet and being inside her was like heaven. Baker came down to his elbows and buried his nose in the skin beneath her ear. He inhaled her scent as if he was a dying man and she was the oxygen he needed to live. Her own musky essence, along with plumeria, would forever be burned in his memory.

This was not fucking; this was making love to the woman Baker couldn't live without.

It didn't take long. Not with the memory of her taking her own pleasure as she sat on his cock fresh in his mind. When Jodelle leaned up and gently bit the lobe of his ear, Baker started coming immediately. He planted himself as far inside her as he could get and shuddered in her arms as his balls seemed to turn inside out.

Her breath whispered along the sensitive skin of Baker's ear as she held him tight and whispered how sexy she thought he was. How she couldn't believe he was hers. How he was the best thing that had ever happened to her.

When Baker felt as if he could breathe again, he lifted his head. His hands came up and cradled her face as he kissed her gently. His cock had finally gone soft, but because he was so long, he was still lodged deep within her body. It felt good. Right.

"Am I squishing you?" he asked.

Jodelle shook her head. "No."

"This uncomfortable?"

"No."

"Good. Because I'm not sure I can move."

She chuckled. "I think that's my line."

Baker caressed her eyebrow with his finger. "I love you," he said quietly.

Her eyes immediately filled with tears.

"I do. I'm not saying that because I'm overcome by your magic pussy, although I kind of am. I love you because you took in a teenager who needed someone to give a shit. I love you because you look out for the kids at the beach. I love you because you work hard, but still make time to enjoy life as best you can without your son. I love you because you refuse to let Mana fade into the background. I love you because of everything you are, Jodelle. I wasn't kidding when I told you I believed that souls reincarnate together. I've been trying to find you my entire life, without really knowing what I was looking for. I'm going to do everything in my power not to fuck this up."

"You can't mess up perfection," Jodelle said softly. "I love you too. I think I have for years. Since the first time I saw you come out of the ocean in your wet suit, your surfboard under your arm, looking all silver foxy and gorgeous. You smiled at me, making me feel as if I were the only person in the world in that moment."

Baker closed his eyes. He'd never forget this night. Ever. He'd treasure it. No one would fuck with what was his. He'd lived a life of hell...and in return, he'd been gifted Jodelle. He'd make sure not one day went by that she didn't know she was appreciated and loved.

"Not that I'm complaining, but are we going to spend the rest of the evening in bed? I mean, I like you here, but..." As soon as Jodelle finished speaking, her stomach growled.

Baker's lips twitched.

She returned his smile. "Sorry. I didn't eat much for lunch. I was working on that website and forgot to stop for food."

Baker nodded. He needed to get up and make sure his woman was fed. "This is just the start of us," he promised.

Jodelle didn't even blink. "No, it's not."

Baker frowned.

"The start of us was when you refused to leave my house because Ben was here and you wanted to make sure I was safe," she said. "And for the record...I'm glad you didn't insist we go to your place. I like my house. I know it's small, but it's mine. I paid off my mortgage last year. And this is where Mana was."

"I'll put mine on the market," Baker said without hesitation.

Jodelle looked surprised. "I didn't mean..." Her voice faded.

"What *did* you mean then?" he asked.

"Well...I *want* to say that I don't care where we live, as long as I've got you by my side, but that isn't true. I know Mana's gone. I know material things don't mean much and that memories are what's important, but I'm not sure I can give up this house."

"And I'd never ask you to. You have a problem with me being here?"

"No," Jodelle said with a shake of her head.

"Then I'll sell my house and we'll live here. Because I can't give up *you*."

She smiled. "Okay."

Fuck, Baker loved this woman. "Have to admit..." he said, not finishing his thought.

"Yes?" Jodelle asked.

"I don't really want to move at the moment. I like where I am."

Jodelle's grin widened, and she shifted a bit under him. "I like where you are too. And where I am. But I'm thinking if we stayed here, we might starve to death. Then Ben would come home and see your butt."

Baker burst out laughing. Hard enough that his cock finally slipped out of the warm, safe haven it had found.

"Damn," he said, still chuckling.

Jodelle laughed with him.

"For what it's worth, don't care if Ben sees my ass. As long as *you're* covered."

"You're sweet," Jodelle declared.

Baker shook his head. "No, I'm not."

"You are to me."

"That's true. You want to shower together?"

"Yes."

Again, no hesitation and not coy in the least. Baker liked that a hell of a lot. "You always going to be this agreeable?" he couldn't help but ask.

"No," she told him. "You'll know if I'm upset, and I'm sure I'll give in and tell you why without you ever having to dig. I get moody, Baker. You haven't seen it yet because of everything that's going on, but I do. Mana's birthday is always hard for me, and I'm not a huge fan of Christmas."

"We'll do something special to honor his birthday. And we can travel for Christmas if you want," Baker told her.

Jodelle shook her head. "You're too good to me."

"No such thing."

"Are you going to let me spoil you too?" she asked.

"You already do. Come on. We need to get up, get showered, eat dinner, and try to appear respectable when Ben gets home, so you don't get embarrassed when he takes one look at you and knows what we've been doing."

"Do you think he will?"

"Tink, you're fuckin' glowing. If he doesn't, he's pretty damn stupid."

"Ben's not stupid," Jodelle complained.

Baker raised an eyebrow at her.

"Right. So, we need to get up, you need to stop being so darn sexy, and you need to help me figure out how to stop glowing so I don't get embarrassed when Ben comes home."

Baker burst out laughing again. He couldn't remember when he'd laughed so much. When he'd arrived earlier, he'd been in a pretty dark place. He'd spent the day bargaining with drug dealers, which was risky at the best of times, and calling in a couple of the favors he'd spent a lifetime collecting. But he'd do anything for Jodelle, and getting an asshole like Rowden off the streets and no longer preying on the young kids in the area was worth every lost marker.

"Come on," he said, rolling to sit up on the side of the bed. "Shower, food, then relaxing until curfew."

"Baker?" Jodelle said, putting her hand on his back.

"Yeah?"

"Love you."

Baker's throat got tight. He didn't think he'd ever get tired of hearing that. "Love you too." Then he stood, held out his hand, and sighed in contentment when the woman he loved took it and let him help her off the bed. They walked hand in hand, butt-ass naked to the bathroom, and nothing had ever felt more natural in his life.

# CHAPTER TWENTY

Jody's life felt as if it were moving a million miles an hour lately. Having Ben around was one of the best things that had happened to her in the last five years, but it also meant she was busier. Trips to the grocery store were more frequent, she helped him with his homework when he got stuck, and yesterday, he'd asked if she would teach him how to cook, a task that Jody was looking forward to undertaking.

Then there was Baker. She was worried about how intensely he was working to take down Al Rowden so he could keep them safe. She was doing her best to be there for him and make his evening hours as stress-free as possible. Her favorite time of the day was when she and Baker went to bed. He held her tightly, as if trying to protect her even in his sleep. They hadn't made love again, but he touched her much more openly and freely since their sex a few nights ago, and she always caught him staring at her with a tender and longing look in his eyes.

She was also still working on her own job, still making sandwiches and snacks for her surf kids, still group chatting with her new friends. It was a lot, but Jody had never been happier.

Yesterday, Kenna had texted everyone to try to pin down a date for the next sleepover. With everything going on, Jody wasn't comfortable leaving. Baker hadn't tried to pressure her either way, had just said, "Do what feels right."

So she'd told the group that she wasn't going to be able to get away right now, but she definitely *did* want to get together with them in the near future, when her life settled down a bit. That had set off a flurry of concerned messages, which touched Jody deeply. It had been a long time since people worried about her like these women seemed to. And she hadn't even met half of them.

Currently, she was standing in the kitchen waiting for Ben to get home from school. She'd just finished making snacks for the kids for tomorrow morning, and Baker had just returned from his own house. He was working extremely hard on both the Rowden thing and the projects he had going on with the government. Jody had just explained that she'd declined the sleepover and was hopeful she'd feel more comfortable going to the next one.

He pulled her into his arms. "Gotta say, I'm not all that upset. I would've missed you something fierce if you went. I'm used to holding you at night. That week I was gone sucked, but at least I was busy. Sleeping in your bed without you next to me wouldn't feel right."

Jody squeezed him tight. "How do you think I felt? But the sleepovers are only one night."

"I'm fifty-two, don't have unlimited nights left, Tink."

Jody rolled her eyes. Baker was being overly dramatic. She pulled back and put a hand on his cheek. "You're a badass former SEAL, and you traipse around the world hobnobbing with bad guys. I think you'll be able to handle one night without me."

Baker leaned his face into her hand for a moment, before turning and kissing her palm. "We're gonna need to get creative," he said.

"Creative?" Jody asked with a frown.

"I like Ben a lot. Have no problem with him being around. But at night, when I want to make love to my woman, don't want you being embarrassed if he hears us."

Jody blushed. Yeah, she didn't want that either. "Well, he *is* at school all day," she said with a shrug.

Baker's eyes glinted. "I can work with that," he told her.

Jody definitely could work with daytime nookie with Baker. She smiled up at him.

"Fuck. Now I want to drag you to bed."

"Ben's gonna be home any minute now," she said regretfully.

Baker nodded. "Yeah." He leaned down and kissed her forehead. Then his lips covered hers, and he kissed her deep.

Jody loved him so much. He was a good man. Yeah, he could be overly intense sometimes, but she wouldn't take him any other way. "Did Ben tell you what his plans were tonight?" Jody asked. "It's Friday, so I'm guessing he'll be doing something with Tressa."

"I'm not in charge of his social calendar, Tink," Baker said with a smirk.

"I know, but I thought maybe he would've said something to you."

"He didn't. But he'll be home soon and you can ask him." As Baker studied her, Jody did her best to not let any worry show on her face. But of course he saw it anyway. "What's wrong?"

"Nothing."

"Tink, talk to me."

"I just don't want to say or do the wrong thing. I'm not his mother, I know that. But I also don't want him staying out all night or getting in with the wrong crowd at school. I realize this is his senior year, and he'll be gone soon, but still. I also want to talk to him about what he's planning on doing after he graduates, but again, I don't want to overstep. Even giving him a curfew feels weird. I mean, he's been cool about it, but tonight's Friday, he's probably going to want to stay out late, but nothing good happens after midnight. And then there's his stepdad. Who knows what *he's* planning. I just don't want Ben to resent me."

Baker took her face in his hands and said, "Breathe, Tink."

Jody took a deep breath.

"First off, Ben's not stupid," he said. "He knows he's lucky as fuck to have landed here. He's not gonna do anything to screw that up. Second, he's a good kid. I don't know how; it wasn't as if he had much guidance from his mom or that asshole Rowden. He was strong enough to know he needed to stop breaking into cars and walk the straight and narrow. He's not gonna stay out too late and worry you."

Jody grabbed hold of Baker's wrists and nodded. "I love you."

His face gentled. "And I love you. Ben's lucky as hell that he's got someone like you on his side. You want to talk about his plans after graduation, do it. He'll probably be glad someone's interested."

"I like Tressa," Jody said softly. "I think Ben really does too."

"I agree."

"He's learning how to treat a woman with care by watching you," Jody told him.

Baker blinked, and it was obvious how much her words meant to him.

"You're a wonderful role model for him," Jody said.

"Took me way too fucking long to find you," Baker growled.

Jody frowned in confusion. "What?"

"Wish I would'a found you sooner. The amount of time I got left in this world isn't nearly enough to spend by your side."

"Baker," Jody whispered, touched.

"If Ben learns to grab hold of what he wants...to treat his woman as if she's the most important thing in his life...then I'm all right with being his role model."

Jody leaned forward and he dropped his hands from her face. She rested her forehead on his chest as she wrapped her arms around him. "Now I'm going to cry," she mumbled.

"If you're crying when Ben walks in here, he's gonna worry," Baker said with a laugh.

"Then you need to stop being so nice. I can't handle it."

"Bullshit. You're gonna have to learn to deal with it because nice is all you're gonna get from me for the rest of your life."

Jody sniffed again. "See? There you go again."

Baker laughed a little harder now. "Come on, Tink. Dry your eyes. Ben'll be home soon, then you can badger him into doing his homework tonight instead of waiting until Sunday —which is crazy, but if that's what you want to do, knock yourself out. Then you two can decide what we're having for dinner and you can teach him how to cook it. I'm guessing you're right, that he'll want to spend the evening with Tressa. Maybe tell him his curfew is midnight...that'll give us time to be alone for a few hours."

Jody looked up at him and took a deep breath. "What if he wants to bring Tressa here?" she asked.

"Then we'll have a quiet evening getting to know her better, and we'll go to bed after Ben gets back from seeing her home."

"You won't be upset that we can't...you know?"

"I'm not with you because of sex, Jodelle. I like being with *you*. Sitting quietly on the couch, watching you putter around the kitchen, seeing you create magic on your computer, hanging out with you on the beach while you keep an eye on your kids. When the time's right, we'll make love again, and we'll both enjoy the hell out of it. But I don't need sex to love you. I just do."

"Right answer," Jody whispered.

They both heard the door open a split second before Ben called out, "Hey!"

Jody turned in Baker's arms and smiled at Ben. "Hey, how was school?"

"Everything all right?" he asked, instead of answering her question. "Has Al done something else?"

"No! We're good. Everything's fine," Jody said quickly.

"Then why do you look like you've been crying?" Ben asked with a scowl.

"Because Baker's being nice," she informed him.

The boy looked confused. "You're crying because Baker's being nice," he repeated.

"Yeah."

"Tip: don't try to figure out the mind of a woman," Baker told Ben.

"Right. So...you're good?" the teenager asked, not taking his eyes from Jody.

"I'm good, Ben. Promise."

"Okay."

"You have much homework?" she asked, pulling out of Baker's arms but loving that he kept a hand on the small of her back.

"He just walked in the door, Tink. Give him a second to breathe," Baker scolded.

"He'll have a better weekend if he does his homework now. Then come Sunday, he can relax and not worry about it."

"Or he can relax now, knowing he doesn't have to do any school work *tonight*," Baker retorted. "That he's got the next two days off from that shit."

"I don't have much, Miss Jody," Ben said with a small grin. "I'll get it done after dinner. If it's okay, I'm gonna hang out with Tressa tonight."

"Of course it's okay. What are your plans?" Jody asked.

"Not sure. We didn't get a chance to talk about it much today. I'll text her later and we'll figure it out."

"You're welcome to come back here," she told him.

"Thanks. But I'm sure you're sick of having me around. You and Baker probably want to be alone. We'll go to a movie or something."

"I'll never get sick of having you around," Jody told him gently. "I know my house isn't all that big, and there's not much privacy to talk with Tressa, but you'll *always* be welcome to bring her here."

"Thanks," Ben said quietly. "I'm gonna go change."

Jody nodded at him.

He turned around when he got to the hallway and said, "This house is the perfect size. It's nice that we can't go days without seeing each other, that there aren't rooms that are off-limits." Without waiting for a response, Ben headed for his room.

Jody took a deep breath and stared down at the countertop. She felt Baker come up behind her. "I really don't like his mom and stepdad," she said in a low voice so Ben wouldn't overhear.

"Me either," he said as he rested his chin on her shoulder.

Jody struggled to regain the mellow feeling from minutes ago. When she had herself together, she asked, "Pork chops or parmesan chicken tonight?"

Baker kissed her temple and said, "Chops."

"Ben!" Jody yelled.

"Yeah, Miss Jody?" she heard him say from inside his room.

"Get a move on! We're having pork chops and you want to learn how to cook. Tonight's as good a time to start as any."

"Be there in a sec!" Ben yelled.

"You want to learn how to make pork chops with us?" Jody asked Baker.

"Fuck no. But I *do* want to watch my woman impart her knowledge to a kid who's starved for motherly love. So I'll sit at the table with my laptop and observe."

"You gonna set up a meet-and-greet with rival terrorists in order to prevent World War Three while we cook?" Jody asked.

She felt his chest rumble with a laugh against her back. "Did that yesterday," he joked. "Tonight, I'm moderating a meeting with the president and Chinese leaders about global warming."

Jody turned and stared at him, not sure if she should believe him or not.

Baker burst into laughter. "Kidding, Tink. Jeez."

"I truly wouldn't be surprised if that was on your agenda, Baker. You're kind of amazing."

He shook his head. "Love you, woman. So damn much."

"I love you too."

"Okay, I'm ready!" Ben said as he entered the room wearing a different pair of jeans than he had on a minute ago and a blue polo shirt. The color brought out the blue in his hazel eyes, and he'd also brushed his hair. If Jody wasn't mistaken, he'd even put on some cologne, or at least used some of the body spray she'd seen on the counter in his bathroom. He was definitely gussied up to meet with Tressa later.

Jody did her best to hide her smile and said, "All right, get in here and we'll get these chops started."

\* \* \*

Two hours later, Baker hid a grin as he observed Jodelle "helping" Ben with his homework. It was obvious the kid didn't require assistance, but it was just as obvious that he wanted Jodelle to feel needed.

Dinner was delicious, and Ben was proud that his first attempt at cooking had turned out so well. It was mostly because Jodelle hovered, making sure he did things exactly right, but Baker had a feeling Ben would retain everything she'd taught him tonight. The kid soaked up her attention like a sponge.

They were discussing his government assignment when Ben's phone vibrated. The teenager glanced down at it—and every muscle in his body coiled. He stood abruptly, his chair crashing to the floor behind him. He rushed to his room and was back within seconds, car keys in hand.

Baker and Jodelle had quickly stood as well, and now Baker went to the boy, grabbing his arm, preventing him from rushing out of the house. "What's wrong?"

"I need to go," Ben said between clenched teeth.

"Talk to me," Baker ordered.

"Let me go," Ben cried, trying to jerk his arm out of Baker's hold, but he didn't relent.

"Not until you tell me what the fuck's going on," he demanded.

Looking into Ben's eyes, Baker saw anger—and unadulterated fear. Whatever message he'd received, it was bad.

"He's got Tressa!"

"What? Who does?" Jodelle asked.

But Baker didn't need to ask. He knew. Rowden was making his next move.

Baker held out his hand for Ben's phone. Their eyes met, and even in the middle of whatever crisis was happening, it felt good when Ben trusted him enough to unlock his cell and hand it over.

Baker didn't let go of Ben, not wanting him to rush out of the house as he read the text the boy had just received.

ROME

> Hey man, thought you'd want to know. I
> heard from Lani, who heard from one of her
> friends who's close to Tressa, that they're all
> at your house for the big party tonight.
> Apparently, she thought you'd be there.

"Rowden's having one of his parties tonight?" Baker asked.

Ben nodded. "Yeah. Everyone was talking about it at school. I didn't discuss it with Tressa because I didn't want her anywhere near there."

"You think Rowden knows you and Tressa are dating?" Baker asked.

"I'm sure he does. Alex Flores is one of his most loyal minions. We used to be close, but when I stopped breaking into cars, he decided I was a pussy and now he hates me. Feeling's mutual too. Anyway, I'm sure he set this up. Tressa can't get involved with this shit, Baker!" Ben said in a low, desperate voice.

"She won't. Text her. Right now. Tell her you're on your way to pick her up," Baker said, handing his phone back.

"If she's in the basement, where the parties usually are, the message won't go through. Al's got some sort of jammer or something. He wants everyone concentrating on getting wasted, not worrying about what he's doing with some of the kids in the garage attached to the house. That's where he teaches them how to break into cars," Ben said.

Baker let go of Ben and walked to the glass bowl on the counter. He grabbed his keys and held them out to the boy. "Go start my car. I'll be there in a second. Do *not* leave without me, or I'm gonna be pissed. And I'm already pissed. You don't want me even angrier."

Ben nodded once, took the keys, and headed for the door.

"Baker, what're you doing?" Jodelle asked.

He returned to her and put his hands on her face. As

usual, she grabbed his wrists. Her eyes were big in her face and she looked worried as fuck.

"You heard. Tressa's at Rowden's. He's having one of his parties. We need to get her out of there."

In the blink of an eye, the worry in Jodelle's expression turned to anger. "He's trying to get back at Ben for leaving by recruiting his girlfriend. What a *dick*! Go get her, Baker. Make sure she's safe. And please try to keep Ben from murdering his stepfather. I don't want to have to visit him in the penitentiary for the next forty years."

Baker wanted to chuckle at her words, but he was way too fucking pissed. "Depending on what condition she's in—not sure if someone will have convinced her to take some MDMA or not—we might not come straight home."

"You'll do whatever you need to do."

Baker tilted his head. "You aren't upset that I might not bring them both right back here?"

"No. I trust you."

Those three little words sank into Baker's psyche and warmed him from the inside out. "You trust me?" he asked.

"Yes. I just said that."

"No, Tink. You *trust* me?"

She stared up at him.

"You told me that's what you think you're supposed to learn in this life."

"Yeah," she said quietly.

"Kills me that we aren't gonna get our quiet night, but I swear you'll never regret trusting me," Baker said.

"I know. Now, I'm thinking you probably need to get out there and go get Tressa, before Ben gets impatient and decides to risk your wrath and leave without you."

"Right. Jodelle?"

"Yeah?"

"He's gonna pay. Hate that he made this play now, when in

a few days he'll be way too fuckin' busy to mess with his step-son. But that asshole's done for. *Soon*."

"Good. Go, Baker. Call or text me when you can to let me know what's going on."

"I will. Lock the door, don't leave the house. Okay?"

"Okay."

Baker tilted her face up, kissed her briefly but with all the love he had in his heart, then turned and headed for the door.

* * *

Ten minutes later, Baker pulled up behind a long line of cars on the street in front of Rowden's house. It was in a nice neighborhood, each property at least five acres, giving enough space and room for Rowden to throw his parties without the neighbors getting too upset over noise or a street packed with cars. Ben had described the layout of the house while they drove. Five bedrooms, huge basement that was more like a bunker. Two garages, one at the front of the house, and a larger one in the back, where Rowden taught kids how to break into cars.

Baker turned to Ben. "Wait here."

"No fucking way," Ben said. "I'm coming with you."

"No, you aren't," he told him. "Look, I know you want to get to your girl, but I don't want you to step foot on this property. Rowden knew you'd come for Tressa. Was planning on it. I don't want him blackmailing you into staying. No offense, Ben, but if you go in there, make a scene and possibly throw some punches, he'll have more shit to use against you."

Ben's nostrils flared and it didn't look like he was ready to agree. The only thing on his mind was getting to Tressa. Baker could respect that, but he also needed to be smart.

"He'll probably use your mom to get to you if using Tressa doesn't work," Baker said. "Maybe some sob story about how she's not doing well. Or he'll tell you he's gonna have her committed again. He'll use her against you, and neither of you need that. Trust me to get your girl out, Ben."

"What if he tries to blackmail *you?*" Ben asked.

Fuck, he really was a good kid. Worried about everyone other than himself. "Not gonna happen. You think I'd leave you *or* Jodelle vulnerable? No fuckin' way. He's screwed, Ben. I just need a few more days to pull the trigger. Now trust me to get Tressa out for you."

Ben turned and looked at him. The anguish in his eyes was painful to witness. "All right, Baker."

Without wasting another second, he nodded, more relieved than he could say that Ben was trusting him with this. "Stay here. I'll send her out to you."

Baker had met Tressa once, when she'd come to the beach to watch Ben surf, but he wasn't sure she'd recognize him tonight. It was dark, she'd probably be confused about why Ben wasn't at the house when someone had told her he would be, and she might be scared. Or even drugged. But all that mattered was getting her out and to Ben. She'd be all right once she saw him.

Baker climbed out of the car and headed up the long driveway toward the front door. He considered doing recon of the house and property, but that would take too much time. If someone had slipped Tressa some MDMA or taken advantage of the fact she was there without Ben, he didn't have any time to lose.

Walking right up to the front door, Baker pressed his finger on the doorbell. He didn't let up either. He leaned on it, hoping the obnoxious tones of the bell would bring someone to the door, stat.

Within seconds, the door was wrenched open by a kid who looked to be around fourteen or fifteen.

"Fuck, give me a chance to open the door already!" the kid bitched. Then he looked up and saw Baker, and swallowed. Hard.

"Go get Tressa."

"Um, who?"

"Tressa Dixon. Long black hair, around five-three. She's fuckin' gorgeous. I know you didn't miss her."

"Oh, her," the boy said. "All right. Uh...I'll go and find her," he said as he began to shut the door.

Baker put a palm on the door and shoved it open. The kid looked startled and took a step back. "Hey, you can't do that!"

"I just did. Go fuckin' get Tressa. You've got about three seconds before I lose my temper."

The kid scurried away just as a deep voice asked, "I'm sorry, who are you?"

Baker looked up and saw Al Rowden in the flesh for the first time...and wasn't impressed. He wore designer clothes that screamed he was trying too hard to be cool. His hairline was receding and it was obvious he dyed his hair, trying to look younger than he was; the gray roots needed touching up. He was about twenty pounds overweight and carried it well.

But it was the look of contempt in his eyes that Baker picked up on immediately.

"I'm here for Tressa," he said without answering his question.

"Again, I'll ask who you are. It's not safe to let my son's guests go off with just anyone who comes to the door."

"But it's safe for them to be in your basement with drugs and alcohol being freely provided?" Baker countered. He couldn't show his hand too soon, but he so badly wanted to call the man out for all the ways he was corrupting these kids.

"I've got security," Rowden said, looking up at a camera focused on the door.

"Yeah, I know," Baker said. He'd already had a friend hack into the system, and he had plenty of video evidence of this asshole happily inviting teenagers into his home last week-end, and those same kids leaving, drunk or high off their asses, at o-dark-thirty in the morning.

Rowden's eyes narrowed. "If you don't tell me who you are, I'm calling the cops."

The last thing Baker wanted was the police interfering in his plan. There were some on the force who were in Rowden's pocket. They were going to go down along with this fucker, but Baker didn't have time to deal with that bullshit right now.

"Name's Baker Rawlins," he said.

No recognition flared in Rowden's eyes. "I don't know you," he said after a moment.

"Nope. But I know *you*," Baker said, not able to help himself.

A noise from behind Rowden made him turn, and Baker saw Tressa being escorted toward the door. There were two girls behind her, obviously just snooping for gossip. Tressa looked confused and nervous about who could possibly be at the door asking for her. When she saw him, her eyes widened.

"Mr. Baker!"

"Time to go, Tressa," he said.

"Holy shit, he's a total DILF!" one of the other girls stage-whispered.

Rowden had the nerve to hold out his arm, blocking Tressa's path to the door. "Not so fast," he said.

But Baker was done. "Come on, Tressa," he said in a low, hard tone.

She immediately obeyed, scooting around Rowden's arm until she was standing on the front porch with Baker.

"My car's the black one, last in line. Ben'll meet you there," he said.

Her eyes lit up in relief. "Ben's here?"

When Baker nodded, she visibly relaxed. Yeah, she hadn't enjoyed being here and was more than willing to leave. She ran off the porch without hesitation.

Baker was glad that it didn't seem as if she'd taken any

drugs either. Her pupils were normal size and she didn't seem jumpy, which was another good sign. She was wary and a little skittish, but that was to be expected after coming to a large party hoping to find Ben, then learning he wasn't there.

"My son is here?" Rowden asked, looking around Baker, as if he might be able to see through the darkness.

"Ben is *not* your son," he said, taking a step back. What he really wanted to do was punch this asshole, but then Rowden would definitely call his cronies on the police force and Baker would have to deal with that bullshit, and it might delay Rowden's fiery takedown. Not to mention, it would worry Jodelle, and that was the last thing he wanted to do right now. She didn't need the added stress on her shoulders.

"I'm married to his mother," Rowden barked arrogantly.

"Which doesn't mean shit. Speaking of which, where's Emma?" Baker asked.

"She's sleeping," Rowden said snidely.

"Right. Because there's a huge fuckin' party in her house and she's able to sleep. Of course. I should've known."

He needed to get Ben and Tressa out of there. But it was literally torture to leave knowing there were other kids in the house who shouldn't be. Who Rowden was corrupting. Unfortunately, Baker had learned a long time ago that he couldn't save everyone, as much as that sucked. And right now, his focus was on Ben, Tressa, and Jodelle.

"You fucked up," Rowden growled. "I'm gonna find out everything there is to know about you, Baker Rawlins, and you're gonna wish you hadn't fucking messed with me."

He couldn't help but laugh. First of all, this pissant wouldn't find shit on him. Nothing that he didn't want found. His life was locked up tight, unlike this asshole's. Once he knew exactly what to look for, it wasn't much of a challenge to find all the skeletons in his closets...and they were all stuffed with them. He was going down. Hard.

"Have at it," Baker said as he turned his back and headed down the walkway.

"You're gonna regret this!" Rowden shouted, outraged.

Baker merely lifted his hand and raised his middle finger as he walked away. He heard the door slam behind him and picked up his pace to a jog as he headed for his car.

Ben was outside the vehicle, holding Tressa. He cradled her face in his hands, like he'd seen Baker holding Jodelle more than once. They were talking quietly, and as much as Baker wanted to give them space, he needed to get them out of this neighborhood and somewhere safe.

"Inside, Ben. We need to go."

"He coming after us?" Ben asked, turning so Tressa was tight to his side, his arm around her shoulders.

"No. But that doesn't mean we should hang around."

"Right," Ben said. He opened the back door, helped Tressa inside, and climbed in after her.

Baker's lips twitched. He never would've seen the day he'd be playing chauffeur to a couple of teenagers, but he honestly didn't mind. He got behind the wheel and pulled out, vowing that the next time he was at this house, it would be to watch Al Rowden being led away in handcuffs.

Ben and Tressa spoke quietly in the back seat, but Baker tuned them out. He drove to the parking area of Sunset Beach and cut the engine.

"Baker?" Ben asked in confusion.

"There's nothing that clears the mind better than a walk in the sand and feeling the ocean spray on your face. Take Tressa for a walk, Ben. *Talk* to her." Baker wasn't sure if Ben would tell his girl everything that was going on, but she needed to know why it wasn't a good idea to go to his house ever again.

"Right. Thanks."

"I'll stay here," Baker said. "Take as much time as you want. I'm not going anywhere."

"Miss Jody?" Ben asked.

For the hundredth time, Baker was reminded of this kid's good heart. "I'll call her. She'll be fine."

Ben nodded. He obviously wasn't ready to smile yet.

"We'll take Tressa home when you're ready," Baker said.

"Thanks, Mr. Baker," Tressa said quietly.

"It's just Baker," he told her.

She nodded.

The kids got out and stepped toward the beach. Ben paused in front of the car and crouched in front of Tressa, mostly out of Baker's view. When he stood, he placed her sandals on the hood of the car. Then he took off his own shoes, placing them beside Tressa's, before grabbing her hand. They headed toward the surf.

The beach wasn't deserted, but it definitely wasn't as busy as during the day. It was also dark, but there were enough lights from houses along the shore that Baker was confident the teenagers would be all right. Ben would make sure nothing happened to Tressa.

Baker exited his car, took his phone out of his pocket, and clicked on Jodelle's name.

"Is she all right?" she asked in lieu of a greeting.

He had a feeling she'd been pacing the house and worried sick the entire time they were gone. She might trust him, but that didn't mean she didn't worry. "She's fine."

He heard her sigh in relief. "And Al? Is he still alive?"

Baker snorted. "Yeah, Tink."

"Was it bad?" she asked.

"Yes and no. The kid who answered the door luckily didn't give me shit and immediately went to find Tressa. Rowden showed up. We had some words, then we left."

"I think you're leaving some things out, Baker," she accused.

"Asshole threatened me," he told her with a chuckle.

"What? That's not funny in the least!" Jodelle complained.

"It's fuckin' hilarious," he countered. "He thinks he can use his connections to get dirt on me. First of all, he's not gonna find anything. Second of all, he's not gonna have time to even start those wheels turning before he's busted."

"Right. Where are you now? Are you coming home?"

"I took Ben and his girl to the beach. They're walking and talking. I'm staying here until they get back. I want to make sure they're both good before we drop her off and come home."

"All right."

"You upset we aren't coming home immediately?" Baker asked.

"No. You're with them. They're safe. It'll probably be good for you and Ben to have some time alone after you take Tressa home. You can talk to him, reassure him that you have everything under control. I'm sure he's kind of freaked out but doesn't want to act like it in front of his girlfriend. I also don't want him getting any crazy ideas in his head about retaliation. So yeah, I'm okay with you being gone a little longer."

Baker lowered his head, eyes on the sand under his feet in the parking lot. He was leaning against the driver's-side door, had been prepared to have to convince Jodelle that Ben needed this time alone with Tressa. But he should've known better.

"That said, if he continues to fuck with Ben, he's gonna have *me* to deal with," Jodelle seethed.

"Wrong," Baker said, standing up straight once more.

"Baker, seriously, using a sixteen-year-old girl to try to get back at Ben, or try to control him, is just messed up!"

"It is," he agreed. "But you aren't going anywhere near that motherfucker."

"I can't promise not to do anything crazy. I lost Mana. I'm *not* losing Ben."

It took Baker a second to absorb that blow. No matter how much he loved her, no matter how happy he made her, he'd never be able to bring back her son. "And I can't lose *you*, Jodelle. It would literally rip me apart. I'd never recover. I need you to be safe."

"And I need the people I love not to be blackmailed or forced to do things they don't want to do, like break into cars, do drugs, and become horrible, awful people. He had his chance with Ben, as did his mother. They failed, so I'm stepping in! However I need to do that."

"Fuck," Baker swore.

Jodelle sighed. Then, to his shock, he heard her giggle. "How about this—I promise to keep you informed if I plan on doing anything crazy. That way, you can come bail me out if I need it."

"How about you inform me if you plan on doing something crazy, and you let me talk you out of it, and I take care of whatever's bothering you instead?"

"I'm not weak," Jodelle said.

Baker frowned. "I didn't say you were."

"I don't need taking care of."

"No, you don't. We should probably have this conversation face-to-face, but since you brought it up—in no way, shape, or form do I think you're weak. In fact, you're one of the strongest women I've ever met. More so than even Elodie and the others. Yes, they went through seriously bad shit, and I'm proud that they came out the other side because of their inner fortitude and a fuck-ton of luck. But you, Jodelle... you've taken some blows that would bring most people to their knees permanently, and you kept going. Not only that, but you *did* something when Ben needed help the most. Most people would've felt bad but kept on with their lives, not willing to get involved. You not only got involved, you invited him to live in Mana's room, sharing yourself and the huge amount of love you've got inside you.

"Having him there, in Mana's room, the same age your son was when he was taken from you, hearing him talk about his friends, watching him surf the same waters that took Mana...that's *strength*, Tink. But you aren't bulletproof. I told you once that my shit doesn't leak onto you, and I meant that."

"Al Rowden isn't your shit," Jodelle said quietly.

"Yes, he is. Because I'm *making* him my shit," Baker countered.

Another sigh. "Baker?"

"Yeah, Tink?"

"Once this is all done, I'd really like to get back to my boring life. You know, working on graphics, watching surfers, and having the worst thing to happen being the occasional burnt dinner."

"That sounds awesome," Baker said.

"Will you text when you're on your way home?"

"Yeah, Tink. I can do that."

"And tell Tressa I'm glad she's okay."

"Right."

"And let Ben know his curfew is suspended as long as he's with you."

Baker chuckled. "You okay with me keeping him out until two?"

"Um..."

"Right. Didn't think so. We'll be home well before midnight."

"All right."

"Gonna let you go," Baker said. "Try to relax. Ben's good. Tressa's fine. This shit'll be over soon."

"Okay. Love you, Baker."

"Love you too."

"Baker?"

"Yeah?"

"I'm thinking Ben might want to see Tressa tomorrow. You know, to make sure she's all right after everything that happened tonight. And if that's the case, and since I usually take Saturdays off and all...I thought if you weren't too deep in your plans for Al Rowden's downfall...we could maybe spend some quality time together."

"If you're talking about making love, fuck yes," he growled.

"Great. It's a date."

Baker's heart swelled. "Yeah, Tink. It is."

"Okay. Be safe. It's dark. And the later it gets, the more drunk drivers there'll be on the roads."

"Right."

"See you soon."

"Yes, you will," Baker agreed. "Make sure the door's locked."

"It is."

"Double check it," Baker pushed.

"Fine. I will."

"Love you."

"Love you too. Bye."

"Bye."

Baker pocketed his phone and stared off toward the ocean. He could just see the white foam from the waves crashing on the shore. He needed to send a few messages to make sure things were still moving smoothly, but that would have to wait until he could get to his computer and access the dark web and the untraceable communication network he'd built.

Rowden's charmed life was coming to an end—and Baker couldn't fucking wait.

# CHAPTER TWENTY-ONE

Jody sat on what she thought of as *her* picnic table at the beach on Monday morning and watched her kids surf. Ben was out there, and Jody was relieved that he seemed to be all right after what had gone down on Friday night. He'd spent all day Saturday hanging out with Tressa at her house, and on Sunday, while he didn't actually see his girlfriend, they spent most of the day texting and talking to each other on the phone when he wasn't doing chores around the house and helping Jody with dinner.

This morning, Baker had convinced him to go surfing, and now here they were.

"You good?" Baker asked from beside her.

Turning, Jody studied the man she was head over heels in love with. It was almost scary how much Baker meant to her. They'd spent Saturday morning in bed together, which had been just as mind-blowing and amazing as it had been the first time they'd made love, then they'd showered, eaten, and Baker had gone down on her right in her living room. It had been one of the best sexual experiences of her life. After Jody reciprocated, sucking Baker's cock until he'd exploded, he'd heartily agreed.

Sunday, Baker talked about moving some more of his stuff to her house. He hadn't brought over his computer equipment yet because he wanted to do some modifications in order to make her internet connection more secure. When she'd asked what that meant, he started talking about the dark web, covering his tracks, and VPNs, and Jody promptly tuned out.

She just told him he could bring over anything he wanted, do anything he wanted to her house, and she'd be all right with it...because it meant he'd be there more often.

So after everything that had happened, even the crap with Ben's stepdad, she was feeling fairly mellow today, even though Baker had just said he had to go down to the Naval base for a while this afternoon.

"Jodelle?" Baker asked in concern. "You all right?"

"Sorry. Yeah, I'm good."

"I wouldn't leave if it wasn't important."

Jody looked at him and nodded. "I know. And it's fine. I'm not a helpless ninny who can't survive one day without her man."

Baker's lips twitched. "I know. I guess *I'm* not comfortable with leaving you two right now."

Jody leaned over and put her head on Baker's shoulder. His arm immediately wrapped around her waist and held her tightly. "You said you needed another day or two to get everything set up where Rowden's concerned," she said.

"Yeah," Baker agreed.

"So today's going to be just another day," Jody reassured him. "You do your thing, I'll do mine. We'll be fine. I was thinking about teaching Ben how to make lasagna tonight. That work for you?"

"Anything you make works for me, Tink." Then he took a deep breath. "I'm hoping to be done with my meetings by four. I'll head home right after that, so I should get back around five if the traffic's not too bad."

"Okay."

"I might not be accessible for most of the day," Baker warned.

Jody picked her head up and looked at him with a frown. "Everything okay?"

"Yes. But sometimes the things I have to discuss with the higher-ups require a bit more security. A complete lockdown of the room, including jamming cell signals. It's just a precaution, but that means except for breaks and lunch, I'm gonna be out of reach for most of the day. You need something, you call Mustang. You can't reach him, you call Midas. If he's not available—"

"I know, I know, call Aleck or Pid or Jag or Slate," Jody finished for him.

"Right. But you leave me a message and I'll get to you as soon as I can."

"Nothing's gonna happen," Jody soothed.

"I've learned that shit has a tendency to hit the fan when you least expect it," Baker told her. "And the closer I get to go-time as far as Rowden is concerned, the more nervous I become. I would've put off this meeting I have today, but I can't."

"I'm gonna stay home all day. I don't need to go to the store. I've got everything I need for lasagna already. I'll meet Ben here at the beach this afternoon. He already said he's gonna bring Tressa and stay onshore with me and teach her more about surfing by talking her through what his friends are doing in the water."

"I pissed Rowden off Friday night," Baker said. "He's the kind of man who's gonna want to save face. He's gonna try something."

"Should we stay home? Not go to the beach?"

Baker pressed his lips together then sighed. "Ben's stressed. He's got so much more going on than most teenagers. I hate to take away the one thing that helps him alleviate that stress. I think it'll be okay since it's a public beach, but keep your eyes peeled for trouble. Keep your phone handy at all times. Don't confront Al if he happens to show up."

"You think he will?" Jody asked.

"Honestly? No. It's too public. He'll want to stay under the radar, but that doesn't mean he's not a threat."

"Your hellfire and damnation will rain down on him before he can execute any plans he might have," Jody told him with a small smile.

"I hope you're right."

"I am," Jody said with more bravado than certainty. Al was obviously a huge asshole, not caring if he corrupted young people, got his wife hooked on painkillers—keeping her drugged out in the process—and sold stolen goods for drugs and gambling money. He was living in a house of cards, and Baker was about to blow it all down. Jody felt a little blood-thirsty in her desire to see Al Rowden get his comeuppance, though she also felt bad that Ben's mom would probably get caught in the crossfire. But they were adults. His mother made her choice, and now she and Rowden both had to deal with the consequences of their actions.

Baker turned his head and kissed Jody's temple. "Love you, Tink."

"I love you too."

They sat with their arms around each other, watching the kids surf until it was time for them to come in and head to school. Baker put two fingers to his mouth and whistled loud and long. It was very effective, and Jody was kind of jealous that the kids immediately responded by paddling toward the shore.

She got them sorted with breakfast sandwiches and stayed until the last one pulled out of the lot. Jody put her cooler in the trunk of Baker's car, while he got Ben's board situated on the roof rack. On the way back to her house, he reached out and took her hand in his. It was a simple thing, not sexual in the least, and Jody felt more content in that moment than she had in a very long time. Five years, to be exact. Life had a way of throwing curve balls at her, but if she'd learned anything from Kaimana's death, it was to appreciate what she had in the moment.

When they got home, Jody went inside and got coffee started while Baker stashed Ben's surfboard in the small garage off the side of the house. It was full of boxes and other crap Jody had accumulated over the years and hadn't gotten rid of.

When Baker came in, he said, "My next job, after this shit with Rowden is finished, is to clean out your garage so there's room for your van in there."

"I don't mind parking in the driveway," she told him. "It's not like I ever have to scrape ice off my windows or anything."

"Yeah, but only two cars fit in the driveway, which means either Ben or I have to park on the street. Don't want to do that permanently because it will annoy the neighbors, and the chance someone could sideswipe the car is higher with every day one of them sits out there."

Jody bit her lip. "Baker, this house isn't very big. If you move in, I have no idea where we're going to put everything. So we'll probably need the garage to store *more* stuff, not less."

Baker walked up to her and kissed her gently. "When, not if."

"What?"

"*When* I move in, not if," he told her. "And you don't have to worry about my shit. If it doesn't fit, I'll sell it, or give it to Theo, or Lexie can find someone she serves at Food For All who needs it."

"You can't give your stuff away," Jody said, exasperated.

"Why not?"

"Well...because it's *your* stuff," she said lamely.

"Jodelle, I don't give a shit about material things. All I care about is you. And why do we need two couches when the one you have is perfectly comfortable? We don't need two beds, or two tables, or two sets of dishes. I'm thinking we can upgrade your TV with mine, since it's bigger, but if you're attached to the one in here, that's okay too."

"Baker," Jody whispered, overwhelmed.

"All I want is for you to make room for *me* in your life. In this house. Everything else is immaterial."

"Okay," she said, loving this man more than she had a minute ago. "Will you help me go through Mana's things? I couldn't bear to give everything away. Some of the stuff in the garage is from his room...things I just couldn't get rid of."

"Of course I will," Baker said gently, pulling her into his arms.

This was one of Jody's favorite places to be. Plastered against his front while he held her tightly. They stood like that for a long minute, before Baker reluctantly pulled back. "I need to shower and get on the road," he said regretfully.

"I know."

Baker lowered his head and put his lips on hers. The kiss wasn't short. It was passionate, and Jody could feel the love he had for her through the intimate meeting of their lips. He pulled back, kissed the tip of her nose, her forehead, then he nuzzled the skin under her ear and inhaled deeply.

Jody smiled. She loved how he always did that. As if he couldn't get enough of her scent.

He palmed her cheek and ran his thumb over her lips, before finally dropping his hand and heading for the bedroom.

It took Jody a moment to regain her equilibrium, but when she finally felt stable, she turned to the coffee maker with a huge smile on her face. It was safe to say she was happy. There had been a time not too long ago when she couldn't imagine ever feeling this way again. But Baker, and Ben, had done the impossible.

* * *

Later that afternoon, Jody was sitting on her picnic table, waiting for her kids to arrive. She'd gotten to the beach a little early to talk to the other surfers and get an idea of the conditions so she could let the high schoolers know before they headed out.

Baker had sent a text around lunch, asking how her day was going and confirming that he'd be leaving around four.

It was now three-thirty, which meant he'd soon be out of his meeting and on his way home. If the traffic wasn't too bad, which was always a crapshoot down in Honolulu, and even on the highway leading up to the North Shore, he might get home in time to help her and Ben make the lasagna.

She was lost in her thoughts when she heard her name being called from behind her.

"Miss Jody! Miss Jody!"

Turning, Jody saw Felipe and Lani running toward her from the parking lot.

Dread instantly filled her at their expressions, and for a second, Jody couldn't move. She'd just managed to stand up when the two kids reached her. They were out of breath, their eyes wide. Both started to talk at once, and Jody had to hold up her hand and say sternly, "One at a time. What's wrong?"

Lani took a deep breath. "It's Ben!"

For the second time in a minute, dread almost overwhelmed her. Then Felipe picked up where Lani left off.

"Ben got jumped at lunch! Alex and some of his friends beat the hell out of him. It was *bad*, Miss Jody. He was just lying there moaning by the time teachers pulled everyone off him."

The thought of Ben being hurt made Jody's adrenaline spike. "Why?"

"No one knows," Lani said. "Although *everyone* knows they don't get along, even though they used to be close."

"Where is he now?" Jody asked.

"I'm guessing at home," Felipe said. "The principal suspended Alex and the others who jumped him, so that's good."

But Jody had tuned out the last part. She'd been home all afternoon, and had just come from there. If Ben had gotten hurt at lunch, he should've been home before she'd even left for the beach. Then another thought struck her. "What do you mean, *home*? What home?"

Felipe looked confused. "Well, *his* home. His dad came and picked him up. I'm assuming he took him to a doctor, then probably brought him home to recover."

No. *Nonononono!* The panic inside Jody increased tenfold. If Al Rowden had picked up Ben and brought him to his house, that wasn't good. Not at all.

In the next second, panic instantly disappeared as determination swam through her veins.

She turned and headed for the parking lot without another word.

"Miss Jody?" Lani called. "Where are you going? What about your cooler?"

Jody didn't stop. She didn't give a shit about her cooler. All she could think of was Ben in the hands of his stepfather. A man who didn't give even one little shit about him. Who was about to crash and burn at *Baker's* hands. Who was probably still outraged that Ben had escaped his grasp. And if Ben was hurt, he was especially vulnerable. Jody wouldn't put it past Al to use Ben's injuries as an excuse to hurt him more and get away with it.

She climbed into her van and dialed Baker's number as she drove like a bat out of hell toward Al Rowden's house. The phone rang a few times then went to voicemail.

"Baker, it's me. Ben's been hurt. Alex and some other kids beat him up at lunch. Al picked him up and brought him home. To *his* home. At this point, he's been there for hours. I'm headed over to see if I can get to him. Love you."

She clicked off the phone. Apprehension threatened to overwhelm her, but Jody pushed it down. Call it motherly instinct, call it a premonition, call it whatever you wanted, but she knew she couldn't wait to get to Ben.

She tried calling Baker three more times, praying he might have gotten out of his meeting early, but each time, the call went to voicemail. She didn't bother leaving another message. She had no doubt whatsoever that as soon as Baker knew what was happening, he'd get there as fast as he could.

Jody was a little nervous knowing he was all the way down at the Naval base and wouldn't be able to immediately get to her and Ben, but she had no doubt that he *would* get there. She just had to find Ben, assess the situation, and do whatever needed to be done in the meantime.

It wasn't until she'd parked her van right in front of Al's house that she remembered she was supposed to call Mustang. She dialed his number, but it too went to voicemail. The longer she sat there, the more she panicked. Ben was somewhere inside that house, and she needed to see him with her own eyes to make sure he was all right. Not wanting to wait another second, Jody leaped out of the car and jogged toward the house.

She pounded on the door with her fist at the same time she rang the bell with her other hand.

"Open the door!" she yelled, looking up at the camera Baker had told her about after his visit to the house. "I know you're in there. I want to see Ben! Open the door!"

Amazingly, the door opened. Jody had kind've expected to be ignored and left standing there all night.

Al himself stood in front of her with a nasty smirk on his

face. "I see the tables have turned. Now it's you who wants inside *my* house."

"Where is he?" she demanded.

"Who?"

"You know who! Ben. Where is he? I know he's here. I was told you picked him up."

Al clucked his tongue. "He's not doing well, Miss Spencer. We appreciate your concern, but he's resting."

"Fuck you," Jody spat. "I'm not leaving until I see him. Ben? *Ben!*" she shouted loudly, not caring if anyone in the neighborhood heard. Hoping they *did*, actually.

To her shock, Al grabbed her arm and yanked her inside the house. "Shut up!" he growled.

"Let go of me!" she hissed back. She was scared, angry, overwhelmed, and more desperate than she'd thought possible. The thought of Mana being around someone like Rowden made her clench her teeth in determination. Mana wasn't here—but Ben was. And she'd be damned if she let him down like so many other adults who were supposed to love and care about him had.

"I have no idea what you see in the little jerk," Al bitched. "He's a fucking *punk*. A juvenile delinquent. He needs a firm hand, and all your damn babying isn't doing him any good."

"If he's a punk, it's because you *made* him that way," Jody retorted. "Instead of teaching him right from wrong, you encouraged him to become a criminal. And for what? So you could use the money to drug his mother? To buy ecstasy to keep his friends under your control? To gamble it all away like a loser? You're pathetic!"

Jody had a moment to flinch at seeing his arm swinging, but she was too slow in turning away. Al's fist struck her cheek, only his bruising hold on her arm keeping her upright. Stars swam in her vision for a moment and she had to take a deep breath to keep herself from passing out. She'd never been hit before, and it hurt. A lot.

She realized too late she shouldn't have let Al know Ben had told her everything. She should've played it cool. But she'd been *so* pissed! She hadn't thought before speaking.

Now she'd put both herself *and* Ben in danger.

When the pain in her face morphed into a deep throbbing instead of intense stabbing, she looked at Al. He was grinning maliciously, as if he'd truly enjoyed hitting her.

"I'm calling the cops now," he told her. "I'm gonna tell them you pushed your way into my house. They'll arrest you for trespassing."

"You grabbed hold of *me*. You hit me and you're detaining me unlawfully." She wasn't actually sure what the laws said about dragging someone into your house, but it sounded good to her. "I'm not afraid of you, or the police," she taunted, lifting her chin. "You're nothing but an over-the-hill asshole. Especially compared to *Baker*."

At the mention of Baker's name, Al's lip curled. His hand tightened on her arm, but he didn't speak. Jody was determined to push him harder. Wanted to hurt him as badly as he'd hurt his stepson.

"Ben looks up to Baker. Idolizes him. He can do no wrong in Ben's eyes. And it's no wonder. He's not only good-looking and smart, he's noble and a literal Naval hero." She snorted a laugh. "I even heard one of the girls called him a DILF. What do they call *you*? Overweight, balding, and *pathetic*! I bet those kids are laughing behind your back about the pitiful old man, trying to pretend he's still young."

Al dropped her arm and drew his other fist back to hit her again.

Jody was ready for him this time. She turned to avoid a direct hit to the face, his fist slamming into her shoulder. It still hurt, but not as badly as the shot to the face. The force sent her stumbling backward. She banged her hip on the corner of a table against the wall in the foyer and fell, smacking her cheek against the tile floor as she landed.

Al lunged forward and kicked her in the thigh, then the side, as she did her best to curl into a ball to protect herself. After a few more kicks, he reached down and hauled her upright. He was panting, his eyes wild—and it was obvious she'd pushed him *too* hard.

"You want to see that little fucker?" Al seethed. "Fine!"

He marched her toward a staircase. Jody stumbled and did her best to stay on her feet, because she had a feeling Al would drag her by the hair if she fell. After reaching the top of the stairs, he pulled her down a hallway to a door at the very end. He pulled a key from his pocket and stuck it in the lock.

Not surprised he'd locked Ben in a room, she gasped when he shoved her inside with a hand on her back. Once again, Jody fell to the floor, but she quickly got to her feet and turned to face Al.

"You shouldn't have come, Miss Spencer," he said darkly.

"Whatever," she said with a shake of her head, doing her best to hide her aches and pains. "Call the cops. Do it. I dare you!"

"I've changed my mind. I'm not calling anyone. You're going to have to suffer the consequences of your actions."

"You can't keep me here. That's kidnapping," she told him.

"No one will know," Al said. "I'll have Alex or one of the others take your van and park it somewhere. I'll tell anyone who asks that you were here, but you left after ensuring Ben was safe. And they'll believe me. I'm a fucking judge. I'm *loved* around here."

He was completely crazy. Jody swallowed hard, realizing that she'd dropped her purse with her keys and phone inside when she'd fallen downstairs. "Then what?" she asked. "You just going to keep me here forever? You have to know people won't stop looking."

"Overdose," Al muttered. "It'll be a shame when they find your body washed up on a beach."

If Jody wasn't so scared, she'd laugh. He was grasping at straws. She'd never done drugs in her life. No one was going to believe she'd overdosed. And she might not have a lot of friends, but the ones she *did* have definitely wouldn't let anyone get away with killing her and trying to blame drugs.

"Let her go," Ben mumbled weakly from behind her.

Jody spun. How had she not seen him before now? How had she forgotten the entire reason she was here? She hurried to the side of the bed, whimpering at seeing Ben's poor face. His eyes were almost swollen shut, his nose at an odd angle, and his face was already completely black and blue.

"Oh, Ben," she sobbed, reaching a hand toward him. She stopped herself just in time. The last thing she wanted to do was cause him more pain by touching him.

"Let her go, Al," Ben mumbled again. "She has nothin' to do with this."

"She didn't until you shot your mouth off and told her too much," Al growled. Then he turned on his heel and slammed the door behind him.

Jody heard the door locking again but she didn't care.

"I'm so sorry, Miss Jody," Ben whispered.

"Don't be. This isn't your fault. Are you all right? What hurts?"

Ben chuckled, immediately wincing in pain as he did. "Well...everything?"

"Okay, don't move. We'll get you to the hospital and they'll check you out. You're going to be fine."

"Um...how are we gonna get to a hospital when Al locked us in and he's planning to dump your van, stuff you with drugs until you overdose, then leave your body somewhere?"

Ben's voice had risen at the end of his question, and Jody could tell he was panicking.

"Baker," she said.

"What?"

"Baker's coming for us. He'll take care of Al, and then we'll get you some help," Jody assured him calmly. Strangely, she *felt* calm. Baker wouldn't be happy she'd come here by herself, but she couldn't *not* be here. And at least she'd tried to call him, as promised. Jody winced as she sat on the edge of the mattress and reached for Ben's hand. His knuckles were bloody and swollen, proof that he'd fought back, but she grabbed hold and held on anyway.

"He hit you," Ben said brokenly.

Jody shrugged, ignoring the pain the movement caused. She was going to be sore for quite a while, but Ben was worth it. "Yeah. But anyone who sees me will know Al put his hands on me, and if he tries to make up some story about how I was here voluntarily to see you, everyone will know he's lying."

"Or the marks could work to *his* advantage if you're found washed up on a beach," Ben mumbled.

"True, but he's not going to have time to put together a plan to kill me and dump my body," Jody retorted.

Ben still looked worried.

"Baker's on his way," she said firmly. "He'll probably show up with a contingent of police and badass Navy SEAL friends in tow. We just have to hang on and wait."

"He's gonna lose his mind when he sees Al hit you," Ben said.

He wasn't wrong. But Jody trusted her man. He wouldn't be happy, but he'd promised not to do anything that would get himself in trouble and take him away from her. "He'll get a handle on it," she told Ben. "Now...what happened today?"

Ben looked skeptical, but said, "I was on my way to have lunch with Tressa when Alex and his asshole friends jumped me. There were four of them, and I did my best to fight back but it was no use. Based on the little Al said on the drive here, I'm pretty sure he told them to do it, so he'd have an excuse to come get me."

"Assholes!"

Ben looked surprised. "Miss Jody! You don't swear."

"I've definitely used more than my fair share of curse words today, but I'm thinking the situation warrants it. All of those jerks are gonna pay for this! And if they damage my van, I'm not going to be happy," Jody said.

Ben stared at her for a second before shaking his head. "I feel as if I'm in the twilight zone. I can't believe you aren't more upset or scared."

"I'm upset that you're hurt," Jody told him. "I'm upset that your stepfather is a jerkhead and your mom is nowhere in sight. She should be moving heaven and earth to protect you. But whatever—I've got your back. And Baker has *our* backs. I called him, Ben. He knows I'm here. I promised I'd call and let him know if I was about to do something crazy, so I did. Not that I think coming here to get you myself is crazy, but I'm guessing Baker won't agree. I still trust him to keep his shit together when he finds us."

"I hope Tressa's all right," Ben said quietly.

"I'm sure she is. She's probably worried about *you*," Jody said.

"Yeah, and that sucks. But I'm glad they messed with me and not her," he said firmly.

Jody looked around the room, irritated when there wasn't a bathroom attached. She had no way of wetting a washcloth to try to clean the blood off Ben's face. She wasn't going to even think about having to pee. Baker would be here before that was an issue. She had no doubt.

"Miss Jody?"

She looked down at him, wincing at the pain he must be in. "Yeah, Ben?"

"I'm never going to forget you coming to my rescue today."

She smiled at him and squeezed his hand gently. "I'm not rescuing you. That's Baker's job. I'm just here to hold your hand and make sure you know you're loved."

He blinked at her words, then closed his eyes. But not before a tear escaped from the side of his eye, rolling down his temple into his hair. Jody gently pushed his hair off his face, then leaned over and kissed his forehead. "Relax, Ben. Baker's got this."

She did her best to swallow a moan as she sat up.

That made Ben's eyes open once more. "You need to lie down," he said.

"I'm okay."

"You aren't. You're gonna have a black eye, and I can tell by the way you're moving that your side hurts. Did he hit you there too?"

"Kicked me," Jody admitted.

Ben scowled. "Lie down," he repeated, this time more firmly.

"All right, all right," Jody said, moving slowly until she was lying next to Ben on the queen-size bed. She clasped his hand and held it tightly as she stared up at the ceiling. Lying down did feel better than sitting up. She inhaled deeply, happy when that didn't hurt.

"He's really coming?" Ben whispered after a minute or two had passed.

"He's coming," Jody said with confidence. "We'll get you checked out. Then we'll go home. I was gonna teach you how to make lasagna tonight, but that might need to wait a day or two. I'll make us some tomato soup, you can call Tressa to reassure her that you're okay, and we'll take the next day or two off before getting back into the swing of things."

Ben chuckled. "You have it all worked out."

"Yup." Jody turned her head and saw Ben had done the same, looking at her through his swollen eyes.

"I'm thinking I need to call Tressa sooner rather than later."

Jody smiled at him. "Yeah, I think so too. You can use Baker's cell."

"I still say he's gonna lose his shit when he sees you. If I saw Tressa with a black eye and walking slow because she'd been kicked, I would definitely not take it well."

"He'll be pissed, there's no doubt. But he'll keep himself under control. Want to know why?"

"Yeah."

"Because he promised. Because if he beats the crap out of Al, it might gain the jerk some sympathy. Because Baker's been working his butt off for the last week to take your step-father down. To ensure he can't hurt anyone else. If he loses control when he sees me, it will jeopardize all that he's done to keep you safe. And Tressa. And me. And every twelve-year-old kid who might think it's cool to break into a car or take a pill that makes him forget everything for a little while."

Ben studied her, then nodded. "You're right."

"I know," Jody said smugly.

"You're also crazy," Ben said with a shake of his head.

"Nope. I trust my man, and I love you. There was zero chance I was leaving you at Al's mercy for one second longer than I had to. I would've been here sooner, but I just found out what happened."

"You really love me?" Ben asked in the smallest voice she'd ever heard from the boy.

"Yes," Jody said, squeezing his hand again. "So much."

"Because I remind you of Mana?"

"No. Because you're *you*, Benjamin Miller."

He fell silent then, and Jody did the same. She hadn't lied. This young man had snuck under her radar. She respected him, liked him, and yes, she loved him deeply.

Lifting her left hand, wincing at the pain the motion caused, Jody saw that it was four-thirty. It was hard to believe an hour had passed since she'd called Baker. But that meant he should be here soon.

Smiling, Jody relaxed against the covers. Al Rowden had no idea the shitstorm that was about to descend upon him.

# CHAPTER TWENTY-TWO

Baker was completely focused. He'd walked out of his meeting at five minutes till four and smiled when he saw he had a voicemail from Jodelle—until he saw she'd called several more times after. Then his adrenaline spiked.

He was already on the move by the time he'd finished listening to her message.

Several calls later—calls to Mustang, and the connections he'd made while researching Rowden—and Baker had a police escort headed north. His adrenaline was so high, his hands were shaking. All sorts of worst-case scenarios were swirling through his brain. He wanted to think he'd arrive at Rowden's house only to find Jodelle had been there, then left with Ben, but he knew better.

Rowden thought he was untouchable. He'd gotten away with too much for too long. He was conceited and vain and secure in the knowledge that the men and women he had in his pocket would always have his back.

He was wrong.

Rowden was going down. Today. Right now.

Baker just hoped he wasn't going to bring Jodelle down with him.

Worry for her kept Baker hyper-alert as he sped north. His role in what was about to happen was minimal. Yes, he set the wheels in motion, but he wasn't a main player when it came to the actual takedown. He'd have to sit back and let the SWAT team do their thing. The Honolulu PD chief had received a search warrant signed by a judge minutes ago, even as they raced toward the North Shore. The director of the local FBI office was on his way. As was a representative from the DEA.

All of the law enforcement agencies on the island were in some way involved in what was about to happen, thanks to Baker's intel.

Not to mention the dealer Rowden bought his drugs from had agreed to refuse him service ever again. The bookie he used to place his bets was no longer willing to take Rowden's money.

Basically, the man was screwed. The empire he'd spent years building had crumbled under his feet. Now it was just a matter of getting the man in custody before he hurt anyone else. He'd surely attempt to use the information he had on people to his advantage, but he'd lost his leverage. He could attempt to blab all he wanted but if he was smart, he'd worry about himself, not taking others down with him.

Everything was happening about twenty-four hours earlier than expected, but Baker was pleased the various agencies had jumped to do what needed to be done. They'd understood the urgency and acted accordingly.

Baker wanted to be mad at Jodelle for going to Rowden's house, but he couldn't. She'd done just what she'd promised. She'd contacted him, tried to get his assistance. She'd also called Mustang, as well. But she could no more leave Ben vulnerable than she would've been able to ignore her own son if he needed help. Her tender heart was one of the many reasons he loved her.

Baker mentally kicked himself as they neared the neighborhood where Rowden lived. He should've insisted on putting off today's meeting with the base admiral. He should've waited until Rowden was behind bars. He'd underestimated the man, which wasn't something he did. Ever.

And his mistake had put Jodelle in danger. Ben too.

The police cars surrounding him turned off their lights and sirens as they got closer, moving in with stealth. The last thing they wanted was for Rowden to do something rash if he thought he was about to get busted. Baker didn't think he would. The man was too arrogant. He thought he was bulletproof, that no charges would ever stick. He was wrong.

There was a SWAT van already parked on the street, down a bit from Rowden's house. Baker looked around but didn't see Jodelle's van. He wasn't sure if that was a good sign or a bad one. Once more, he prayed that it meant she'd arrived, picked up Ben, and left. But the rolling in his gut told him that wasn't the case. Rowden had brought his stepson here for a reason. He wasn't going to let him go easily.

Baker jumped out of his car and stood with his hands fisted by his sides as the officers gathered to make entry into the large house.

Mustang and Midas came up beside Baker. They'd jumped into Midas's car back at the base and had joined in the convoy. The rest of the team was waiting back in the Honolulu area. Watching over the women and children, just in case shit went south in some unexpected way. There was no indication that it would, but with everything that had happened in the past, no one was taking any chances.

"You good?" Mustang asked.

"No," Baker said between clenched teeth.

His friend was smart enough to avoid platitudes about how he was sure Jodelle was fine. Mustang knew better than most how stressful this was, not knowing if your woman was okay. He'd been through something similar with Elodie.

Luckily, the SWAT team was prepared and didn't take

long to enter the house. Baker watched with his teeth clenched as they pounded on the front door, demanding for Rowden to come out. They gave him less than twenty seconds before using the battering ram to knock down the thick, ornate door.

Baker heard shouts and orders for people to get down. He lunged forward a step before Mustang stopped him by grabbing his arm.

"Wait. Give them time to secure everyone."

That was easy for Mustang to say. It wasn't *his* woman in danger this time.

"Fuck waiting," Midas disagreed. "Go. We've got your back."

Baker knew his friend's reluctance to wait stemmed from the fact he'd almost arrived too late to save Lexie. If he hadn't skipped the simple act of stopping for her favorite coffee the morning she was attacked, her outcome might've been very different.

Baker hurried toward the door, now lying catawampus on its hinges. He expected someone to stop him, but no one did. He entered the house and paused, tilting his head as he listened to the officers still clearing the house.

There were four teenagers lying on the tile in the huge entryway, hands behind their backs, but no sign of Rowden. Lifting his chin, Baker yelled, "Jodelle?"

Two of the officers guarding the teenagers jerked at the sound, but to their credit, they didn't otherwise move.

He yelled her name again. "Jodelle!"

"If she's here, the officers will find her," Midas said.

Baker wasn't willing to wait. He needed eyes on her. Pronto.

To his surprise, he heard his name. It was faint, but Baker immediately turned to the stairs and took them two at a time. The house was obnoxiously huge, but he didn't stop to admire the paintings on the walls or the Berber carpet.

As he passed a bedroom, he saw two officers restraining Rowden on the floor, while two others were checking a woman lying motionless on a large bed in the middle of the suite. Rowden was screaming that they were making a mistake, that the officers were going to pay with their jobs, but Baker kept going. His concern wasn't Rowden, it was Jodelle.

"Jodelle!" he yelled once more.

"Baker!" he heard from one of the rooms at the end of the hall. "We're in here!"

Almost lightheaded with relief at hearing her voice, Baker ran toward the sound. He opened two doors, finding empty bedrooms, before he tried the third. Locked.

"Step back!" Baker shouted.

He thought he heard Jodelle chuckle, but that couldn't be right. She had to be scared to death.

"You back?" he bellowed.

"Yes!" she returned.

Baker lifted a foot and with one mighty kick, the door was no longer standing between him and the woman he loved.

Moving recklessly, not caring if someone might be in the room with a weapon pointed straight at him—Jodelle would've found a way to warn him if that was the case—he burst into the bedroom. He briefly took in Ben lying on the bed, looking like complete hell, but then his eyes locked on Jodelle, sitting on the mattress next to the teenager.

His gaze flew straight to her smiling lips.

Fucking hell. She was *smiling*!

"Hi," she said.

Baker thought he heard Mustang chuckle behind him, but he was so damn relieved Jodelle was all right, he felt dizzy. He swiftly bent and put his hands on his knees, attempting to stave off the blackness moving in from the corner of his eyes. Jesus, the last thing he needed was to fucking pass out right now.

"Baker?" Jodelle asked, alarmed. Then he felt her hand on his shoulder.

Moving too fast, he stood upright and grabbed her.

The dizziness sent him collapsing right to the floor, Jodelle in his arms.

She didn't struggle to get up. Simply snuggled into him with her knees on either side of his hips, holding on just as tightly.

"Dammit, Baker. You know you aren't supposed to be in here until we give the all-clear," an annoyed voice bitched from the doorway.

"You were taking too long," he told the head of the SWAT team without remorse.

"Careful with her," Ben said from the bed.

Lifting his head, Baker caught the teenager's eye. "What?"

"She's hurt. Be careful."

All the relief he'd felt at seeing Jodelle faded instantly. Every muscle in Baker's body tensed. He put his hands on her shoulders and lifted her off his chest, gently, so he could get eyes on every inch of her body.

"I'm okay," she said quietly.

That was when the bruise on her face finally registered. And the marks in the shape of fingers on her upper arm. And the way she held herself stiff, as if attempting to mitigate some other injury he couldn't see.

"Get the medics up here. Now!" Baker demanded.

"Yes, do," Jodelle agreed. "But not for me. For Ben. Al had those boys beat him up. And he's been lying here covered in dried blood and hurting for *hours*," Jodelle said, obviously outraged. "He needs to be looked at. And he needs clean clothes. Oh, and he wants to call Tressa to let her know he's all right. She has to be worried sick."

Baker couldn't take his eyes off the mark on her face, getting darker by the minute. Anger raged inside him, almost obscuring his vision.

"Call my lawyer! This is illegal! You can't barge into my house like this!" Rowden yelled from the hallway.

Without thought, knowing beyond a shadow of a doubt that it was Rowden who'd put his hands on Jodelle, Baker moved. He had no other thought in mind but to show the asshole what happened to men who touched someone weaker than them—especially *his* woman.

"Baker," Jodelle said softly as she grabbed his hand.

Somehow, he'd stood up, put Jodelle to the side, and taken a couple steps toward the door without even realizing it. It was only her touch on his hand that brought him out of his red haze of fury. Baker looked down at her.

"I need you," she said softly. "*We* need you. Al had the kids take my van somewhere, along with my phone and purse. We need you to take us to the Kahuku Medical Center so Ben can get treated. He'll need help changing into scrubs or something, and I'm sure he'd rather you be the one to do that than me. If you hit that asshole, he'll try to have you arrested. Find a way to use that to make this search, or whatever it is, inadmissible or illegal or something. And the last thing I want is you hurting your hand on top of all that."

Baker still struggled with what his head and heart were telling him to do. He wanted to make Rowden pay—but he also knew Jodelle was right.

"I knew you'd come," she said, squeezing his hand. "I told Ben that you'd be here just as soon as humanly possible. He was worried, but not me."

Her trust in him was humbling.

Taking a deep breath, Baker did something he'd rarely done in his adult life—he left dealing with the bad guy to someone else. He'd done the leg work, delivered Rowden to the Feds on a silver platter. The man was going to prison, no matter how much he squawked and postured.

Baker stepped closer to Jodelle and gently ran his thumb over the dark mark on her cheek.

She placed her hand over his and leaned her head on his palm. "I might've taunted Rowden and pushed him a little too far," she said quietly. "But...at least if the cops came, I knew they'd take one look and know he hit me."

Baker growled, but kept a tight grip on his control.

"The medics are here," Midas said.

Baker opened his mouth to tell them to check Jodelle, but she turned and pointed to the bed. "Good. Ben needs to be looked at. He was jumped at school by several kids. I have no idea if anything other than his nose is broken or not, but he's in a lot of pain."

The paramedic nodded and made a beeline for the bed.

"When you're done ordering them around, will you let them look at you?" Baker said with a small grin. He couldn't fucking believe he was smiling right now, but how could he not?

"I'm okay," she told him. "I just need a long hot bath and for my man to hold me."

"Done," Baker said. But if she thought she was going to get out of a full examination, she was kidding herself.

Jodelle stepped closer, put a hand on his chest, and went up on her tiptoes. Baker leaned down, and she put her lips next to his ear.

"Thank you," she whispered. "Thank you for being someone I can trust. I know you're pissed, but thank you for holding yourself together for me. I love you, Baker. I knew you'd come. I *knew* it."

Then she went back down on the flats of her feet and smiled.

Baker was still pissed. He couldn't just turn off his anger like flicking a switch. But for Jodelle, he'd control the adrenaline still pumping through his veins. He leaned down and kissed the mark on her cheek. Then her forehead. Then her nose. Then finally, he covered her lips with his own. He kissed her softly, not wanting to hurt her any more than she already was.

When he lifted his head, he took a deep breath and turned to Mustang without letting go of Jodelle. "Think you can get one of the officers to talk to the punks downstairs, find out where they took Jodelle's van?"

"Yeah, I can do that," Mustang said with a smile.

Baker then turned to Midas. "And can you let everyone know what's going on? That Jodelle's good? Ben too? I'm guessing Lexie and the others have probably gathered their pitchforks and are ready to storm the castle if they don't hear something soon."

Midas chuckled. "You aren't wrong, brother. I'll take care of it."

"Thanks."

"We'll meet you at the clinic," Mustang said from the doorway.

"That's not necessary," Baker said.

"We'll meet you at the clinic," Mustang echoed more firmly, and with a glare thrown in for good measure.

"That would be great. Thank you," Jodelle told him.

Baker nodded at his friend.

Mustang gave him a chin lift, then disappeared down the hall.

"You were lucky," the paramedic said to Ben as he helped him slowly sit up on the bed. Ben winced but nodded. "You're gonna be sore for a while and have some pretty nasty bruises, but it doesn't seem as if you have any internal bleeding. I can't tell if your ribs are cracked or not, you'll need an X-ray for that, but as far as I can tell, you did a decent job of protecting yourself."

Baker's jaw tightened, and the hatred for Rowden welled up inside him once more. But just like before, all it took was Jodelle's touch for him to get his anger under control.

It took a few minutes of discussion but eventually the

paramedics decided on using a stair chair to get Ben down the stairs and into the ambulance. The teenager insisted he could walk, but Jodelle, and the medics, were having none of that.

When Ben was strapped into the chair and ready for transport, he looked up at Baker and asked quietly, "My mom?"

Baker wanted to feel bad that he hadn't even thought about the woman, other than to note her presence in a room when he'd walked by. He opened his mouth to tell the kid that he had no idea when Midas spoke up.

"She's being taken to Honolulu, to a detox clinic. She's pretty out of it."

Ben sighed and nodded. "I figured as much."

Jodelle walked over to him and put a hand on Ben's shoulder. "She's getting help. Finally. Maybe this will be the push she needs to get off the drugs and get her life back together."

Ben shrugged.

Jodelle frowned as the paramedics began to wheel Ben out of the room and into the hall. Baker gently wrapped his arm around her waist. She wasn't as steady on her feet as she'd like to pretend she was. Still, Baker couldn't help but be impressed by her strength.

She looked up at him. "I feel bad for her."

"She had to know what the hell her husband was doing," Baker told her.

"Maybe, maybe not. But she's losing the best thing to ever happened to her. Ben. That sucks. I'm hoping once she's clean, or at least not so drugged, she'll get her head out of her butt and do what she has to in order to salvage some sort of relationship with her son."

"Come on, Tink. You can work on saving the rest of the world another day. Right now, we need to get to the clinic and make sure Ben's good. Then you need to be looked at. Then we'll go home and I'll get that bath ready for you."

Jodelle leaned against his side, giving him most of her weight. "I love you, Baker."

"I love you too. More than you'll ever know. Now, come on, let's get out of this fuckin' house."

"Gladly," she said on a sigh.

\* \* \*

Hours later, long after the sun had set, after she and Ben had seen a doctor and been cleared to go home as long as they both took it easy, after she'd taken a long bath, after Mustang had gone out and picked up dinner from a sandwich shop in Haleiwa, after her van had been returned safe and sound, and after Ben had gone to his room to call Tressa, Jody sat on the couch in her living room.

She'd gotten text after text from Elodie and the others, who wanted to check on her and make sure she was all right. She'd done her best to talk them out of coming up in the morning. It felt good that they were concerned about both her and Ben, but Jody needed some time before she'd feel up to entertaining anyone.

Mustang had left not too long ago, and she was currently watching Baker through a window. He was in her backyard. He'd gone out there after his friend left, claiming he needed a moment to himself.

Jody wasn't offended in the least. He'd been by her side every second since he'd kicked in the door to the room where Al Rowden had locked up her and Ben. The second she'd heard him bellowing her name, she'd relaxed. Baker had arrived, as she knew he would, and she and Ben were safe.

The amount of restraint Baker had shown after seeing her injuries was admirable. But Jody wasn't an idiot, she knew that self-discipline had taken a toll. He was a man used to being in the thick of things. Taking down bad guys himself. For him to step aside and let others deal with Rowden, to not even get one minute alone with Ben's stepdad...to tell him what a douche he was, or inform him that *Baker* was the reason he'd likely spend the rest of his life behind bars...had to be eating at her man.

So Jody gave him the space he needed.

When he'd first gone outside, his fists had been clenched and his jaw tight. He'd picked up a mango that had fallen off a large fruit tree in her backyard and thrown it as hard as he could toward the trunk. He'd hit it dead on, and the mango had shattered, sending sticky fruit pulp everywhere. Then Baker picked up another and did the same thing.

He threw the rotting fruit over and over again, until there were no more available for him to throw. Then he closed his eyes, tilted his head back, and stood stock still.

A tear escaped and slid down her cheek, but Jody didn't take her gaze from her man. Eventually, his fists unclenched and he took a deep breath. It took another five minutes before his shoulders relaxed and he turned to come back inside.

By now, Jody's face was wet with tears, and she was sniffling nonstop. Baker stopped in his tracks when he saw her.

"Fuck," he muttered.

Jody sent him a watery smile. "No, I'm good. I just...I love you so much."

Baker looked down at his sticky hands and immediately headed for the kitchen sink. Jody turned, wincing at how the move sent a small twinge of pain shooting through her torso. But that didn't stop her from keeping her eye on her man. He washed and dried his hands, then made a beeline for where she was sitting on the couch. He sat down and carefully lifted her, settling her on his lap. He sat back, cradling her against him, and sighed.

"Feel better?" she asked.

"Yeah." He grabbed a tissue from the box on the table

next to the couch and brought it up to her face. He dried her cheeks, then held it to her nose. "Blow."

Jody rolled her eyes and grabbed the tissue from him. She blew her nose, causing another twinge in her torso, then settled back against him when he took the used tissue and threw it back on the table. Her cheek rested against his chest, and she could hear the rhythmic *thump thump thump* of his heartbeat.

"I'm sorry."

"For what?" he asked.

"For putting myself in that situation. I know you have to be mad."

"I'm not mad. I would be if you hadn't called me though."

"I knew you'd be almost done with your meeting," Jody told him. "But I didn't want to wait. Ben had already been there for hours, and I had no idea what Al was capable of. No, that's not true. I know exactly what he was capable of. Sending a bunch of kids in to beat up his stepson so he could get him back under his roof and try to blackmail him some more."

"What'd he say to you?" Baker asked.

"What do you mean?" Jody asked, stalling for time. The police chief had agreed she should receive medical treatment immediately, and in deference to Baker, said she could make her statement tomorrow. So he'd yet to hear the details.

"You know what I mean. Ben hinted that Rowden said some pretty bad shit."

Jody shrugged. "He was desperate. He was losing control over Ben, and he had to know his leverage against him was shit, and I think he was scared about what it could mean for him when I showed up."

"What'd he say?" Baker repeated.

"I don't want you to have to go outside and take your anger out on my poor mango tree again," Jody said, not really kidding.

"I'm good. I just needed to release some of the tension and stress I've been holding onto since I listened to your voicemail."

She sighed. "He said he was gonna force me to overdose. Then throw me into the sea."

Every muscle under her went taut, and for a second, Jody was afraid for her poor mango tree again. But Baker reined in his emotions and squeezed her gently.

"I hated that Ben had to hear him say that, but I knew it wouldn't happen," she said.

"He could've killed you," Baker said in a low, tortured tone.

"I know. And I was scared. But I had no doubt you would get there before he had a chance to do anything he was planning."

Baker shook his head. "You couldn't have known that."

Jody sat up and looked him in the eye. "Yes. I did. Baker, you were fifteen, twenty minutes away from getting out of your meeting. You were coming, I knew that as well as I knew my own name. I feel bad because you actually suffered more than I did today. You were worried sick for me and Ben, not knowing what we were going through, and all we were doing was lying on a bed waiting for you to show up."

"You're amazing," Baker whispered.

"I'm not," she insisted. "If I didn't have you, I would've been a hot mess. But I watched you work tirelessly to take him down. I had every confidence in you. Trust, Baker. I've learned it. *You* taught it to me. I don't know if I fully believe the soul business like you do, but if you're right, I've more than learned what I need to in this life. Because of you."

"I'd have to agree," Baker said. "And because of you, I've learned the true meaning of love."

"Baker," Jody whispered.

"Sucks that it took so long for me to find you though," he

muttered as he scooted down until Jody was plastered on top of him on the couch.

"You know we have a perfectly good bed, right?" she asked with a smile.

"Yeah. But we can hear Ben better from out here. Just in case he needs something."

The love Jody had for this man seemed to get bigger and bigger every day that went by.

"He's gonna struggle with what happened," she said softly. "Especially over his mom."

"Yeah. But he'll have us to talk to. He'll be good," Baker said confidently.

A full minute went by before Jody asked with a grin, "How long do you really think we have before Elodie and the others descend?"

"A day at most," Baker said without any angst in his voice. "But if you truly aren't ready, I'll talk to Mustang and the others."

"It's okay. I really do want to get to know them all. As well as your friends. And I want to meet Theo. And have dinner at Duke's with them. And see Food For All and the mural Theo painted on the wall."

Baker chuckled. "Then that's what we'll do." He turned and kissed her temple.

Jody relaxed against her man, and even though she had the best intentions to stay awake, to make sure Baker was truly okay after everything that happened, the second her eyes closed, she fell into a deep healing sleep, secure in the knowledge that the people she loved most were safe under her roof.

\* \* \*

Baker didn't sleep. He couldn't. He couldn't turn off his brain and the visions of all the different ways today could've gone differently. When he heard his phone vibrating on the kitchen counter, he managed to slip out from under Jodelle without waking her, which just showed how exhausted she was and how today had taken more of a toll than she was willing to admit.

He saw it was Slate calling. He stepped outside so he could talk without waking Jodelle or Ben. "What's up, Slate?"

"I know it's late, I'm sorry. How's Jodelle? And Ben?"

"They're okay. Sleeping."

"Glad to hear it. Midas let us know the doctors say they've only got superficial injuries and should heal up fairly quickly, yeah?"

"Uh-huh."

"Good. Anyway, I'm calling to make sure you know what's going on with Rowden."

Baker straightened. "And?" He'd planned on making some calls in the morning to his contacts to find out what was happening, but having intel now would be better.

"Even though he was crying for a lawyer at the house, he agreed to talk to the Feds without one when they arrived in Honolulu. He denied everything. But after the Feds started laying out the evidence against him, he started talking. Fast. Tried to blame everything on Ben at first, saying he was the one who got *him* involved in the break-ins. Then claimed Ben was the one buying MDMA for the parties. When the Feds didn't buy that bullshit, he turned against Emma. Saying she was desperate for the oxy and begged him to get it for her."

"What a fuckin' douchebag," Baker said.

"Yeah. He didn't have much to say about the gambling, but the bookie you talked to has very good records—not to mention audio and video recordings of their meetings. By the time they started showing him the interviews with the kids you tracked down, the ones who worked for him and he'd been blackmailing, Rowden shut down. He couldn't deny anything. And finding the older kids who'd stood up to him, and ended up in adult prison for shit Rowden forced them to do, was the nail in his coffin. He's got a shitload of charges looming, but the corruption charges alone, because of his position as a juvenile judge, will send him to prison for a very long time."

"Good," Baker said, not hiding the relief in his voice.

"For the record..." Slate said. "You're fucking scary sometimes, Baker. But my wife and I are very glad to call you a friend. That being said, friends are there for each other. So I'm giving you a heads-up that there'll be a caravan of people headed your way tomorrow afternoon. The women agreed to give you the morning, but they aren't waiting a few days, like Jodelle suggested. They're coming to see with their own eyes that you, Jodelle, and Ben are all good."

"Fuck," Baker sighed without heat.

Slate chuckled. "We've got your back," he said. "Today, tomorrow, and in the future. Prepare to be invited to baby showers, renewal-of-vow ceremonies, birthday parties, graduations, barbeques, and anything else the women can think up. We might not have the connections you do, but that doesn't mean we aren't here for you however you need us."

Baker was almost overwhelmed with emotion...which never happened. He blamed it on everything that had gone down that day. He'd always felt alone, which had never bothered him before. Now he not only had a woman who loved him, he had a teenager who looked up to him, a team of SEALs who treated him as if he was still one of them, and their women, who wanted to smother him with affection simply because their men considered him a friend.

Baker was a lucky son-of-a-bitch, and he knew it.

"If someone can wrangle some malasadas...Jodelle would appreciate it."

"Done," Slate said.

"Oh, and we're running low on strawberry Pop-Tarts."

Slate laughed. "Do I want to know what that's about? Because I know *you* aren't eating that shit."

"They're for Jodelle."

"Say no more. Anything else?" Slate asked.

"Just...thank you."

"We'll see if you're still saying that tomorrow when we all descend on you. Glad Jody's all right," Slate said quietly. "And Ben."

"Thanks for the update."

"Can't believe I knew something you didn't. You're slipping, Baker."

He chuckled. "Whatever. Was cuddled up with Jodelle on the couch. That's way more important than getting the deets on that fuckin' asshole."

"True," Slate said.

"Besides, I'm good. I knew he wasn't gonna get out of the shit hole he dug himself into."

Slate laughed. "You're an arrogant asshole, but you aren't wrong."

"See you tomorrow," Baker said, smiling himself.

"Tomorrow," Slate returned.

Baker clicked off the phone and stared out into the dark night for a moment. Then he turned to look inside. Jodelle was still lying where he'd left her. The bruise on her face had darkened further throughout the day, which still infuriated Baker, but the love and admiration he had for her overshadowed his anger at Rowden.

He slipped back into the room, put his phone on the counter, and headed for the couch once more. He maneuvered Jodelle until she was draped against his side, sighing in contentment.

"Everything okay?" she mumbled sleepily.

"Yeah. Go back to sleep, Tink."

"Love you."

"Love you too."

Baker would never get tired of hearing or saying those words. He was an idiot for resisting her pull for so long. He'd kick his own ass for that for the rest of his life. But she was his now, just as he was hers. There was nowhere he'd rather be than right where he was in this moment.

Holding her in his arms and thanking his lucky stars that their souls had once again found each other.

# EPILOGUE

*One Year Later*

Jody wasn't sure why Ben was so insistent on going to the beach. She'd actually planned to take the afternoon off, since he was visiting. He was a freshman at the University of Hawaii down in Honolulu and had come up for the weekend. After everything that had happened last year, and in the months since, Ben had recovered from his pseudo-kidnapping and beating without issue.

Jody had thought she'd do the same, but she'd had nightmares for weeks after. Mostly about running through a huge empty house screaming Ben's name and unable to find him. But every time she woke up in Baker's arms, with him stroking her hair, telling her she was safe. That Ben was fine. She was good. He hated seeing her struggling, but he'd been her rock, and she had no idea what she would've done without him this past year.

While Jody liked to think Ben visited as much as he did to see *her*, instead of spending his weekends with his new friends at the university, she knew he came back to the North Shore mostly to see Tressa. The pair was still dating, she was finishing up her senior year, and they were as close as ever.

"Come on, Miss Jody! We're gonna miss the good waves," Ben cajoled from near the front door.

Jody rolled her eyes. "I'm coming. Jeez! Keep your pants on."

Ben merely smiled at her.

She grabbed her keys out of the glass bowl on the counter and headed out the door. Baker had left about ten minutes ago, taking her cooler with him, and said he'd start handing out snacks to the kids.

Jody smiled at her van as she approached. She'd been so relieved that Alex and his cronies hadn't ruined her vehicle when they'd ditched it at Al Rowden's request a year ago. They'd punctured the tires, but those were easily fixed. The passenger-side window had also been broken, but again, Baker's friends had arranged to have it replaced within a couple of days.

Once they were on their way, Jody asked, "How've you been doing, Ben? Now that the trial's finally over?" It had taken longer than both Jody and Baker would've liked for Rowden's case to go to trial, but it was done. He'd fought until the very end, refusing to plead guilty even though the evidence against him, thanks to Baker, was overwhelming.

"I'm good," Ben said in a casual tone.

"Seriously, honey, how *are* you?" Jody insisted.

Ben turned to meet her eyes. "Honestly, I'm fine. He got what he deserved."

"Yes, he did." Al Rowden would be spending most of the rest of his life behind bars. By the time he was released, he'd be an old man...which was more than all right with Jody. "How's your mom?" she asked.

"Last I heard, she's back in rehab."

Emma Rowden hadn't had an easy time of trying to kick her oxycodone habit. She'd been in and out of rehab ever since the night the police raided her house. She'd get clean, go into a group home for recovering addicts, then relapse and the cycle would start all over again.

"I'm sorry," Jody said.

Ben shrugged. "It is what it is." Then, more quietly, "I don't think she's gonna make it, Miss Jody."

Her heart sank. "Oh, Ben."

"She's suffering. Every day is hell for her. I hate seeing her struggle so hard."

"Yeah," Jody said sadly.

"She's not strong enough to fight through it. Sooner rather than later, I have a feeling I'm going to get a call telling me she's gone. And I'd be at peace with that. Her suffering would be over, at least."

Jody inhaled deeply trying not to cry. The situation with Ben's mom was so damn sad. The fact that Ben didn't hate her was a testament to what a good person he was.

"But enough of that. I'm looking forward to surfing with Baker. He's still pretty amazing for an old guy."

Jody chuckled. "Don't let *him* hear you say that."

"Never," Ben said, sounding genuinely horrified.

As they pulled into the parking lot, Jody was surprised to see it so crowded. "Is there a competition today that I didn't know about?"

"Not sure...there's a spot!" Ben said, pointing.

Jody pulled in and turned off the ignition. She got out and was surprised when Ben linked his arm with hers and quickly steered her toward the beach.

"Aren't you forgetting something?" she asked with a laugh. "You're gonna need your board if you're going to surf."

"I'll come back and get it," Ben said.

For the first time, Jody started to get suspicious. Baker leaving before them, Ben being adamant about getting to the beach today instead of hanging out with Tressa, leaving his board in the van...it was adding up to something going on that she wasn't privy to.

As they walked toward the beach, Jody saw a large crowd of people, most of whom she recognized. All of Baker's SEAL buddies were there, as were their wives, with Kenna looking as if she was about to give birth at any second. Charlotte, Monica's daughter, was toddling precariously with her dad right at her heels, waiting to catch her if she fell.

Along with the SEALs and their families, Jody saw Kal, Lani, Brent, Rome, and Felipe. Even Tressa was there, along with some of the parents of the other kids she watched over while they were surfing.

"What in the world?" she asked, looking up at Ben.

"You'll see," he told her with a smile.

Baker approached them and Ben relinquished his hold on her arm.

"Thought you were never gonna get here, Tink," Baker said.

"If I'd known there were shenanigans afoot, maybe I would have hurried a bit more," she retorted.

He grinned, leaned down and kissed her briefly, before pulling her toward the waiting crowd. Without pause, he escorted her to "her" picnic table and turned both of them to face everyone.

"I'm gonna keep this short and sweet because the waves are bitchin' today, but thank you all for coming. We all know what Kaimana Spencer did at this beach over six years ago. He sacrificed himself to save the life of another. He was giving, selfless, and a hero in every sense of the word."

Baker turned to Jody, and she couldn't help but tear up. He put his hand on her cheek and spoke again. This time it felt as if they were the only two people in the world. "From here on out, this is Mana's spot. And yours." Baker gestured to the picnic table behind her, and Jody glanced at it in confusion. It looked just like it always did...except now it had a metal plaque screwed into the top. She leaned forward and read:

**While doing what he loved. Surf on, brother.**
**"Out of the water, I am nothing," ~Duke Kahanamoku**

The tears in her eyes spilled over and fell down her face.

"He'll never be forgotten. Ever. His legacy will live on forever," Baker said as he pulled her into his arms.

Jody hung on tight, not taking her eyes off the plaque.

Everyone around them cheered, and Jody struggled to get herself together. "Did you arrange this?" she asked Baker.

He shrugged. "Ben had the idea, I just ran with it."

"I love you," Jody told him.

"Love you back. Now...kiss me, then go mingle with your friends."

"Our friends."

"Yeah," Baker agreed.

She went up on her tiptoes, but Baker met her halfway as he always did. He kissed her long and deep, not caring that they were in front of all their friends. Jody felt off-kilter by the time he lifted his lips from hers. He smirked and brushed a finger over her cheek.

"I know that look," he said quietly.

"Yeah, it's the look of you getting me all hot and bothered before you head off into the ocean," Jody quipped.

Baker simply smirked wider.

"I met Baker at this exact spot," Monica said from next to them.

"Yeah, you saw my tattoo and it freaked you so much, you fell on your ass," Baker retorted.

"This was also where Baker pulled his scary-guy routine and warned me if I hurt Midas, I'd be in big trouble," Lexie said, grinning. She and Midas had finally tied the knot a few months ago in a quiet ceremony. His parents and siblings had all been there, and the party Kenna had thrown for them afterward on the beach at her condo was large, loud, and extremely fun.

"Lots of memories here for sure," Carly said as she joined the others, Elodie, Kenna, and Ashlyn at her heels.

"On that note, I'm goin' out into the waves with Ben," Baker said. He kissed Jody's forehead, then jogged toward the parking lot to grab his board from his car.

"I think we scare him," Ashlyn said with a smile.

Everyone chuckled.

"You all right?" Elodie asked. "We weren't sure surprising you with this was a good idea, but Baker insisted that you'd be okay with it."

"I'm definitely okay with it," Jody said immediately. "I have no doubt Kaimana would've done great things in this world. He would've been remembered for his kind soul and amazing energy. My greatest fear has always been that he'll fade from people's memories, and now he won't. Anyone who sees this will read his name, and that act alone will keep him from disappearing forever."

Carly's eyes filled with tears.

Jody eyed her suspiciously. "Um...are you pregnant, Carly?"

The other woman looked surprised for a moment, then she laughed. "Can't hide anything from you, can I?"

Immediately, all the others were congratulating the other woman while hugging her.

A short while later, the surfers were all in the waves and the others were getting ready to leave when Elodie came up to Jody.

"How'd you know?" she asked with a wistful look in her eyes.

"Carly's not usually so emotional. Besides, she's been telling us for months that she and Jag have been trying to get pregnant. Honestly, it was a wild guess."

Elodie nodded.

Jody reached out and put her hand on her friend's arm. "It'll happen for you and Scott. I know it."

Elodie sighed. "It's been over a year," she said with a shake of her head.

"Don't give up," Jody said sternly.

"I'm not, it's just...It's frustrating. The next step is seeing a fertility doctor. If that doesn't work, we'll look into adoption. There are a ton of kids out there who need a foster home too. We don't need a child to be a family, but I know Scott really wants one."

Jody gave her a hug. "You and Scott will be the best parents. No matter if that's a baby of your own, or a teenager who needs a safe place to land."

Elodie gave Jody a small smile. "Ben's a good kid."

"Yeah, he is."

"He's lucky he has you."

"No, we're the lucky ones," Jody said.

Elodie's husband came up then, putting his arm around her waist. "You ready to go?"

"Only if you promise we can stop at the Dole Plantation on the way home and get a Dole Whip."

"I wouldn't dream of passing that place without stopping," Mustang said with a smile. He gave Jody a chin lift and said, "See you soon?"

"Of course. I'm guessing we'll all be gathering at the hospital for the birth of Kenna and Aleck's baby sooner rather than later," Jody said.

"Very true," Mustang said. He gave Jody a short hug, then headed for the parking lot with Elodie under his arm.

An hour later, it was just Jody left on the beach, sitting on Mana's picnic table, staring at her man as Baker walked up the sandy beach toward her.

She stood and held out a towel for him and watched as he dried himself off. He'd pulled his wet suit down to his waist, and Jody couldn't help but stare. He might be fifty-three, but Baker still made her knees weak.

"You stare at me like that any longer, I won't be responsible for my actions," Baker warned.

Jody rolled her eyes. "Whatever. You know you're hot," she told him.

"Don't give a shit about that. Only care about you loving me," he retorted.

"Well, lucky for you, I do."

"Good." He reached into the small pocket in the side of his wet suit and got down on one knee right there in the sand. He held up a beautiful one carat or so ring, with small diamonds surrounding a flawless topaz gem in the center. "It's Mana's birthstone, I figured it was appropriate. Will you marry me, Jodelle? I'll never let you down. I'll bend over backward to keep you safe and content. I'll—"

Jody didn't let him finish. She threw herself at him while exclaiming, "Yes!"

He caught her and fell onto his back in the sand, laughing.

"Shit, Tink, I almost dropped the ring!" he complained with a smile.

Jody lay on top of the man she loved more than she ever thought possible. "This is the best day ever."

"Yeah," he agreed as he slipped the ring down her finger. Then he wrapped his arms around her and kissed her.

"Hey, you two, Sex On the Beach is a drink, not something you should do literally," Ben said, the humor easy to hear in his voice.

Jody reluctantly pulled her lips from Baker's and held up her hand. "He asked me to marry him," she told Ben with a huge smile.

"Congrats!" he said. Though he didn't sound all that surprised. He obviously knew what Baker had planned. "Tressa and I are gonna head out."

"Are you going to be home for dinner?" Jody asked as Baker helped her stand.

"Are you making lasagna?" Ben asked.

"Uh...yes?"

"Then I'll be home for dinner," he said with a smile. "Can Tressa come too?"

"Of course," Jody told her. "You're always welcome."

"Thanks," Tressa said.

As they walked away, Baker said, "He's gonna marry her."

"Yup," Jody said without feeling the least bit of angst about that.

"Love you, Tink. I'm never gonna let you down. Ever."

"I know," she told him. "You think we can go home and celebrate the fact that we're engaged?"

Jody had never seen Baker move as fast as he did after that question.

She laughed and felt lighter and happier than she had in years. Before they left the beach, she ran her hand over the plaque on the table. "Love you, Mana," she whispered. Baker squeezed her hand in support, and she smiled up at him. "Let's go home."

"Home," he echoed.

*1.5 years Later*

Jody stood in Jonny's backyard overlooking Waimea Bay. He was a former professional surfer Baker knew, who'd graciously allowed them to use his yard as a venue for their wedding ceremony. Jody was extremely curious as to how the two men had met, but she had a feeling neither would admit to the real story, so she let it go.

Neither she nor Baker had wanted anything big or fancy. A gathering of their close friends, overlooking the spot where

Kaimana loved to surf and where he'd watched competitions with the hopes of someday being among the participants.

They'd planned a short but heartfelt ceremony. This wedding was as different from her first as she could get. No huge church. No big reception. No fourteen-member wedding party. No expensive dresses, tuxedos, and people she didn't know watching her vow to obey and honor her husband.

It was noisy. Kenna's five-month-old baby boy was crying and Monica's daughter was babbling nonstop to anyone she could get to listen. Lexie had shared that she was pregnant with a baby girl, and Carly was so pregnant, she was about to pop. Jody prayed she wouldn't go into labor right there on the manicured lawn. Ashlyn and Slate had brought the eight-year-old girl they were fostering, who was doing her best to make sure Charlotte didn't fall over as she toddled all over the lawn while babbling to the adults.

Theo had come with Midas and Lexie, and he was currently sitting under the patio with a piece of paper and his pencils, drawing. Jody had met him several times now, and she was always impressed all over again with his talent. He was a little antisocial, but no one minded in the least. He had a huge heart and was always welcome at their get-togethers.

The best thing about the day was that everyone was at ease, having a good time, and dressed casually. The latter was the one thing Jody had insisted on.

She was wearing a yellow sundress with little cap sleeves, the skirt falling to her knees. She had on a pair of white flip-flops with a large yellow flower at the toes. Jody had left her hair down, and when it kept blowing in her face during the ceremony, Baker had moved so he was standing next to her instead of in front of her, wrapped her hair in his fist, and held it out of her eyes as he gazed lovingly down at her.

He looked exceedingly handsome in his black board shorts, white shirt, and a pair of black flip-flops on his own feet. Jody had to keep pinching her arm to reassure herself that this really was her life. It wasn't as if she had low self-esteem, she was just still in awe that someone as wonderful and hot as Baker was with her.

"You may now kiss the bride," the officiant said. Jody had met him right before she and Baker walked together across the lawn, toward the spot at the edge of the yard with the best view of the bay, where they were saying their vows.

The hand in her hair tightened when Baker tilted her head back and lowered his own. As she always did, Jody went up onto her tiptoes to meet him halfway. His free hand wrapped around her, holding her steady, and Jody wrapped her own around his neck.

She'd received many wonderful and toe-curling kisses from Baker in the last year and a half, but this one seemed to outdo them all. Maybe it was the cheering and whistling from their friends in the background. Maybe it was because it was their first kiss as man and wife. Maybe it was because Jody had never been happier in her entire life. Whatever the reason, she knew she'd never forget this moment. Ever.

Baker had just lifted his head to smile at her when the heavens decided to open up. Rain fell in sheets, but Jody was feeling too happy to care.

Their friends laughed and all made a beeline for the large covered patio on the back of Jonny's house. But Jody and Baker stood in each other's arms, oblivious to the rain that soaked their skin in seconds.

Baker smiled wider. "Happy wedding day," he told her.

Jody tightened her arms around his neck. "My husband."

"My wife," he countered. Then he shook his head. "Honestly never thought this would happen to me. Figured I'd die serving my country."

"I'm glad you didn't."

"Me too," he said with a small grin. Then he sobered. "All the shit I've seen and done...you're my reward."

"Baker," Jody whispered.

"It's true," he insisted. "You're too good for me. I know it, my friends know it, but I don't give a shit. I'm never gonna do anything to fuck this up. Ever."

"I know. Me either," she told him.

He leaned down and kissed her briefly once more.

Jody sighed in contentment. She turned her head and looked over Waimea Bay. The waves were huge, most likely because of the storm that had rolled in. "I feel as if he's here," she said.

"He is," Baker agreed. "I'd like to think this is Mana's way of telling you he approves of me."

Jody tore her gaze from the waves and looked up at her husband. "He would've loved you for me," she reassured him. "Even at seventeen, he was protective. He always worried about me being alone after he graduated and moved out."

Baker nodded, then took a small step back from her. His hand fell from her hair and the wet strands fell over her shoulders. Jody looked up at him in confusion a heartbeat before he took one of her hands in his and wrapped the other around her waist. Then he began to dance with her. In the rain, with their friends watching from the shelter of the patio, with the waves crashing far below.

She didn't think it was possible, but Jody fell more in love with Baker at that moment.

They danced their first dance, soaking wet, with the wind and rain beating against their bodies, and nothing in Jody's life had ever felt more perfect.

*Two Years Later*

Jody stood with Baker's arm around her shoulders, watching Ben. They were at Ka'ena Point and Ben was spreading his mom's ashes in the ocean. Emma Rowden hadn't had an easy life in the last two years. She'd tried so hard to kick her drug habit but in the end, had been unsuccessful.

Ben, being the amazing kid...no, *young man* he was, had done his best to keep his mother in his life. Even after all she'd done to him, or more correctly, all she hadn't done, he'd still found it in his heart to forgive her and keep in touch.

Tressa stood about ten feet behind Ben, giving him privacy, while at the same time providing him the support he needed. They were closer than ever. Tressa had started attending the University of Hawaii after graduating from high school, and Jody had a suspicion she was spending more time at Ben's apartment near campus than she was in her own dorm room.

Ben stood, and Tressa immediately went to his side. From Jody's vantage point about thirty feet behind them, she could see they were having an intimate conversation.

"I hate this for him," Jody said softly.

"I know," Baker said, holding her tightly.

When Ben had asked her if she thought the Point would be a good place to spread his mom's ashes, she'd agreed wholeheartedly. When he'd picked up her belongings from the last halfway house she'd lived in, and where she'd been found by one of the other residents, there had been a letter addressed to him.

Ben had let Jody read it, and it was one of the saddest things she had ever seen.

*Dear Ben,*

*I know I haven't been a good mother, and I'm so sorry. You deserved better. I will be forever grateful for Jodelle. She was there for you when I wasn't. I know you're going to do great things. It's not fair of me to ask, but maybe you'll think of me once in a while.*

*Remember the good times we had when you were little. We struggled, but I realize now, too late, that we were happy.*

*I'm proud of you. You're the best thing I ever did in my life, and I almost screwed that up too. I did screw it up. Again, I'm sorry. Thank you for forgiving me. It couldn't have been easy, but know it means the world to me.*

*I'm just so tired, Ben. So damn tired. I can't fight anymore. Don't be sad. This is what I want. I just want the pain to stop. Go be awesome, son. I have no doubt you will be.*

*I love you. I didn't always show you the way I should've, and I'll always regret that.*

*Love, Mom*

Somehow, Emma Rowden had gotten hold of a lethal dose of methamphetamine. As far as Jody knew she hadn't ever taken the potent drug. But she'd purposely injected double the dose even a hard-core addict would normally use to get high.

Ben had been sad, but not really surprised. He was aware of how hard his mom was struggling because he'd continued visiting her every now and then.

Jody watched as Ben blew a kiss to the ocean, then turned and headed toward where she and Baker were standing.

"You okay?" Jody asked quietly.

"Yeah," Ben said.

It was obvious he wasn't all right, but Jody didn't call him on the lie. The quartet walked the two or so miles back to the parking lot in silence, each lost in their memories...good and bad.

That night, Tressa stayed for dinner. The mood had lightened and they played a few rounds of Uno. By the time Tressa left to go home to see her folks, it was late. Ben would be driving back down to Honolulu the following afternoon. He had plans to surf with Baker in the morning, then they'd all go to lunch with Tressa and her family, before the college kids went back to school.

After saying good night, Ben headed to his room, a room Jody hadn't changed since he left for university two years ago.

Baker headed to bed after checking the locks on the doors and windows, as he did every night without fail. Seeing him carry out his routine made Jody sigh in contentment. Her man never stopped looking after her. She was as much in love with him today as she was over two years ago when he refused to leave her alone in the house with Ben there. Protective to the core, that was Baker.

After tidying the kitchen, Jody headed to bed herself. She stopped outside Ben's door on the way, knocking softly.

"Ben? You awake?"

"Yeah."

Jody cracked the door and peeked inside. Ben was sitting on the edge of his bed, still in the clothes he'd worn all day, staring down at the letter his mom had written him. Jody's heart nearly broke.

She went inside and sat next to him, putting her arm around his broad back. She didn't speak, just hugged the man-boy she'd come to love as if he were her own.

Ben turned, hitching his knee up on the mattress, and wrapped his arms around Jody, buried his head into her shoulder, and cried.

Jody held him as tightly as possible, doing what she could to comfort him. Emma Rowden wasn't a good mother. She hadn't lied in the letter she'd written to Ben. She should've protected her son. Should've done whatever she had to do in order to make sure he was safe. And she hadn't. But that didn't mean she didn't love him, or that Ben didn't love her.

Ben cried on her shoulder for several minutes before his sobs finally tapered off. He sat up and wiped his tears on the sleeve of his shirt. "I'm sorry," he said softly.

Jody put her hands on his face and shook her head. "Don't

ever be sorry for showing your emotions, Ben. *Never* be sorry for that."

He nodded, and she dropped her hands.

"I love you," Jody told him. Ben's gaze came up to meet hers. "You're amazing, and your mom was right, you're going to do awesome things in this world."

"Thanks," he said. "I love you too, Miss Jody."

Jody smiled. She would never get tired of hearing him call her that.

"Get some sleep. Baker's gonna want to kick your butt in the waves tomorrow."

Ben rolled his eyes and used his palms to wipe off the remnants of tears on his cheeks. "As if." Then he leaned forward and hugged Jody once more. A long, emotional hug. "Thanks for everything. I mean it."

"Of course," Jody said into his hair. "I've said this before, and I'm sure I'll say it again, but oh well. I might not be your biological mom, but you're like a son to me, and you'll always have a place here, Ben. Always."

He nodded and pulled back. Jody took that as her sign to go. She stood, squeezed his hand, then headed for the door. She pulled it closed behind her and, knowing she was going to lose it, made a beeline for the one person who could always make her feel better.

The second Baker saw her enter their bedroom, he threw back the covers and came to her.

Jody wrapped herself around him as if she was going to fly into a million pieces and he was the only person who could hold her together. Without a word, he led her to the bed and somehow got them under the covers without letting go.

Jody cried then. For Ben. For Emma. For the pain they both suffered.

"He'll be okay," Baker said in a low voice after she'd somewhat gotten herself pulled together.

"I know," Jody mumbled into the bare skin of his shoulder.

"He's got you. And me. And Tressa and her family."

"I know," Jody repeated. Then said a little roughly, "I hope Al's having a horrible time in prison."

Baker chuckled. "It's not exactly a five-star vacation home, Tink."

"Still. I want him to be hungry. And cold. And wondering where he went wrong in his life. I want the other prisoners to treat him like shit, and for him to be lonely and terrified that someone's gonna jump him every second for the rest of his life."

"Damn, woman," Baker said.

"You've got connections. You could make that happen, right?" she asked, looking up at Baker.

"I can, but I don't need to. He's already feeling all that and more."

"Promise?" Jody asked.

"Promise," Baker said firmly.

Jody nodded. She'd never asked about his connections, but if Baker said Al Rowden was suffering, she knew without a shadow of a doubt, he was. "Good."

"Bloodthirsty," Baker mumbled as he gathered her against him once more.

"He hurt Ben," she said simply.

And it *was* that simple. No one hurt the ones she loved. She'd do whatever it took to protect Ben. It didn't matter that he was twenty years old now. It wouldn't matter when he was thirty or forty. She'd always want to protect him. "I love you, Baker," she whispered into his skin, running a finger over one of the tattoos on his chest.

"Love you too, Jodelle. You gonna be able to sleep?"

"Yeah," she said with a small nod. "And even if I couldn't, you'll be here."

"Damn straight," Baker mumbled.

Jody squeezed her man and sent a silent prayer to Kaimana, thanking him for sending both Ben and Baker to her. She was certain he'd had a hand in bringing them into her life. She fell asleep in the arms of the man she loved, having no doubts whatsoever that he loved her just as much in return.

*Four Years Later*

Jody was so proud of Ben, she thought she was going to burst.

Today was his graduation ceremony from the University of Hawaii and he was going right into grad school, studying marine biology. Jody knew he was going to achieve all his goals and would get to spend his life working on the ocean that he'd learned to love at a young age.

She and Baker had come down to Honolulu and spent the previous night in a hotel, so they wouldn't have to fight morning traffic and risk being late for the ceremony. Baker had splurged and gotten them an ocean-view suite, and while they didn't make love every day, not even close, they hadn't been able to keep their hands off each other last night.

Her husband still made her feel as if she was the most beautiful woman in the world, even though she'd put on a few pounds over the years. He'd worshiped every inch of her body, whispering words of admiration and praise as he sent her over the edge with his mouth and fingers before entering her and making her orgasm once more, while taking his own pleasure.

They were about ready to leave when a knock on their hotel door surprised Jody, as she wasn't expecting anyone.

Baker didn't seem startled in the least as he strode over and opened the door. Ben walked in—and Jody couldn't help but frown.

"What's wrong? I thought you were going to the ceremony with Tressa?"

"I am. I wanted to talk to you first though," Ben said.

That didn't exactly lessen Jody's trepidation. She looked at Baker in concern, but his face was blank. "Oooo-kay," she said nervously.

Ben glanced at Baker, and her husband nodded at him reassuringly. That was the first clue that Baker was in on whatever was going on.

"Come sit," Ben said gently.

Jody went over to the couch and sat, holding her breath that she wasn't about to hear something bad. Like Ben wasn't actually graduating, or that he and Tressa had broken up—which would totally break Jody's heart—or that he was running off to join a traveling circus or something.

For the first time, she noticed that Ben was holding a piece of paper. He stared down at it and fingered it nervously before taking a deep breath and meeting her eyes.

"I talked to Baker about this, and he thought it was a good idea. But if you don't think so, if you aren't happy, you have to be honest with me. I'll be all right either way...but I just wanted to do something to let you know how much you mean to me."

Just like that, Jody calmed, her focus on reassuring Ben. She hated seeing him this nervous. She reached out and put her hand over his. "Whatever it is, it'll be all right," she said gently.

Ben's lips twitched. "You don't even know what I'm gonna say and you're trying to comfort me."

Jody shrugged. She was. She couldn't deny it.

"Right, so...you know I never took Rowden's name when my mom married him. It wasn't really my choice either way, my mom just never did the paperwork to change it and that asshole she married didn't want to adopt me. So I kept my mom's maiden name. She never told me who my biological father was, and he never really mattered to me anyway. But I started thinking...and I got an idea. It might be stupid, and you might not like it, but...I thought maybe I'd change my last name to Spencer."

Every muscle in Jody's body went tight. She blinked, not sure she'd heard him correctly.

"As I said, I talked to Baker, and he told me about how you didn't want to change your last name when you guys got married, because of Kaimana. Because that was his last name, and it felt as if you were losing a part of him if you changed yours to Rawlins. And since you're the only mom I have left, I wondered if you might be willing for me to share your and Mana's name. When I get married, I'm hoping my wife will change her last name to mine. And our kids will have it too. I filled out the paperwork." He gestured to the piece of paper in his hand. "But haven't filed it yet, because I wanted to get your permission and blessing first."

Ben's words were rushed there at the end, as if he wasn't sure what her reaction would be and wanted to be sure to get his entire argument out before she said no.

But Jody had no intention of saying no. No one in her entire life had done something for her that touched her so deeply. Baker hadn't had any issue with her keeping Spencer as her last name, but the thought that Ben wanted to take her name floored her.

She stared at the young man in front of her for a beat, then promptly burst into tears.

Ben looked freaked out, but Baker didn't hesitate. He sat down on Jody's other side and pulled her close. Jody leaned against him, hiccupping with the force of her sobs.

"Jesus, Tink. Take a breath."

She tried, but Jody was simply overwhelmed.

"Is that a yes? Or a no?" Ben asked hesitantly.

Jody pulled herself out of Baker's arms and threw herself

into Ben's. "Yes! Oh my Gosh, yes! I can't...that's...I don't know what to say!"

Ben hugged her tightly, then gently gave her back to Baker, as if he didn't know what to do with a crying woman.

It took her another few minutes to completely get control of herself, but Jody couldn't stop smiling. Never in her wildest dreams would she have imagined this moment.

"I'm gonna file this paperwork next week then," Ben said, sounding much more relaxed and like himself as he stood.

Baker pulled Jody to her feet, keeping his arm around her waist.

"You better get going," he told him. "You wouldn't want to miss your own graduation."

"Right," Ben said. He hugged Jody again. "Love you, Miss Jody," he said softly. Then he pulled back and headed for the door.

Jody's eyes filled with tears once more, but she battled them back. Today was a happy day, and she didn't want to cry anymore. The second the door closed behind Ben, Jody turned to Baker. "I can't believe you knew about that and didn't warn me!" she said as she slapped him lightly on the chest.

Baker grinned. "He wanted me to keep it a secret. So I did," he said simply.

That was so like her husband. He'd promised years ago to never let his secrets and what he did touch her, and they hadn't. Not once. Last month, he'd retired from his job with the government. It took longer than he'd wanted, but he would no longer be going on trips overseas to "visit" with nefarious people to make deals and exchange information. He still used the dark web to find intel, but Jody was relieved he wouldn't have to do the trips anymore.

"I'm thinking you might want to fix your face before we leave," he told her gently.

Jody chuckled. She was sure she looked a mess. She went

up on her toes and kissed Baker. It wasn't a short kiss either. When she pulled back, they were both breathing hard. Baker glanced over at the bed, and Jody laughed out loud. "No time for that, sorry," she said.

"Glad we're staying another night," Baker said with a shrug and a grin that made Jody's toes curl. "Go on, Tink. We need to get out of here so we can get a good seat."

She nodded, picked up Baker's hand, kissed the palm, and headed for the bathroom. When she looked back right before she entered, she saw Baker hadn't moved. He was still standing where she'd left him, staring at her with a smile on his face. When he caught her gaze, he gave her a small chin lift.

Jody could only smile back and marvel for the four millionth time over how lucky she was.

*Six Years Later*

"So, after six years..." Elodie said, then paused and looked up at her husband, who was standing behind her with his arms around her waist and his chin on her shoulder. "We're finally pregnant!" she announced.

Everyone went crazy. Yelling and cheering, surrounding Elodie and Mustang and hugging them exuberantly.

Jody stood back and took in the scene with a huge smile on her face.

"They're seriously happy," Baker said from behind her. He was standing much as Mustang had been, his chin on her shoulder, his hands clasped around her belly.

"Yeah," Jody agreed.

"Mustang's fuckin' scared out of his mind though," Baker added.

Jody looked up at her husband. "You knew?"

355

He simply raised a brow in response.

"Of course you knew," Jody said, answering her own question.

"Triplets," Baker said softly.

Jody spun in his arms. "Seriously?"

"Yeah. It's gonna be a high-risk pregnancy. After four years of fertility treatments, this was gonna be their last attempt before they went the adoption route. The doctors implanted six embryos with the hope of at least one of them being viable."

"Three," Jody breathed. "Holy crap."

Baker chuckled and his chest vibrated under her hands. "Yeah."

They were standing in the middle of the grassy area behind the Coral Springs Condos. Kenna and Aleck still lived in the same condo with their now five-year-old son. They still had regular get-togethers, and now that everyone had children, the gatherings were even crazier than ever.

Lexie's son was almost three and her daughter was now four, and the latter was best friends with Kenna's son. Monica and Pid had two daughters, and a son who was born last year, and they both claimed they were done having children. Carly's daughter was four and a half and her son was six months old. Ashlyn and Slate had fostered over two dozen kids in the last four years, and had just finalized the adoption of their latest fosters, a set of siblings who were ten and eight.

So yeah, any get-togethers they had now were full of laughter, sometimes tears, and lots and lots of love. And through all of them, Elodie and Mustang had smiled and wiped faces and chased toddlers, treating everyone's kids as if they were their own. But Jody, and everyone else, knew how hard it was for the couple. They'd wanted children for so long, but it hadn't happened.

They'd endured four years of fertility treatments, along with disappointments so crushing, Jody had begun to worry for Elodie's mental health. So the news today that she was finally pregnant was overwhelming and joyous.

"I'm so happy for them," Jody said. "Although three? At once? Oy!"

"That was my thought too. Good thing they have lots of friends to babysit and to help when things get too crazy."

Jody nodded, her thoughts already turning to what she could do to help the couple.

"Should I be concerned about those wheels spinnin' in your head?" Baker mumbled.

Jody smiled up at him. "Maybe," she said honestly.

"If there's anything in my life I regret, it's not giving you babies," Baker said.

Jody's heart melted. "We would've made beautiful kids," she whispered.

"Yeah," Baker agreed. "But the good thing about our friends having the kids and not us, is that we can give them back at the end of the day when they're cranky, or hyped up on sugar, or exhausted."

"Oh, yeah, totally agree," Jody said.

"Get over here, you two!" Lexie called out. "We're gonna do a group picture!"

"How long do you think it's gonna take this time?" Jody asked Baker quietly as they turned to join the group. They'd begun taking the group pictures every time they got together. Jody forgot who suggested it, but everyone had agreed they wanted to document the progress of their "little family."

"Too fuckin' long," Baker said under his breath.

Jody couldn't help but laugh. Trying to get everyone to stand still and all look in the same direction was almost an impossible feat, but that was part of what made the pictures so awesome. There was always a baby crying, or someone looking the other way, or making a weird face.

As they huddled together, Jody got the chance to talk to

Elodie for a moment. She gave her a big hug. "I'm so happy for you," she told her.

"Me too," Elodie said. "But what if—"

"*No.* No what-ifs. Positive thinking, always," Jody scolded.

"You sound like Scott," Elodie said with a smile.

"Always thought your husband was a smart man," Jody quipped.

Elodie hugged her again. Then whispered in her ear, "It's triplets."

Jody smiled. "I know," she whispered back.

Elodie rolled her eyes. "Should've known. Baker knows *everything.*"

She nodded. "You're going to be fine. As are your babies. Mark my words."

"All right, everyone! Smile at the camera!" Kenna yelled.

Jody felt bad for Robert, who had finally retired from working as the concierge at Coral Springs but was still invited by Kenna to attend their get-togethers. He reveled in being a sort of grandfather figure to everyone's kids and never hesitated to volunteer to take the group pictures. Theo was also there, off to the side, drawing as usual. To no one's surprise, he got along so well with the children. He tolerated them using his drawing pencils and papers, but the adults usually tried to bring crayons and their own paper so the kids didn't bother Theo too much.

Baker came up behind Jody and took her in his arms again, sighing in her ear as the usual chaos began and Robert tried to get everyone to smile at him at the same time.

Jody had no problem smiling. She loved her life. Loved her friends. Every now and then she'd get sad because Kaimana wasn't here to meet everyone, but Baker seemed to know when she was down and did everything in his power to cheer her up. But for the moment, Jody was content. She looked up at Baker, and he put his hand on the side of her head and bent down to kiss her.

The picture of their get-together was taken at that moment. With Jody and Baker kissing, half the kids not looking at the camera, Carly's infant screaming his head off, and Elodie and Midas both with their eyes closed. When Jody saw it the next day after Kenna had emailed it to the group, she'd laughed her head off and immediately printed it to hang on her wall.

*Ten Years Later*

Baker stood against the wall of the reception hall and watched as Jodelle danced with Ben in the mother-son dance. The last ten years had been full of laughter, as well as disagreements, a bit of angst here and there, and more love than he'd ever felt in all of his sixty-two years combined.

God, how in the hell had he gotten to be in his sixties? Most days he didn't feel a day over thirty...okay, maybe forty. But not sixty-two. He still went surfing now and then, but most of the time he was content to sit on the shore with Jodelle as they watched their kids.

Of course, their kids changed over the years, but there were always teenagers to keep an eye on as they surfed the sometimes dangerous waters. Jodelle still did graphic design work, and she was damn good at it. Baker was constantly surprised at her creativity and how she could create such intricate and beautiful graphics for her clients.

As for him, Baker didn't think he'd ever be able to completely stop digging for information on people. The satisfaction he got when he found what he needed to help someone, or bring down a bad guy, never waned. Nowadays, he passed along any intel he dug up to someone else to act on, but he still had plenty of connections in the world.

Jodelle looked radiant tonight. She always did in his eyes

though. Whether wearing the floor-length, flowy mother-of-the-groom dress she had on right now, or in a pair of shorts and a tank top sitting on top of the picnic table at the beach, or wearing nothing at all, lying replete in his arms. He loved her so much, it was almost scary. Baker wouldn't change one thing in his life if it meant he'd end up right where he was in this moment.

Ben and Tressa's marriage vows had been heartfelt and moving, and the party was now in full swing. Jodelle had been beaming all night, and he couldn't blame her. When the couple had been pronounced Ben and Tressa Spencer, Jodelle lost it, turning to him and crying on his shoulder.

Ben had a great job working with a marine biology research firm, and Tressa was working as a paralegal for one of the many law firms in the city. They'd moved in together two years ago, right after he'd proposed. Baker had insider knowledge that Tressa was expecting, and he couldn't wait for Jodelle to find out. She was going to be an amazing grandmother, if the way she doted on Elodie's three and a half-year-old triplets was any indication.

Baker didn't have any desire to be out on the dance floor, but he loved watching his wife laugh and dance with all of Ben's younger friends. The photographer Ben and Tressa had hired was going a little crazy with all the pictures, but Baker had no doubt Jodelle would treasure each and every one.

Their little house was full of pictures. Every inch of the walls covered with photos, and there were small picture frames propped on every available surface as well. Older ones of Kaimana and Jodelle, photos from their own wedding, pictures of their friends' children, and as many of the group shots as Jodelle could find room for. There were also shots of Ben and Jodelle, Ben and Tressa, even Ben and Baker. Everywhere he turned in their house, Baker came face-to-face with love and happy memories.

There wasn't a day that went by that he didn't regret not

meeting Jodelle earlier, but he did his best to enjoy every moment with her to the fullest. He couldn't go back and change anything in his life, but he could damn well make sure Jodelle knew without a shadow of a doubt that she was loved.

For the rest of the evening, Baker kept his wife hydrated, bringing her lots of water as well as making sure her champagne glass never went dry. By the end of the night, Jodelle's high heels had been abandoned under their table, her hair had fallen from the elaborate updo it had been put in earlier that morning, and she had a flush on her cheeks from dancing and from all the alcohol she'd consumed.

Ben and Tressa had left an hour ago, and now Baker wanted to get his wife to their hotel room. She didn't drink a lot, but when she did, she tended to lose all her inhibitions—and became absolutely insatiable in bed. Baker was more than ready to get that portion of their evening started.

She snuggled against him in the taxi on the way to their hotel, plastered herself to his side as they rode the elevator up to their room, and the second they were alone, she reached for his tie.

As much as Baker wanted to act on the thoughts he'd had all evening by unzipping her dress and watching it pool around her feet, he wanted to give her the present Ben had asked him to give to her. Ben knew Jodelle well. He didn't want to make her cry at the reception...any more than she already had during the wedding.

"Let go for a second, Tink. I need to give you somethin'," he said.

She smirked and her hand snuck down the front of his chest, heading for his cock. "I know what you can give me," she said suggestively.

Baker chuckled, grabbed her hand, then towed her over to the small couch in the room. He sat her down, then reached for the eleven-by-fourteen wrapped frame Ben had given him earlier. He knew what was in it, and he was ready for Jodelle's tears when she saw it.

She grinned when she saw the gift and reached for it eagerly. His wife was a sucker for presents. He did his best to give her as many gifts as possible, simply for the joy of watching her open them.

She ripped the white and cream wrapping paper as Baker spoke. "It's from Ben. He gave Theo a picture from our own wedding and asked if he'd recreate it in a drawing for you."

Amazingly, Theo Merkl had become one of the most sought-after artists in Honolulu. Years ago, Lexie had started selling some of his drawings so he could have some spending money. She'd began by taking ten of them to a street fair—and had sold all of them within thirty minutes. His popularity had just grown exponentially from that moment until now. The man had an uncanny ability to depict extreme emotions in his works.

He didn't draw for the money, as he didn't have a strong grasp on the whole concept of saving and what it meant to be rich or poor. He was happy living his life the way he always had. Lexie and Midas had opened an account for Theo and invested his earnings. As a result, he'd definitely never be homeless again.

There was a waiting list for his creations, but Theo loved drawing for his friends more than anything else. So Baker had no doubt when Ben had tracked him down and given him the picture of Miss Jody, standing with her new husband in the pouring rain, staring up at him with all the love she had for him shining in her eyes, that Theo had probably jumped on the chance to recreate the moment.

Baker watched as Jodelle's eyes filled with tears as she stared at the drawing. Her fingers brushed over the glass with reverence before she looked up at him with watery eyes.

"It's us," she said unnecessarily.

Baker nodded and pulled her against his side as he gazed

at the picture. He hadn't seen it before, and he was just as awed now as he was every time he saw one of Theo's drawings. The man was a master. He might be mentally deficient, but his talent was unmatchable.

"But look, it got smudged," Jodelle said with a frown. She ran her thumb over a noticeable smudge in the artwork. It was right over her shoulder, and even through the sheets of rain Theo had drawn, it was easy to see.

Something caught his eye in the wrapping paper on the coffee table in front of them, where Jodelle had thrown it in her exuberance to open the gift.

He picked up the small envelope and handed it to Jodelle. She set the framed picture on her lap and opened it. Pulling out a piece of paper, she read the contents aloud.

"Miss Jody, I figured on my wedding day, a reminder of your own was appropriate. I can only hope Tressa and I stay in love just as deeply as you and Baker have. Love, Ben. PS. I asked Theo about the smudge on the drawing, and he told me that every time he's around you, he sees a small 'floating ball of mist' near you. Said he puts it in all the drawings he does of you. I've never noticed it before, but if Theo says it's there, I'm sure it is."

Jodelle looked up at Baker in confusion. "Have you noticed it in his other drawings?" she asked.

In response, Baker pulled out his phone. He'd taken a picture of every drawing Theo had given them. They were so good, he wanted to be able to look at them wherever he was, not just when he was at home. He pulled up one of Jodelle holding Elodie's triplets. Her arms were obviously full, but her head was thrown back as she was laughing hysterically at something someone said. Looking closer, Baker saw a small smudge near her right elbow that he'd never noticed before. He pointed it out to Jodelle, then scrolled to the next picture.

It was of Jodelle with her arm around Ben. They were sitting on her picnic table at the beach. It was drawn from behind and, sure enough, there was a small smudge near her ankle near the bottom of the picture.

Every single picture Baker looked at, Theo had included that small smudge. All of them were located near her arms or legs, which was most likely why Baker hadn't noticed before. He always concentrated on the happiness and love in Jodelle's eyes and face.

He picked up the newest drawing Theo had given them and stared at that smudge for a long moment—then suddenly, his eyes filled with tears.

Jodelle didn't miss his reaction. "Baker?" she asked with concern, putting her hand on his thigh.

Turning to his woman, Baker whispered, "It's Kaimana."

"What?" Jodelle asked in confusion.

Baker ran his thumb over the smudge once more. "I know this sounds crazy, but I think this is Mana. He's been watching over you."

Jodelle looked at him in awe. "It doesn't sound crazy," she told him. "I feel him sometimes. But I figured everyone would say that was just me being a grieving mother."

A tear fell from Baker's eye, and Jodelle's thumb brushed it away.

Then she shifted to her knees on the couch and kissed his cheek. "Don't cry, Baker. Not about this. I've always felt that he's around. I absolutely love that Theo confirmed it."

Baker did his best to get control of his emotions. Only this woman could bring that part of him out. He nodded at her.

"You good?" she asked.

Baker sighed and kissed her briefly. "Yeah, Tink. I'm good."

"Does that mean we can get naked now?"

Baker snorted out a laugh. In response, he stood, reverently placing Theo's drawing on the table. He took the time to touch the smudge and send a silent message to Kaimana, vowing once more to always take care of his mama, before turning, picking Jodelle up, and heading for the bed.

She wrapped her arms around him and giggled. He dopped her legs next to the mattress and curled a hand around the back of her neck. She rested her hands on his chest and gazed up at him.

"You have a good time tonight, Jodelle?"

She sighed. "Oh, yeah. Tressa was beautiful. And Ben so handsome in his tux. I'm so happy for them."

"How do you feel?"

She scrunched her nose at him. "About what?"

"Physically, Tink," he said with a grin. "You feel sick at all?"

"Oh. No. Tipsy, yes. Horny, definitely. Sick? Nope."

"Okay, good. I've got a box of Pop-Tarts in my bag for the morning," he informed her.

Jodelle beamed up at him. "You'd think I'd have grown out of that by now."

Baker shrugged. "You do, let me know. Otherwise, I'll always bring them for you."

"Always having my back," Jodelle said quietly.

"Absolutely," Baker confirmed.

Then Jodelle shocked him by tipping her head back and saying, "If you're here, Mana, it's time for you to go for a little while. I'm gonna make love to my husband, and I don't need you around for *that*."

Baker chuckled, but when Jodelle's gaze met his, he sobered.

"I love you, Jodelle Spencer. So damn much, you don't even know."

"I *do* know," she countered. "Because I love you the same way, Baker Rawlins." Then she reached around her back for her zipper.

Baker stopped her immediately by grabbing her hand and lowering the zipper himself. "I've been dreaming of doing that all evening, you aren't gonna deny me," he said sternly.

"Then get to it," Jodelle demanded.

"Gladly." Then Baker got busy making love with his wife.

\* \*

Thank you all for reading the SEAL Team Hawaii series. I've always had a soft spot in my heart for the state of Hawaii. I'm sure you'll continue to see Baker pop up in future books, I have a feeling he's like Tex...always got his nose in other people's business.

And don't worry...there are more Navy SEALs lurking in my mind, waiting impatiently for their stories to be told.

Be kind. Read on. And stay strong.

*Want to talk to other Susan Stoker fans? Join my reader group, Susan Stoker's Stalkers, on Facebook!*

**Scan the QR code below for signed books, swag, T-shirts and more!**

## _Also by Susan Stoker_

### SEAL Team Hawaii Series

_Finding Elodie_
_Finding Lexie_
_Finding Kenna_
_Finding Monica_
_Finding Carly_
_Finding Ashlyn_
_Finding Jodelle (July)_

### Eagle Point Search & Rescue

_Searching for Lilly_
_Searching for Elsie_
_Searching for Bristol_
_Searching for Caryn (April)_
_Searching for Finley (Sept)_
_Searching for Heather (Jan 2024)_
_Searching for Khloe (TBA)_

### The Refuge Series

_Deserving Alaska_
_Deserving Henley_
_Deserving Reese (May)_
_Deserving Cora (Nov)_
_Deserving Lara (Feb 2024)_
_Deserving Maisy (TBA)_
_Deserving Ryleigh (TBA)_

### Game of Chance Series

_The Protector (Mar)_
_The Royal (Aug)_
_The Hero (TBA)_
_The Lumberjack (TBA)_

## SEAL of Protection: Legacy Series

*Securing Caite*
*Securing Brenae (novella)*
*Securing Sidney*
*Securing Piper*
*Securing Zoey*
*Securing Avery*
*Securing Kalee*
*Securing Jane*

## Delta Force Heroes Series

*Rescuing Rayne*
*Rescuing Aimee (novella)*
*Rescuing Emily*
*Rescuing Harley*
*Marrying Emily (novella)*
*Rescuing Kassie*
*Rescuing Bryn*
*Rescuing Casey*
*Rescuing Sadie (novella)*
*Rescuing Wendy*
*Rescuing Mary*
*Rescuing Macie (novella)*
*Rescuing Annie*

## SEAL of Protection Series

*Protecting Caroline*
*Protecting Alabama*
*Protecting Fiona*
*Marrying Caroline (novella)*
*Protecting Summer*
*Protecting Cheyenne*
*Protecting Jessyka*
*Protecting Julie (novella)*

## ALSO BY SUSAN STOKER

*Protecting Melody*
*Protecting the Future*
*Protecting Kiera (novella)*
*Protecting Alabama's Kids (novella)*
*Protecting Dakota*

## Delta Team Two Series

*Shielding Gillian*
*Shielding Kinley*
*Shielding Aspen*
*Shielding Jayme (novella)*
*Shielding Riley*
*Shielding Devyn*
*Shielding Ember*
*Shielding Sierra*

## Badge of Honor: Texas Heroes Series

*Justice for Mackenzie*
*Justice for Mickie*
*Justice for Corrie*
*Justice for Laine (novella)*
*Shelter for Elizabeth*
*Justice for Boone*
*Shelter for Adeline*
*Shelter for Sophie*
*Justice for Erin*
*Justice for Milena*
*Shelter for Blythe*
*Justice for Hope*
*Shelter for Quinn*
*Shelter for Koren*
*Shelter for Penelope*

## Ace Security Series

## ALSO BY SUSAN STOKER

*Outback Hearts*
*Flaming Hearts*
*Frozen Hearts*

## **Writing as Annie George:**

*Stepbrother Virgin (erotic novella)*

# ABOUT THE AUTHOR

*New York Times*, *USA Today*, #1 Amazon Bestseller, and #1 *Wall Street Journal* Bestselling Author, Susan Stoker has spent the last twenty-three years living in Missouri, California, Colorado, Indiana, Texas, and Tennessee and is currently living in the wilds of Maine. She's married to a retired Army man (and current firefighter/EMT) who now gets to follow *her* around the country.

She debuted her first series in 2014 and quickly followed that up with the SEAL of Protection Series, which solidified her love of writing and creating stories readers can get lost in.

If you enjoyed this book, or any book, please consider leaving a review. It's appreciated by authors more than you'll know.

www.stokeraces.com
www.AcesPress.com
susan@stokeraces.com

f facebook.com/authorsusanstoker
twitter.com/Susan_Stoker
instagram.com/authorsusanstoker
goodreads.com/SusanStoker
BB bookbub.com/authors/susan-stoker
a amazon.com/author/susanstoker

Made in United States
North Haven, CT
05 July 2023

38574495R00212